A WINDOW OPENS

A NOVEL

ELISABETH EGAN

SIMON & SCHUSTER

NEW YORK   LONDON   TORONTO   SYDNEY   NEW DELHI

Simon & Schuster
1230 Avenue of the Americas
New York, NY 10020

First Simon & Schuster hardcover edition August 2015

For information about special discounts for bulk purchases,
please contact Simon & Schuster Special Sales at
1-866-506-1949 or business@simonandschuster.com.

The Simon & Schuster Speakers Bureau can bring authors to your live event. For more information or to book an event, contact the Simon & Schuster Speakers Bureau at 1-866-248-3049 or visit our website at www.simonspeakers.com.

Interior design by Ruth Lee-Mui

Manufactured in the United States of America

1   3   5   7   9   10   8   6   4   2

Library of Congress Cataloging-in-Publication Data
Egan, Elisabeth.
A window opens : a novel / Elisabeth Egan.
pages   cm
I. Title.
PS3605.G354W53 2015
813'.6—dc23
2014047742

ISBN 978-1-5011-0543-2
ISBN 978-1-5011-0546-3 (ebook)

For Ethan, Louisa, Simon, and Frances,
my lights at the end of the Lincoln Tunnel

We shall not cease from exploration,
And the end of all our exploring
Will be to arrive where we started
And know the place for the first time.

                        —T. S. Eliot, "Little Gidding"

And the moral is: If you ever find yourself in the wrong story, leave.

                        —Mo Willems, *Goldilocks and the Three Dinosaurs*

I drag my suitcase out from under the bed and start packing.

The Ramona books go in the elastic pocket intended for socks and under-wear; the yellow-spined Nancy Drews go in neat towers on the luggage floor. Around these, I wedge Anastasia Krupnik, Pippi Longstocking, Emily of New Moon, Harriet the Spy, Betsy, Tacy and Tib, the All-of-a-Kind Family.

When the luggage is full, I sit on its lid and yank twin zippers around the periphery until Strawberry Shortcake's canvas face is distorted from overstuffing. Then I grab the yellow plastic briefcase handles and lug the suitcase down the hall to my brother's room, where he's working on the final side of a Rubik's Cube.

Will immediately kicks the door shut with the toe of his Reebok and, in his unfamiliar new deep voice, says, "Get out, Alice."

I heft my suitcase of books downstairs and make my way to the kitchen, where my mom is on the phone, receiver tucked between ear and shoulder, olive green cord wrapped around her waist.

I carry my wares to the backyard.

My dad is sitting on a lounge chair in the sun, his head in a cloud of pipe smoke, reading. When he sees me, he puts down his pipe and Ed McBain, lifts his legs off the bottom half of his chair and gestures for me to set up shop. "Welcome, Book Lady. What's on the reading list today?"

One by one, I lift the books from the suitcase, showcasing them in my hands the way Vanna White does on Wheel of Fortune. *I explain the concept of Choose Your Own Adventure and read a short poem from* Where the Sidewalk Ends.

My dad listens intently, puffing on his pipe, pretending he hasn't heard every one of my sales pitches at least ten times before. When I'm finished, he makes a show of examining the books, lingering for a moment over battered spines and flipping a few over so he can read the descriptions on the back. I scratch my mosquito bites and attempt to French-braid my hair and wonder which of my friends will be at the pool in the afternoon. I'm a little dizzy from the hysterical thrum of the cicadas.

Finally, my dad says, "I'll take this Encyclopedia Brown. And can you recommend a good book for my wife?" We both glance back at the kitchen window, where my mom is still gabbing on the phone, most likely railing about the scourge of Atari.

"So. How much do I owe you?"

"A dollar."

He fishes into his pocket and hands me a stack of quarters, saying, "Save this for a rainy day."

Instead, I buy twenty watermelon Jolly Ranchers at the pool. Later, while the grill is cooling after dinner, I'll come back out to the yard to collect the books my dad bought so I can sell them back to him again next week.

Being the Book Lady sets me up for two things: a mouthful of cavities and a deep appreciation for the heft and promise of a book. Eventually, I will learn that the first is a small price to pay for the second.

SPRING

1

In my book, January and February are just frozen appetizers for the fillet of the year, which arrives in March, when you can finally wear a down vest to walk the dog. That's when I commit to my annual resolutions: become more flexible in all senses of the word, stop snapping at my family, start feeding the parking meter, take wet laundry out of the machine before it mildews, call my mom more, gossip less. Throughout my thirties, the list has remained the same.

On this particular sunny and tentatively warm day, I was driving home from spin class, daydreaming about a pair of patent leather boots I'd seen in the window of a store near my office. They were midheight and semi-stylish, presentable enough for work, with a sole suited for sprinting through the aisles of Whole Foods. Maybe I recognized a little bit of myself in those boots; after all, I fit the same description.

When I stopped for a red light in front of the high school, my phone lit up with a photo of Nicholas. The snapshot was three years old, taken on wooden bleachers at the Y while we were waiting for our son, Oliver, to finish basketball practice. Splayed across Nicholas's chest was the paperback edition of *The Cut* by George Pelecanos; while he grinned at my then new iPhone, our daughters, Margot and Georgie, each leaned in and kissed one of his cheeks.

"Hey, what's up? I'm just driving back from Ellie's class. Since when does 'Stairway to Heaven' qualify as a spin song?"

Silence on the other end. I noticed a spray of white crocuses on the side of the road, rearing their brave little heads. "Nicholas? Are you there?"

"Yeah, I'm here."

Another pause.

"Nicholas? Are you okay?"

"Yeah, I'm fine. I just—"

More silence.

I watched as a group of high school kids trampled the crocuses with their high-tops and Doc Martens. The light turned green.

"You just . . . what?"

"Listen, Al, I'd rather not have this conversation on speaker while you're driving. Can you call me when you get home?"

I felt a slow blossom of anxiety in my throat. When someone starts talking about the conversation in the third person, you know it's not going to be pretty.

"Nicholas. What's going on?"

"I can't . . . You know what?" I heard a noise in the background that sounded like a big stack of papers hitting the floor. "Actually? I'm coming home. I'll be on the 11:27 train. See you soon." There was a strain in his voice, as if someone had him by the neck.

"Wait—don't hang up."

But he was gone.

Suddenly, I felt chilly in my sweaty clothes. I distractedly piloted my minivan down Park Street, past a church, a temple, a funeral home, and a gracious turreted Victorian we'd lost in a bidding war when we first started looking for houses in Filament.

My mind raced with possibilities: Nicholas's parents, my parents, his health, an affair, a relocation. Was there any chance this urgent conversation could contain *good* news? A windfall?

What was so important that Nicholas had to come home to say it to me in person? In the seven years we'd lived in New Jersey, he'd rarely arrived home before dark, even in the summer, and most of our daytime conversations took place through an intermediary—his secretary, Gladys, doyenne of the Stuyvesant Town bingo scene.

I called Nicholas back as soon as I pulled into the driveway of our blue colonial. When the ringing gave way to voice mail, I suddenly felt dizzy, picturing the old photo pressed to my ear. The girls had grown and changed since then—Margot's round face chiseling down into a preteen perma-scowl, Georgie's toddler legs losing their drumstick succulence. But what struck me was Nicholas's jet-black hair. It had been significantly thicker in those days, and a lot less gray. I couldn't remember the last time I'd seen him kick back with a book, let alone look so relaxed.

I was about to find out why.

I spent the next hour repairing damage wrought by the daily cyclone of our kids eating breakfast, getting dressed, and supposedly cleaning their rooms but really just shoving socks, towels, and Legos under their beds. Eggshells in the garbage disposal, Leapin' Lemurs cereal in the dustpan, Margot's tried-on-and-discarded outfits directly into her hamper even though I knew they were clean. I filled out class picture forms—hadn't I already paid for one round of mediocre shots against the backdrop of a fake library?—and called in a renewal of the dog's Prozac prescription: "His birthday? Honestly, I have no idea . . . He's not my son! He's my dog!" Cornelius lifted his long reddish snout and glanced lazily in my direction from his favorite forbidden napping spot on the window seat in the dining room.

I kept checking my phone, hoping to hear from Nicholas, but the only person I heard from was my dad. Ever since losing his vocal cords to cancer, he'd become a ferocious virtual communicator. His texts and e-mails rolled in at all hours of the day, constant gentle taps on my shoulder. The highest concentration arrived in the morning, while my mom played tennis and he worked his way through three newspapers, perusing print and online editions simultaneously. Many messages contained links to articles on his pet subjects: social media, the Hoyas, women doing it all.

That day, in my state of anticipation and dread, I was happy for the distraction.

Dad: Dear Alice, do you read me?

Alice: I do!

Dad: Just wondering, are you familiar with Snapchat?

Me: Sorry, not sure what this is.

Dad: Reading about it in WSJ. Like Instagram, but temporary. Pictures only. No track record.

Me: I'm not on Instagram either. Have nothing to hide anyway.

Dad: I can educate you. These are great ways to stay connected.

Me: I'm on FB. That's all I can handle.

Dad: Yes, but why no cover photo on your timeline?

Dad: Hi, are you still there?

Dad: OK, TTYL. Love, Dad

We live four houses from the station, so I headed over as soon as I heard the long, low horn of the train. By the time I'd walked by Margot and Oliver's school and arrived at the steep embankment next to the tracks, Nicholas was already on the platform. He looked surprisingly jaunty, with his suit jacket hanging from his shoulder like a pinstriped cape.

He kissed me on the cheek—a dry nothing of a peck that you might give to someone who baked you a loaf of zucchini bread. He smelled like the train: newsprint, coffee, vinyl. I shivered inside my vest and pulled him in for a tight hug, wrapping my arms around his neck.

"What is going *on*?"

Nicholas sighed. Now I smelled mint gum with an undernote of—*beer*? Was that possible?

The train pulled out of the station and we were the only two people left on the platform. I was vaguely aware of a gym class playing a game of spud on the school playground behind us. "I called it and he moved!" "I didn't move, she pushed me!" Nicholas leaned down to put his leather satchel on the ground. It was a gift from me for his thirtieth birthday: the perfect hybrid of a grown-up briefcase and a schoolboy's buckled bag. As he straightened his back, his green eyes met mine. He put his hands through his hair and I thought of the photo, my chest tightening.

"Alice, I didn't make partner."

At first, the news came as a relief. A problem at work was small potatoes compared to a secret second family or an out-of-control gambling problem or the middle-age malaise of a friend's husband who said, simply, "I don't feel like doing this anymore," before packing a backpack and moving to Hoboken.

Just a *backpack*!

Then: the lead blanket of disappointment descended gently but firmly, bringing with it a sudden X-ray vision into our past and our future. The summer associate days when we dined on Cornish game hen and attended a private Sutherland, Courtfield–sponsored tour of the modern wing of the Met; the night Nicholas's official offer letter from the firm arrived, when we climbed a fire escape to the roof of our apartment building and started talking—hypothetically, of course—about what we would name our kids; the many mornings I'd woken up to find him, still dressed in clothes from the day before, with casebooks, Redwelds, and six-inch stacks of paper scattered willy-nilly across the kitchen table. You don't know how big a binder clip can be until you've been married to a lawyer.

What next, if not this?

But first, *why*?

"Oh, Nicholas. I'm so sorry. I mean, just . . . Really. Wait, I thought the partners' meeting wasn't until November. Why are they—"

"It's not. Until November, I mean. But I had a feeling—"

"You had a *feeling*? Why didn't you tell me?"

"Alice, I don't know, okay? I'm working with Win Makepeace on this bankruptcy—the one I told you about with those bankers who wanted to go out for karaoke? And he let slip that it's not going to happen for me. Actually, he said it, flat out, as if I already knew. Should have known."

I pictured Win in his spindly black chair with its smug Cornell crest, how he would have smoothed a tuft of sandy hair over a bald spot that was permanently tanned from a lifetime of sailing on Little Narragansett Bay. Who names their kid *Win*, anyway? Not Winthrop, Winston, or Winchester, just *Win*. I was proud to come from a family where all the men are named Edward.

Then I snapped back into the moment, shaking my head as if to dislodge a pesky thought. "So, wait, he just *said*, 'Nicholas Bauer, you are not going to make partner at this law firm'?"

"No, not like that. I made a tiny mistake on a brief—a comma instead of a period—and he said, 'Bauer, let's face it, you're not Sutherland, Courtfield partner material.'"

"He did *not*."

"He did."

"Nicholas, is this even legal?" I grabbed his hand and pointed us in the direction of home.

"Of course it is. He just stood there in his fucking houndstooth vest and basically told me I had no future there. That, in fact, the partners decided *last* November, and they weren't going to tell me until a year from now—"

The swings on the playground were empty, swaying lazily in the breeze by their rusted chains. Sadness kicked in at the sight of them. Hadn't Nicholas given up enough for this law firm? How many times had I watched him knot his tie, lace his dress shoes, and board the train on a Saturday? How many vacations had been interrupted by urgent calls from clients and arbitrary deadlines from partners?

Nicholas kept going, spelling out the logistics of how these decisions are made and the arcane, draconian methods law firms use for meting out information to their unsuspecting workhorse associates. But I already knew the drill. My dad was a retired partner at another midtown law firm; I grew up hearing about the personality quirks and work ethics of candidates who didn't quite make the cut. There had been eighty aspiring partners in Nicholas's so-called class at Sutherland, Courtfield; by the time they were officially eligible for lifelong tenure—the proverbial golden handcuffs—they would be winnowed down to five, at most. Even knowing this, I'd never imagined Nicholas would be part of the reaping.

By this point, we were in our kitchen, where Cornelius wove among our legs, whimpering anxiously as if he sensed the tension. I made a fresh pot of coffee that neither of us would drink. Nicholas and I were rarely home alone without our kids, but my mind didn't go where it normally would in such a situation.

Only two weeks before, my parents had taken the kids for the weekend, and before their car was even out of the driveway, we'd raced upstairs to our room. Suddenly, Georgie had materialized at the foot of our bed, looking perplexed. "Wait, why are you guys going to *sleep?*"

Nicholas and I leapt apart, and he grabbed a book from the floor and made a show of reading it. I tucked the sheet under each arm and reached for her hand, which was dwarfed by a plastic ring from the treasure chest at the dentist's office. "Georgie! You're back so soon?"

"Pop brought me back. I forgot Olivia." Olivia is a pig in striped tights; she came with a book by the same name, and she's a key member of Georgie's bedtime menagerie, which also includes Curious George and a stingray. "What are *you* two doing?"

Nicholas put down the book: *Magic Tree House #31: Summer of the Sea Serpent.* "We're . . . napping."

Georgie chewed the end of her scraggly braid, beholding us suspiciously with hazelnut (her word) eyes.

"Okay, well, don't do anything I wouldn't do!" She turned on her heel and ran downstairs. The minute we heard the front door close, we picked up where we'd left off.

•   •   •

Now Nicholas leaned against the counter, absentmindedly peeling the clear packing tape we used to hold our cabinets together. Our kitchen was in dire need of a facelift—the black-and-white checkered floor was so scratched, it looked like the loading dock at a grocery store. We'd been saving up for a renovation.

"But at least you can stay at the firm until you find a new job, right?"

"No, that's another thing."

"What?" I envisioned sand pouring through a sieve: vacations, restaurant dinners, movies, a new car, college savings, retirement—every iota of security spilling out and away.

"Alice, I can't stay there."

"What do you mean you can't stay there?"

"Oh, come on. You know how it is. 'Up or out.'" Nicholas's shoulders slumped and I rubbed his back in wide circles, as I did when one of the kids threw up on the floor in the middle of the night. *It's okay. It's okay.* He unbuttoned the top button of his shirt with a defeated air. "Now that I have this information, I really need to move on. It would be humiliating to stay—I'm a dead man walking."

I pictured Nicholas in an orange prison jumpsuit, shackled at the ankles and cuffed at the wrists. "I get that."

"So, I've been thinking—and this isn't the first time it's crossed my mind—now might be the time to hang out a shingle. Bring in my own clients; run my own show."

"Really?"

"Really." Nicholas leaned over the sink, turned it on full blast, and threw water at his face in little cupped handfuls. Then he turned back to me with glistening cheeks, shiny droplets clinging to his eyebrows. He looked ashamed instead of refreshed. "Alice, I have to tell you, I didn't react well to the news."

"What do you mean?"

"I mean . . ." Now Nicholas opened the fridge and grabbed a bottle of beer. After he flicked off the cap, he lifted it by its brown neck and tilted the bottom in my direction in a gesture that telegraphed both "What have

I got to lose?" and "Here's looking at you." I raised an invisible bottle of my own, although my mood was anything but celebratory. Even though he was a borderline teetotaler, I didn't need to be told that this wasn't Nicholas's first beer of the morning.

"Yes?"

"I lost it when Win told me I wasn't going to make partner."

"Lost it . . . how?"

"I threw my laptop across the room." He crossed his arms and closed his eyes briefly, as if to block out the reality of what he was saying, which was horrifying and surreal. An angry Nicholas was a silent Nicholas, icily folding laundry or staring straight ahead at the road for hours while driving. In all our years together, I'd never seen him throw anything except a ball and once, when we took a pottery class together, a tragically misshapen bowl.

"Wait . . . *what?* I'm sorry. Did you just say you *threw your laptop across the room?*" My mind flashed on the possibility of having my own beer, but I thought the better of it—the last thing I wanted to do was arrive at school pickup with alcohol on my breath. A spark like that could ignite a firestorm of gossip whose fug would follow me for years; I'd seen it with a mom who was spotted at the Scholastic book fair with a tiny bottle of something in her satchel purse. It could have been hand lotion or hair spray (this being New Jersey, after all), but the die was cast. The woman was never invited to be a class parent again.

Nicholas fiddled with the refrigerator magnets, arranging the unused alphabet letters in a little line at the top of the freezer door. *QPITZLSF.* "Yes, I threw my laptop across the room. But we were in a conference room, and there was a lot of space. And the laptop was closed, so . . . well, I guess that doesn't make it any better, but at least it didn't shatter."

"That's something." No mess to clean up, no injuries. Still, I felt a little light-headed. I closed my eyes and pressed my index fingers onto their lids until I saw orange kaleidoscope patterns.

"Yeah, I guess."

"Did it . . . make a lot of noise?"

Nicholas looked sheepish. "Yes."

"Well. At least . . . you're going out with a bang?"

We both laughed, halfheartedly. Nicholas tilted his head back and took a long swig from his beer. His neck looked smooth and young; he might have been twenty, pounding a Natty Light in the office of the college newspaper.

"Glen—remember him from my basketball team?"

"Yeah?"

"He has space I can rent in North Caldwell. I think I might have a few clients who would jump ship, and I've been coming up with ideas for bringing in new ones. I want to give it a whirl."

"Wow. Nicholas! You've really thought this through." I didn't believe this, not for a minute. Nicholas and I are hardly models of perfect communication, but we keep each other in the loop when it comes to major decisions.

"I guess. I won't miss the commute, or feeling like a minion all the time. But it'll take a while to get up and running. That's what scares me."

"Are you worried that you've burned a bridge?" (I really wanted to say: Aren't you worried these people will think you are *out of your mind*?)

"Maybe? But for me that was a bridge to nowhere."

We were quiet for a minute, both standing there like characters on a movie set. I knew what my line was and I delivered it without hesitation: "Nicholas, we'll make it work."

"I know. I'm sure it will turn out to be a good thing, I just—"

"It's already a good thing. Nobody should have to stay in a place where they want to throw something across a room. We're going to figure this out. I'll find a new job. Full time. We'll survive."

I tried to sound cheerful, game for anything, but the truth is, I was petrified. I wasn't sure if I was ready to up the ante on the work front. Our kids were still little. I loved my part-time job at *You* magazine. I worried that it would take years for Nicholas to start his own firm and that he was now unemployable thanks to this understandable but completely uncharacteristic violent outburst in his past.

Nicholas unthreaded his cufflinks—little elastic knots that he had in every color of the rainbow. "Actually, that's not a bad idea."

"Which part?"

"You working full-time."

And just like that, the page turned. We were on to a new chapter.

At bedtime, Georgie picked *Sylvester and the Magic Pebble*, which I can read with my eyes closed. Normally, it's only the two of us for stories; Oliver and Margot like to read to themselves in their own rooms. But tonight they were shoehorning their bodies into Georgie's single bed by the time I finished the first line: "Sylvester Duncan lived with his mother and father on Acorn Road in Oatsdale."

If March is the fillet of the calendar, this is the fillet of parenthood: that one, brief part of the day when lunchboxes are unpacked, bickering is suspended, and everyone smells like toothpaste. Margot didn't move away when my thumb found the cleft in her chin, and I didn't flinch when Oliver's bony shoulder wedged painfully into my spleen. Georgie pulled her knees underneath her stretchy Tinker Bell nightgown and sidled further up the bed to make more space.

2

Nicholas and I have been married for thirteen years. We met when we were freshmen at our tiny arty/crunchy college in Vermont; in fact, he was one of the very first people I met on my first day there. My roommate and I were lugging her baby-blue futon up the stairs to the fifth floor when the door opened on the second-floor landing, and a smart-looking boy with circular wire-rim glasses stepped through. He asked if we needed help. We did.

We didn't start dating—insofar as people "date" in college—until senior year, when I was an editor of the college newspaper and Nicholas was one of my writers. He stopped by the newspaper offices on a night when we were "putting the issue to bed"— how I loved the urgency and insiderness of this expression—and took me to task for excising the word *elephantine* from an article he'd written about the football team.

"I just didn't think the players would appreciate being described that way," I explained. "And for what it's worth? These changes are at my discretion. Editor trumps writer. Sorry."

Nicholas rolled his eyes. "Whatever. Hey, Alice, have you seen *Pulp Fiction* yet?"

That Friday night, he borrowed his roommate's car so we could drive to a megaplex in Burlington to see John Travolta make his comeback. We ended up lingering for so long over Moons Over My Hammy at Denny's, we never made it to the movie. I don't remember what we talked about, but I know we were both wearing green corduroy zip-up shirts. The waitress asked if we were twins. At the time, we thought the question was hilarious. Yes, the two of us are Irish and German sides of the same coin: dark hair, green eyes. But I have freckles; Nicholas has dimples. I tan; he burns.

On our way back to school, a deer jumped out in front of the car, and Nicholas swerved to the side of the road to avoid hitting him. We rolled to a stop and he exhaled, loudly. "Did you see how scared he was?"

"I did," I said, my head full of the quick pulse of blood through my ears. The deer had been so close, I'd seen the wild look in his eyes and the razor-thin grooves in his antlers.

Looking past Nicholas, through the driver's side window, I noticed three rolls of hay in a field lit by the moon. Along the horizon, the Adirondacks rose and fell in a dark line, looking like a row of women in strapless dresses wearing body glitter made of stars.

We sat there for a minute before pulling back onto the narrow ribbon of Route 7. We were quiet. This wasn't when he kissed me for the first time; that was later, on a pleather college-issue couch, in the middle of a video of *Fast Times at Ridgemont High*. But that pause in the car was the beginning of something, and I knew it was important.

"Alice?"

"Yes?"

"Can I ask you a favor?"

"Anything." We were lying in bed, staring at the ceiling.

"Can we not tell anyone about this? It's really embarrassing."

"Of course. But, Nicholas, this happens to a lot of people. Law firms are notoriously—"

"No, I'm serious. I'm going to need clients and I don't want anyone thinking of me as some sad sack."

"Who would think that? Are you kidding?" (The words *passed over* flashed through my mind like subtitles in a poorly translated movie. I banished them immediately.)

"Alice, I'm serious. You need to promise this is just between us."

"I promise."

"Especially your dad."

"What about my dad?"

"I don't want him to know."

"Okay, Nicholas, but eventually we'll have to tell him."

"I know. I just want to . . . live with this decision a little bit before I hash it out with him. He'll have his own opinions and—well, honestly, I don't want to hear them right now."

"Okay."

I remembered my dad at Nicholas's law school graduation, his lanky frame folded into a plush chair at Carnegie Hall. The dean was firm about holding applause until the last juris doctor accepted her diploma, but when Nicholas strode across the stage, baby-blue robe shining in the spotlight, my dad rose up in the middle of the audience. Just stood there, ramrod straight, no sound except the thump of his chair folding closed, wearing an ecstatic grin.

My mind reeled with people I might talk to in strictest confidence—my brother, Will; my mom; my friend Susanna; one of my college roommates—but then I focused on my own potential to be a hero in this private family drama. I would forge ahead, quietly, full of grit and grace. I would channel my grandmother, who moved to Boston from County Roscommon when she was eighteen, married an underemployed charmer who died when she was pregnant with their sixth kid (my dad), raised her family on the top floor of a Dorchester triple-decker while cooking for a fancy family in Winchester, and still found time to crochet afghans and serve as prefect of the sodality at church.

Until this point, I'll admit, I was the tiniest bit smug about my work–life balance. When other moms complained about the never-ending tread-mill connecting home and work and everything in between, I kept quiet, knowing how lucky I was to have a part-time job I loved. I wasn't part of the high-powered commuter set and I wasn't a PTA insider, but I got to dip into both worlds.

On Mondays, Wednesdays, and Fridays, I was the books editor of *You*, a position I'd held since Margot was a baby. My job consisted of reading books sent to the magazine by publishers, picking the ones we would review, then writing the reviews. Sure, the magazine was geared to a demographic Nicholas and I half-jokingly referred to as sorority girl health nuts. But my colleagues were like family, and the job offered the perfect combination of intellectual stimulation and access to the last word in spin shoes from the fitness closet. Best of all, I still had time to actually spin, when I wasn't refereeing play dates and having coffee with friends.

On a Tuesday, I might take an early shift at a bake sale in the school gym, selling whole-grain organic blueberry muffins to voters on their way to the 8:16 train, and the next day, I'd be waiting on the platform with those same people, this time wearing heels instead of Converse. I kept two bags on the red bench by our front door: one Orla Kiely tote stocked with Band-Aids and flavor-blasted Goldfish; the other, a Furla shoulder bag containing manuscripts and magazine layouts.

I loved those weekday afternoons with my kids, even though there was often a shrill edge to my reminders to put away play dough/crayons/baseball cards/hockey guys/Apples to Apples. And despite their constant grumbling about walking Cornelius and the weird bread I packed in their lunches, despite the hundreds of shapes of pasta I swept off the kitchen floor over the years and all those microscopic Polly Pocket shoes I felt guilty throwing out, nothing gave me greater pleasure than glancing at the rearview mirror of my minivan and seeing our trio. There was Margot, her blue glasses eternally halfway down her nose; only the top of Oliver's head visible as he buried his nose in the *Dictionary of Disgusting Facts*; and Georgie, sporting an impossible bounty of hair accessories— ribbons fastened to metal alligator clips, candy-striped bobby pins, plastic Goody barrettes shaped like butterflies and poodles.

Our house is so close to their elementary school, I can actually see each of the kids in their classrooms, depending on what grade they're in (hello, therapy). When the red doors opened at the end of the day, I waited for them to burst out and race toward me as quickly as was humanly possible beneath the weight of their massive backpacks. On the days we didn't have soccer or swimming or hip-hop, they each brought a friend home and we crossed over together midway down the block, a chain of seven happy people holding hands.

On my work days, Nicholas and I relied on Jessie, the babysitter we'd hired from Craigslist seven years earlier, when she was eighteen and we were new transplants to New Jersey. She was our first friend in Filament and was still our coolest, by a wide margin. When she wasn't coloring Shrinky Dinks or carpooling our kids, Jessie was the lead singer with the Prenups, northern New Jersey's premier wedding band. Thanks to her rocker influence, Oliver could pick out "More Than Words" on her Fender before he even learned to write his name. All three kids could play a mean air guitar.

With her nose pierce, dahlia tattoo sleeve, and blue-streaked hair, Jessie is the opposite of Mary Poppins, but she's as unflappable as I am easily flustered. On a typical night, I came home to find her in the kitchen, pulling a lasagna out of the oven while teaching Margot how to reduce fractions while supervising a craft project involving Georgie, popsicle sticks, and Elmer's glue. If Oliver happened to be tap-dancing on the ceiling, I wouldn't have been surprised.

Nicholas and I knew how lucky we were. At least, I hope we did.

•   •   •

A few days after Nicholas's revelation, I was at the *You* offices, stuffing a stack of publishers' galleys in my bag, gearing up to race for the 6:09 train back to Filament, when I noticed that the features editor, Annika, was alone in her office. I tapped on the wall next to her door. "Do you have a minute to chat?"

"Alice! Always. Come in, sit." With one elegantly muscled arm, she gestured at the Ultrasuede swivel chair in front of her desk, her wide-set Jackie Kennedy eyes narrowing with concern when I slid the shower-style door closed behind me. "Oh no. Is this serious?" Her expression rearranged itself from "ready for harmless gossip" to "I'm sorry to hear you have a suspicious mole."

"I wanted to see if by any chance you guys might have a full-time position for me. My circumstances have changed at home, and well, I need to step it up. Financially." My unrehearsed explanation sounded unintentionally dire. I corrected my posture, as we were often exhorting women to do in *You*: spine straight, shoulders back, chin up. My imaginary sister hoisted a pair of pom-poms and cheered me on: You've got this. You go, girl.

Annika furrowed her brows, which were groomed, like mine, by an opinionated aesthetician who set up his tweezers, scissors, and powders in the photo department once a month. "Is everything . . . okay?"

"Yes! Everyone is healthy. Nicholas and I are fine. It's just—we're facing some financial challenges. Also, the kids are all in school now so I don't really need to be at home so much anymore." The words felt strange in my mouth, *need* being very different from *want*. My throat tightened. I could picture the expression on my own face since I saw it so often on Margot's: eyes wide, lips tight, nostrils flared. Determination with a side of hesitation.

"Okay. I hear you. Listen, Al, I can ask around, but with ad pages shrinking—and really we don't do as much as we used to with books—I'm not optimistic. I wish I could be. You know we love having you here." Annika's voice quavered. We'd known each other for years; *You* was a place where I once bared my pregnant belly in a meeting to show the younger editors my crazy highway system of bright-blue veins. The boundary between professional and personal had long ago evaporated.

"No worries, I get it." On the wall behind Annika's desk was an arty photograph of a large broken egg. I could see my reflection in the glass over the yolk: forehead crinkled, hair a little frizzy despite its thrice weekly drubbing by flat iron. "Annika, I think I need to start looking for a new job."

We sat quietly for a minute, staring at each other over her desk.

Annika gestured at her mega-Rolodex, which contained the stapled-in cards of every editor in New York City, not to mention celebrity gynecologists, pinch-hitting babysitters, pet behaviorists, and Ivy League matchmakers. "Alice, anything I can do to help. Just say the word."

> **Dad:** Dear Al, are you out there?
> **Me:** Yes. On train, heading home.
> **Dad:** How was your day? What's the news?
> **Me:** Nothing to report. You?
> **Dad:** Mom and I are going to the Saint Patrick's Day parade in Newark.
>   Join us?
> **Me:** No, thanks. Bagpipes depress me.
> **Dad:** OK. Dinner Sun?
> **Me:** As long as corned beef and cabbage are not on the menu.
> **Dad:** Lamb, mint jelly, Yorkshire pudding. CU! Love, Dad.

"It's not that they don't *like* me, but Annika doesn't think they have a full-time position in the budget. She said if I was interested in covering beauty, maybe, but otherwise . . ." Nicholas and I were in the basement, separating empty cans of Happy Hips dog food from flattened cereal boxes and tying newspapers in preparation for recycling day. Some couples have date night; we have our weekly powwows over the plastic bins by the dryer.

"And you couldn't do beauty?" Nicholas's laser focus annoyed me. Had it escaped his notice that I barely wore makeup and polished my boots more frequently than my nails?

"No, I can't do *beauty*. Nicholas! I'm a books person. And I've been at *You* for too long. Current circumstances aside, it's time to start looking for a new job."

"Can you not put it like that? 'Current circumstances'? It's not like I'm leaving my firm to run a lemonade stand. I have a plan, Alice."

"I know. But your plan is going to take a while to implement, and I want to make sure we're . . . secure." I sliced my thumb on the edge of a Rice Krispies box, then paused to shake it frantically in the air.

"I appreciate that. But I'm not wild about the subtext of what you're saying. It's not like I—"

"I'm just worried. Suddenly I'm married to a man who threw a computer across the room and that makes me nervous. I'm sorry, but it does."

"Alice, I told you, it was *closed* and we were in a *conference room*. Nobody got hurt."

"I know, you keep saying that, but the bigger issue is: you just destroyed your credibility in that corner of the legal community and I don't think—"

"Exactly. You're right. I did. But the truth is I don't want to be in that corner anymore, and Win Makepeace just happened to be the person who forced my hand. I'm trying to look to the future. What's next? I'm about to find out. Sounds like you are, too."

At Nicholas's parents' fortieth anniversary party, one of their old friends gave a toast about how he'd never expected their relationship to last. Judy and Elliott had been a pair of hippies, hopeless dreamers, who got hitched on a lark. But their relationship turned out to have legs: my in-laws traded their Beetle for a Buick, their fondue pot for a crockpot, became homeowners, parents, churchgoers, scout leaders, business partners, Reiki masters.

This evolution could have been their undoing, but—said this bearded man whose martini listed dangerously to the side—instead Judy and Elliott managed to change alongside each other, and that, he believed, was the key to their contentment. And most likely the key to the dissolution of his own marriage because his ex hadn't been able to expand her vision of their future together to accommodate his dream of opening a mobile hookah lounge.

The speech ended on an awkward note, with everyone assuring the guy that he should *of course* go into the hookah business. Meanwhile, I held on to one memorable phrase: *change alongside one another*.

There's something to it. Nicholas and I certainly aren't always completely in sync—he's an introvert and a cynic; I'm an optimist. He considers people guilty until proven innocent; I collect new friends wherever I can find them. But changing together? We're good at that.

Oliver, Nicholas, and my dad were wrapped up in March Madness, cheering loudly for the Hoyas. While Nicholas and Oliver whooped and yelled, my dad had his own unorthodox way of expressing enthusiasm. Since he couldn't make a peep without holding a little electric wand to his neck, he simply pressed the button on the side of his electrolarynx so it emitted a steady vibrating buzz, the sound of an electric razor. The kids called the device Buzz Lightyear.

My mom and I were in the kitchen, wiping down the counters and preparing a tray of green cannolis for dessert. (In Essex County, everybody is Irish in March, even Italian bakers.) "Mom, have you heard anything from Will?"

She shook her head, her amethyst earrings making a little tinging sound. "Not in a few weeks. I know the boys are getting ready for their recital, so that's probably keeping everybody busy." My nephews are Suzuki prodigies—two apples who fell really far from their father's tree. When my brother was their age, he was a garden-variety dirt bike–riding, baseball-playing, noogie-giving troublemaker. The only bows he knew were the ones he used to tie me to the tetherball pole in our backyard.

3

To: Alice.Pearse@gmail.com
From: pearseparents@gmail.com

Dear Alice,

I hope you'll forgive the intrusion; I know Mondays are busy for you with work and little ones. Out of the blue, I just heard from my old friend John Enzo who shared some surprising news: that Nicholas intends to leave Sutherland, Courtfield at the end of the month? To start a private practice here in New Jersey?

Alice, WTF! (Sorry, just learned this one.)

Seriously, I hope you know that I try not to meddle in the lives of my kids. And I hate to raise this subject via e-mail; but given my communication limitations, it's what makes the most sense.

My mom looked up from her ministrations at the sink. "How do you think he looks?"

"Who?" Of course, I knew we weren't talking about Will anymore.

"Daddy. Do you think there's something funny about his color?"

"No, Mom. I think he looks great."

"Are you sure? Not sort of yellow?"

"I'm sure. He looks good."

This was our usual call and response. My dad had rebounded from the initial devastation of his diagnosis, with its life-altering treatment. He'd been forced into an abrupt retirement—what good is a lawyer who can't talk? Now he filled his days with gardening, exercise, newspapers, mysteries, crosswords, and grandchildren. My kids and their cousins found his Darth Vader voice both horrifying and fascinating. They begged him to come over and answer the door for trick-or-treaters on Halloween.

My mom was the one still in the watchtower, constantly scanning the horizon for the enemy. She organized my dad's vitamins, medications, stoma tubes, and diabetes supplies with military precision. Every night, she charged Buzz Lightyear on her side of the bed and then placed it on his pillow first thing in the morning so he could grab his voice before he opened his eyes.

Usually, I was right there with her, scrutinizing my dad for any sign of a recurrence, but now I was too busy worrying about my own family. We had two months of Sutherland, Courtfield paychecks in our future. After that, we would rely on savings and my meager paycheck until Nicholas's new business was up and running. Of course I couldn't reveal this to my parents—I'd promised Nicholas. The pressure was on.

Why didn't you tell me and Mom about this news? Remember, Alice, I've been a senior associate, too. I know it was a different time, but I recall how hard it was and how rarely I saw you and Will.

I'm concerned that the challenges of starting a law practice almost from scratch will be even more daunting. Forgive me for getting down to the nitty-gritty, but do you have enough savings to cover your mortgage until money starts coming in? Does Nicholas have clients lined up? Will they pay up front? Even in the best-case scenario, he may not make any money for three to six months.

I'm wondering if the two of you would consider a loan from me and Mom. We could help pay Jessie, for instance.

Once again, I'm sorry to pry into your personal affairs. I respect your decisions and, of course, Nicholas's.

I would appreciate an update when you have time.

Love,
Dad

PS. Your mom thinks I should mind my own business.

"Different time"—*ha!* When my dad was an associate, Dictaphones and telex machines were cutting-edge. There were no smart phones; you never left work with your office in your pocket. I remembered my dad working in the living room, using his Hartmann briefcase as a makeshift lap desk, but he wasn't expected to be reachable at three o'clock in the morning via e-mail, IM, text, or FaceTime. He never had to stand on the sidelines of my brother's baseball games, whispering furiously into a little metal rectangle that was like another member of the family. At some point, his workday came to an end—unlike Nicholas's, which bled into the weekend and onto vacations, depending upon the whims of Win Makepeace, who could snap his fingers from his weekend home in Watch Hill and derail our plans three states away.

I highlighted the subject of my dad's message—"News?"—and clicked the garbage pail icon in the upper left-hand corner of my screen. Technology could be so convenient.

> To: Alice.Pearse@gmail.com
> From: pearseparents@gmail.com
>
> Dear Alice,
>
> Just confirming that you received my e-mail message from earlier today. You never know with these things. I noticed you liked one of Will's pictures on Facebook, so I'm assuming you had a chance to log some computer time. Anyway, send up a flare, will you?
>
> Love,
> Dad

If I didn't respond to my dad's second e-mail, I could expect to receive a letter by certified mail. Like all lawyers of his generation, my dad took correspondence very seriously.

> To: pearseparents@gmail.com
> From: Alice.Pearse@gmail.com
>
> Dad,
>
> I did get your message(s). I appreciate your concerns and assure you Nicholas and I have discussed each one. Thankfully, he isn't the sole breadwinner—we'll still have my salary, so we won't need to borrow

from you. (I *implore* you not to bring this up with Nicholas, who would be mortified.) Of course, we're realistic and know that we'll have to cut corners here and there, but I'm committed to helping Nicholas build a professional life where he's happy, fulfilled, and home more. People our age don't stay in the same job for decades—it's a quirk and a perk of Gen X. Thanks for checking in.

I love you.

Alice

I put out all kinds of feelers, the way you do when you look for a new job. I made a list of all the people I know who I thought might be able to help; however, I stopped short of calling them "contacts," since many are friends I have lunch with a few times a year, whom I trade tips with about books and husbands and stores that sell non-low-rise jeans that don't scream *mom*.

The tone of my e-mail was breezy: "I'm starting to think about exploring other options, so I'd love to set up a time to chat with you about any fun positions at [INSERT NAME OF MAGAZINE/NEWSPAPER/PUBLISHING COMPANY/WEBSITE HERE]." My first response came from an old friend who had recently been named editorial director at Mama.com: "Total shot in the dark: are you pregnant or considering adoption? We're looking for an expectant mommy blogger. The pay is crap but we could throw in some free products and board books . . . ?"

A guy I knew from the train invited me to meet him in the third car that night to talk about a position at his copywriting firm. I was half asleep by the time we arrived in Filament.

Nicholas's distant cousin wondered if I had any experience in newsletters. She said Nabisco was looking for someone to educate consumers about a new line of energy-boosting crackers. No thanks.

The most interesting lead came from a former colleague who put me in touch with her cousin, the director of guidance at a well-known private school, who was looking for college essay coaches. In a brief phone conversation, I learned that I could earn up to $3,000 per client. The work sounded easy enough, but the conversation hit a wall after I described the most recent personal essay I'd edited for *You*. It had been a moving piece by a woman who suffered from trichotillomania, a disease that caused her to pull out her eyebrows and eat them. The guidance director cleared his throat: "Well, then. I'm afraid that's not the kind of material colleges like to read about."

Another door, closed.

One morning, I was sitting at my desk at *You*, parceling books into stacks like a dealer at a blackjack table: serious novels, fun novels, tragic memoirs, witty memoirs, thrillers to send to my dad, cookbooks to hoard under my desk until Christmas or school auction time, when they would be bundled into raffle baskets with a set of cutting boards. I was killing time before a features meeting, anticipating the inevitable slightly tardy e-mail from the assistant to our editor in chief, with the subject line: "She's ready. Please gather in her office."

Suddenly, an unfamiliar name popped up in my in-box. This wasn't unusual, since at least half of my e-mail came from publicists I didn't know, pitching books or stories on subjects *You* would never cover: geriatric beauty tips, government spy programs, "Top 10 Tips for Re-Caulking Your Tub." Usually I didn't even open these messages, but the one from Genevieve Andrews had me at the subject line: *do you want to be part of the future of bookstores?*

No caps.

Uh, *yes*.

I clicked. The message said,

To: Alice.Pearse@gmail.com
From: GenevieveAndrews@scroll.com

Dear Alice: I hope you won't mind that I'm tracking you down out of the blue like this. I believe we follow each other on Twitter, where I always

look forward to your opinions on what to read next. I'm writing now
because I've just started a new job as the lead for the New York division
of Scroll and I'm looking to hire forward-thinking booklovers to help
create an unforgettable reading experience for our customers. If you're
interested in learning more, might we meet for coffee at Shakespeare's
Sister (SoHo branch) next Friday at 4 p.m.?

Yours,
Genevieve Andrews

Imagine being discovered on Twitter, of all places! I couldn't wait to
tell Nicholas, who thought social media was a huge waste of time.

I floated into the features meeting on a cloud of optimism and goodwill.
While other editors reclined on cheetah-print sofas, cheerfully debating
the merits of gargling with coconut oil for twenty minutes a day, I sat on
the floor and daydreamed about becoming a forward-thinking booklover.

Of course, I remembered Scroll from a recent article on the front page of
the *New York Times*. It had been a big story, including a jump to the business section, about the Cleveland retail giant MainStreet expanding into
virtual bookstores. I'd skimmed the piece while eating Fage yogurt; now
I reread it on my phone while I waited for the train home.

MainStreet is a family business, owned by the Rockwell brothers, Sam
and Dan, who are beloved by Wall Street for their runaway success with a
chain of high-end suburban shopping malls. My in-laws, Judy and Elliott,
live outside Cleveland near Heritage Towne, the first in a fleet of dozens
of MainStreet's "lifestyle centers," which mimic the hometown vibe of the
very mom-and-pop stores they put out of business. Cobblestone, gaslit
lanes connect Johnny Rockets with Hollister; phone-charging stations are
coyly housed inside old-fashioned phone booths; easy-listening rendi-
tions of folk favorites are piped to the furthest reaches of the parking lot,
for the brave souls who forgo valet service. Heritage Towne has a gym, a

movie theater, a band shell, a medical center, and its own Whole Foods. The Residences at Heritage Towne are currently under construction.

According to the *New York Times*, a third Rockwell brother was joining the empire. Under his aegis, MainStreet would open a nationwide chain of reading lounges, known as Scroll, which would "reinvent the bookstore experience," according to an unnamed MainStreet spokeswoman. Customers would be able to browse e-books on docked tablets and then download files directly to all their devices at once. Plans for the lounges included fair-trade-certified coffee bars and eco-friendly furniture sourced from reclaimed local materials.

Scroll would be based in New York—"the epicenter of the literary universe." The industry's most discerning, community-minded tastemakers would be hired to curate the e-book collection for Scroll, whose site would be tethered to the MainStreet homepage so patrons could buy, say, a wheelbarrow along with their gardening book.

"As Cervantes put it, 'No limits but the sky,'" said the unnamed spokesperson.

Interesting, I thought, as I scanned the big board in Penn Station for my track number. Being a tastemaker sounded like fun. And I was certainly community-minded—after all, I'd been the co-planner of the Flower Street block party for six years running.

On the train, I reread Genevieve's e-mail. I didn't want to get my hopes up, but the future was starting to look a little bit brighter. The timing was almost too good to be true.

My original post-college plan had been to live in Vermont for the summer, then to move to New York and find a job in book publishing. After graduation, I shared a house with seven other women (not girls; we were clear on this point). We were all waitresses with editorial assistant dreams; we loved Mary Cantwell, Sylvia Plath, Joan Didion. While we counted out our tips at the kitchen table at two o'clock in the morning, we'd plan our lives in New York, in our minds a strange outdated jumble of beatnik Greenwich Village and slices of cheesecake at the Automat.

Meanwhile, my brother had just started the analyst training program at Lehman Brothers. What little free time he had, he spent Rollerblading around the Loop in Central Park and trying to pick up "Betties" at sunset happy hours in South Street Seaport. At my graduation, he took me aside and said, "Alice, I know you think you want to be a poet, but you need to find a job where you make *bank*. That's the only way to have any fun in the Big Apple." Will's version of New York was one I wanted to avoid at all costs.

One night, I came home with a business card belonging to a friendly customer who turned out to be an editor whose colleague was looking for a new assistant. The card was a little damp, having traveled atop my cocktail tray among countless rounds of Otter Creek Copper Ale, but my roommates passed it around the table and admired it: "Alice, you are *set*. If you get this job, you'll be hobnobbing with the literati while we're stuck restocking croutons and rolling cutlery."

Nicholas showed up, smelling like popcorn from the theater where he worked as a projectionist, and someone shoved the card at him: "Look, your girlfriend already has an in."

"Really? That's great!" He smiled, squinting at the card. Even then, he was a reader of fine print. "An in . . . in textbook publishing?"

Okay, so maybe I wouldn't be working with Anne Tyler or Isabel Allende. The point was to get my foot in the door.

The card led to an interview, the interview led to a job offer from a textbook publisher, and the job offer came with health insurance and twice-monthly paychecks for $649—just enough to afford me two suits from Labels for Less, a pleather bag from Strawberry, a year's supply of generic macaroni, and a windowless, closetless bedroom above Let's Pet Dog Grooming in Cobble Hill. My life in New York had officially begun.

From college engineering textbooks, I moved on to Page-A-Day calendars: cats, dogs, horoscopes, Bible verses, cars, Magnetic Poetry. In this job, I learned the hard way how to be detail-oriented—but for the keen eye of a copy editor, Valentine's Day would have fallen on February 15th in the 1996 Sagittarius calendar—and I collected a lifetime supply of crossword clues and useless trivia. A cat with extra toes? Polydactyl. Planet ruled by Pisces? Neptune. First automobile with a compass on the dashboard? Templar Touring Roadster.

From calendars, I moved to magazines, where I was happy. Trust me, there is no better place to work than a women's magazine when you're newly engaged: the *squeals*! The endless admiration of your emerald-cut diamond! The shower with an exquisite buttercream cake and Veuve Clicquot champagne and a gift certificate for a couples massage at Bliss!

But still, I remained on the fringes of the professional world I'd hoped to be part of. When I waited in line in the basement of Coliseum Books to have my copy of *Bridget Jones's Diary* signed by Helen Fielding, it was not the hilarious author I had my eye on but the young cardigan-wearing woman to her left: the editor. What was it like to be the person who chose books readers would fall in love with, buy for their mothers, and remember forever after, the way you never forget a delicious meal?

Nicholas was thrilled by the e-mail from Genevieve—and tickled by the way she found me. "Maybe Twitter isn't so pointless after all," he said, begrudgingly. "And Scroll! They're supposed to be a great company."

"You're just biased because of the Cleveland connection."

The Rockwell brothers are natives, too. In every profile for *Fortune* or *Businessweek*, they wax poetic about eating Notso fries at Yours Truly in Shaker Square (you don't want to know) and their annual viewing of *A Christmas Story*, which was filmed in the Tremont neighborhood of Cleveland, even though the family in the movie is supposed to live in northern Indiana. The brothers deliver this line interchangeably: "When we decided to start our retail business, there was only one place to go: Cleveland. For us, that's where MainStreet starts."

"Do you think I'll get an employee discount at all the MainStreet stores, or just Scroll?" We were driving up the gradual slope of Bloomfield Avenue, on our way to a neighboring town to look at office space for Nicholas. He wanted to sign a lease immediately; I thought he should set up an office in the basement until he was established.

"Alice! Pace yourself. You're meeting this woman for *coffee*; I mean, I'm sure she'll want to hire you, but it's hardly a done deal."

"I know. I wonder what Genevieve is thinking I'll do there?"

"I guess you'll find out soon enough. Which reminds me: I hope you won't mind, but I told your dad about your interview with Scroll." Nicholas angled his Accord into a parking lot behind a bagel store and a Mexican restaurant. "And here we are."

I glanced at the stucco facade of his new building, a far cry from the mirrored skyscraper he was leaving, and put a hand on his arm. "Wait, *what*? You're the one who just pointed out, it's *coffee*, not an interview. Why would you bring it up with my dad?"

Nicholas grimaced. "Sorry, he was trying to give me advice and I couldn't understand what he was saying, so I just . . . blurted it out, I guess." He paused to fish Glen's key off a carabiner attached to his belt loop, a look which reminded me depressingly of the dozens of keychains dangling from the zippers of each of our kids' backpacks. "Anyway, your dad was excited, Al! Really excited. It was a nice way to sidestep a weird heart-to-heart with him about my future."

"My dad isn't a heart-to-heart kind of guy—you know that. He just wants to be in the loop."

"That's the thing, though. I don't really want him in the loop right now, okay?" Nicholas squinted through his windshield into the window of the Mexican restaurant, where two men were removing pits from a mountain of avocados. "I don't want to get into the specifics of *why* I'm leaving Sutherland, Courtfield. You get that, right?"

"Of course. Fine. Let's go check out the new digs."

Actually, I *did* mind that Nicholas had taken it upon himself to spill news of my interview. But at least I knew why the morning's deluge of texts from my dad had contained two articles about MainStreet—one from *Forbes*, one from *Wealth*. Those Rockwell brothers were outrageously young! In their Warby Parker glasses and Hugo Boss shirts, they looked like boys dressing up as businessmen.

We walked by a Dumpster overflowing with cardboard boxes and slipped inside a door propped open by a brick wrapped in duct tape. "You have to use your imagination," Nicholas explained. "The place is bare bones but it has potential."

I pasted a supportive smile on my face and toured the new office. The Flor tiles were stained and the filing cabinets might have been salvaged from the set of *9 to 5*, but the light was good and the skyline view couldn't be beat, even if it did look incredibly far away.

I was still surprised to find myself living on this side of the Hudson. For me, growing up in New Jersey, New York was true north on the compass, the place you looked for from the highest point in town. For a Clevelander like Nicholas, it might as well have been Oz. The first time he rode the subway, he bought an extra token to send home to his mom.

I didn't miss the city, exactly, but I got whiplash when I reflected on my own transformation from post-college East Villager hanging out at Veselka to downtown mom with Gourmet Garage bags hanging from the handles of my stroller to Filament commuter navigating the hordes in midtown. Now, no matter how authoritatively I strode toward my office building in Times Square, I always found myself on the receiving end of a sales pitch from a representative of Big Apple Bus Tours. "Buy the all-day pass! Including the Cloisters, the Statue of Liberty—"

"I *live* here," I said, brushing by imperiously in my best approximation of Anna Wintour, if Anna Wintour wore a raincoat from Strawberry.

One night, a year after we got married, I met Nicholas after work at his summer associate event at the New York Public Library. There were speeches from the heads of the different practice groups and signature cocktails with names like Expert Witness and Blind Justice. The ice luge was bigger than our whole apartment.

While Nicholas was shouldering his way up to the bar, I approached three Nehru-jacket-wearing men who looked friendly enough. "Hi, I'm Alice Pearse, Nicholas Bauer's wife!"

The men looked surprised, as Sutherland, Courtfielders often did when confronted with a wife who had not taken her husband's name. One of them said, "Hi. Do you need a cocktail napkin?"

"No, thanks, I'm all set. So . . . are you guys with the bankruptcy group?"

"We're the caterers, actually."

"Oh. Well, I love your jackets."

Suddenly, I felt a very strong hand on my shoulder. I spun around to see Win Makepeace, the head of the bankruptcy group, towering over me with a self-satisfied expression on his face. "Alice, is that you? Let's let these fine gentlemen get back to their canapés. Come meet my wife, Lucinda—she just went on the South Beach diet, so I'm sure you'll have a lot to discuss."

As Win steered me in the direction of a frail blonde with unnaturally smooth skin and bubble hair, I waggled my fingers at the caterers, who smiled sympathetically. They were probably as baffled by the legal life as I was.

Nicholas and I were the last ones to leave and my feet were killing me, so we sat down on the front steps of the library between the marble lions, Patience and Fortitude. Nicholas was still chuckling over my gaffe.

"How was *I* supposed to know? Those guys were the friendliest people there!"

"Exactly, which should have been a dead giveaway that they weren't Sutherland, Courtfield material!"

We leaned comfortably into each other's shoulders, enjoying the warm breeze and unexpected pocket of peace on Fifth Avenue. I felt the cool stone of the stairs through the thin fabric of my skirt. I watched the street vendors quietly shouldering their closed-down carts in the direction of Tenth Avenue, then looked up at the elegant arcs flying atop the Chrysler Building.

"Nicholas, you know I adore you, right?"

He looked surprised, then tickled. "Alice, I adore you, too."

"Good. Now that we have that ironed out, I have something to tell you."

"You *do?*" As he glanced over at me, his expression leapt from relaxed and content to alert and ecstatic. He didn't give me a chance to answer; I didn't need to. "No. Way. You *are?*"

"I am!"

"Are you sure?"

"I'm sure. I just took the test. Two tests, actually."

"Just *now?*"

"I figured, why wait?"

"Wait, you mean you just took a pregnancy test in the middle of the welcome party for summer associates?"

"I figured the library was as good a place as any."

We grinned at each other. We adored Cornelius, our jointly adopted dog, so we'd made a split-second decision to expand our household, figuring parenthood couldn't be so different from pet ownership. I don't need to explain how many times we've marveled at our naivety since then.

"Oh, Alice." Nicholas buried his face in my shoulder. For a minute, I thought he was crying, but then I realized he was shaking—with excitement, I thought, and maybe with fear. "A *baby!* We'll have a little New Yorker!"

I imagined a jelly-bellied toddler wearing frog rainboots, twirling in the blue glow under the whale at the Museum of Natural History.

It was another beginning, the best one. Falling in love and getting married were nothing compared to Margot.

When Margot was five and Oliver was three, we decamped from our one-bedroom apartment to Filament. We wanted more space and, between preschool tuition and Nicholas's school loans, we were having trouble keeping up with our bills. The commute seemed like a worthwhile price to pay for a front porch and a fenced yard for Cornelius, even one pocked with the roots of a dogwood tree, which turned a Slip 'N Slide ride into a death wish.

But what really sold me on our ramshackle house was its proximity to Blue Owl Books. The first time we visited, I paused at the front door and took in the beamed ceilings, the walls stenciled with names of local authors, and tables piled high not just with best sellers, but also art books, travel books, cookbooks, and poetry. An entire wall of shelving was dedicated to books about New Jersey: diners, lighthouses, amusement parks, the Pine Barrens, the parkway, the shore. There was even a kids' biography of Thomas Edison and a board book about Jersey tomatoes. I remembered my mom saying she had been *overcome* the first time she saw the rose windows in Chartres Cathedral. That's exactly how I felt the first time I beheld the Blue Owl.

That day, I bought the tomato board book, a new volume of the *Nutshell Library* (ours had been chewed to pieces by humans and a canine), and two copies of *Goldilocks and the Three Dinosaurs* by Mo Willems— one for our new house, one for my parents'.

The red-haired woman who rang up my purchase said, "You can never have too much Mo. 'If you ever find yourself in the wrong story, leave.' Isn't this the one where he says that?"

"Yes! It's one of my favorites. You can probably tell."

From there, Nicholas and I went straight to our home inspection, where we heard all kinds of dire warnings about termite damage and basement dampness. Given the proximity of these problems to the bookstore, nothing could dissuade me from offering the full asking price.

The red-haired woman at the Blue Owl was Susanna, but I didn't really get to know her until a year later, when Georgie was a baby. By then, I'd mostly adjusted to the rhythms of suburban life, grateful for luxuries like slipping into a car after coming out of a movie on a cold night or sipping a glass of sauvignon blanc on the front porch while our kids circulated among the neighboring yards. I still missed the playground culture of the city; friend-making in Filament was a little like casual dating—you hoped she'd call, but she might not. The moms were friendly and generous with their farm shares and recommendations for electricians, but none of my relationships had progressed to the next level. I feared I might have to host a dinner party in order to find my soul mate.

Then the fire alarm went off during music class, and I ran into Susanna in the parking lot outside the Y. Rather than wait for the green light to return to our positions on the floor of the gym, we chose the same moment to escape from the pack of unimpressed babies and their exhausted, egg-maraca-shaking adults.

"I'm never going back," I muttered under my breath to Susanna, who fell into step beside me with the familiarity of a kindred bookworm.

"Me neither. This is my third kid! I don't have time to play the bongos." She was a full head taller than me and had the graceful carriage of a woman who grew up alongside a ballet barre. She carried Violet effortlessly, like a very light bag of groceries. With her cheek resting on Susanna's shoulder, Violet looked down at Georgie in her stroller and the two exchanged gummy smiles.

It wasn't long before the four of us were tucked into a diner booth. The babies bobbled around in their booster seats, smashing saltines to smithereens, while Susanna and I chatted over the first of hundreds of cups of coffee sipped in our kitchens, at PTA meetings, and on the bleachers at our older girls' swim team practices. (Black for me; milk and two sugars for her.) Violet and Georgie grew up alongside each other, first strapped into neighboring car seats, then toddling around playrooms, bickering like biddies over Slinkies, tea sets, Hexbugs, and which of them got to be the mom.

Meanwhile, Susanna and I became students of each other's lives: college boyfriends, childhood pets, parenting styles of our parents. I knew that she had spent her senior year of high school recuperating from scoliosis surgery and that her parents had announced their divorce to their kids on the drive home from Rye Playland. Our husbands go camping together every fall; our kids are honorary cousins. When Susanna's husband, Paul, was diagnosed with soft-tissue sarcoma, I organized dinner deliveries and made sure the kids were busy every day after school. One day, their four-year-old son, Judd, said, "Alice, please can't you take us home today? Cancer isn't contagious."

A month after Paul's final treatment, Susanna threw a party at the Blue Owl to celebrate the all-clear they'd just gotten from their oncologist. The two of them circulated among relieved friends and neighbors, laughing and smiling, while all our kids banged out a raucous soundtrack on a xylophone in the children's section at the back of the store. As Nicholas and I distributed slices of Star Tavern pizza and plastic cups of champagne, I caught snippets of conversation: *He looks good, Susanna is so strong, This family has been to hell and back, God bless.* I almost cried when Paul's dad paused, mid-conversation, to grab his son's face and plant one powerful kiss on each cheek: "*My boy.*"

When the crowd dispersed, Nicholas and I collected our kids. With their dark hair and pale skin, the three of them reminded me of characters from a fairy tale: a little bit ethereal, with just enough earthliness to outwit the witch (me).

Nicholas and I carried the younger two all the way home while Margot trailed drowsily behind us. "Mommy, do you think Olivia Kidney and Junie B. Jones are, like, BFF?"

I grinned at Nicholas in the dark. "I'm pretty sure they are."

Now Susanna and I were in Ray's Luncheonette, the cozy coffee shop all the local moms landed in post spinning, post Bar Method, post hot yoga, or post hip-hop. Eighty percent of the women in the restaurant were dressed in full-body Lululemon. If I sifted through the white noise underneath the sound of clinking diner mugs and cutlery, I could hear snippets of familiar conversation about plumbers, beach house rentals, ideas for coaxing a reluctant reader to hit the books, and directions for whipping up a homeopathic remedy for warts.

We were planning the next meeting of the No Guilt Book Club. This was a seasonal event we'd hatched together: a night where we invited our friends to the Blue Owl, and for a small fee they got unlimited wine, a discount on all purchases, and our recommendations for what to read next. This was my kind of book club: the one where you trade suggestions but skip the part where you have to exclaim over your host's Santa Claus cheese spreader.

Susanna opened her meticulously handwritten Moleskin calendar and clicked the bottom of a ballpoint pen. "So. I wanted to brainstorm about incentives. What do you think about raffling off a beach bag full of summer books? We can throw in sunglasses, SPF, stuff like that?"

"I love it. One for kids' books, one for adults'? And I'd love to do something with Father's Day . . . Maybe you fill out a quiz about the man in your life and it guides you to just the right thriller or Dave Eggers book?"

"Great, great." Susanna was furiously jotting notes. "And will you give the welcome this time? You're so much better at that than I am."

I smiled. Susanna is an expert businesswoman and knows how to play matchmaker with a clueless customer and table of books, but put her in front of a roomful of people and she reverts to her roots as a wonky academic. Perhaps because I'm more on her customers' wavelength, I never lose sight of the fact that most No Guilt ladies are in it for the wine— not for an in-depth analysis of how mentors shaped Sonia Sotomayor's career.

"Hey, have I mentioned that I'm interviewing for a new job?" I tried to keep my tone light; of course, I knew I had told Susanna no such thing.

She looked up, a line forming at the center of her forehead. *"What? Wait, why?"*

Even though we often mined the most intimate topics, from sex to occasional ambivalence about motherhood, we rarely talked about my work life. The Blue Owl was our shared interest—her vocation, my avocation—and somehow *You* seemed petty in comparison. Maybe I sensed Susanna's disdain for women's magazines, or maybe I'd been a little too pleased with my part-time schedule and the semi-glamour of the magazine world. As a small-business owner, she never gets a break. I winced, remembering the time I collected my kids from Susanna's house after taking a whirlwind day trip to Washington, DC, to interview Jill Biden for the back page of *You*. When Susanna opened the door, looking exhausted in reading glasses and a ripped Oberlin sweatshirt, I bellowed, "White House Frisbees for all!" Unfortunately, the one I launched across the living room knocked a menorah off her mantel.

Now I felt deeply uncomfortable not being able to share my real reason for leaving *You*. But I'd promised Nicholas, and I knew he would respect such a request from me if the tables were turned. I could not betray his confidence.

"I'm just ready, you know? And this cool thing came up. I'm sure you've heard of it. Scroll?"

Susanna slowly brought her fork back to her plate, where a bite of spinach and feta omelet cooled before my eyes. "You have *got* to be kidding me."

"No, actually, I'm serious. They got in touch with me; I'm meeting with them next week."

"Alice, you would *not* lower yourself."

"Susanna, stop! I'm just meeting with them—not joining a cult!"

She sat up straighter in her chair. For an instant, I pictured us as twelve-year-olds in a middle school cafeteria: Susanna in her scoliosis brace, me in my Coke bottle glasses. You never really leave those people behind, do you?

"Alice, are you fucking kidding me?" She spoke with such emphasis, her red curls bounced under her Athleta handband. "What is going *on* with you?"

The waitress came over to top up our coffees and then made a show of backing away, as if she'd encountered an invisible force field. Odd move, I thought; in my waitressing days, I couldn't get enough of customers who scrapped it out at my tables.

"So, *seriously*. You would really work for an operation that will be the final nail in the coffin of the Blue Owl? You can kiss *real* bookstores good-bye." Susanna picked up a knife and started aggressively smearing jelly across the face of her multigrain toast. I had to admire the way she cleared the flat plastic Smuckers packet of every lick of purple.

"Susanna, you're being a little bit dramatic. Honestly, I thought you'd be excited about Scroll. The more people who read, the more books are sold. A rising tide lifts all boats, right?"

Actually, I had been petrified about telling Susanna. But given my impending financial situation, I also felt a twinge of annoyance; after all, she had opened her store with the help of a generous nest egg from her grandfather. The sum total of my grandparental inheritance consisted of a claddagh ring and a locket with tooth marks on the back.

"Not exactly. I'm sick of people using my store as a showroom and then buying books freaking *online* for half the price. Scroll will just make it easier for them to get the same crazy deals in person. It's maddening."

Susanna is an avowed Luddite; she only has a smart phone because it came as a free upgrade when her flip phone died. And a visit to the Blue Owl website will get you the address of the store—that's it.

"Can we take this down a notch? I could use more coffee and the waitress won't come back here until we change the subject to the swim team carpool." I smiled hopefully and breathed deeply. "Susanna. I'm sorry. Someone from Scroll e-mailed me, and it seems shortsighted not to meet with her."

We paused to nod in deference to a just-arrived mom of six who placed third in her age group in the Ironman and has a successful catering business, No Small Affair. Everyone suspects she's on meth but still, the woman commands respect.

"Seriously, Scroll just wrote to you out of the blue? How did they even know who you *are*?"

I ignored the subtext of her question. "The woman who e-mailed me follows me on Twitter."

Susanna's laugh warbled up from the back of her throat. Normally that sound was one of my favorite things about her, but now it rankled. "They *found you on Twitter*? Oh yeah, that sounds like a legit way to recruit future employees. Maybe I should start looking for salespeople on Pinterest. Shit. Just think of all the money I've wasted on classifieds in the *Filament Illuminator*!"

Once again, I employed all my powers of restraint and ignored the outburst, which struck me as a little bit rude. I felt the tickle of a sob at the back of my throat. "Gee, Susanna, I hoped you'd be more enthusiastic— or at least *civil*—but fine, I had a feeling you wouldn't be. I get that. So I'll tell you the real reason I'm looking for a new job . . ."

And then I told her everything. How could I not? Susanna is full of bluster and unsolicited opinions, but she was also the president of my sounding board and I couldn't keep a secret from her—especially when I knew Nicholas would eventually go public about why he was opening his own office. Susanna's husband, Paul, would most likely be among the first to know. And I needed my own support network, right?

I finished up, "Of course it goes without saying, I might not even be interested in what Scroll is offering, or they might not be interested in me. This whole conversation could end up being completely moot, except for the part about me looking for a new job."

Susanna sliced an end off her omelet and shoveled it onto my plate. "Fine, I get it. Now eat this. You're going to need sustenance. And for what it's worth, it's your turn to pick up the big girls from swimming."

As hopeful as I was about my meeting with Genevieve, it seemed prudent to investigate other options. On MediaBistro, I noticed a posting for a job editing political nonfiction for Plum Books, a small press in SoHo. I clicked the link and submitted my resume directly to the company, even though my political experience was limited to one year as president of my seventh grade class.

It was so easy to apply for jobs online! The last time I'd sent out my resume, you still had to buy a box of special paper, and you had to make sure you printed your credentials with the watermark facing the right way.

Surprisingly, I heard from the publisher immediately, and we scheduled a meeting for the next day. Visions of lunches at Dean & Deluca danced in my head. I imagined regular visits to the Scholastic store. I saw myself skipping down cobblestone streets, lugging a manuscript in the crook of each arm.

The minute I arrived at Plum Books, I knew my fantasy was not to be. Their suite of offices on Prince Street happened to be right next door to my old ob-gyn's office, which was weird enough. Then the door opened a crack and a man who looked like a very young Fidel Castro peered out at me. He had a patchy beard and a thin cigar tucked behind his ear. He wore a tight-fitting black T-shirt with the silhouette of a dog on it and the message Mutts Against Mitt.

"Hi, you must be Gus. I'm Alice." I stuck out my hand.

"Heeeey, Alice. Wow. Well. Come on in." Gus held the door open to reveal a loft space painted glossy orange with industrial-looking metal pipes snaking all over the pressed-tin ceiling. There were bumper stickers on every surface: Friends Don't Let Friends Vote Republican, More Trees Less Bush, Vulture Capitalist. I was painfully aware of my faux-tweed skirt from Ann Taylor Loft and my oversized pearl earrings. Why hadn't I worn something a little edgier? I felt like Nancy Reagan.

Gus introduced me to his comrades, who were sprawled on beanbag chairs drinking coffee from mugs emblazoned with still more slogans (No More Nukes; Think Globally, Act Locally). I lowered myself down beside them and spent the next half hour hollering over the widest generation gap I'd ever encountered. When I mentioned my adolescent admiration for Geraldine Ferraro, Gus wrinkled his forehead.

His deputy editor smirked beneath an ironic mustache. "Do you mean Gennifer Flowers?"

"Actually, no. I mean Geraldine Ferraro. Walter Mondale's running mate in 1984 . . . ?"

Crickets.

Of course. These boys had been *born* in 1984. Geraldine Ferraro was as irrelevant to them as Spiro T. Agnew is to me—maybe even more so, since she never actually made it to office.

When we parted ways, Gus said kindly, "You seem like a really cool woman. Best of luck finding your thing."

4

We had tickets to see Blue Man Group on the day of my coffee date with Genevieve, so Nicholas and I drove into the city with the kids and, by some stroke of luck, happened to find a parking spot right in front of Shakespeare's Sister. The plan was for the rest of the family to have an early dinner at the Time Café and then meet me at the theater after my interview. Of course, Nicholas would learn that the Time Café is no more: like many restaurants we were fond of in the late nineties, it has been replaced by a French bistro specializing in moules-frites.

Genevieve hadn't asked to see my resume, but just to be on the safe side, I brought a copy with me in a brass-cornered leather folder. Aside from this throwback successory—the job seeker's equivalent of a picture of a whale's tale with PERSEVERE printed underneath—the only other thing in my bag was a Ziploc of Veggie Booty.

The restaurant was nearly empty when I walked in, so it was easy to spot Genevieve.

I'd scrutinized her Tumblr and Pinterest, read two years' worth of her tweets, and performed multiple Google searches, image and otherwise, using various combinations of her name, with quotation marks and without. I knew that Genevieve volunteered for Badass Brooklyn Animal Rescue, was a graduate of Carleton College, and was married to a man named Lance who blogged about hydroponic gardening. She appeared to be fond of quotes, especially one from John F. Kennedy, which she'd pinned two times: "Change is the law of life. And those who look only to the past or present are certain to miss the future."

Genevieve was seated at a table for two with her back to the door, so my first impression of her included the heart-shaped bentwood of the café chair as part of the snapshot. When I approached the table, faux-tentatively since I knew I was in the right place, she held up a finger and smiled—closed lips, no teeth. It was an efficient smile. She was on her phone.

I slipped out of my coat and draped it over the back of my own chair, carefully, in order to spare Genevieve a view of its torn satin lining. When I sat down, she made the universal "I'm just wrapping up this call" gesture. Her brown eyes remained fixed on a spot above my head, which made me self-conscious about the root touch-up I had applied to my hairline in the rearview mirror of the minivan. Did it look like clumpy mascara? *Please no.*

"So we'll take this offline until Monday, then circle back . . . Fine . . . Fine . . . Done."

No good-bye—but this didn't register until later, during replay and postgame analysis with Nicholas. In the moment, I was surprised by the deep timbre of Genevieve's voice, which didn't at all match her pixie stature. She had Mia Farrow's haircut from *Rosemary's Baby*, but hers was light brown instead of strawberry blond. In pictures, she had come across as elfin and cute. In real life, she was attractive in a powerful way, like a compact car with impressive pickup—the human equivalent of a Fiat. She exuded energy.

"Alice. I've heard so many great things." Genevieve smiled again, for real this time. *Heard so many great things . . . from who?* I wondered. She cast a pointed glance at my dorky folder. "This is purely a meet-and-greet—me trying to determine whether you would be the right fit for Scroll. From there, we can talk next steps. Sound good?"

"Absolutely."

"So why don't we order some drinks and jump right in?"

I perked up a little, thinking we'd upgraded from coffee to wine, but in a dizzying flurry, the waiter materialized and Genevieve ordered a cup of humdrum peppermint tea. I leaned over, peeked at the menu card in its Rolling Rock stand, and ordered an exotic-sounding Japanese hojicha green tea.

Then it was just the two of us. She smiled, widened her eyes, and held both arms out in a way that said, *Where to start?* The gesture was charming, since we'd never met before and I suddenly had absolutely no idea what to say.

"Tell me, Alice, how do you like to read?"

"Oh—well. I *love* to read! It's my favorite thing to do. I—"

Genevieve crinkled her eyes a little and her face softened. I noticed she was wearing a tiny gold ampersand on a delicate chain around her neck. "I mean, do you use an e-reader or . . . ?" She leaned forward slightly, like she wanted to reach over and catch my answer in her hands.

"Of course. I have a Kindle, first generation. I also read galleys, manuscripts, hardcovers, basically whatever I can get my hands on."

"So you're agnostic."

"Actually, I was raised Catholic, and I've fallen pretty far from the flock, but I still consider myself a *spiritual* person, if that makes any sense?" (Why was she asking about religion? Was this even legal?)

"Good to know. But I meant *platform* agnostic, meaning you toggle back and forth between your device and carbon-based books."

Carbon-based books?

"Sorry, yes. I do toggle. I'm a toggler." OMG, stop acting manic. Breathe, Alice. Think *confident, grounded businesswoman.*

The waiter arrived and deposited two mugs on our table as I struggled to heed my inner voice, which tends to be more sensible than my actual one. (Bossy, too.) The restaurant was starting to fill up, and the waiter quickly moved on to other customers—but not before Genevieve said briskly, "Just the check when you have a chance."

I looked down at my mug and transferred my dismay over Genevieve's apparent rush to what I saw inside. Floating in the brackish water was a big hairy ball of undulating brown leaves, lashed together by a loose fiber that looked like nude pantyhose. I had no idea how to navigate this unappetizing spectacle: sip around the ball? Remove the ball from the mug and dump it . . . where? There wasn't a saucer in sight; it would make mincemeat of a cocktail napkin, and extraction would be a two-spoon job, so I made a split-second decision to leave the ball in the water. Once, I had choked down a link of my Irish uncle's homemade blood pudding; I could certainly soldier my way to the bottom of this cup of tea.

The first sip was the worst, with the seaweed leaves brushing wetly against the tip of my nose. The tea tasted earthen, with an undernote of Tabasco.

Genevieve bobbed her neat teabag up and down by its string, looking pensive as she watched me swallow, hard. She said, "You're adventurous. I like that."

Her vote of confidence washed over me like a spell from a magic wand, relaxing my shoulders and dislodging intelligent conversation from the thorny bramble of my nerves. I *am* adventurous, but I hadn't had a chance to act on the impulse in years.

When we were finished—tea choked down, questions answered, night just beginning to fall on SoHo—Genevieve shook my hand (firm downward movement, release) and said, simply, "We'll be in touch."

At Blue Man Group, our seats were so close to the stage, we had to wear ponchos to protect our clothes from the paint and Cap'n Crunch cereal being hurled into the audience by the show's mute yet oddly peaceful stars. A trio of imitation iPads hung from the ceiling, with three different feeds—text, numbers and symbols, video clips—scrolling across their movie theater–sized screens at lightning speed. When I peeked at my kids, their eyes darted in every direction, attempting to take in the visual assault in a way that left me disheartened.

"So do you think it went well?" Nicholas was at the wheel; we were midway through the Lincoln Tunnel and already our passengers were sacked out behind us.

This is one of my favorite dynamics in parenthood: being with the kids without being constantly interrupted by them.

"Hard to say. I couldn't tell if she liked me or not. She asked a *lot* of questions. I think she's really smart."

"Did she get into what they'd want you to do, exactly?"

"Not really. She mentioned that they're looking for Content Managers, but I'm not sure if that's what she has in mind for me." I glanced over at Nicholas, who glanced over at me in the same instant.

"What's a Content Manager?"

"I have no idea!" We burst out laughing. When I glanced behind us to make sure everyone was still asleep, Oliver was resting his head on Margot's shoulder. Everyone's cheeks were flushed pink.

"Well, did you ask?"

"No, I was too embarrassed."

"*Embarrassed?* Alice."

"I know. Lame. Anyway, she mostly talked about the kind of people she wants to hire. She says she wants disrupters." The two of us exchanged a knowing look; I'm more of an envelope calligrapher than an envelope pusher. "Strange, right? But you know what? It would be fun to be at the *beginning* of something. How many years have I been listening to the death knell of magazines?"

"How did you leave things?"

"She said she was trying to figure out if I'd be a good fit in the Scroll culture. If she decides I am, they'll have me come in for meetings."

"Do you feel good about it?"

"You know what? I do. I guess we'll see what happens, but I'm really excited. I hope I get a chance to find out more."

As it turned out, I heard from Genevieve at six thirty the next morning, which was a Saturday. She wanted me to come in and meet the team the following Friday.

Dad: Dear Alice, how did it go?

Me: Went well. Going in to meet other Scrollers.

Dad: Nice. Does it sound like interesting, fulfilling work?

Me: It sounds like a job, which is what I need.

Dad: Yes, I get that. But some degree of satisfaction is nice, too.

Me: Dad, I already read What Color Is Your Parachute. Now I need the sequel: Your Husband's Parachute Is Broken. Kidding, but still.

Dad: Life is long. It will work out. Remember, I raised you to bring home the bacon!

Me: Ha

Dad: Mom & I off to see Don Giovanni. G2G. Love, Dad

5

Nicholas and I were twenty-six when Margot was born. We were the first of our crowd to have kids—to the extent that, when we told our friends I was pregnant, more than one wondered whether we were planning to keep the baby. Like many prospective parents, we were excited but wary, with no idea what we were in for. We fantasized about tossing our baby in a straw basket and placing her on restaurant tables alongside wine bottles and tea lights.

Right away, I was on a different track from everyone I knew. My friends were taking the GMAT or the LSAT, working at start-ups, writing for blogs, and staying out till all hours with the very people they played Nerf basketball with during the day. In a stunning about-face, my brother quit his job at Lehman and moved to Hurricane Island, Maine, to become a wilderness instructor for Outward Bound. The timing wasn't great—my dad was in his first round of chemo—but I think we were all happy for Will to put his days as a frat bro behind him. I almost couldn't square the guy I remembered doing shots at Stuff Yer Face in New Brunswick with the one who sent long missives on recycled paper flecked with bits of twigs and leaves. "Big Al, you're not going to believe this, but I'm learn-ing to live with only what I can carry in a canoe. The natural beauty here is humbling; I've never felt such a sense of home. Hey, have you read any Thoreau? Dude is really worth checking out."

In August of 2001, Nicholas and I moved, too: we upgraded to a big-ger apartment in Battery Park City to be closer to the firm. By then, Mar-got was four months old, and I had been a mom long enough to know that the restaurant table plan was pure fantasy. Bath time was the new cocktail hour, with Avent bottles in lieu of cosmos. But we loved watch-ing the sunset behind the Statue of Liberty and the stealthy uptown glide of cruise ships arriving in the harbor at dawn. At night, we strolled the esplanade by the Winter Garden, where Walt Whitman's poetry was sol-dered onto a low fence: "City of tall facades and marble and iron! Proud and passionate city! Mettlesome, mad, extravagant city!"

On the morning of September 11, 2001, I was in our apartment four blocks south of the World Trade Center, changing Margot's diaper when the first plane hit. I heard the sound and looked out the window, expect-ing to see a car accident at the mouth of the Brooklyn Battery Tunnel. Instead, I saw pigeons flying through the air. When I put on my glasses, I realized they weren't pigeons; they were papers. Was there a tickertape parade for the Yankees?

Nicholas had been on his way to Citibank in Tower One, and he ran back home when he felt the impact of the first plane in the sidewalk under his feet. He closed the door to our bedroom, which had a view of the tow-ers, and started filling the bathtub, lugging pots of water from the sink to the stove.

"*What* are you doing?" I burst out laughing.

"Alice, I'm telling you, that was not a small plane. I'm worried we're going to be stuck here for a while."

"Nicholas, you're *crazy*. I'm sure it's no big deal." This exchange per-fectly illustrated our dynamic at the time—and for years after, until our roles reversed just recently, post–Sutherland, Courtfield, and I became the worrier.

The second plane hit, the first tower fell, and we ran down the stairs to our lobby, hoping to seek shelter in the basement. There was no basement. The doormen were soaking gym towels and throwing them over the heads of hysterical residents so we wouldn't breathe in the noxious gray dust that rushed through the cracks between the front doors. Someone threw a towel over Margot's head. "Get that baby *out of here!*"

"Get your hands off my baby," I hissed, in a voice I'd never heard come out of my mouth before.

We stampeded back upstairs to our fourth-floor apartment with strangers, assuring them that we could safely jump out the window in a pinch, even though it was a forty-foot drop to the ground below. When the second tower fell, I was sitting on the living room floor, holding the hand of a woman I had never seen before and wouldn't see again until five years later, when we bumped into each other during rush hour in Penn Station and both burst into tears on the spot.

I hadn't been to church since college, but I whispered a Hail Mary quietly into the top of Margot's fuzzy head. Nicholas paced the room, stopping every so often to look out the window, even though there was nothing to see; at ten forty-five in the morning, the world was dark in every sense of the word. I thought we would die.

I wondered, is this how my dad feels every day?

Then: a soft knock on the door, from a Red Cross volunteer, warning us of a bomb threat in Battery Park; next, the distribution of white masks, including a child-sized one that covered Margot's entire face; then, the evacuation by police boat, where a father shook his head at the receding, smoldering city and said to his teenaged son, "I don't know. I just don't know."

We spent the day in the mess hall of a Jersey City army barracks. Fellow evacuees carried paintings, wedding albums, birdcages, jewelry boxes. One woman wore oven mitts on her feet. Our proximity to Ellis Island was not lost on us. Nor was the fear on the face of a young soldier in full fatigues, brandishing a machine gun—an unfamiliar sight back

then—barking, "Stop asking questions! Our country is in a state of Alpha Omega! This is the state of highest alert!"

I kept looking around for movie cameras. That guy over there with the eyebrows . . . was he Oliver Stone?

When we finally made it to my parents' house, my dad met us in the kitchen—vertical for the first time since his surgery and crying for the first time ever, in my memory.

"Dad, have you seen something like this before?"

He came of age in an era of bomb drills, assassinations, riots, tear gas, the draft. Now he was mostly bald and he wasn't strong enough yet to learn how to use the electrolarynx. But when he mouthed a single word—"Never"—I understood.

"We had a lockdown drill at school today," Margot made this announcement offhandedly, as I spritzed No More Tangles into her hair.

"Really? Wow." I shuddered at the thought of the principal's voice blaring over the PA system: *Active shooter in the school. Active shooter. In. The. School.*

On warm days, when the windows were open, I could hear the state-mandated announcement from our front porch.

"Where's your, um, hiding place?"

"This year we're in the coatroom. We have tape on the floor. If you step over it, the bad guys will be able to see you from the door."

"Ah, I see."

"After, we had popsicles for Mason's birthday. The lime kind."

"Yum."

When Margot ran off to brush her teeth, I started to worry about commuting into the city five days a week. What if there was a real emergency and I needed to get home?

I didn't even have the job yet and I was already agonizing about accepting it.

But there was also a little flame of excitement at the back of my mind. I could do this. I was ready to spread my wings. This was a chance to do something new, to get involved with a start-up ten years after my friends had taken the plunge at Kozmo.com, Pets.com, and Drugstore.com. In those days, I'd been too busy having babies and going to my dad's doctor appointments to consider introducing any more uncertainty into my life, even if there were stock options attached.

Of course, I agonized about what to wear to the interviews. I plied Susanna with coffee and she stretched out on my bed, her back propped against my Ikea headboard, while I modeled various outfits: straight skirt with a blousy shirt (too Virginia Woolf); flowered dress with cable tights (too Louisa May Alcott); red dress with a cute peplum flounce (too Belle Watling).

I stood in front of my closet in a Blue Owl T-shirt and threw up my hands in dismay. "Seriously, Susanna? I'm at a loss. Don't you have anything I can borrow?"

"Sure, if you want to wear overalls or hemp." We both laughed; Susanna buys most of her clothes at Whole Foods. "Seriously, Al, you should just wear green. Send them subliminal reminders of cash—at the end of the day, that's all Scroll cares about anyway."

"Please? Can we not? These aren't the shopping mall people, remember—these are the *book* people. They're readers, not bean counters."

"Oh yeah? I'll believe it when I see it. These Scrollers have another trick up their sleeves, I'm telling you."

"Susanna! Enough. This might be my big chance. I need you in my court."

We settled on black pants and a gray cashmere sweater with an industrial zipper up the back. Susanna recommended pairing this ensemble with black ballet flats, but I ruled them out—too Holly Golightly—and opted for mod boots instead. I couldn't shake the feeling that Susanna was trying to sabotage my chances.

•   •   •

"We're very nimble here at Scroll, so we're going to throw a lot at you today and see how you do. I have no doubt that you'll do just fine," said Genevieve. She took a perfunctory glance at my resume and ran through my schedule for the day, which consisted of back-to-back, in-person meetings with two Content Managers, an Analytics Expert, and a Marketing Specialist, and phone interviews with a Quality Control Representative and a Warehouse Engineer in Cleveland.

"Oh, I'm nimble," I assured Genevieve. I thought of my waitressing days, and the way I'd learned to carry six dinner plates at a time—three on each forearm. Of the picky diners who complained that there were too many peppers in the fajitas; and one grouchy guy who didn't crack a smile when I accidentally served him a raw lobster, its claws bound in navy elastic bands.

"You'll come straight back to my office after your meeting with Analytics, I'll have you sign some papers, and then I'll take you to a restricted area where you'll take the phoners. Good?"

"Great." But I worried about fine print on the papers. Ever since the great Columbia House Music Club debacle of 1988, I was leery of signing my name on a dotted line. (Surely I wasn't the *only* fifteen-year-old who believed I'd get eleven cassette tapes for the low, low price of one penny.)

I was also concerned that I wouldn't be able to find my way back to Genevieve's office. The thirty-seventh floor of the mirrored midtown tower was a warren of white: carpets, chairs, walls, window coverings, white boards. By the elevator bank, the company logo was barely visible against the white wall behind it—a slim white scroll reminiscent of a college diploma, hovering over a white receptionist desk (empty) and a metal cup of pristine white pens. I kept checking my boots to make sure I wasn't tracking in mud, or worse.

•   •   •

The in-person meetings were both dizzying and dazzling.

The Analytics Expert, Rashida, explained the Tenets of Winners, which functioned as both inspiration and rubric for all MainStreet employees. She told me that each of my interviewers had been assigned a different tenet in advance of our interview, ranging from Winners Get It Right (WGIR) to Always Take Action (ATA) to Surprise and Delight Your Customer (SADYC). Their questions were tailored to tease out my commitment to each tenet. At the end of this day of meetings, known as the Chain, the pack of interrogators would meet for a debrief, where they would compare notes and then vote me on or off the island. If one person objected, I would not be offered a spot on the team.

It was surreal to try to come up with business-appropriate examples of how I was a negotiator, a closer, a committer, and an experienced analyzer of data. My mind kept boomeranging to examples starring dog training (not many success stories there) and my kids. For instance, when Oliver was a ferocious toddler, Nicholas and I used to refer to him as the terrorist—as in, "We do not negotiate with terrorists." And when I thought about data, it wasn't in terms of Excel, which I'd never used, but in terms of weight and height charts from the pediatrician's office, or the printout I examined with the orthodontist while he showed me, degree by degree, exactly how he would shift Margot's teeth into submission.

"Our mission is to reinvent reading the way Starbucks reinvented coffee," said the Marketing Specialist, whose name I missed. Caleb? Ethan? Anyway, he was a bearded guy in his twenties, the doppelganger of every other bearded guy I passed in the minimalist hallway. "We've targeted the experience our customers will most value, and we'll deliver it along with steep discounts, membership opportunities, and the chance to spend peaceful, uninterrupted time at the intersection of the past and the future."

I sighed reverently; the words *peaceful* and *uninterrupted* make me weak in the knees. Then I leaned forward in my seat—a white leather sling suspended from a chilly metal frame. "Can you talk a little bit

more about that? Membership opportunities and the part about the
intersection . . . ?"

The Marketing Specialist nodded knowingly. "Of course—we just
get so excited about this stuff, we forget our thought process isn't really in
the zeitgeist yet. Note, I said *yet*. Okay, so firstly, we're crafting a membership model for frequent fliers. A flat monthly fee will net you four
titles of your choice, one title we select for you via our ScrollOriginals
series, and unlimited access to the SSR area."

"Sorry, SSR—?" Oh, how I wished I'd caught this guy's name.

"Alice, I just love your inquisitiveness." The Marketing Specialist unbuttoned the cuffs of his denim cowboy shirt and rolled them up, one fold
at a time, with the precision of a doctor scrubbing in for surgery. His fore-
arms were slim and elegant like hairless cats. "SSR stands for *sustained
silent reading*. These areas consist of leather armchairs reserved for our
most serious readers. We're talking waitress service, foot massages, complimentary biscotti, cup holders with mini hot plates to keep your coffee
warm . . . oh, and unlimited gummy bears. Market research shows that
Haribo gummies are the leading candy consumed by voracious readers."

I nodded vigorously, dumbfounded.

"I'm sure you've logged time in the Virgin Atlantic Clubhouse when
you travel?"

"Of course." I hadn't, actually; I'm steerage, born and bred.

"Then you're familiar with our model for SSR. We want to deliver
that first-class experience to our literary lounges."

"Wow. That sounds amazing." It really did. Like Barnes & Noble su-
perstores in their heyday but better. The gummy bears alone were reason
enough to covet the job. "How much will the monthly membership cost?"

His jaw tightened slightly. "We aren't able to talk about pricing at
this time."

"Oh, that's fine, I was just curious. And wait, can we rewind for a
minute?"

He nodded his head warmly. (Was it Seth? Keith? I knew it was something gentle, the name of a kid my brother would have beaten up in grade school, when he was still known as Billy.) "Absolutely. How can I illuminate you?"

"Can you explain the part about the intersection of the past and the—"

"Future? Abso-fuckin'-lutely. As a lifelong booklover, I'm *so* stoked about this. Now, our primary focus is on the future of reading: e-books. Forward progress, et cetera. But here at Scroll, we feel it's important to provide a familiar touchstone from the great literary traditions. As a result, our lounges will also offer—drumroll, please—a line of carbon-based books in first editions. *The Grapes of Wrath*, *Catcher in the Rye*, what have you. These books will be available for purchase."

The Marketing Specialist rubbed his thumb against his pointer and middle fingers, mouthing the words *"Money money money."* I banished Susanna's smug smile from my mind.

Then, out loud, he continued. "You may be interested to know, new hires are entitled to one first edition title of their own selection. When you accept your offer, you name your dream title and it will be waiting on your desk on your first day of onboarding."

"Wow," I said. Suddenly my signed copy of *Angela's Ashes* didn't seem so exciting. "What did you pick?"

"Sorry?"

"What was your dream title?"

"Ah. Mine was *A Fan's Notes*. By Frederick Exley? Do you know it?"

"Oh, of course. I've never read it, but my husband—"

"Yeah, it's some deep shit. And in the spirit of transparency, I'd like to give you a shout-out for raising the bar right there."

"Raising the bar?"

"That's our name for when a prospective employee takes it to the next level. I liked how you admitted you've never read Exley. Lots of people in your shoes would bullshit their way through the conversation. Well done."

• • •

Genevieve slid a single sheet of paper across her desk. "Before we move on to the confidential portion of the day, I just need your John Hancock. What you're about to see is totally classified—not to be shared with any of your contacts, including family."

The little hairs on the back of my neck went up; this felt like an episode of *Law and Order* where I was about to see a taped-off murder scene. Still, I scribbled my signature at the bottom of the nondisclosure agreement without reading a word of it. "Of course. My lips are sealed." I gestured as if I was closing a Ziploc bag, knowing perfectly well that I'd call Nicholas or Will to spill all classified information on my way home.

"But first, I thought you might appreciate what I have in here . . ."

When I looked up, Genevieve was unlocking a cabinet over her desk. Then she snapped on a pair of latex gloves and started pulling books off a shelf. "Let's see, where to start . . . Faulkner's *As I Lay Dying*, Cather's *My Ántonia*. Didn't you mention that you're a Harper Lee fan? Take a gander at this." In fact, I had mentioned no such thing, but of course Scout Finch and I went way back; she'd held a prime spot in my suitcase just before I abandoned the Book Lady for horseback riding. And now, suddenly, *To Kill a Mockingbird* was in my hands: brown dust jacket, "Harper Lee" stamped on the spine in mint green letters. It was wrapped in plastic, so I assumed it was a first edition.

"That's *my* dream title," said Genevieve, watching me with the pleasure of a kid sharing a beloved toy with a new friend.

"This is *so* cool. What was it like to read?"

"Pardon?"

"I mean, I've only had the pleasure of *To Kill a Mockingbird* in paperback. Was it amazing to reread it the same way Harper Lee probably did when it first landed on her doorstep?"

Genevieve furrowed her brow, charmingly quizzical. "Can you believe, I haven't *actually* taken off the plastic? Guess I need to put that on my action item list." She gently lifted the book from my hands, put it back in the cabinet, and locked it up with a tiny silver key.

We sat there for a minute in silence. Genevieve's office was peaceful, spare—and, of course, white. There were no stacks of paper, tangled electrical cords, or pump-dispensers of hand cream. It was so different from the bustling hive of *You*, where my reading was constantly interrupted by beauty editors looking for mascara testers or Reggie, the mail guy, placing yet another crate of books on the floor of my cube. I thought, I could get used to this. Like working at a spa!

Genevieve and I smiled at each other. The meeting had the feeling of a successful first date. I liked her confidence and economy with words. I liked that she appeared to like me. I felt a surge of ambitious energy. I want this, I thought. I wanted my own neat white office and efficient haircut. The chance to bring books into the twenty-first century—that was just the icing on a very enticing cake.

"Alice, before you proceed to your final discussions, I wanted to talk to you a little bit about how we would envision your role. Because with your qualifications, naturally you're interviewing us as much as we're interviewing you." Genevieve smoothed a tendril of hair off her forehead and flicked open the single, paperbag-brown file folder on her desk.

I waited. What could I say? I desperately need this job and would kill to be part of something so cool?

Genevieve cleared her throat. "I envision you in a hybrid role of tastemaker and curator—of course, contributing to ScrollOriginals would fall into this bucket. And I'm also thinking you might be a nice fit for a role we've cooked up, known internally as ScrollCrier."

I tilted my head to the side, curious.

She went on. "You see, we're looking for someone to liaise with the publishing community at large. As you can imagine, we've received an exceptionally warm reception to our Scroll concept—who doesn't want to see more bookstores, right? But we'd like to have a designated staffer who makes sure these contacts are up-to-the-minute on our mission as it continues to evolve. Does that make sense?"

"You mean, just keep the publishing community in the loop about what's happening with our plans?"

"Exactly. An ambassador of sorts."

"That actually sounds like it could be right up my alley."

Genevieve grinned. "You'll learn, nothing at MainStreet, or at Scroll, is set in stone. We're experts at dealing with ambiguity, which can be both liberating and frustrating, I'm not going to lie."

"I get that. Remember, Genevieve, I'm a magazine person. We've relaunched *You* three times in the past five years—and every time the editors have had to embrace a new look and message. That's been an exciting part of my job."

Genevieve stared at me for a long second, then nodded. "Okay, then. Well. I have a good feeling about you, Alice Pearse."

Awkwardly, I said, "I have a good feeling about you, too, Genevieve Edwards. I mean, *Andrews*!" I cringed. How could I have gotten her name wrong?!

Genevieve motioned for me to follow her, and we walked down the long white hall to a door marked Authorized Visitors ONLY. She paused, her hand on the brushed metal doorknob. "Now. This is our simulated Scroll lounge. You'll have your phone interviews in here. But before we proceed, I have to underscore the importance of the NDA you just signed. This area is highly confidential, only for the eyes of employees above Level Five and our most serious recruits."

I nodded and held up two fingers. "Scout's honor." Serious recruits? This job was actually within my grasp—a mind-boggling stroke of luck.

The door swung open on a high-ceilinged circular room painted a warm buttercup yellow. The floors were dark, wide-plank wood, and the ceiling soared into a pale blue dome. We stepped in and Genevieve gestured for me to pick from a small army of leather armchairs, each accompanied by its own gooseneck reading lamp topped off with a different-colored glass shade. I selected a red one, settled in, and was surprised when the bottom of the chair coughed up a padded footrest.

Genevieve giggled. "Yeah, they don't look like recliners. But we've

learned that readers want the La-Z-Boy feel. The Rockwells commis-
sioned these chairs specially for Scroll—the idea being that chic library
feel with a down-home yet decadent touch."

"Decadent is right. Wow. This place looks like the private screening
rooms on *House Hunters: Million Dollar Homes.*"

"So true. I love that show!" We laughed. I resisted the impulse to
ask Genevieve if she watched *The Bachelor,* too. Forget a successful first
date—this was starting to feel like love at first sight. She went on: "Before
you call in to Cleveland, can I grab you a warm beverage, Alice? We're
not staffed up with baristas yet, but I can make you a coffee from one of
our instant cold-press machines. We have a roaster on the premises so we
know our beans have been treated humanely."

"Sure, I'd love a cup. Are you sure I can't get it myself?"

"Please." Genevieve pressed my shoulders down into the chair and
made her way over to an oak counter next to a glass case piled high with
scones, muffins, and madeleines. "Can I interest you in an earth-friendly
baked good? We're fine-tuning our gluten-free, wheat-free, dairy-free
menu. That's one of the perks of the job—you get to taste everything."

"Thanks, they look delicious, but I'm fine. I just can't get over these
bookshelves!" Around the perimeter of one side of the room, the shelves
ran from the floor to the bottom of the dome—oak, gently curved, with a
sliding ladder connecting the bottom shelf with the top.

"Pretty spectacular, right?" Genevieve grabbed a chunky clay mug
and gestured for me to spin my chair around. "Don't miss the screens
on the other side of the room. Get it? Past meets future? I'm sure Keith
told you about our ScrollFirst program. We'll store those books on the
shelves; and then you can just swivel your chair around and order an
e-book for your device. Milk? Sugar?"

Keith! So that was his name. Indeed, Will had gotten into hot water for
pummeling a classmate by this name during a game of four-square in 1983.

"Just black, thanks. Wow. I like the idea of marrying e-books with
real—I mean, carbon-based books. The old with the new. It's very . . ."

"Inclusive?"

"Yes, exactly."

"Inclusion is one of our most valued tenets. See, Alice, you'll fit right in here."

As soon as my last interview was over, I called Nicholas from the lobby of a hip hotel around the corner from the Scroll offices. I had forty-five minutes to kill before the next train to Filament and I was more than happy to sink into a maroon velvet couch with a large goblet of white wine. Even though I'd barely moved all day, I felt sore and drained to the point of catatonia. But I did have the wherewithal to notice that I was the only person in the vicinity not wearing a wool skullcap and also the only person clad head to toe in clothing from the Boden catalog.

"So?"

"I'm exhausted. My face hurts from talking. But . . . *Nicholas!* I love Genevieve. And you should *see* this place."

"Are the offices nice?"

"Gorgeous. Just . . . unbelievably *stark*, but in this really elegant way. Genevieve showed me what their stores are going to look like, and basically it's like the most beautiful library you've ever seen, with bookshelves on one side and high-tech flat-screen monitors on the other."

"Wow. When do they open?"

"Ha. Not soon enough. And Nicholas, one thing the *New York Times* story didn't mention? They're selling *first editions* along with e-books, and you can get a membership that gets you into this upgraded area and a little hot plate for your coffee and access to books you can't get anywhere except Scroll. I'm telling you, it's *amazing*—" In the background, I heard a soft hiss and then a clink. "Nicholas? Are you still there?"

"I'm here. Sorry. Just opening a beer. Wow—cheers, Alice, this all sounds great! Did they love you?"

"Wait, are you in your office?"

"No, I came back early and sent Jessie home. I'm just hanging with the kids."

"Oh. Okay. What time is it, anyway?"

"I have no idea. Four thirtyish?"

"Wow, cocktail hour starts early in your line of work. Hey, one weird thing: the subject of the kids hasn't even come up yet."

"Of course the kids haven't come up yet! It would be illegal for them to ask if you have kids, and why would you volunteer the information? It's irrelevant."

"Irrelevant? Well. The kids are . . . my life, I guess. They're my best work."

Nicholas laughed—warmly, but still. "Just relax. We'll see what happens."

I wrote thank-you notes to all my interviewers on outrageously expensive cream-colored cards printed with funky red reading glasses. I thought they struck the right balance between hip, intellectual, and modern.

Oliver paused at the dining room table, soccer ball tucked under his arm. He studied the translucent box of cards—harder to open than a CD wrapper—and said, "Mommy, are you writing a letter to our eye doctor?"

"Our eye doctor? No! I'm writing to the people I met with about a job."

"Do they wear glasses?"

"Some of them."

"Did you tell them kids used to call you 'four eyes'?"

"Actually, no. My eyesight didn't come up."

"Why not?"

"It just didn't."

"Mommy, can we get an Xbox?"

"No."

"Why not? Everyone has one but us."

"Because we're *readers* in this house."

"But Mommy—"

"Oliver! Please throw the Frisbee around with poor Cornelius; he hasn't been out since this morning."

This wasn't the first time the subject of an Xbox had come up. A kid in Oliver's second-grade class got one for his birthday and that opened the floodgate of lobbying for Kinect Sports, FIFA Soccer, Sonic Generations, and Kinectimals, which Oliver assured me would be "just the thing" for Georgie. "It's animals, Mommy! And you can get Harry Potter for Xbox! The games are educational!"

If Oliver was eager for a gaming console, I was equally unenthusiastic about having one in the house. I already had enough trouble monitoring television and computer use, which skyrocketed on weekend mornings when Nicholas and I were desperate for extra sleep. Anyway, why couldn't Oliver go outside and play real basketball or take our real dog for a real walk? As for Harry Potter, he belonged inside a book. End of story.

6

When Nicholas's time at the firm dwindled to six weeks, he started lugging bags and boxes back from his office in the city. We designated a corner of the basement for storage of items that would go to the new office when his lease started: file folders, legal pads, stapler, a framed drawing of the New York Public Library.

Less important items never made it to the basement but got absorbed into the flotsam and jetsam perpetually at sea in our house. In the playroom, I discovered an unfamiliar toaster among the plastic bowls and utensils in Georgie's miniature kitchen. Upon closer inspection, I realized it was a Lucite deal toy from GE, sent to my husband by investment bankers at the close of a particularly grueling transaction. There were a squadron of these trinkets lined up along his windowsill on Park Avenue, all tiny replicas to commemorate whatever had been at the crux of a particular deal: a cement mixer, a magnifying glass, a pill bottle. Each one represented months of dinners in a conference room and fresh shirts hastily purchased by Gladys from the Charles Tyrwhitt around the corner.

Was he really going to walk away from the past ten years of his life without a backward glance?

One night, we were in the basement, sorting the recycling together, and I discovered that the glass bin was too heavy for me to lift. "I got it," Nicholas said, throwing on a Red Raider hockey sweatshirt left over from his high school days. "Can you grab the door?"

As he strode past, holding the towering pile of brown bottles and one lone Hellman's jar at an arm's length, I said, "Do you think we're drinking more than we used to?"

"No, why?" Nicholas made his way gracefully to the curb, sidestepping hula hoops, a pogo stick, and two soccer balls, one deflated. The still-round one he kicked into Oliver's soccer goal, using a fake sportscaster voice to say "Score!"

I let the screen door close behind me, making a mental note to buy more mayonnaise.

My mom called to check in. Will called to check in. The timing of their outreach indicated that they had consulted one another first and taken it upon themselves to give me pep talks.

"Good things come to those who wait" was my mom's theme. If I didn't get the job, we would have the "Things happen for a reason" conversation; if I did, we would go in the direction of "Hard work and persistence are always rewarded."

My mom is a docent at the Thomas Edison Museum in West Orange. Two days a week, she leads tours of schoolchildren and senior citizens through Edison's newly refurbished lab, where they can see the little cot he slept on so he wouldn't have to go home and be bothered by his eight kids; the wax-faced dolls Edison wired to sing "Mary Had a Little Lamb"; and the hulking tarpaper Black Maria movie studio where Edison screened early silent films like *The Great Train Robbery*.

Will and I grew up steeped in Edisonia. In fact, above the crucifix in my still-intact childhood bedroom is a quote from the great inventor, cross-stitched by one of my aunts: "Our greatest weakness lies in giving up." Open the closet and you'll also find a picture of River Phoenix, long ago clipped from *Tiger Beat* and still clinging to the door with yellowed tape twenty years after its subject's death.

My brother's call was more transactional: "Look, Alice, if you get this job, great; if not, you can continue to help women achieve their lifelong goal of having flat abs."

Will always had a snide attitude toward my job at *You*, possibly because his wife, Mary, is blessed with a perfect physique and doesn't have time for the frippery of disposable reading. Her subscriptions are to journals, publications with indices instead of perfume strips. Mary is an ophthalmologist; Will owns Jersey Boy Portage, a kayak school on Bailey Island, in Maine, where they live with my two sweet nephews, who write music and show no signs of their father's brutish behavior from childhood.

Even though my wrists were always red from Will's Indian burns and he'd ruined my favorite doll with a Mets "tattoo" in permanent ink, the two of us had been close as kids. Now we're respectful of each other. Sometimes I wonder what happened to the guy who bought rounds of tequila shots for everyone at Dive Bar on Broadway on my twenty-second birthday. His solemn outdoorsman replacement is so earnest, I feel like I have to watch my language when we're together.

"Gee, Will, thanks for the vote of confidence."

"So what does your bookstore friend think of Scroll? A little healthy competition?"

"Will? Don't be a dick."

"Alice, no need to get vulgar." (See?)

"Anyway. What are you guys up to this weekend?"

Will and his kids were going paddling in Casco Bay while Mary volunteered at a pop-up eye clinic in a disadvantaged neighborhood of Portland. My family and I were going to see *The Lorax* at the Willowbrook Mall, with Cinnabon on the agenda for dessert. I told Will we were running a 5K to raise money for a literacy program in Newark; in fact, I had only donated to the cause on behalf of a neighbor—and not very generously, either.

> **Me:** My Visa was just declined at the gas station. I paid in cash but what's up with that?
> **Nicholas:** No worries. I charged my office stuff on there, and I guess the amount was high enough to trigger a fraud alert. Just sorting it out now.
> **Me:** I thought you were renting the office furnished?
> **Nicholas:** I am! Just incidental things. An Aeron chair—got a good deal on eBay. And I splurged on a bar cart to give the place that *Mad Men* vibe.
> **Me:** Um. Wish you'd consulted me before making these purchases. Calling you now.

I was on my way home from dropping Margot at an art class on a Thursday afternoon when a number with a Cleveland area code popped up on my phone. Judy and Elliott happened to be visiting for a few days, and I knew they were on the other side of Filament, retrieving Oliver from a friend's house. Assuming they were lost, I steered my Honda Odyssey minivan (eighteen cup holders, no rear-seat entertainment) to the side of Essex Avenue and answered. Cornelius sat in the passenger's seat, panting, his tongue hanging out of one side of his mouth. "Hey. What's up?"

"Hello, may I please speak to Ms. Alice Pearse of 14 Flower Street, Filament, New Jersey?"

"Oh! Um, this is Alice."

"Alice, my name is Chris Pawlowski, and I'm a recruiter from MainStreet. Do you have a few moments?"

"Of course." Cornelius's panting was now a low-grade whine, so I grabbed his collar and pushed him into the backseat.

"It's my pleasure to extend an offer to you for a position of "—a brief pause, papers shuffling—"Content Manager–slash–Industry Liaison.

Salary commensurate with experience." While Chris prattled on, I frantically scribbled notes on the back of an Exxon receipt using a Yo Gabba Gabba pen grabbed from the floor: vesting schedules (stocks!), signing bonuses (two!), starting date (as soon as possible), time-off balance (ten days—seriously? In the whole *year*?).

"Chris, thank you! I'm so happy to hear this news! You made my weekend." There I was in my Gap Body pants and purple Under Armour sweatshirt, receiving an offer for a position with punctuation in its title. I had arrived.

"I'll tell you, I'm breaking protocol by sharing this, but I set up a shit ton of Chains for candidates for this very position, and Genevieve Andrews nixed every one." Chris lowered his voice. "Alice, you charmed the pants off everyone. They loved you."

"Thanks, Chris. That's nice of you to say. So, is it okay if I check back in with you on Monday? I'd like to take the weekend to think about . . . everything." There was nothing to think about, really—but I sensed Scroll would respect scrappy negotiating and I didn't want to let them down.

It was time for Alice Pearse to step up to the plate. I remembered my dad and Will cheering for Ron Darling when he pitched at Shea Stadium: "Hey batta batta, *swing*!" I was already winding up my arm.

I poured wine for Judy and Elliott in the living room and gestured for Nicholas to come into the kitchen. "I got the job!" I whispered. His eyes lit up when I showed him the numbers on the Exxon receipt.

"Alice, are you *serious*? This is big money."

"Of course I'm serious! I'm so excited, I can't *believe* it!"

He lifted me into a hug that would have turned into a graceful spin if we were sitcom stars. Instead, we collapsed into the side of the refrigerator.

"Nicholas, we're going to be *fine*! My job will keep us afloat."

Nicholas looked momentarily taken aback, even mildly insulted. "Of course we're going to be okay. I'm not worried! Why are *you* so worried?"

"I don't know, maybe because our kitchen cabinets are falling off the walls and college tuition is expensive and we like to buy artisanal yogurt at Whole Foods? Seriously, why *aren't* you worried?"

"Forget it, we should be celebrating. Yes, we're heading into a lean phase—but less so now, thanks to Scroll. I'm proud of you."

He leaned down and kissed me—a long, slow kiss. Margot walked into the kitchen and said "Yuck" before turning on her heel and walking out of the room.

Me: Dad, I GOT THE JOB!!!
Dad: That's my girl. LOL.
Me: Wait, why are you laughing?
Dad: I'm not.
Me: LOL means Laughing Out Loud.
Dad: Oh. Well, in my book, it means Lots of Love.

7

I was sitting on my front porch when I noticed Ollie standing next to a bench across the street, on the side of the school lawn furthest from our house.

Now that Oliver and Margot were in second and fifth grades, I'd implemented a plan whereby they met each other at the bench and walked home together. This raised eyebrows among other parents, even when I pointed out to concerned parties that our house is literally a stone's throw from the school, and the crosswalk is manned by a crossing guard who could have been a bouncer in another life. Still, the principal requested a letter absolving the school district of responsibility.

On the days I was at work, Jessie continued to retrieve the kids herself instead of letting them walk home. She said she was hoping to catch a glimpse of Filament's very own celebrity meteorologist, who sometimes came to school to pick up his daughters. When I asked if she thought Margot and Oliver were still too young to make their way alone, Jessie said breezily, "Not my call! You're the mom." (Which, of course, gently meant *yes.*)

On this particular Friday, I was home alone waiting for Margot and Ollie. Georgie went directly to a friend's house from preschool. Now Margot appeared to be taking her time collecting her brother, and so Oliver stood by the bench—slightly hunched, hands shoved deep into the pockets of his too-small navy windbreaker. Even from down the block and across the street, I could tell by the set of his narrow shoulders that he had a defeated, exhausted look about him. He needed a haircut. I made a mental note to put him to bed early.

Did I walk over and escort Ollie across the street? No. I went inside to grab a can of seltzer, certain that Margot would eventually catch up and bring her brother home.

On Monday, after spending the morning on a middle school tour with Margot, I called Genevieve from my dining room table. Once Chris told me I'd need to raise this particular issue with my immediate team members, I wrote out my spiel and rehearsed it with all my trusted advisors. I said, "Your offer is incredibly generous. I'm thrilled about it. But I do have one logistical issue I wanted to raise."

"Of course, go ahead!" Genevieve's cheerful voice trilled through the phone.

"My deal is, I'd like to work from home on Fridays." The request sounded naked and unadorned, but I resisted the urge to explain or embellish. Instead I drew little question marks on the cover of Margot's social studies textbook—an infraction that later earned her a demerit for defacing school property.

Genevieve said she heard my concerns but she needed to "run them up the flagpole."

The next day, I was on the train into the city when Genevieve called back. We were tearing through Secaucus, moving full throttle past the Meadowlands and the turnpike view made famous by the opening scene in *The Sopranos*. In an instant, we would head into the tunnel under the Hudson and I'd lose the signal.

"Alice? We shared your ask with Cleveland. Unfortunately, they weren't receptive. It's a real butt-in-the-chair operation out there, but of course we're a satellite office, so we can be flexible on an à la carte basis." There was a pause. We sped through the Secaucus station, which has a deep track so I glimpsed a blur of ankles belonging to people waiting for another train. Genevieve continued, "Let's leave it like this: you'll be in the office five days, but you can work from home as needed. As long as I know where to find you."

My seatmate shifted, elbowing me in the side. I winced. "Well, thanks for trying. Also, I forgot to ask: is there any wiggle room on the vacation time? Ten days seems . . . stingy, if you don't mind my saying so."

"I admire your candor, actually. I had the same concern before accepting my job, and I'm sorry to report, the vacation policy is ironclad. It's MainStreet policy for executives and managers to receive the same packages as people on the retail side. Leadership doesn't get preferential treatment."

I swallowed my disappointment and focused on the unfamiliar experience of being pegged as a leader. "In that case, Genevieve, it's my pleasure to officially accept this job."

"Fabulous! Welcome to the team. Would you mind holding for just a moment?"

I heard the sound of a button being pressed, but the phone wasn't on mute, as Genevieve must have intended it to be. So I heard her bellow, loud and clear: "Alice Pearse is in! Tell Chris to hold off on making an offer to the greeting card chick!"

Greeting card chick? Was she a tastemaker, too?

"Alice? I'm back. Let's be in touch when you've given notice and we can talk start dates and all that good stuff. But in the meantime, I'm absolutely thrilled to have a chance to work with you." The way she said *aPsolutely* reminded me of Susanna; I wondered if Genevieve and I would also end up being kindred spirits.

"Thanks. I feel the same way." By now, my seatmate was getting antsy, muttering under his breath about people who think they're so important.

But Genevieve wasn't finished. "Before we hang up, I have one more question."

"Yes?"

"Alice Pearse, what is *your* dream book?"

I smiled out the window. This was an easy question to answer. "I'd love *A Room of One's Own.*"

"Consider it done."

We hung up.

I thought of a line that was underlined and circled in my old Penguin paperback of the Virginia Woolf classic: "The beauty of the world . . . has two edges, one of laughter, one of anguish, cutting the heart asunder." This pretty much summed up how I felt about my new job: overjoyed and petrified.

Then I concentrated on a simple mantra from a less-complicated book: *I think I can, I think I can, I think I can.*

The No Guilt Book Club was thinning out after a night of revelry at the Blue Owl. We'd depleted almost two cases of wine, and the tables at the front of the Blue Owl were stripped of the hardcovers we'd piled on them earlier in the evening. The cookbook shelves looked like a mouth with many teeth missing, and the memoirs were so pillaged, I pitied the employees who would have to re-shelve them in the morning.

As I bustled around grabbing empty cups and cocktail napkins, I caught snippets of conversation: "If you love Anne Rivers Siddons, you must read Elin Hilderbrand," and "No, Jonathan *Tropper.* Trust me, he's a lot more fun than Jonathan Franzen."

Susanna and I headed to the back of the store to grab cardboard boxes and tote bags for friends who needed extra reinforcement to haul their bounty home. She threw an arm around my neck and leaned her cheek on my shoulder. "Another successful night. What would I do without you, my friend?"

I inhaled her familiar scent of cloves and Kiss My Face shampoo and placed my red-lettered Scholastic box carefully on the floor. "Susanna, there's something I have to tell you."

"OMG, please don't tell me you're switching Margot to the Piranhas." This was the rival of our girls' swim team, the Panthers. Margot and Susanna's older daughter, Audrey, were part of the same undefeated relay team; we joked that our families' longstanding friendship would be the subject of a personal interest segment when they made it to the Olympics together.

"No, not that. It's a little more serious." Now Susanna started to twist the detachable bottom of her plastic wineglass. I worried that she was going to spill it on an attractively spiraled stack of *Tiny Beautiful Things*. "I accepted the job at Scroll."

I didn't embellish or elaborate. I owed Susanna honesty, not an apology.

Her hazel eyes flicked around at her own floor-to-ceiling shelves, then down to the blue owl inlaid in the blond-wood floor in glazed tile. There wasn't a swiveling armchair in sight, but this was still my gold standard of bookstores; she knew that. She had to. "Thanks for letting me know, Al. You understand my concerns, right?"

"I do."

"I get it that you need to do this for your family, but you'll be working for a major competitor of mine."

"I know. Susanna—"

"They could put me out of business."

"Honestly, I don't think that will ever—"

"You know what, Alice? It's a job. We're bigger than this." She grabbed my hand and I held on, even though my engagement ring was twisted in such a way that it wedged painfully into the side of my pinky.

•   •   •

Even with Nicholas's dramatic pay cut looming, I was a little dazzled by my new salary.

One morning I dashed off a handful of checks for summer camps—two weeks of acting, $650; one week of lacrosse, $280; two weeks of fashion design, $900, not including a sewing machine.

"She better be the next Gloria Vanderbilt when she's done with that one," grumbled Nicholas. Gloria Vanderbilt? And he teased *me* for suggesting Mary Lou Retton as a subject for Oliver's report for Women's History Month (#stuckinthe80s).

I picked out two summer dresses, an eyelet blouse, and a cropped cardigan at a local boutique. I also bought a yellow perforated leather bag at Anthropologie and a pair of gold ballet flats. Two other shoppers admired a similar pair and one said, "Too bad, I wouldn't have anywhere to wear them."

I would.

I looked at myself in the mirror, which was slanted in a cunning way so as to trim a few inches off the waistlines of the middle-aged women of Filament. Even with that minor mercy, I was still thicker than I would have liked to be and my hair had the maroon halo that announced "I will not go gently into gray hair." Otherwise, I liked what I saw. At least my ankles were still in good shape.

I swore I'd never wear clogs again.

When my dad took me to Howard Savings Bank to open my first-ever account, I marveled over how easy it had been to earn the paycheck we were depositing: "All I had to do was sit there!"

I was fifteen, a lifeguard with a crush on a boy who worked at the snack bar. The summer was shaping up nicely; I couldn't believe I was getting paid to drink Slurpees and teach kids how to blow bubbles.

My dad asked the teller to cash the paycheck, and then he handed me a thick stack of bills. "That's what $472 feels like. Nice, right?"

I shrugged. "I guess so."

"My first paycheck at Howard Johnson's was a lot less, I can tell you that." He was proud. Even through my new Ray Bans, which I wore inside, the glow was unmistakable. Then he handed the money back to the teller. "This all goes into savings."

To this day, I remember the cool heft of those bills in my hand.

A week before my first day at Scroll, I gave Jessie the day off and took the kids to a store called Our Name Is Mud. The plan was for them to paint a penholder for me to keep on my new desk, but the mission immediately devolved into misery. It turned out, Georgie didn't really want to paint a penholder; she wanted to paint a tiny bisque dog for $19.99 ("He can be twins with Cornelius!"); Margot wanted to tackle a platter that could hold a Thanksgiving turkey (or two); and Oliver loudly wished he were on the slide at the playground across the street.

Through gritted teeth, I hissed, "You guys, *we are here to paint a penholder.*" I almost said "a fucking penholder" but didn't. I picked the one I wanted and plunked it down on the table while the scandalized, aggressively nice saleswoman showed us how to sponge down the piece before applying paint.

Is it possible that I was the first grouchy mom ever to paint pottery with her children?

As the kids painstakingly started to paint navy and yellow stripes (my choice) up the side of the penholder, I was reminded for the millionth time how like Nicholas they are. I would have slathered on the paint and been done with it. These three were meticulous and quiet, focused on the task at hand just long enough for a seed of doubt to germinate in my mind.

Why was I committing to this job at the very moment when my kids had reached the ages I'd been waiting for since they were babies? They were eleven, eight, and five. I could take them anywhere and they had interesting things to say. They could entertain themselves, which meant I no longer had to participate in games or dress-up or pretend to like puzzles.

Why was I doing this?

For the money, that's why. And for the chance to spread my wings in a way I hadn't since they were born. Was that so much to ask?

Just as my eyes started to well up, Oliver grabbed Georgie's wrist and said, "Not like *that*, dummy. You're messing it up!"

"Oliver, she can do it however she wants. *You're* the one whose part looks ugly." Margot is always quick to defend Georgie, especially when she has the chance to antagonize Oliver in the process.

"Yeah, you're not the boss, *Ollie*. I'm doing it how *I* want to do it."

Oliver started to cry. He's a stoic soldier of a boy, so I was unaccustomed to the sight of fat tears rolling down his freckly cheeks. He didn't make any noise. He just put his chin down on his chest, shoulders shaking with sobs.

I patted Oliver softly on his back, moving the palm of my hand in small circles under the hood of his Adidas sweatshirt. "Shhh, it's okay, Ollie. You did a great job. I'll think of you guys every time I reach for a pen!"

I tried to sound reassuring, then upbeat, but had trouble croaking out the words.

On the way home, I cranked up Z-100 and rolled down all the windows, much to everyone's delight. While Margot, Oliver, and Georgie shouted out their dance moves—The sprinkler! The typewriter! The shopping cart!—I cried quietly in the breezy solitude of the front seat. I kept thinking of Oliver waiting by the bench, alone.

8

The morning of my first day at Scroll, my phone was abuzz with texts from mom friends wishing me luck. These were women who had slathered my kids with sunscreen, whose children's birthday parties I'd attended, who knew all the ups and downs of my marriage thanks to endless poolside analyses and post drop-off coffees.

"We're proud of you," Susanna wrote. "We'll be cheering from this side of the river!"

Nicholas was at the counter when I left for the train station, six slices of bread in front of him, assembling school lunches with the loving care I could never bring myself to apply to such a thankless operation. He looked at me very seriously and said, "You can do this."

His first week in his new office was fast approaching, so I said, "You can, too."

Cornelius met me at the front door with his red leash in his mouth. I smoothed the worry lines on his soft forehead. "Sorry, big guy."

I expected the departure to be bittersweet but instead felt elated as I walked down the street, past the line of cars jockeying for position in front of the school. Before I turned the corner, I glanced back at my house and saw all three kids framed in the front hall window. Georgie's nose was flattened against the glass. Margot appeared to have an arm slung across both her siblings' shoulders. It was such a rare moment of sibling solidarity, it might have been a mirage.

I blew a kiss and hustled off to join a stream of commuters rushing for the 8:16.

While I was standing on the platform, I texted Jessie, "Big day is here! WML. You'll take good care of my little people, right?"

Her response arrived just as the train rolled into the station: "Of course I will, you know that. This is your moment, Al!"

It was.

My new commute was twenty minutes longer than my old one, bringing door-to-door travel time up to a grand total of eighty minutes. That first day, I floated uptown from Penn Station, propelled by adrenaline and possibly starvation, since I'd been too nervous to eat breakfast. As I speed-walked past my old building, I felt a homesick pang for *You*'s colorful elevator lobby decorated with photos of models doing healthy things like meditating and eating watermelon.

But Scroll is an *exciting* place to be, I reminded myself.

I pictured Nicholas that day at the train station—"Alice, I didn't make partner"—the defeated slump of his shoulders, how alone he'd looked. Now we were in it together, both pitching in equally to keep ourselves afloat.

Another image floated into my head, unbidden: a line of editors saying good-bye on my last day at *You*. Proud frowns on their dear, familiar faces; women who had been mine alone during a time when everything else—food, sleep, sanity—half belonged to my kids.

Then I thought of my dad, a camera attached to a tube threaded through his nose and down his throat, watching his own cancer on a flat-screen TV. "Subglottic laryngeal fungating, friable tumor with heaped-up

edges and multiple areas of necrosis and surrounding areas of hyper-
emia." The doctor had dictated these ugly words to a nurse, who closed
her eyes briefly before jotting the verdict on my dad's chart. My mom and
I froze like statues, eyes glued to the film.

And the patient? He looked away first. He reached out his freckled
hands and gently lifted Margot, who was only three months old, from my
lap onto his.

Oh, I know courage. It runs in my family.

Scroll's Office Support, David, answered the door when I buzzed. He was
a transplanted Clevelander, and he wore the chunky gray plastic glasses
befitting a recent Columbia grad living in a hip neighborhood of Brooklyn. I liked him immediately.

Scroll's new Purchasing Manager, Ellen, happened to be starting on
the same day, so David showed us the ropes together. Ellen was whippet
thin and serious-looking like Emily Dickinson. She, too, wore statement
glasses, but hers were silver cat-eye. David ushered the two of us into
a bright-white conference room and handed over two heavy laptops. I
tried to have a good attitude about switching from a Mac to a PC, but
the red foam track button on my graceless black ThinkPad immediately
called to mind Darth Vader with a pimple on his face.

Genevieve had warned me that I would have to share an office. I'd
acted perturbed when I learned about this—noise level had been a factor
in my thwarted case for a day to work from home—but the truth was,
I'd never even *had* an office before, so sharing one was no problem. My
new officemate, Matthew, worked from a standing desk and wore noise-
canceling headphones. He was Content Manager, Non-Fiction. He lifted
the headphones a few inches away from either ear and said, "Welcome,
Scroll employee #305."

Matthew was very tall, with a thick head of blond hair, bushy blond
eyebrows, and a beard that looked like it had been planted with a different
kind of seed—dark brown and coarse. He wore shoes with an individual

receptacle for each toe. Normally I found this style disgusting, but Matthew managed to pull it off.

"Thanks! Are there really that many of us?"

"Indeed there are. We multiply overnight like . . . I don't know what. Let me know if you need any help getting settled in. I'm glad to have company in here." Matthew planted his feet shoulder-width apart and turned back to his work.

Of course, the office was white, but when I arrived that morning it was bathed in a yellow glow in the very shade Georgie uses when she's drawing a big smiling sun. My desk was next to the window and it had a view of the rooftop garden atop the Museum of Modern Art. If I stepped into the low window well and looked east, I could see one distant spire of Saint Patrick's Cathedral. Far below, the garbage trucks and yellow taxis were Matchbox-sized, making their way haltingly down 55th Street.

My desk was made of simple pine, painted white, held together with industrial metal brackets. The chair was white molded plastic, with a dangerously responsive metal button on the side that controlled the height of the seat. One wrong move and you'd be on the ceiling before you knew it. Everyone who worked at Scroll—and MainStreet, at large—had the exact same workspace, known as the Prodigy Setup, hearkening back the Rockwell brothers' early days working from their parents' garage.

A Room of One's Own was sitting in the middle of my desk in a pool of soft light from a lamp that was the miniature of the ones I'd seen in the simulated lounge area during my interview day. Otherwise, the desk was empty, so the book looked like it was on display in a very chic modernist museum. I picked it up gently, admiring the homespun navy design on the cover, and felt dumbfounded by my luck. Underneath was a note printed on brown paper: "Welcome, Alice Pearse. We hope these words inspire you to take your literary work to even greater heights. Please treat your dream book with the care it deserves. First editions may not leave the premises under any circumstances."

"I can't believe this is *mine*." Matthew didn't respond and I realized he couldn't hear me underneath his headphones. I waved my hand to catch his eye and he lifted up one padded ear cup. "I'm just admiring my dream book. What was yours?"

"*The Jungle* by Upton Sinclair. Not the most upbeat subject, but . . ."

"Well. The author of my book drowned herself, remember? So where is yours now?"

Matthew tapped a metal bin over his desk. "I keep it in here. If you read the fine print, you'll see that you're not supposed to take the plastic off, although I did one time. I needed to smell the pages."

I knew we would get along.

After hours of "onboarding," which consisted of memorizing PIN numbers, reading the wiki page on MainStreet's intranet, and collecting my employee ID badge, I met Genevieve for lunch at the Union Square Café. I'd been there once before, dining on a gift certificate from Sutherland, Courtfield.

As soon as we sat down, Genevieve told me she had to rush back to the office by one thirty for a phone call with Greg. "A million apologies," she said. "This lunch is seriously the highlight of my day."

We'll be cutting it close, I thought, and then I wondered, who is *Greg*?

There was a birthday celebration happening at the table next to ours, and the guest of honor was a stocky middle-aged woman. Her companions were a broomstick-thin man and two little girls who were accompanied by two American Girl dolls wearing the same dresses in miniature. Naturally, I knew the dolls by name: Julie Albright and Kit Kittredge; their clones lived in my third-floor playroom.

"I'm going with the tasting menu. Who can pass up monkfish prepared the right way?" Genevieve snapped her menu closed. "You?"

"Same here." The mussels made me nervous, but I didn't want to damage my reputation as an adventurer.

She leaned over the table in the universal stance of women having fun together in restaurants, smiling broadly. She had one crooked eyetooth, which gave her the rakish air of a girl I might have climbed trees with as a kid. "So, what are you reading right now?"

"At this very moment? *Gone Girl* by Gillian Flynn. It's a galley I took from *You*—not out until June—but mark my words, it will be big. How about you?"

Genevieve fished a well-thumbed paperback from her leather bag, which was structured like a briefcase, with a hot-pink seersucker lining. "Don't you dare laugh."

She held up the book for me to see. It was *The One Minute Manager*. I laughed. "I can't say I've read that one."

"I know, I know, it's very B-school of me, but I need all the help I can get in this role. Anyway, you should definitely check it out, especially as you rise through the ranks at Scroll. Be sure to add it to your TBR list."

"Wow. Thanks." I was disarmed by Genevieve's candor. Warm as everyone was at *You*, the editor in chief functioned like the matriarch of a large, very stylish family: she never second-guessed herself and she certainly never touched the bread basket at lunch. Genevieve's openness and hearty appetite were a pleasant change. "Wait—TBR . . . what's that?"

"To Be Read! All the books you can't wait to get your hands on."

"Yes! I have one of those." I pictured the towering stack of hardcovers on my side of the bed. With a lamp and my glasses on top, it doubled as a night table. I smiled at Genevieve; she flashed her infectious grin right back. The moment reminded me of the underwater "tea parties" I had with Margot in the summer: both of us beaming at each other through bubbles, pleased to find each other at the bottom of the pool even though we'd orchestrated the reunion ourselves only two seconds earlier.

Like blind daters trading relationship histories, we compared titles. We both loved *The Immortal Life of Henrietta Lacks* and *Zeitoun*. Genevieve had never read *Random Family*; I confessed I'd seen the movie *In Cold Blood* but never read the book. We promised to fill in these gaps and report back to each other.

Genevieve started building a little pile of poppy seeds on the tablecloth with her index finger. "So, Alice. Scroll has a really interesting corporate culture, which you'll figure out when you head to Cleveland."

"Yes, I'm really looking forward to it! I don't know if I mentioned but my husband is actually from Cleveland, so—"

"No! That's awesome! Although I'm pretty certain you'll find that MainStreet is a different environment than what you're used to out there." Now Genevieve leaned forward, glancing conspiratorially around the restaurant as if to check for stray Rockwells. "Before you go, you may want to invest in a few blazers. That seems to be the uniform for Main-Street women. The guys wear hoodies; the ladies wear power clothes."

"Oh. Okay." Would I need a floppy paisley tie, too?

"Also, you should definitely make sure you're up-to-the-minute on community outreach. That's a top priority for Greg."

"I made a list of team members I'd like to introduce myself to—"

"You mean, who you *will* introduce yourself to, right?" Genevieve reached across the table and gave my shoulder a gentle shove. I hoped she couldn't feel my bra strap, which was drooping halfway down my upper arm. "Alice, I'm going to encourage you to speak only in the most declarative terms. It's an important part of how we message ourselves. Scroll is a very *certain* company, you'll learn."

I laughed and nodded vigorously. "Got it."

Our plates arrived, drizzled with creative oils and accompanied by ancillary cutlery whose purpose eluded me. When our trio of waitstaff finished their ministrations, Genevieve raised her water glass and said "Bon app!"

"Yes! Mangia!" I hoped we wouldn't go back and forth in this vein, since I couldn't remember how to conjugate *comer*.

With a forkful of fish on its way up to her mouth, Genevieve said, "You have three kids, right?"

I nodded my head around a mouthful of monkfish, which was scrumptious. I figured Genevieve had pieced together the highlights of my personal life through the same kind of detective work that led me to her generous donations on behalf of at-risk dogs.

"Wow. What's that like?" Genevieve lowered her fork to her plate and looked at me expectantly. I never know how to respond to this question, which is usually followed by "Did you always know you wanted a third?" (The answer is yes, although Nicholas required convincing.)

I thought of Margot and Oliver boogie boarding on Long Beach Island, their faces glowing as a wave deposited them on either side of Georgie, who squatted right at the water's edge, dribbling sand on her ample thigh. Three giggling, salty little people with gigantic smiles and pruned fingers, fearless and fun—moments like this are the whole point of parenthood. Then there's the flip side: the same three kids in a dark room on a beautiful day, wearing faded pajamas, bickering wildly over the final crumbs at the bottom of a bag of Cool Ranch Doritos, with *Elf* blaring in the background. Welcome to the yin and yang of parenthood: the moments when you feel like you won the motherhood jackpot, and the ones when you feel like a zookeeper breaking up a brawl among primates.

Genevieve waited expectantly.

"It's . . . a wild ride. A grand adventure. Honestly, it really depends on the day." Resisting the urge to elaborate or inquire about Genevieve's plans to have kids, I steered the conversation gently back to Scroll. "Tell me more about what I can expect these next few weeks."

"Well, people in Cleveland are firing on all cylinders. You'll see that soon enough. If Greg pings you at breakfast, he expects an answer by lunch." She tucked an invisible strand of hair behind her ear and smiled conspiratorially. "Scroll has its roots in retail; they play by retail rules. You'll do great, I have no doubt."

"I'm just excited to get my feet wet"—get my feet wet?—"and pick some great books for the stores."

"Lounges." Her face hardened a bit, taking me by surprise.

"Sorry?"

"Greg wants to cement the idea of Scroll as a literary salon, not just a center of commerce. So we're drilling down on the idea of a lounge, as opposed to any old bookstore. With better coffee, too."

"Well, in that case, maybe they should think about serving wine!"

"We."

"Yes. We."

Genevieve laughed. "I'm with you on that, one hundred percent."

There was an awkward silence. A truck thundered down the street, rattling the bottles behind the bar.

"So. Will Greg be there when I'm in Cleveland?"

"I imagine he will be, yes."

"Will he be in orientation, too?"

Genevieve gave me a long stare.

"Alice, Greg is the president of Scroll. Greg Rockwell? He's the third brother. He's been with the company since the beginning; he's a member of the L Squad. Greg dabbled in some writing of his own—westerns, I think— then got his start at MainStreet in appliances. He has some revolutionary ideas about selling books. You'll see."

"Oh yes! Great. Well. I look forward to getting to know him."

Appliances? L Squad? I felt the red crawl of mortification on the back of my neck.

This was starting to remind me of the sushi business lunch where I was too embarrassed to tell my dignified, cultured magazine editor boss that I'd never eaten edamame before. She looked on, aghast, as I popped a whole pod in my mouth without divesting the beans of their prickly shell. She was the same boss who broke me of my native New Jersey habit of saying, "draw" instead of "drawer" and "mira" instead of "mirror," then softened the blow by giving me my inaugural sweater set in pink cashmere. ("They're meant to be worn together," said the card.)

Moments after dessert arrived, Genevieve had to rush back to our office for her phone call—but not before giving me a list of goals to add to MainStreet's employee portal, GatheringPlace. "Okay, so *great* chit-chatting, but here's the scoop: I need you to set up meetings with at least thirty agents and editors. I need you to establish yourself as an arbiter of impeccable taste by assembling a collection of four hundred twenty-five top titles to sell in our lounges. Are you with me, Alice?"

I was momentarily distracted by a delivery of white petit fours to the girls at the next table; they squealed with delight, exactly as mine would have at the sight of mini cakes topped with marzipan bunnies. "Absolutely. I'm right with you."

"Great. I'll also need you to educate yourself about the ScrollOriginals program and brainstorm about a subscription model for elite readers. You should be prepared to present these thoughts to key influencers when the time comes. Make sense?"

Genevieve delivered these instructions without pausing—*ratata-tattat*. I couldn't remember ever being so *definite* about anything, except maybe cutting crusts off sandwiches. (I have a firm policy against that.)

Before I could respond, she said, "Great. You're awesome, and I'm so psyched to have you aboard. I think we'll have a lot of fun together." Then she hustled out of the restaurant, weaving her way among tables and grabbing a thickly shoulder-padded trench from the coat check before disappearing through the heavy door.

I quietly ate my plum upside-down cake, with a sinking sensation that I'd already forgotten my password for GatheringPlace. When I rooted around in my bag, looking for Chapstick, I found a note from Margot: "Good luck today, Mommy! UR a star." I folded it up quickly and held up my hand for the check.

On my way back to the office, I called Nicholas. "What does it mean to 'drop' a meeting on someone's calendar?"

"I'll show you when you get home." I could hear the amusement in his voice.

I'd never used Outlook before, so I was baffled by the patois of Scroll calendaring: OOTO (out of the office); WFH (work from home); DA (doctor's appointment); BL (business lunch); VIM (very important meeting); EOD (end of day); SHHY (should have happened yesterday); WTFAIDH (What the fuck am I doing here? Okay, fine, I made that one up). Aside from my Outlook calendar, where meetings, appointments, reminders, and admonitions appeared and disappeared, seemingly willy-nilly, I continued to maintain my Google Calendar—color-coded by family member and rife with orthodontist appointments, basketball clinics, and pottery classes (not my own).

Overwhelmed as I was by the newness of everything, I also felt like I was floating on air, seeing everything in the crispest detail. The sensation was like getting a prescription for new glasses when I hadn't realized I was overdue. My stomach churned with excitement every time I passed the Scroll logo on my way to the watercooler. Pretty soon, that logo would be above storefronts all over the country and I would be partially responsible for the unique and stylish wares inside.

Right before I left to catch the 5:45 train, we had our first all-hands meeting. Genevieve explained that this would normally be a forum for us to update the team on "big wins" in each of our categories, but for now, with so many new people, she just wanted us to introduce ourselves. There was Keith, whom I remembered from my Chain, and Matthew, of course; and Rashida, who was in the process of "pivoting" out of her role as Analytics Expert and into one as Environmental Lead, where she would create Scroll's hip intellectual vibe; Jess (Associate Content Manager); Mariana, our resident Book Hunter, who traveled the globe collecting first editions to sell in the lounges; and David (Support).

I didn't need anyone to tell me that David would not run out and get decaf skinny lattes for us at four p.m., as his contemporaries did at *You*. Nor would he handwrite 250 sweet sixteen invitations as I had at his age for a former editor in chief, whose daughter's party had been at the Pierre. ("No gifts; your presence is present enough.")

While Genevieve stepped into the hallway to take a call from Greg, Mariana said, "So you're a Virginia Woolf fan?"

"I am! My husband gave me *Mrs. Dalloway* in college and I've been hooked ever since. I have to tell you, Mariana, I'm happy with my job, but yours sounds pretty unbelievable, too. Searching for beloved old books? Come on. How did you get into this line of work?"

She laughed; clearly I wasn't the first person to point out what a nice deal she had. "Well, I got my start in rare books at Sotheby's—"

Genevieve pushed open the frosted-glass door of the conference room and Mariana whispered, "We should go out for a drink sometime!" I was flattered by her assumption that I would ever be free to go out for a drink after work.

Rashida and Genevieve welcomed everyone aboard and told us newbies how lucky we were to be in these shiny new offices. Six months earlier, they'd started out in a windowless room in a different Main-Street building. They didn't even have a watercooler! Or air conditioning on weekends! Their delivery reminded me of the subtle power grab of veteran moms getting acquainted with first-timers: "You think *you* have it bad? *I* lived in a one-bedroom in Park Slope when *my* first baby was born. Can you imagine lugging your Bugaboo up the front steps of a brownstone? So I carried him everywhere in a Bjorn—*hell-o*, sciatica!"

Everyone else at the square blond conference table had a laptop in tow; I had the same blue spiral notebook I'd used at *You*—right side of the page for work, left side of the page for personal. "That is *such* an interesting system," said David, eyeing the notebook with suspicion. I felt like I'd shown up at SoulCycle wearing Jane Fonda's aerobics outfit.

When it was my turn to talk, I felt surprisingly calm. I told the group how excited I was to take a flying leap into a new world, while hanging on to the best part of the old one: reading. I said, "If you'd asked my ten-year-old self to describe my dream job, this is the one I would have described. I read so much, my mom had to lock me out of the house to get me to play outside."

When I looked around the table, my youthful colleagues were smiling and nodding as if they, too, were once kids who got socked in the stomach with the red ball at recess. So what if several of them hadn't learned how to read yet when I graduated from high school? I was among bookworms and we would venture forth together, united by three-letter

Scrabble words and casual references to Kafka's *Metamorphosis*. I felt like the human version of one of those little plastic capsules my kids get in goody bags at birthday parties: pour water on them and they expand into a little towel or a T-shirt, or even a foam dinosaur.

I was a mom capsule expanding into an innovator.

There was a horse-drawn carriage in front of the Scroll building when I left, and I was in such an expansive mood, I almost hired the driver to whisk me away to Penn Station. What better way to celebrate my arrival at the intersection of literature and commerce?

I came back to earth when Genevieve emerged from the rotating doors behind me. Aside from the ridiculous expense and practical nightmare of navigating midtown rush hour by horse, I would have died of embarrassment if Genevieve had spotted me tucking myself in under the green velvet lap blanket. Friendly as she was, she didn't seem like the fairy-tale type.

On the train home, I traded texts with my dad, who was eager to hear about my first day and to tell me about his first day of jury duty. Then I checked Facebook and noticed that he had commented on several photos I'd posted in 2007, spurring a round of speculation from friends, along the lines of "Wait, you guys are in Maine? I thought you were starting your new job." And finally, I caught up on the texts that had been piling up during the day. Several were from my mom, who never mastered punctuation on her flip phone keyboard. She spells it all out instead.

> **Mom:** scan at sloan kettering on mon at 2 care to join question mark dying to hear about first day period zowie exclamation point
>
> **Me:** Sorry, I'll be at work—not much flexibility in this gig. But it's great so far! Xoxo

I felt a flash of annoyance that my mom still expected me to be able to drop everything when I suspected Will wouldn't even know about my dad's appointment until it was over.

> **Susanna:** I was thinking of you all day. Sincerely hoping you loved it.
> **Me:** Thanks, S. So far, so good. I may need to check your impeccably curated shelves for ideas . . .
> **Susanna:** Don't push it, bitch.

> **Nicholas:** So? Should I break open the bubbly?
> **Me:** I have arrived, in every sense. See you in a few.

Finally, I tweeted this, the result of a search for "fresh start" on BrainyQuote.com:

@alicepearse . 1m

"Daring ideas are like chessman moved forward; they may be beaten but they may start a winning game." —Goethe [1 retweet by Genevieve; 1 favorite by my dad]

By the time I looked up, forty minutes had passed and we were pulling into my station. As I made my way down the hill between the tracks and North Edison Avenue, I saw a little figure running toward me, dribbling a soccer ball and smiling broadly: Oliver. He was there to meet my train. He had never done this before, and I felt so proud—of him, of me.

We walked home together, holding hands.

When we arrived, Nicholas was waiting on the front porch. "I thought we should celebrate," he said, nodding in the direction of a bottle of champagne—already open, already half-empty. I grabbed its icy neck and took a long swig before we went inside for dinner.

9

By my second week on the job, I started to feel like I was in the groove. I recognized some acronyms here and there and I'd completed a series of mandatory video tutorials on issues like confidentiality and sexual harassment in the workplace. Every afternoon at four, I joined my colleagues for a coffee break and pastry tasting in the simulated Scroll lounge, known as the Sim.

The young Brooklyn hipsters were an impressive bunch. They answered e-mails after midnight while tending their chickens and building lamps from spare parts salvaged at flea markets. They baked artisanal macarons and wove their own reusable coffee filters and trained for weekend mud runs upstate. "Mud . . . what?" I asked David, when he mentioned plans to participate in the Tough Mudder.

"Oh, Alice, you should try it! It's hard but amazingly fun."

"I'll stick to spinning, thanks."

We brainstormed and bounced ideas off each other and promised to "noodle that over" when we didn't have answers. The whole vibe was invigorating. I enjoyed working with this crew in the same way I loved baby-sitting when I was in college, when kids were a rare species in everyday life.

And I had to admit, it was thrilling to be surrounded by people who understood so little about my "real" life at home.

"I can't believe you have three kids!" they'd say.

Or "You look so great for . . . I mean, you know. You don't look like a mom."

To: alicepearse@scroll.com
From: nbauer@bauerassociates.com

First day in the new digs; just wanted to give you a shout-out. It turns out my building is dog friendly, so it looks like I'll be able to bring the big guy in every now and then. Guess I'm not in the Big Apple anymore. How is it over there? Know anyone who needs a lawyer?

To: nbauer@bauerassociates.com
From: alicepearse@scroll.com

Sorry for radio silence—have been in a strategy meeting all day. Did you know there are more bookstores in the US today than there were in 1930? Who knew? Hey, listen, I might be late for dinner—a couple of us are grabbing early drinks—but save some lasagna for me!

To: alicepearse@scroll.com
From: nbauer@bauerassociates.com

Things were really quiet so I came home early. Lasagna in the oven and I'm on the porch with a Sam Adams. #thissuburbanlife

Dear [INSERT NAME OF AGENT OR EDITOR],

I hope you won't mind that I'm tracking you down out of the blue like this. I just left my post as books editor at *You* to start a new adventure as a Content Manager at Scroll, an innovative new addition to the MainStreet family. We will be setting up retail lounges across the country where bookworms can browse and purchase e-books in a relaxing, inspiring environment. Coffee will be served.

I'm on the prowl for news of your authors' latest and greatest novels and memoirs so we can make sure to include them on our list. I'm a huge fan of [INSERT NAMES OF AGENT OR EDITOR'S TOP AUTHORS] so I thought I would connect with you directly about the possibility of partnering for our ScrollOriginals program, where authors and bookstores have a unique opportunity to meet on the same page.

When you have time, I'd love to take you out for lunch or coffee so I can tell you more about our exciting plans. I look forward to hearing from you soon!

Alice Pearse

This e-mail was an adaptation of a template passed along to me by David, who inherited it from Matthew, who received it from Genevieve. The message contained some language I found borderline cringeworthy—especially the use of the word *partner* as a verb—but I went with it.

I struggled with the sign-off. "Best" and "Yours" and "Looking forward" were all the rage at *You*, but they weren't really my style—or Scroll's, for that matter. Several of my new colleagues went with "Cheers," which I felt should be reserved only for full-blooded Brits.

I sent out a slew of these e-mails and was surprised by how quickly people wrote back. Seconds after I hit send, an editor wrote back: "Alice, thank you for reaching out. Really eager to hear what you guys have up your sleeves. Looking forward to hearing what the future has in store for booklovers! I'm tired of buying online; ready to go back to the old way."

I responded, "Great! I can't wait to meet you!" and then forwarded the whole exchange to Genevieve, feeling downright tickled by the fun of it all. She responded promptly: "Want to grab lunch later? Hale & Hearty has a delicious mulligatawny. And hey, in the future? Please avoid using exclamation marks in your e-mails. Grazie."

Standard lunchtime was 12:30, and choices included sushi, nouveau American, Mediterranean, farm-to-table, or any place that had an over-priced chopped salad on the menu. I always paid; my expense reports were astronomical. The best meals were with agents and editors, who peppered me with so many questions about Scroll, I barely had time to eat.

"Will you bundle an author's previous titles with new ones?"

"Are you open to selling children's books?"

"Is the ScrollOriginals program limited to nonfiction?"

"Will the subscription program extend to all branches?"

"Do you have plans for an outpost in [Topeka/Milwaukee/Fort Lauderdale/wherever the agent or editor's mother lived]?"

I covered basic logistics over sparkling water and Diet Coke; then, by the time main courses arrived, I moved in with the features that hadn't been mentioned in *Publishers Weekly*: the first editions, the sumptuous furniture, the sustained silent reading—SSR—areas, the lending library that would allow members to read any e-book for free while they were on the premises.

I knew my companion's jaw would go slack with shock, then awe. It turned out, many members of the New York publishing community were tired of buying books from the solitude of their own living room. "Scroll will bring the community experience back to book buying," I said, spearing a piece of grilled chicken or shrimp, then popping it into my mouth with gusto.

When my dining companion raised the thorny subject of independent bookstores, I trotted out my friendship with Susanna. "You know who my best friend is? An independent bookstore owner." I explained how the Blue Owl functions like a little community center, how I couldn't imagine life without it. "But lots of towns all over the country don't have a bookstore anymore, so Scroll will fill that void."

"What about stores that have survived the rise of the website: how will they fare with a competitor selling e-books for less money right down the street?"

"I'm sorry, I can't talk about pricing right now. But we believe that a rising tide will lift all boats."

If the agent or editor was around my age, I reminded them how threatened the networks had been by the advent of cable. It was going to be the end of television! And now the networks and cable coexisted alongside each other, with different kinds of programming but definite overlap in their audiences.

"Scroll is like cable," I said. "We're not trying to put anybody out of business. We're just trying a new approach to book sales."

"That is so cool. How lucky are you to be part of such an amazing idea?"

"I know. It really is a dream job."

With cappuccino on the table, while the agent or editor nibbled on complimentary biscotti or mini meringues, I changed the subject. Evangelizing about Scroll started to feel a little bit like telling the story of how Nicholas and I got engaged—in Labyrinth Books, where he planted the question on a postcard of the Manhattan skyline inside Pablo Neruda's *100 Love Sonnets*. I loved telling the story, but I'd told it so many times, I worried it might start to sound stale.

My dad came into the city to meet me for lunch. When the elevator doors opened on our pale-peach lobby, he was paying for a roll of Mentos at the newsstand, wearing a navy blazer and a maroon paisley ascot over his stoma. It had been a few weeks since I'd seen him and he looked a little thin.

"Dad! Weren't we meeting by the LOVE statue?" I glanced around surreptitiously to see if anyone from Scroll was behind me. Proud as I was of my dad's mastery of Buzz Lightyear—no easy feat—I didn't want to introduce him to my colleagues. They would be kind and appropriate, of course, but I could already envision the polite queries when I went back upstairs: "So, your dad. Was he always . . . like that?"

I remembered the one laryngectomee I knew before my dad became one himself. He was a retired policeman, very tan, who played the harmonica all day at the deep end of the pool where I worked; he was highly regarded by the stoner lifeguards for his rendition of "Another Brick in the Wall." And then, one summer, he showed up on opening day with a hole in his throat. He had a new hobby—cards—and he was always trying to recruit opponents for rummy, spades, spit. "Name your poison," he'd croak, pressing a gunmetal gray device under his chin. Nobody wanted to play. The guys in the snack bar called him Robocop.

"My train got in early, so I thought I'd check out your new place," my dad said, gesturing grandly at the high ceilings and the single file of bamboo stalks growing out of white gravel in the middle of the lobby. At the sound of his voice, a woman in a suit looked up sharply from her iPhone. Mind your own beeswax, said my inner third grader.

"Well, great. Welcome!" I reached up to give him a hug—an experience akin to embracing a lawn chair; we Pearses are not touchy-feely by nature. "What do you think?"

"Fancy. I like the vegetation."

I smiled, moving swiftly in the direction of the revolving doors. "Shall we? I was thinking maybe Le Bonne Soupe? They have a quiet upstairs—"

My dad held up his hand, shook his head, then moved the other hand under his chin. "I made a reservation. It's a surprise."

I followed him out the revolving door on 55th Street and we headed east. I knew better than to try to keep the conversation afloat on such a bustling stretch. Buzz required dexterity (hard to walk and talk at the same time); plus it couldn't compete with the rumble of cars bouncing over potholes or bike messengers howling epithets as they narrowly missed colliding with taxi doors and each other. Even without the normal patter of conversation, I could tell my dad was pleased to be back in midtown, his old stomping grounds.

Halfway down the block, he stopped, opened a glass door and motioned for me to go inside ahead of him. We were dining at Michael's, a beloved if slightly timeworn media hot spot. Back when I was an editorial assistant, I had their maître d' on speed dial and I would request the best tables by number. If my boss had an early appointment after lunch, I even ordered her the Cobb salad ahead of time so it was ready when she arrived.

My dad and I were swiftly ushered to the worst table in the restaurant. Michael himself seemed to sense that there was something different about our party, although he probably couldn't put his finger on what it was since I was the one who had announced our name at the front desk when we arrived. He led us to the back of the first dining room—there was Barbara Walters, Dr. Oz, Chris Harrison from *The Bachelor* (would it be rude to snap a picture?)—then to the back of the second dining room. Michael kept checking over his shoulder to make sure we were with him. He pulled out both our chairs, opened each of our menus, and said, with a small bow, "Thank you for dining with us."

My dad nodded, and smiled warmly.

"Will you be having still or sparkling water today?"

"Still," I answered for both of us.

When we were alone, my dad fished Buzz out of his breast pocket. He pressed it to his neck, which was scarred from multiple surgeries and courses of radiation. "Now that you're part of the media elite, I thought this was the right choice."

"It was. Thanks, Dad." My heart broke a little, imagining the search history on his Internet browser. (*Midtown publishing hot spot not too loud.*)

"Have you been here before?"

"Once or twice." I'd eaten at Michael's a million times on my *You* expense account. "May I recommend the bay scallops? They really can't be beat."

I offered my dad a roll, which he declined.

"Seriously?"

He shrugged. "Saving room for lunch."

I did most of the talking: about MainStreet, about Georgie's refusal to wear any color except pink, Oliver's new obsession with Greek mythology, Margot's futile campaign for an iPhone, and Nicholas's networking to attract new clients. My dad was engaged and curious on all subjects, as always. He wanted to know, did Oliver have *D'Aulaires' Book of Greek Myths*? Had *I* read *Mythology* by Edith Hamilton? I had not but made a mental note to add both books to our family's TBR list, which tended to double in length after a visit with my dad.

At some point in the meal, I noticed he wasn't eating his lobster bisque; he was swirling it around in the bowl and rearranging the pattern of parsley flakes on its surface.

"Dad, is there something wrong with your soup?"

He held up Buzz and tried to speak twice before he found the right spot on his neck. Two diners behind him looked curiously in the direction of the buzzing sound, then went back to scrutinizing their *Playbill*s with a magnifying glass.

"No, nothing wrong. I'm just having some . . . problems. Swallowing."

Had I been in my own personal state of Alpha Omega, this response would have triggered a choir of alarm bells. But I was too preoccupied with the incongruity of being at Michael's with my dad and—fine— maybe by nagging worry that someone I knew would walk in.

I said, "Really? Do you think you should get that checked out?"

"No need to get worked up. It's just a cold, probably." As if on cue, he coughed, covering his stoma with his hand. I held my breath, hoping no bodily fluids would stain the ascot. When I established that they had not, I changed the subject.

10

I'd wound down most of my school-related volunteer activities, but I still had to get through the dance I'd agreed to organize for Louisa May Alcott School. The theme was Beach Bash, which had caused some controversy at a PTA meeting.

"Not to be crazy"—all the moms say this, we can't help ourselves—"but didn't we have a Summer in January dance last year? Shouldn't we consider other concepts?" This feedback came from a second-grade mom who made it her life's work to fight for the rights of allergy sufferers everywhere, even though only one of her two daughters had had a minor allergy that she'd outgrown before kindergarten.

"Thanks, I took that into consideration, but you see we still have inflatable palm trees and duct tape lifeguard stands from Summer in January, so I thought I'd put them to good use for Beach Bash in April. All in favor of recycling?"

Of course, I knew green was the ultimate trump card.

I ended up splurging on some new decor from Oriental Trading Company, abhorred purveyor of crap for kid parties—in this case, foam sunglasses to be decorated with aquatic-themed stickers by kids who don't like to dance. I corralled Capri Suns and individually wrapped nut-free treats for the snack bar, to be sold by Margot and her fellow fifth graders to raise money for their graduation carnival. I obtained a permit from the fire department and stuffed an envelope with overtime cash for the custodian, who I see every morning when I go outside in my pajamas to collect the newspaper.

On the afternoon of the dance, which was a Friday, I was at my dining room table, working from home (WFH, in Outlook parlance), when the phone rang. "Hello?"

"Hello, is Mrs. Alice Pearse available? This is the Filament Board of Education calling."

"This is Alice." It's not every day I receive a call from Central Office, as it's known, so I didn't bother to point out that I'm not technically a Mrs.; Pearse is my maiden name.

"Mrs. Pearse, are you the organizer of tonight's dance at the Louisa May Alcott School on Flower Street?"

"Yes, I am the organizer."

"Mrs. Pearse, I regret to inform you that you have neglected to secure a $500,000 insurance policy in case of emergency, as advised by district protocol. You need to file the appropriate paperwork by six p.m. Otherwise, you will be in violation of Section B of Clause Two of the safety code and your dance will be uninsured."

In order to secure the insurance policy, I needed permission from the principal, permission from the PTA president, a copy of the fire permit, a head count for students expected to attend . . . the list went on. In the background, my work computer sounded a symphony of arriving e-mails. *Tingtingting.*

The stress rose in my ears like a noise.

For the next hour, I listened to a conference call on mute while inflating fifty beach balls and fifty blue and white balloons. When it was my turn to weigh in on which first editions would eventually be included in Scroll's television commercials, Rashida said, "Alice, are you sick?"

"No, I'm just working from home."

"I'm so glad. You sound really out of breath."

"Really? It must be a touch of . . . asthma." I shoved my chair back from the table, pressing a balloon into the dining room wall. Of course, it popped. *BOOM.*

"Alice? Are you still there?"

"Is she okay?"

"What was that noise?"

"Sorry, guys! I'm fine. A truck just backfired in front of my . . . where I live." No need to remind my colleagues that I didn't live in a loft apartment like everyone else.

After the conference call, I picked up my kids at school and then made the rounds of the fire department, the Board of Ed, and Town Hall, collecting signatures in triplicate for the insurance policy. I bribed Oliver and Georgie with red Gatorade and promised Margot I'd buy her blue nail polish if she rang the doorbell of the PTA president's house and asked for her signature on the appropriate form. I was too irritated and embarrassed to do it myself, but I faked a friendly smile as the PTA president glanced around my kids and out to my car.

When Margot got back into the minivan, I said, "So?"

"She said she never sees you anymore. She misses you."

"And what did you say?"

"I told her you're busy because you work."

"You said it just like *that*?"

"Yeah, pretty much." She popped her head up from the backseat and started applying Bonne Bell Lip Smacker in the rearview mirror, her mouth forming the same O my mom's does when she puts on lipstick.

"Margot? Just so you know, all parents *work*, whether it happens in the home or outside the home."

"I know, Mom. Can you change the station?"

By the time the DJ arrived at six thirty, I was 99 percent sure the insurance policy was in place. Still, I held my breath when the third-grade boys practiced backspins by strobe light. One kid said, "Can you believe there are no party favors? This dance sucks, big time."

On Mother's Day, I ate fried eggs in bed and read my crayoned, construction paper, glue-laden cards while propped up on pillows, sipping a Bloody Mary (Nicholas's contribution). Ollie's said, "Dear Mommy, You are the Werld. I will never take you for granite." Margot's was a little cooler than it had been the year before, but she still made a Top Ten list of her favorite things about me, with open circles as the dots over each i. Number one on the list: "You're always there for me." Luckily, she doesn't remember the winter I made her wear snow boots she hated, cried over, refused to walk in—only to discover, in April, that their toes were still packed with the tissue paper from the store.

Georgie's family portrait featured a gargantuan mother with hands even bigger than her head. The armchair psychologist in me wondered if these oversized mitts indicated power or if this was her subconscious allusion to the times I've grabbed her delicious upper arm and maybe squeezed a little too hard while encouraging her to sit *down* and at least *try* what the rest of us were eating. (Georgie survives on peanut butter and jelly sandwiches. Cut into triangles, not with organic peanut butter—only Jif—and preferably with the jelly slice facing the plate.)

After breakfast, I packed for Scroll orientation in Cleveland. It was Nicholas's turn to settle back on the pillows, watching, while I filled a duffel bag with an array of dresses, boots, hair drying and straightening devices, three pairs of pajamas, and even a vanilla-scented candle to give my first-ever solo hotel room that cozy vibe.

"What? Say it. You think I'm a rookie."

"No, I don't. I'm just glad you opted not to go with the chocolate sauce."

I'd gotten it into my head that I should bring a little East Coast souvenir for each of the Cleveland team members. When I was at the cash register in our local ice cream store, about to purchase eighteen mini jars of chocolate sauce, Nicholas stepped in and staged an intervention. He admitted that the plan gave him severe secondhand embarrassment. ("Seriously, Alice, people just don't *do* stuff like this.") For once, I listened.

At the airport, I kissed everyone's foreheads. "Will you guys call me?"

"Mommy, you're going away for four days." Margot rolled her eyes. "Jessie is perfectly capable of taking care of us." This was true. Just that morning, when we were searching for hair elastics, Georgie called down the stairs, "Can you text Jessie? She knows where to find them." Sure enough, Jessie reported that the mother lode was in a jewelry box on the third shelf of the linen closet.

"I'm also perfectly capable of taking care of you," added Nicholas, looking wounded.

"Yeah! It's not like you're going to the moon. But you know something? I *really* will miss you." Oliver offered the top of his head to be kissed, and Georgie held on, arms and legs wrapped around me like a koala.

"Mommy, can I braid your hair?"

"Right here? I don't think so, Georgie. I still have to go through security—"

"Okay, but promise you'll do braids for your meeting? It looks so pretty."

"I'll see what I can do."

"Have fun," said Nicholas. "Remember, you *can* go home again."

This was MainStreet's motto. We tried to work it into casual conversation as often as possible.

The minute I made it through airport security, I updated my Facebook status: "EWR → CLE." It didn't have the same ring as the ultimate high-powered trip, "JFK → LAX," but still. I hadn't traveled alone in twelve years; it was dizzying to walk through the terminal without a stroller.

•   •   •

Our family (including Cornelius) made the seven-hour pilgrimage out Route 80 to Cleveland several times a year, always on the Fourth of July and on alternating Thanksgivings. The challenge of having the car packed up by dawn is our version of adventure travel. If we haven't reached the Delaware Water Gap by seven a.m., we feel we've failed.

I was staying at a Scroll-subsidized hotel in the old arcade downtown, but Judy and Elliott still insisted on meeting me at the airport.

"Alice! It's us!" (As if I didn't know.) Elliott gave me a tight hug.

"Oh, honey, we are *so* excited for you. Just *beyond*. I've been telling all my friends about your new job." Judy held me at an arm's length before bringing me in, giving me a moment to appreciate her fluffy new haircut and earrings made of flattened spoons.

MainStreet is the most beloved resident of Cleveland. They set up shop—literally—after the steel companies moved out and the car plants closed down, and they've brought business to the lakefront, employing entire neighborhoods. Of course, they've also perked up the local retail scene with their six hometown mega-malls.

After I wrestled my luggage off the conveyor belt, Judy, Elliott, and I headed over to Heritage Towne for dinner at Wok 'n' Roll, a do-it-yourself stirfry "experience." I was unclear on what distinguishes an experience from a plain old restaurant—perhaps the long list of trade-marked salads or the custom fortune cookie station.

Judy and Elliott were more than willing to suspend their disbelief after parking in a heated spot in front of a faux parking meter dispensing MainStreet bucks—mini-coupons to Delia's, The Body Shop, and Johnny Rockets. "Oooh, now we'll have to go for milkshakes for dessert," said Elliott, long-haired former sixties radical who now owns a struggling coffee shop on Cleveland's near west side.

"OMG, Alice, we're addicted to the Chocolate Madness Shake. We split one after Zumba, but you'll want your own, trust me." Judy led the way to the restaurant, pointing like a proud tour guide at Heritage Towne's many charming features: baby-changing stations tucked inside tiny insulated cottages trimmed with gingerbread, a clock tower where locals gather to ring in the new year, a fleet of motorized wheelchairs tricked out like hot rods with chrome and tail fins. The attention to detail was mind-boggling, right down to the milk boxes doubling as umbrella stands under the candy-striped awnings outside each store.

By the time we were seated in an oversized booth upholstered in chinoiserie, I was both dazzled and a little sickened by my endlessly clever employer. I'd been thinking of Scroll as a bold literary endeavor, but now I wondered: would it be just another mall store?

"Tell us, how is our son doing?" said Judy, once we'd made inroads in a bottle of what she refers to, simply, as "chard."

"So far, so good. I mean, it's only been a few weeks, but his office looks great—Palm Coast Pale was a great paint choice, by the way— and all his systems are in place. FedEx and well . . . you know." I struggled to think of another system. "Of course, the final touch will be the sign in front: Nicholas Bauer, Attorney-at-Law, but that's still in the works."

Elliott laughed his big guffaw. "Attorney-at-law! That's my son!"

"I'm proud of him. I mean, it will be even better when he gets some clients, but . . ."

I'd already plowed through half a bowl of shrimp crackers and was eager to change the subject. The truth was, Nicholas and I were both pretending not to worry while casually agreeing to eliminate formerly basic amenities like cable and home delivery of the *New York Times*. The one night a week my mom came over to make spaghetti and meatballs for dinner was now one less night we had to pay for dinner—or pay Jessie, whose hourly rate suddenly felt like a tremendous luxury. We'd decided to cut back her hours; two afternoons a week, Nicholas came home early to pick the kids up from school. The idea was that he'd continue to work from home, but he seemed to spend a lot of time sampling microbrews from Oregon. I had never before paid close attention to when my paycheck was deposited; now I resisted the temptation to take it to a check-cashing place around the corner from Penn Station.

"And the kids? Those cuties."

"They're great. They're adjusting to everything really well; they love having Nicholas around more." I didn't mention Oliver's latest observation: "Daddy doesn't get as mad at us when we're having fun. And *he* doesn't make us clean up."

"And you? How are you adjusting?" Elliott furrowed his caterpillar-thick brows.

My eyes smarted. There was something about the combination of his resemblance to Nicholas and the pleasure of being able to understand what he was saying in such a loud restaurant—a luxury I didn't have with my own dad. I pressed a finger tight to my lips before answering, "It's fine. It's all going to be fine."

"Well, Elliott, now look what you've gone and done. Can't you let Alice get used to her big job before grilling her?" Judy defused the moment, and we dug into our udon noodles.

I'd driven by the corporate campus many times, but now my blue employee pass allowed me into MainStreet's inner sanctum for the first time. It consisted of a handful of eight-story waterfront buildings bedecked with solar panels and flanked by special short water fountains for dogs, which were welcome to come to work with their owners. All shrubbery was cleverly groomed with a patriotic theme. In the short walk around the place, I spotted topiaries in the shape of Uncle Sam, the Liberty Bell, and of course, a giant dollar bill.

My first meeting on Monday morning was a general orientation for all new hires—over two hundred of us—in a conference room with a mural on the back wall that said Shop Local. MainStreet prided itself on being the most dog-friendly company on earth, so I wasn't surprised to find canines of all shapes, sizes, ages, and breeds in attendance alongside their humans. They were all remarkably well behaved, unlike sweet but incorrigible Cornelius. I cringed, imagining him plowing down colleagues in his rush to gobble up the dog biscuits on the breakfast buffet.

The presentation focused on the unique culture established by our company's boy genius leaders. We learned that employees took great pride in being wacky; if we passed a special test, we could even win a yellow ID lanyard indicating our wackiness. (I made a note in my notebook: "Investigate wacky test.") We saw a video clip of our leaders' speeches at a ribbon cutting for Heritage Towne: "We don't just sell merchandise, we sell the future."

MainStreet employees referred to the Cleveland office as "Big Daddy." And Genevieve was right: most of the women did wear blazers. The men wore hoodies, and ninety-eight percent of them also had beards. Others had ponytails; many had both. People at MainStreet dove deep, jumped on a call, explored topics from a 30,000-foot perspective, and opened their kimonos to each other. When MainStreeters moved into a different "space," they weren't referring to a new office.

During orientation, we received strict instructions to leave an empty seat at the table in every meeting we would attend during our time at MainStreet. "Why?" I whispered to the guy next to me, a Metadata Specialist who had just relocated from Dubuque.

"For the customer," the guy whispered back, straight-faced, while frantically copying down the Venn diagram our instructor was sketching on the Smart Board.

"Wait. *What?*"

"The empty chair is for the customer. So he always has a presence in meetings."

"Or her," I said, reflexively. "You mean like Elijah?"

Even though every person in the room had endured the same grueling hiring process, our leaders still conducted a thorough review of the Tenets of Winners—with the unfortunate pronunciation of "tenants."

I'd been classified as a Level 6 employee; it turned out, the highest level was 10, but there was no Level 9—just to make the leap from 8 to the pinnacle seem all the more insurmountable. For help with procedural questions, "best practice" was to check the wiki; if you still didn't have the answer you needed, you could file a "trouble ticket." Trouble tickets "lived" in GatheringPlace and were organized by six-digit numbers. Your manager would be cc'ed on any trouble ticket you filed, so new employees were cautioned to file them sparingly or risk flagging themselves as poor problem solvers. Winners Answer Their Own Questions (WATOQ) was the most sacred of all the Tenants.

The hotel room was divine.

I started each day with room service muesli ($22) and, at night, celebrated another day of acclimation by devouring strawberry shortcake topped with a sprig of mint ($15). Orientation was exhausting and baffling, but in the absence of my normal hour-long routine of bath-books-bed, I had enough time to sneak in a long walk and visit my favorite bookstore in Larchmere. I was careful to pay for my purchases with a personal credit card; despite MainStreet's contributions to Cleveland's economy, I knew the bookstore owner would not take kindly to plastic printed with Scroll's telltale white logo.

Like Susanna, many independent booksellers had been vocal in their opposition to our reading lounges. When I mentioned this to Genevieve, she said, "Progress is impossible without change. People who can't change their minds can't change anything." When I repeated her astute observation to Nicholas, he pointed out that Genevieve owed a debt of gratitude to George Bernard Shaw.

By the end of the third day of orientation, I started to feel homesick for the sticky chaos of Flower Street. I half hoped I'd be invited to join a pub crawl organized by a new hire who wore lobe-expanding earrings—but, alas, his chosen revelers hopped on a shuttle bus to Ohio City with nary a glance in my direction. (Maybe it was my reading glasses?)

Back at the hotel, I called home and Jessie answered. "Alice, is that you? Hang on a sec." Her voice sounded cheerful and warm, as if I'd caught her in the middle of a fun jam session instead of the cacophonous symphony of early evening in our house. I depended on a glass of wine to get me through these hours; Jessie cranked up the Beatles and encouraged dance parties in the dining room. "I just tire them out," she'd say. "That's the name of the game."

Now I heard Oliver's basketball pounding in the driveway and I imagined Georgie nearby on the swing set, deep in conversation with herself. The oven door creaked shut, and then Jessie was back. "Sorry, just grabbing the chicken from the oven." She sounded out of breath, which made me happy in a twisted kind of way. See, it's not so easy after all. "So, all is well out there?"

"Yes! I miss you guys! And Jessie, thank you for holding down the fort. I can't tell you how much—"

"Stop. It's my pleasure." Plain as the view of the Cleveland Public Library from my hotel window, I pictured Jessie swatting away my gratitude. I had one friend whose au pair live-tweeted tantrums and another whose nanny dosed her charges with Smarties and kept the good stuff— Adderall—for herself. In my mind's eye, I got down on the fake sisal rug and bowed down before Jessie. "Stop it," she'd say. "I love your kids! And this is not rocket science."

So why did I sometimes feel so out of my depth?

I closed the drapes and started flipping through a leather binder of hotel amenities: gym, sauna, dry cleaning, 24-hour bar.

"Jess, is my husband, around by any chance?"

There was a pause, then Jessie's muffled aside to Margot—"Is your suit on? Susanna will be here in five"—then the clomp of Margot's turquoise Converse across the kitchen floor. I could picture the scene so clearly, right down to the tiny skull hanging from a leather string around Jessie's neck.

"Alice, I'm back! Anyway . . . Nicholas? He's going straight from his office to basketball. He said he might go out after that." Now the water was running; I knew Jessie was busy, but I still wasn't ready to end the conversation.

"Okay, maybe I'll catch him in the car. How was Oliver's science test?"

"Great. He had a little trouble with the vocabulary section, but he said the true/false was easy. Listen, can we talk later? Cornelius is jumping up on the counter—"

"Of course. Go. Give them kisses for me."

I didn't wish I was there, exactly, especially with chicken on the menu (unpopular), but I still couldn't believe I *wasn't* there. I've never tried scuba diving but I imagined this was how it felt to discover you were underwater and still breathing.

> **Susanna:** Just drove by your house & saw N walking M&O across the street. Cute scene. Everyone dressed, happy, carrying a lunch.
> **Me:** You have no idea how much this means to me! Xoxoxo

> **Dad:** So? Are you running the place yet?
> **Me:** Hardly. Lots of stuff to learn, tho. Now watching the sunset over Lake Erie.
> **Dad:** Learning a lot?
> **Me:** Yes. It's pretty exciting!
> **Dad:** Good for you. I'll be first in line to hobnob with the literati.
> **Me:** ☺
> **Dad:** If only I could do anything out loud besides buzz. LOL.

Day 5. My final appointment in Cleveland was a meet-and-greet with the (mid)western branch of the Scroll team. There were about fifteen people in the room, all fitting the profile of the typical Scroll employee, down to the vintage footwear (running the gamut from Tretorns to wingtips) and tongue-in-cheek haircuts (bowl cuts, mullets). When I arrived, there was already a row of people seated along the periphery of the room, although there were still two empty seats at the conference table. I made a split-second decision to claim one; we were only supposed to save a seat for *one* customer, right—not for his mother, too? Age before beauty.

The chairs were the excessively ergonomic kind, threatening to topple over when I leaned back, so I sat there, ramrod straight, waiting for the presentation to begin. When the room darkened, the Smart Board came to life with numbers and graphs, and a disembodied voice delivered a presentation on the projected Scroll customer.

According to market research conducted in MainStreet shopping malls, she was between the ages of twenty-five and forty-five. She lived in an urban or semiurban environment with her partner and one child or more and a "substantial pet," classified as a dog or a cat, which she pampered with organic treats and high-end accessories. She drove a practical car but splurged on extras: navigation, roof rails, remote starter. She washed her hair with economy shampoo but splurged on designer face cream. She shopped for apparel at Anthropologie and Banana Republic, and for home goods at Williams-Sonoma, Room & Board, and West Elm. She subscribed to an average of three publications. She consumed an average of three books a month, selected on the basis of friends' recommendations, positive reviews, and "other," which the disembodied voice described, somewhat patronizingly, as a combination of serendipity and gut instinct.

I felt like I was watching a nature program about myself. *She dwells in that gray area between family obligation and a desire to satisfy her own sense of adventure. Here she is now, coming in for the kill. Watch as the mom sinks her unmanicured claws into the dad's neck. He has failed in his mission to gather food for their young, so she must feed them tacos instead . . .*

Before I left for the airport, I lined up with all the other new hires to collect a trophy for completing the orientation program. It was a hefty piece of hardware, topped with a bronze scroll, engraved in a font reminiscent of the Declaration of Independence: Alice P. I hadn't done anything to earn this distinction (other than show up and eat expensive sugar cookies), yet I felt a surge of pride when I shook Chris Pawlowski's damp hand. Until this point, the only trophy I'd ever received was from my high school swim coach (Best Team Spirit), granted at the same ceremony where Will won a scholar-athlete award that came with a cash prize and a plaque so heavy, our dad pretended to drop it on the way out to the car.

Naturally, like all young athletes of their generation, my kids had more medals, trophies, and certificates than shelf space for all the hardware and accolades. Our sunroom bookshelf (Billy by Ikea) was laden with bobble-headed softball and T-ball players cast in low-grade metals, propped up on plastic squares painted to look marble. Now I had my own barely earned prize to add to the collection.

11

Me: Stuck at Penn—the 6:09 was canceled. Can you pick up M & Audrey
from swimming?

Me: Hello? Do u read me? I just tried to call—no answer.

Nicholas: Srry. Just waking up from a nap.

Me: Where r the kids?

Nicholas: Playing on the iPad.

Me: So much for no screen time during the week. Did you see my
message about the train? Need you to pick up the girls.

Nicholas: Can you ask Susanna?

Me: Why?

Nicholas: Forget it. I'll ask her.

Me: Wait, why can't you pick them up. Or Jessie?

Nicholas: She's not here on Wednesdays, remember?

Me: Right. And you?

Nicholas: I had a few beers while I was cleaning the basement.

Me: Are you kidding?

Nicholas: Alice, lay off, k? I'm fine. Susanna & I will handle this.

When I got home, the recycling bins were already at the curb, hours earlier than we usually dragged them out for collection. Headlights from a passing car lit up a mountain of bottles, artfully stacked. I averted my eyes.

Mom: please call me when you can

The text popped up in the middle of a meeting and I turned my phone upside down so I wouldn't see it again until later. Two seconds later, I received an e-mail from Matthew, who was sitting right next to me (because of course we both had our laptops): "Are you in trouble with your mom?"

I typed back, "I'm late for my curfew."

Before Matthew, the only man I'd ever worked with was a former boss who jotted his measurements on a notecard so I could shop for him at Brooks Brothers. Matthew and I were like a random roommate match that might have appeared disastrous on paper—some housing dean's idea of a funny joke—but we turned out to be pleasantly harmonious. We bonded about how old we were compared to our colleagues. They didn't write anything down! They didn't answer e-mail, either, which could be disconcerting; were we really supposed to learn to IM?

Matthew's side of the office remained as spare as it had been the day I arrived, adorned with one simple black-and-white picture of a typewriter. My side was bristling with book cover postcards push-pinned to the wall, a sketch made by Georgie of a stick figure reclining with a book, a framed WPA poster encouraging reluctant readers to tackle the classics, and a whiteboard with all my projects color-coded in red, green, and blue.

Once I noticed Matthew eyeing my collection of ephemera and my (ever-increasing) stacks of books. "What?"

"Nothing. I'm just . . . a minimalist, I guess."

"Well, avert your eyes, then."

"No, no. It's all good. There's enough black and white in this company. We can use some color."

Me: On the train. How was your day?

Nicholas: Quiet.

Me: Good quiet or stressful quiet?

Nicholas: Playing solitaire on my computer quiet.

Me: Are you regretting your decision?

Nicholas: What decision?

Me: To go out on your own.

Nicholas: Kind of a big topic for texting, don't you think? Not my choice, really.

Me: But it was your choice to throw a laptop across the room and ruin any chance you had of building on the relationships you made at Sutherland, Courtfield.

I looked at this final message inside the white bar on the screen of my phone. Then I deleted it and typed "xo" instead.

Mom: alice, did you get my message question mark please call me exclamation point

This time I was scrubbing a lasagna pan and my hands were slick with Palmolive and ground beef. Once again, I didn't respond.

The principal of Louisa May Alcott was transferred to a different school in the district, and the moms were up in arms. I listened to them rage one Saturday morning at spinning and felt smug about having more important things to think about, like whether Honest Tea or Odwalla juice would be the optimal accompaniment to the reading experience at Scroll. It's not that I wasn't upset about losing our principal. I felt a neighborly kinship with him—and I'd appreciated his sympathy when our kitten was hit by a car—but now I was too busy to get ensnared in the web of venomous texts passed among moms who were convinced this was the end of decent public education as we knew it.

"Alice, we miss you. How's your job going?"

I brought myself back to the group, ashamed of feeling momentarily superior.

For Scroll's sales conference, I wore a green silk dress printed with cheetahs lounging in trees. My kids were horrified when I came downstairs—"You look like a tablecloth"—but on my way to the train I felt like a million bucks.

The new principal had already rejiggered the traffic pattern around the school: instead of an orderly drop-off line, where kids hopped out of cars one at a time, we now had a melee of parents in SUVs jockeying for position within a four-block radius of my house. North Edison was clogged with incoming students and school buses almost all the way to Sunshine Bagels, a quarter of a mile away. I made my way down the line, spiffy and smug, smiling at my friends and secretly judging the families whose tinted windows hinted at the ghostly glow of a movie being screened inside.

"Announcement: The 8:16 train from Filament to Penn Station will be arriving on Track Two in approximately three minutes." I was still in the school parking lot, so I picked up my pace, delivering my usual rushed greeting to the lunch lady whom I passed every morning on her way to my kids' school.

"Have a beautiful day," she said.

"You, too!"

At the sales conference, the Content Managers took turns presenting their Top Ten lists to the fifteen or twenty salespeople in the room, plus another thirty people who dialed in via video conference from Cleveland.

Genevieve had given us talking points, but they were so general, I found myself paralyzed by nerves, too antsy to eat lunch. When I ran into her in the bathroom two minutes before it was New York's turn to present, she said, "Are you ready to rock this?"

I avoided her eyes in the mirror. "Not really. I've never done anything like this before." My experience speaking in front of groups was
limited to giving toasts at weddings; I would have felt more at home with
a deejay behind me—and would have preferred for my audience to be
lubricated with a few cocktails. Instead, a few of them looked downright
dyspeptic, especially the gang in Cleveland.

Genevieve turned to face me, thrusting a paper towel into my hands.
"Alice, you are going to *shine* in there. Just be yourself."

Not surprisingly, Matthew and I had very different approaches to
sharing information about our books with the team. When it was Matthew's turn to present, he leaned back in his conference room chair and
spread his arms over the backs of the two chairs on either side of him,
looking for all the world like a bored college student who knew this material cold. He barely consulted his notes and spoke calmly and intelligently
for his allotted time—no pauses, no frills. The sales reps were rapt as
he quoted Truman Capote from memory: "Failure is the condiment that
gives success its flavor."

Then I was up.

I put a big smile on my face and spoke so loudly, the guy sitting next
to me jumped. But I knew I'd lose the Clevelanders if they couldn't hear
me; I already knew what it was like to be in a conference room halfway
across the country, missing out on every other word of the conversation. I
dove into the merits of a new novel I'd just read, which I thought had the
potential to be a best seller for Scroll. My audience looked a little bored;
Greg stared at his laptop.

In the Content Manager equivalent of a Hail Mary pass, I veered off
topic: "Many of us remember that moment when we realized our parents
need us more than we need them—that the roles have been reversed."

People looked up. I had their attention.

I explained how, for me, this moment came right after my dad first got
sick. My mom needed to learn how to use the ATM machine, and I was
the designated instructor. After she'd collected her bills, my mom leaned
into the machine and said, loudly, "Thank you, ma'am." That was when

I knew she was mine to take care of, at least for the time being. The axis had shifted.

The sales reps laughed warmly, and then they leaned in to listen as I explained how my anecdote related to the book.

I knew my presentation hadn't been as confident or as intellectual as Matthew's, but the head of the sales team nodded her head and smiled when it was over. "Good job," she mouthed across the table. The Clevelanders were hardly effusive with their praise, but at least they were awake and some of them nodded approvingly.

I felt like a Mylar balloon, floating above the conference room table, high on helium and glinting in the sun. *I think I can I think I can . . . I am.* I thought of all the years I'd made work phone calls from inside my closet so editors wouldn't be able to hear my kids watching *Blue's Clues* in the next room. My presentation was no TED Talk—the pièce de résistance among Scrollers—but still, the sales conference left me feeling like I was starting to get a handle on what I was doing. Plus, the danish was delicious.

On the way back to our offices, Genevieve gave me a pinched, "Nice job. Looked like you were having fun up there." Later she sent a message to the whole team: "Good hustle, gang. In future, please stick to the script. No need to introduce personal anecdotes into our pitches."

What happened to being myself? I wondered.

"Mom? It's me."

"Alice! You are a tricky woman to track down. Hold on." In the background: lovebird chirping, the yank of the detergent holder being pulled out on the dishwasher, Cascade pouring in, *snap*. "Okay, I'm back."

"Sorry to be so elusive. It's been a crazy week. What's up?"

"Well. Probably nothing. But I did want to tell you—I mean, it's too soon to worry, but—"

"Mom, what's going on? I'm calling from work." I didn't mean to sound like an irritated sitcom husband, but I knew I did.

"Well, you know we had Daddy's appointment yesterday."

In the beginning, I went to all the appointments—once every three months, once every six months, once a year. I'd missed the last few, but I always kept track of them on my calendar and made sure to call my mom afterward. Talking to my dad on the phone was tricky, but sometimes I asked my mom to put him on so I could tell him how relieved I was that his scans had come back clear.

Now I had the sickening sensation that this conversation was heading in a different direction. Before my eyes, my cheerful kelly-green dress faded to drab olive.

"And?"

"Now, Alice, I know you have so much happening these days and I really don't want you to be upset. But Dr. Davis saw something he didn't like in the exam. We still need to wait for the scans, but he's . . . concerned."

"What do you mean, concerned?"

"I mean, he wants to keep an eye."

"Keep an eye?"

"Sweetie, I wish you'd stop repeating everything I'm saying." I could hear my mom rearranging the pens in the square beige cup by the phone. Sharpies in the middle of the bunch, Bics filling out the periphery like carnations in a bouquet.

"What did he find?"

"A blockage."

"A *blockage*?"

"Yes."

"Where is it?"

"In the throat."

It had been years since we'd disembodied my dad this way: the throat, the esophagus, the stomach, the lungs.

"Where in the throat?"

"Where . . . where the tumor was the last time." My mom rushed through the final part of the sentence, as if it wouldn't be true if I couldn't understand what she was saying. But I understood. Perfectly. The language of illness is like pig latin: no matter how much time has passed since you last heard it, you remain fluent. "Apparently, he's been having some trouble swallowing? He didn't mention it to me. I thought he was eating a lot of soup, but . . ."

I remembered my dad at Michael's, swirling his spoon through the crème fraiche on top of his lobster bisque. I thought of the jaunty paisley ascot he wore that day, of his blue blazer, his penny loafers. I thought of him polishing those shoes in the living room, swiping a cordovan-stained brush over each toe. The smell of Kiwi parade gloss. The tin cigar box of shoe shine supplies stored on a basement shelf between a tackle box and yearbooks from Roxbury Latin. Forever a scholarship student, my dad didn't replace a pair of shoes until the soles were thick with patches, like a roof with too many layers.

"Oh, Mom. What else did he say?" Again: the same old rhythm, the endless inquisition about what the doctor said, what the nurse said, what was the look on her face, did she seem optimistic, did he look worried? Will and I used to joke that someone should wear a wire to the appointments so we could replay, pause, and rewind the conversation at a later date.

"He said it could be scar tissue. That's always a possibility. He might get the scan back and decide to do a minor surgery to abrade the area."

I flinched. Imagine ten consecutive strep cultures and you get the idea of having your throat abraded. One time I watched my dad endure this procedure and had to excuse myself to get sick in the bathroom. "What if it's not scar tissue?"

"Alice, we're really not there yet."

"What do you mean, we're not *there* yet? Where are we, exactly?" I didn't know why I was being so combative with my mom; she was only the messenger. But my whole body was suddenly alight with rage. I could taste it in my mouth, bitter and hot.

"Now, Alice, I can tell you're getting hysterical. We're going to stay calm here. We're not going to panic. We're going to find out what this is and then come up with a plan."

"Mom, I'm not getting hysterical. I'm just—" My eye fell on the framed family picture on my desk: me and Nicholas and the kids in Maine, with the sun setting behind us. It was the rare one where we're all looking at the camera, smiling genuine smiles, wearing clean shirts.

The last time I'd been through this with my dad, I'd only had one baby. Now I had three kids—big kids, who adored their grandfather and would want answers I might not have. I thought of them, passing around Buzz and holding it to their smooth throats. "How do you make it work, Pop?" Oliver had just written an essay about how my dad was his most inspiring person. "He wears his voice on a string around his neck. Sometimes he lets me wear it, but not while I ride my bike."

I also had this new job. I wanted my chance to shine. I felt ashamed of wanting something beyond my dad's good health, but wasn't I entitled to both?

"Mom?"

"Alice?"

"How's Dad?"

She sighed, the wind of information taken out of her sails. "Well. He came straight home and typed up the announcements for the church bulletin. Now he's on the computer ordering from his seed catalogs. You know how he is."

Of course. Actions before words. It was the Jesuit way.

"Mom?"

"Alice?"

"Did you tell Will?"

"I told Mary. Will was out on a boat without his phone." That must have been nice, I thought, ungenerously.

"What did she say?"

"She said we have nothing to go on until the scans come back. Scar tissue is a bitch, she said. We should be cautiously optimistic."

My two least favorite words in the medical vocabulary, a fancy way of saying "I have no idea."

"And how long until we get the scans back?"

"Five to seven business days."

"Is there any way to—"

"Dr. Davis will get the information to us as soon as he humanly can. He's on our team, remember."

When we hung up the phone, I realized Matthew had returned to his side of the office. I had no idea what he'd heard. I rolled slowly back from my desk, grabbed the key from the hook in the hallway, and walked downstairs to the bathroom on the floor below ours. While a stranger brushed her teeth, I locked myself in a stall, closed the lid of the toilet, lifted up my feet and sat there for ten numb minutes. I didn't cry; I just stared at the mint-green metal wall, my mind blank. Then I went back upstairs for a presentation about metadata. Then I went downstairs again, walked over to the front steps of Saint Patrick's Cathedral and called Nicholas. As soon as I heard his gentle voice, I started to cry.

SUMMER

12

Our kids were at home with Jessie, who had arrived with her sewing kit, ready to stitch a hole chewed by Cornelius in Mr. Pibbles, Georgie's beloved stuffed stingray. She'd whistled when I came down the stairs in a new dress from Garnet Hill. It was gray lace with subtle black leather trim; she was the only one who'd noticed its debut.

Now Nicholas and I were at the Appian Way, at a dinner hosted by Volunteer Lawyers for Justice. It was the kind of restaurant where all the tables wore fluffy white skirts, gathered at the top with elastic, and the butter pats adhered to tiny white squares of cardboard. The sauce on top of our side orders of spaghetti was billed as "Jersey's Best Sundae Gravy."

"As in *ice cream* sundae? Or day-of-the-week Sunday?" I whispered as we sat through the first of six speeches by local business people.

"Stop. These are restaurant folk, not editors."

"Nicholas?"

"What?"

"Can I ask you one more question?"

"Yes." He looked crisp in his white shirt and striped tie, like a young politician spit-shined for his first stump speech. He held up two fingers to a passing waiter. "Two Sam Adams, please."

"Oh, not for me, I'm fine with wine."

"Too late. Guess I'll just have to drink both." He'd already had a Brooklyn Lager before we left the house.

A tiny lightbulb went on in my head and I quickly flicked it off.

This was the first time the two of us had been out, alone, in months, and I didn't want to ruin it by nagging Nicholas about how much he was drinking. He'd always been a beer-on-weekends kind of guy; these days, he was tossing back a six-pack a night. The fact that he consumed these beverages over the course of several hours didn't help matters, especially since happy hour commenced before I even left my office. Taking out the recycling was now officially Nicholas's job. I no longer joined him in the basement for the sorting, even though I'd always enjoyed our peaceful chats over the thrum of the dryer.

Think of something else; think of something else; think of something else.

"Hey, Nicholas, are there actually any lawyers who *aren't* for justice?"

"Come on, Alice, just go with it. These people are the keys to my business development."

We were interrupted by a thick-necked man who stopped by our table and stuck out his beefsteak hand for Nicholas to shake. "Nick Bauer, right? Dom Mercadante." (I never call my husband Nick; nobody does.)

"Dom, nice to meet you. This is my wife, Alice Pearse."

I smiled winningly. "Hi, Dom!"

"Hey, so Nick, you were recommended to me by an old basketball buddy—you're renting office space from him?"

"Glen. Of course. He can *play*." Nicholas took a long swill from his beer, grabbing my hand under the table at the same time. That was sweet, at least.

"Yeah, well, he thought you might be able to help out with a situation I've got coming up. My brother, Phil, he's in some hot water on a lease over there in Filament. Opened this deli a while back—great location, top-notch mozzarella, but the parking's a bitch." Dom turned in my direction. "I apologize for my French."

"No need to apologize. I'm fluent myself."

"Glad we have that in common. So, I guess what I'm saying is, my brother has missed his last few rent payments and I'm a little worried he won't be able to cover his costs. He may need to think about filing for bankruptcy. Think you can help?"

Usually Nicholas worked on matters with many more zeroes in the dollar figures, but he didn't hesitate: "I'd love to." He was building a client list, slowly but surely.

On the way out to the parking lot, I grabbed the keys.

Since the days were getting longer, Susanna and I met up halfway between our houses to walk the dogs after dinner. This was my favorite time to stroll around Filament. The tulips were out and the high school lacrosse team wrapped up practice with a huddle and a cheer—"Go Brights!"— which echoed throughout the neighborhood.

We talked about everything and nothing: when Margot and Audrey would get cell phones; where we should take our husbands for their joint birthday dinner; whether I should follow up with the mom who let Oliver play a violent video game at her house.

"What would you *say*, exactly?" I could tell Susanna was skeptical.

"I'd just let her know that I'd appreciate it if she didn't expose my son to that crap." We paused to let Cornelius and Susanna's dachshund, Hotdog, sniff a pair of trash cans on the curb.

"Alice. Really? Do you want to be that mom?"

"Probably not. But I'm really annoyed. The object of the game was to blow up buildings. They're only eight years old!"

"Me, I'd probably take the passive-aggressive approach. I'd just not let Ollie go there again. Her kid can come to your house and be bored to tears by all your wooden toys."

I laughed. "Good strategy. Different subject: how are things at the store? You haven't mentioned."

She sighed and crossed her arms like it was cold, even though it wasn't. "Honestly? Not great. I had to ask one of my full-time people to go part-time. I'm hoping things will pick up again now that the weather is warm. Oh, and I started selling Ugly Dolls. So that's something."

I didn't know how to respond to that. Rashida and the Environmental Team were squarely against any merchandise that would junk up our simple aesthetic, especially toys. We wouldn't sell cards, bookmarks, or fancy notebooks either. "Well, isn't it about time for us to get a No Guilt Book Club on the calendar? That always brings in business, right?"

"Yeah. We'll see."

A train went by, empty except for a few commuters standing in the aisle, waiting to get off.

"In other not-so-great news, my dad's appointment didn't go very well."

Susanna stopped in her tracks. "Tell me."

I took the day off for Margot's fifth-grade graduation—a blisteringly hot affair where I was annoyed with my mom for wearing an oversized straw hat. Did she think this was the Kentucky Derby? I snapped at her for all kinds of minor infractions, then quickly downed two glasses of wine at lunch at the Highlawn Pavilion, the same restaurant where my parents had taken me for dinner after my high school graduation.

I knew why I was annoyed at her: my dad stayed home.

Me: Dad, we missed you today. Hope you got some rest.

Dad: I did. Also got some basil and sage in the ground, so we have that to look forward to.

Me: Did you get those articles I sent you? About the clinical trial at MD
   Anderson?

Dad: Which articles?

Me: The ones from The Lancet, JAMA?

Dad: Yes. Good to have additional info.

Me: What did you think?

Dad: Hey, did you see those pics Will posted? Are those kids getting big
   or what? LOL.

On GatheringPlace, the tally of my accumulated vacation days inched
along at a snail's pace, in halves and quarters inside an icon reminiscent
of a digital clock circa 1983. My current time-off balance didn't permit
me to take two personal days in quick succession, so I found myself in
a company-wide meeting—known as TownGreen—on the day Margot
and Oliver were released from school for the summer.

In the past, the last day of school had been one of my favorites. I invited the kids' classes over to our house for Popsicles in the backyard, and
I stood around chatting with the teachers while the kids played basketball
and blew bubbles and politely shook Cornelius's paw. I'm not a fun mom,
but this was the one fun thing I did.

Now, at the very moment when I knew my kids were lined up at the
ice cream truck for bomb pops, I was in a stark white conference room
with a cactus terrarium in the middle of the table. The New York office
was being beamed in via video to a cool blue conference room in Cleveland, where a rented popcorn machine lent a festive air to the gathering.
We could barely hear anything on our end over the popping and crunch-
ing on theirs.

"Hi, team!" Genevieve slid into the chair next to mine and leaned
over so her shoulder brushed against mine. Then she whispered, "Brace
yourself. This one will be a *huge* snooze."

"Really?" I glanced around the table to see if anyone was listening,
but the other Scrollers were either reading e-mail or chatting loudly with

colleagues in the Cleveland office. "I thought TownGreen was supposed to be like a big pep rally?"

"Ha! You're still a newbie, aren't you? An interminable lecture is more like it."

I struggled to arrange my face in the correct expression: appreciative of Genevieve's humor while mindful of the fact that I was her direct report. I also didn't want to look too buddy-buddy with her in front of Mariana, who joked that I was Genevieve's favorite. (Was *that* why she'd never followed up on the drinks plan she mentioned on my first day?)

The first item on the TownGreen agenda: communicating the Scroll way. The message: keep interoffice e-mails terse, with as much information as possible in the subject line. If you could, in fact, contain all the relevant details in the subject line, it should then be punctuated with [EOM], which stood for "end of message." This SOP (standard operating procedure) would spare your recipient the fraction of a second it took to open the e-mail.

When the Communications Team finished their presentation, the Environmental Team took over. The speaker was Rashida's manager, to whom she reported on a "dotted line." This woman smoothed her parted-in-the-middle hair behind her ears, clasped her hands together, and bowed slightly in the direction of the crowd. "Namaste, y'all. We're here to talk about mindfulness in the arena of office supplies." She paused while everyone clapped. "Going forward, we're launching a campaign known internally as ThinkFirst. The idea being, before we soil a tree-based product with ink, we should ask ourselves, 'Is this necessary?' "

Ellen, the Purchasing Manager, whispered to Genevieve, "By tree-based product, does she mean paper?"

Genevieve smile-smirked, an expression I now recognized as her trademark. "I believe so."

Rashida kept her eyes on her laptop, fingers flying on the keyboard. I knew she was answering e-mail, as everyone did in meetings. If you walked away from your computer for an hour, you'd be snowed under with corporate announcements and missives from Cleveland, each accompanied by a little red exclamation point. The trick was to absorb the scattershot immediately upon its arrival.

The ThinkFirst campaign extended to all office supplies. In an effort to reduce our environmental footprint, we would now file trouble tickets to requisition file folders, notepads, and Post-its—but these little luxuries would only be available in small batches. And there would be no more ballpoint pens; for those unavoidable occasions where it was necessary to put pen to paper, we would be issued fountain pens with replenishable ink cartridges. All Scroll copy machines would be programmed to turn off after reaching a weekly ceiling of paper output. Ditto for laser printers. "Send attachments! Read on the screen! Isn't that what we're all about here at Scroll, anyway?"

Rashida's boss kept getting interrupted by raucous applause, which was accompanied by a few stray whistles from the back of the room. Finally, she held up a hand with a ring on every finger. "In conclusion, the average office worker uses at least ten thousand pieces of copy paper every year. We know that paper takes up over twenty-five percent of Ohio's garbage each year. Can you imagine what that figure might be for New York City?" Her eye flicked to the camera linking our two states, at least for the moment. "You guys, let's start bringing these numbers down. Now. The world will thank us. The world is watching."

I turned in Genevieve's direction and snorted quietly. "The world is watching? Seriously?"

I didn't realize I'd spoken until Matthew said "Oh snap" under his breath.

We clapped our hands politely and flicked off the television. Genevieve nodded gamely. "Seems a little extreme, but we'll go with it."

"Yup," said Rashida. "This comes straight from Greg. Near paperless it is."

"I like where your mind's at, Rashida." Genevieve turned to me, then said loudly so the whole room could hear, "Alice, please try to keep your editorializing to a minimum when we're connected with Cleveland?"

I was too dumbfounded to respond. Wait, *you're* the one who said this was going to be a huge snooze!

"Alice?" She snapped her fingers softly in my face.

"Yes, Genevieve. Of course."

I thought of Margot, Oliver, and Georgie, shimmying into new bathing suits, and for an instant wished I was right there with them in my sensible Nautica tankini.

Most commuters have certain strategies for combating the tedium of the journey from one side of the Hudson to the other. Mine are sacrosanct: I head to the quiet car; I sidle up to the window in a three-seater, thus reducing my chances of having to sit next to somebody, since nobody wants the middle seat; and I pick the side of the train where I'm most likely to catch a glimpse of the sunset over the Meadowlands. It is, as Yeats said of Ireland, a terrible beauty.

With the exception of a handful of kindred spirits, I avoid all conversation with friends and neighbors. I listen to piano music on my way into the city, and on my way home, bracing for the onslaught of kids and chaos waiting for me, I listen to the train sound on my white noise app. This is how a train is *supposed* to sound: a peaceful clickety-clack punctuated by a romantic horn.

One night, I landed in the middle seat of a three-seater on the train home. The women on either side of me were ordering from Fresh Direct and I experienced a momentary thrill about being part of this exhausted, overworked club of working moms thronging to New Jersey.

When the conductor arrived to collect tickets, one of my seatmates couldn't find her monthly pass. She muddled around in her purse for a few minutes before surrendering. "I need to buy a one-way to Glen Ridge."

"That'll be $11.75, including the $6 surcharge for buying on the train." The conductor was unapologetic. In fact, he seemed pleased to deliver the news.

The woman next to me raised her hand. "Wait—I think I have an extra ticket." She pulled one from her purse and handed it over, waving away the other woman's offer of reimbursement. "Are you kidding? Just pay it forward."

This was the snapshot view through the trees as the train pulled into the station: Oliver and my dad playing Wiffle ball in our front yard. Oliver with the yellow bat to his ear; my dad winding up his arm.

In eight years of living six miles from my parents, I couldn't remember a time when either of them had dropped by unannounced.

Knowing, heartsinkingly, what was in store when I got home, I took my time, appreciating the daffodils on the corner of Flower Street and the tapestry hammock rigged by my neighbors on their front porch every summer. A boy rode his skateboard down the front path of the school. Someone on the block was grilling; someone else's sprinkler went *Tsk. Tsk. Tsk.*

Suddenly, Jessie's voice floated through the screen door. "You guys, dinner! Last one to the table has to clear the plates!"

Oliver glanced up at the porch. "Three more pitches, Jessie? I think I can hit it all the way across the street. I'm showing Pop."

I couldn't see my dad's face but he appeared to be waiting for Jessie's verdict. He knew who was boss.

"No, Oliver. Now. The salmon burgers are getting cold."

I thought her tone was a little bit harsh, but Ollie bounced willingly up the front steps, taking two at a time.

When I arrived at the house, my dad and I were alone in the front yard. He wore khaki pants and a short-sleeved, bright-red Izod shirt. His eyes were hidden behind thick tortoiseshell glasses, and his hair was longer than usual, a frizz of black and white. He held up his hands, palms to the sky, and slowly shrugged. From the string around his neck, Buzz Lightyear swung gently to and fro, unnecessary.

On the front porch, we took seats facing each other like opposing counsel at a deposition. He didn't have to tell me why he was there; I knew.

The cancer was back.

When Will and I were kids, the best day of the year was the one when we got to go to our dad's office. We each had our own day, unannounced beforehand. You'd wake up, get hustled out the door in semifancy clothes, grab a doughnut at Bun n' Burger, and then you were off on the train. The big city glittered on the other side of the river, and you were the luckiest kid in the world to be on your way there.

Will loved walking by Madison Square Garden; I loved the different shades of Wite-Out. Pink, pale green, baby blue, canary yellow.

The day consisted of sitting in my dad's office, reading *Harriet the Spy* and cobbling together an art project from copier paper and paperclips fished from a little magnetic holder. I was dazzled by the view from the 38th floor: a straight shot from 42nd Street all the way down Park Avenue to Union Square, populated by little dollhouse people and their microscopic dogs. I watered my dad's ficus tree, filling Styrofoam coffee cup after Styrofoam coffee cup in the little office kitchen and carrying them carefully down the hall, hoping to cross paths with the woman who once said, "Well, hello, young lady. You must belong to Ed Pearse: you're his spitting image!"

Things Not to Say to Someone Whose Parent Has Cancer:

- Are you close?
- Did he get a second opinion?
- Has he tried the Paleo Diet?
- Has he tried meditation?
- Has he read *The Power of Positive Thinking*?

- How long does he have?
- Do you know his end-of-life wishes?
- At least your mom is young.
- At least you have your own family.
- I'm sure he'll be okay.

PS. Saying nothing at all is worse than saying all of the above.

Dinner was over; the kitchen was clean (for once), and I sat at the dining room table with a pile of paperwork fanned out in front of me. Half of it was an exhaustive report from the Scroll metrics team, which might as well have been in Cyrillic numerals, for all I understood of it. The other half was information on recurrences of throat cancer from various hospitals across the country: MD Anderson in Houston, Dana-Farber in Boston, Johns Hopkins in Baltimore. The names of these places were so affable-sounding, I could almost convince myself I was coordinating a reunion of far-flung old friends. Hey, Dana Farber, want to come over on Saturday night? Oh, sorry, I have plans with MD Anderson. Have you tried Johns Hopkins? He'd love your pork ragù.

The phone rang. It was Will, calling from his cell phone and obviously on the move. "Al? I'm driving over to Freeport for a sunset paddle. Just wanted to see how you're holding up. I can only talk for a sec."

I could picture my brother in his Keens and river shorts, sunglasses held in place with a Croakies strap, left elbow resting on the open window of his car. I even knew the scenery: Crystal Spring Farm, Bow Street Market, the Harraseeket Inn, rolling fields full of peaceful cows and Queen Anne's lace all around. I felt a twinge of annoyance. Other than a few evenings at the community pool, I'd barely been outside since the snow melted. Now, here I was, taped inside a hot box of stress while my brother roamed free with a breeze on his ruddy face.

"Will, *you* called *me*."

"Right. So, is there any news?"

"About Dad, you mean?" I didn't intend to sound combative, but I knew I did. Under the table, my knee brushed against something sticky, which turned out to be a big wad of purple gum. In my own home?! You have *got* to be kidding me.

"Of course about Dad." Judging from the volume of the wind rushing past his car, I guessed Will was holding his phone in the hand closest to the window. He was no longer the same guy who frittered away his life savings on a foosball table for the Sig Ep house, but he still couldn't be bothered to use basic grown-up safeguards like a Bluetooth device or even a seat belt.

"Not really. I mean, I think he's still digesting the information and then he'll come up with a plan with Dr. Davis. I'm actually doing a little research on my own right now, but not turning up anything very useful." I dragged my thumb up the corner of one of my stacks of paperwork, flipbook style, only to see a dizzying assortment of medical terms pop out: *Nasopharyngeal. Oropharyngeal. Hypopharyngeal.*

"Yeah, I wanted to ask you about that. Do you know if they're thinking about a vegan diet? A running buddy of mine had prostate cancer a while back and he had some luck cutting out—"

"Will, Dad doesn't have prostate cancer."

"Yes, I'm aware of that, Alice." In his adult incarnation, Will was endlessly patient sometimes. I miss the explosive kid who punched a hole in his bedroom wall when our mom put the kibosh on his plan to camp out for tickets to a Mötley Crüe concert. "I'm just saying, it can't hurt to be open to a holistic approach. Diet, meditation, some herbs. Don't you think?"

Actually, I *did* think—it certainly couldn't hurt to try these strategies, which my dad would almost certainly file away under "New Age." But I resented my brother for shoehorning a phone call with me between leisure activities, for sounding so Zen about everything, and mostly for living in such a beautiful faraway place when I wanted him right there with me in New Jersey, where we could have this conversation over bitter diner coffee.

I took a deep breath. "Will, I'm trying to do my part here to make sure we have all our bases covered, but I have a full-time job and three small kids and a dog. Why don't *you* do a little homework on alternative therapies? I'm sure Dad would appreciate it."

He didn't counter with the obvious response: he, too, had young children (plus two guinea pigs, one pregnant) and ran his own business. "Awesome. I'm on it. Listen, Alice, I need to motor, but I want you to remember: we're a team. Got it?"

"Got it. Bye."

Later, alligator. In a while, crocodile. Those were our old sign-offs, back when we were skulking around the backyard on walkie-talkies, pretending to be Nancy Drew and the Hardy Boys (he was partial to Frank).

I pinched the little bridge of skin between my thumb and index finger, determined not to cry.

Just as I was about to return to my grim reading, Georgie and Margot strolled through the dining room. From the back, they looked like big and little versions of the same person, with shoulder-length wavy hair, narrow shoulders, and long, pale feet. They even wore matching ankle bracelets, woven from periwinkle thread by Jessie and studded with five wooden beads—one for each member of our family. The two girls appeared to be on some kind of mission—most likely to the freezer for lime popsicles—but Georgie paused at the threshold of the kitchen, where she turned to face me and then shimmied up the doorframe like a monkey, hands and feet pressed against each side.

She grinned mischievously when she got to the top.

"Georgie! Get down—you could hurt yourself!" Impressed as I was with her acrobatics, I still had to play my boring mom role.

She looked down at me, wrinkling her nose. "Mommy?"

"Yes?"

"I have a question."

"Yes?"

"What do you daydream about?"

From the kitchen, over the sound of the freezer door unsticking, Margot said, "Georgie, you crack me up."

"I don't know. You guys, I guess? Who you'll be when you grow up?"

Georgie slid down to the floor, crestfallen, her feet landing on the hardwood with a slap. "That's *it*? I would of thought you'd daydream about *funner* stuff."

I called into the kitchen as she disappeared to collect her dessert: "Me, too!"

13

Greg Rockwell arrived in New York for three weeks, with the goal of "team building with my Big Apple peeps." We prepared for his arrival with a flurry of activity—hanging tasteful art in our offices, ordering white melamine plates for the kitchen, creating a personalized guidebook for his family. I wrote up little descriptions of all my favorite kid-friendly places: the Cloisters, the Intrepid, the quiet little garden behind the Cathedral of Saint John the Divine. I even included suggestions for the best places to get ice cream near the Museum of Natural History and the Met so Greg's family wouldn't have to pay tourist cafeteria prices.

"How do you know his kids aren't lactose-intolerant?" asked Matthew, from his perspective high above my screen.

"I don't. Maybe Emack and Bolio's has sorbet?"

"You better hope they do."

We invited Greg to all our meetings, but he came to none, not even the one Genevieve showed up for carrying a big pink box of scones. We invited him out for drinks at a rooftop bar, but he didn't make an appearance there either. He never mentioned the guidebook, which seemed a little silly in retrospect. My time would have been better spent mastering my new vocabulary: merch, omnichannel, POS, transaction data, auth-in. Sometimes I felt like one of the Danish au pairs I made plans with on the front lawn of the school—understanding but not understanding.

Despite his elusiveness elsewhere, Greg was right on time for our 1:1 meeting, which took place in my office. Like a roommate displaced by a college hookup, Matthew had to gather up his laptop and head to the conference room for the duration. Actually, Greg reminded me of someone I might have known but would never have been friends with in college; he would have been the guy doing keg stands in the basement of the frat house—someone Will might have befriended before he found Buddhism. Now, in his adult incarnation, straddling Matthew's chair backward with his shirt untucked, Greg gestured with his chin at the stack of hardcovers on my desk: "You really want to pollute the environment with that crap?"

I laughed. "Excuse me?"

"No, seriously, I just got back from a fact-finding mission at the Strand. That place is a tinderbox waiting to go up in flames. We have to ask ourselves, what kind of impact is all that *paper* having on our planet?" He shuddered.

"Well, I guess that's why Scroll is such a great idea."

"Yeah. You could say that. So, Allison. Tell me how *you* plan to surprise and delight in the marketplace."

"It's Alice, actually."

"Sorry?"

"My name. It's Alice, not Allison."

"Oh, yeah, of course, sorry." Greg was building up his hand strength using two surprisingly loud little devices usually stowed in the top drawer of Matthew's filing cabinet. (Matthew was big on fleeting self-improvement programs; I knew another drawer was filled with protein bars left over from a short-lived diet.)

"As for our literature selection: right now I have about fifty-six titles in all, give or take. I'm also meeting with agents and editors, who are practically jumping out of their skin with excitement about Scroll."

"Really?"

"Of course! Plus I have more submissions for ScrollOriginals than I can handle on my own. We're thinking of bringing in an intern to vet them—"

Greg held up his hand and made a motion as if to turn down the volume. "All good stuff. But we have to ask ourselves, what does the customer really *want*, right?"

"Right." I was still getting used to Scroll speak, which involved a semi-Socratic tic of inserting "Right?" at the end of every sentence. "Wait, sorry, Greg, what do you mean?"

"I mean, does the customer really want *books* with his coffee, or might he enjoy something else?"

"Like . . . ?"

"I don't know. Isn't that *your* job?" Greg gazed at me through heavy-lidded eyes. Was he high?

"I guess I'm not understanding your question."

"I'll break it down for you. What's the best way for us to gain traction in the marketplace?"

"By creating a bookstore experience like no other? By giving customers something they can't get anywhere else. Beyond that, I haven't really thought—"

"Well, start thinking, girl!" Greg dropped the hand exercisers on Matthew's desk with a clunk. He squinted at the picture on my desk. "Hey, switching gears here, is that your family?"

"Yes, the kids are older now but—"

"Let me ask you, what video games do they like to play?"

I laughed. "Much to my son's chagrin, we don't have any video games. I'm not a fan."

"Do you mind if I ask why?"

"Not at all. I just think they're stupid. I want my kids to be readers and to live in the real world—not some fake universe. Not to mention the violence." I congratulated myself on adhering to the sixth tenet: Winners Talk Frankly (WTF).

"Huh. Interesting." Greg looked contemplative. "Hard to do both, right? The kids and the job?"

"I guess, but—well, the alternative isn't really an option for me right now."

"Got it. Anyway. My wife stays home."

"Oh."

"I mean, listen, I'm no rocket scientist, but I think kids need their mom."

Suddenly, on Sixth Avenue, the flow of traffic came to a grinding halt. Distant ambulances silenced their sirens and dogs stopped barking. Or maybe that was just my imagination. I reached up to make sure my hair wasn't standing on end.

"I guess. I mean, yes—kids do need their mom. I like to think—"

"One more question: has Genevieve brought you up to speed on our pivot?"

"Pivot? Actually no, I don't think so." Even as I threw her under the bus a little bit, I felt weirdly protective of Genevieve, who, for all her quirks, was a good-enough feminist not to offer her opinions on major life choices in a business meeting.

Greg made a little teepee out of his fingertips, thumbs touching at the bottom to form a triangle. His stance was prayerful, as if he was about to impart important wisdom or maybe pass me the bong. "I'm sure she'll bring you up to speed soon."

I nodded again, but I was barely paying attention. I was too busy formulating intelligent responses to the topic we'd already closed out moments before. Had he really told me that he thought women should stay home with their kids?

I'd have to get to the bottom of our pivot another day.

I came home to find Nicholas playing quarters on the front porch with Susanna. They were cackling raucously when I pounded up the front steps and then stopped, not believing my eyes. Were those really red Solo cups on my teak coffee table? Were those actual Budweiser tall boys rolling on the floor, mingling among jump ropes and badminton birdies? I felt like I'd stepped through the looking glass into my brother's college years, except Will's frat brothers at least had the decency not to get wasted in broad daylight with children riding Big Wheels nearby.

Before I had a chance to say anything, Oliver zoomed past. "Mommy! Race me!"

This was my cue to start timing his "split"—meaning the time it took for him to bike from the apron of the driveway to the garage and back. I started counting loudly, according to protocol, "One Mississippi, two Mississipi," then, when he was out of earshot behind the house, turned my attention back to the derelict adults in front of me.

Nicholas held up one finger while chugging a beer, then wiped the foam from his upper lip. "Sorry, Al. I realize this is a depressing scenario. Business is slow for both of us so we were just . . . regressing."

"That's a good word for it."

Oliver reappeared and skidded to a stop, inches from the road. "How long, Mommy?" He was red-faced, with a little Alfalfa-style tuft of hair sticking up at the back of his head.

"Only seven seconds this time!"

"Is that a new world record?"

"Oh, I'd say so. Most definitely. *That* is a first."

I brushed past Susanna and went inside to feed Cornelius and then pick up Margot and Audrey from swimming. Paul was in Atlanta on business and clearly our spouses were in no condition to drive.

Me: "What do you want to be when you grow up?"

Georgie: "A bunny holder."

Me: "What do you mean?"

Georgie: "Someone who holds bunnies."

Me: "Like a dog walker walks dogs, you'll hold bunnies."

Georgie: "Yes."

Me: "Wow, you'll have strong arms."

Georgie: "I know. It's the perfect job for me."

•   •   •

My parents had a week-long rental on Long Beach Island (Exit 63), as they had every single summer since I can remember. This year's cottage was a cramped ranch in Holgate, steps from the bird sanctuary at the southern end of the island and across the street from the Jolly Roger convenience store, site of my first taste of Ben & Jerry's Heath Bar Crunch in the summer of 1988. Just seeing the weathered gray building triggered a Pavlovian craving for ice cream and the sense memory of the smell of Coppertone and the chorus of Tracy Chapman's "Fast Car."

Everywhere I go on LBI, I sift through the sands of time. The seedy bar we sneak out to after the kids go to bed used to be Touché, a hip turquoise- and pink-lit nightclub where Will took me to test out my fake ID in college. In the mornings, my mom fetches warm boxes of sticky buns and crumb cake from the Crust & Crumb Bakery, just as her mom did when I was Georgie's age. Even the bike rental place still has the same sign out front— We'll Teach Your Kid to Ride or We'll Buy You a Lobster Dinner—which is how I came to watch my six-year-old nephew master a two-wheeler on the same pebbly sidewalk where his dad learned thirty-five years earlier.

On Saturday morning, after we packed our minivan to the gills with bikes, boogie boards, sand chairs, towels, coolers, buckets, and shovels and were sitting in the bumper-to-bumper traffic on the causeway that leads to the island, I received a message from Genevieve: "Alice, it's too long since we received your input. Please take a moment to share your top three priorities with the team, Cleveland included."

The first time she made this request of me, we had just come from getting our nails done together. I was a little baffled—my Well Red polish was barely dry, after all, and Genevieve and I had just traded honest assessments of each other's eyebrows (verdict: mine were too thin, hers required taming). Then it occurred to me that Genevieve might be implementing a new leadership strategy from the *One Minute Manager*. Befriend, then berate. Was that a thing?

That time I gamely listed my priorities and then spent a good twenty minutes scrutinizing my Monopoly board–sized monitor, reading and rereading the message to make sure all my work was represented and accurate.

Then I hit send.

Within seconds the e-flogging started.

"First off, who *are* you?" (I had to laugh.)

"Why are you pursuing so many titles by women?"

"Why are there no authors from Colorado on this list?"

"When will the detail pages go live for this merch?"

Surprisingly, the hardest question to answer was the first.

This time I put down my iPhone, closed my eyes, turned my face to the sun, and reached my hand over to cup the back of Nicholas's neck. This vacation would do him good, I thought. As furious as I was at him for leaving his job, the stress of starting a new business was way more intense than either of us had imagined, and I feared that my husband was crumbling under the pressure.

Still, Nicholas had definitely stepped up to the plate for my career. Every morning, he made three breakfasts, packed three lunches, and threw dinner in the slow cooker—all before I finished reading the Scroll missives that arrived in the middle of the night. Sure, I unloaded the dishwasher and kept track of who needed new socks and communicated with Jessie and arranged playdates via text, but otherwise I'd abdicated almost all household responsibility.

When we finally arrived at the house, my nephews were waiting on the roof deck, holding aloft between them a huge crayoned cardboard sign that said "Welcome, NicholasAliceMargotOliverGeorgie!" I dabbed the outermost corner of each eye with an index finger. I was so happy to be there, even at the cost of my remaining vacation days.

My mom was playing tennis in Beach Haven; my dad was taking a nap (something I had never known him to do), and we dispatched the kids to the Jolly Roger to pick up sandwiches for lunch. Nicholas and I huddled around a green plastic picnic table with Will and Mary, who were in excellent spirits for Mainers downgrading to the Jersey shore in the prime of their own beach season at home.

"So, how does he seem?" I couldn't help asking; it was so hard to have any perspective on our dad, especially since he always insisted he was hunky-dory.

Will and Mary exchanged a look. *You go. No, you.* As much as I like my sister-in-law, I didn't want her two cents. This was a conversation for siblings, with in-laws as invested observers.

Thankfully, Will spoke first. "He looks . . . old."

A lump the size of an apple spontaneously materialized in my throat. I nodded my head and choked out, "I know."

Will dragged a tan hand down the length of his face, then adjusted the bill of his baseball cap. "And he *reeeally* doesn't want to talk about what's going on. When I asked him if he's in any pain, he looked at me like I was insane."

"I know. And Mom wants to talk about nothing else. She's really on his case about nutrition. And while I agree that a fruit smoothie might be a better breakfast than a Frappuccino, I don't want to get into a big thing with him about it."

A family rode by in a surrey with fringe on top—rented, of course, from the place with the bike-riding lessons. They were impossible to miss: two adults, sweaty and pedaling; two kids kicking back and repeatedly squeezing the black rubber bulbs of their handlebar horns. The girl wore braids, the boy had a crew cut, and both wore the kind of unisex dime-store flip-flops that had been the one item of apparel Will and I shared as kids.

Nicholas chimed in. "Anyway, I don't really think it's your place to tell your dad what to eat. Not your pig, not your farm, right?" This was his mom's favorite expression—mine too, but not in this instance.

"But that's the thing, he *is* our pig." I looked around the table. Even though my sister-in-law's opinion didn't matter to me as much as Will's, it seemed rude to exclude her from the conversation altogether. "Mary, what do you think?"

"I think you want to be there for him, but you're not going to be able to fix this."

The kids were back, lugging three plastic bags bulging with Cape Cod potato chips and Arizona iced tea—the official refreshments of New Jersey summer. As the four of us clambered down the mossy wooden stairs attached to the side of the house, Will said, "I'm scared, Al."

"I am, too."

We had never been the kind of family who rented a surrey with a fringe on top—our mom was too busy antiquing and our dad was too busy doing the crossword puzzle while wearing penny loafers and black kneesocks pulled all the way up. We weren't a sporty family, or an adventurous one.

But our parents had always, always been the ones pedaling. Until now.

We brought drinks down to the beach for cocktail hour, and we persuaded my dad to come along. Usually he avoided sand until the last day of the vacation, when he took his one stroll down to the water with binoculars. He'd look left, look right, and then head back to the house to smoke his pipe and read another book by John le Carré, James Michener, or Elmore Leonard. This time, he settled quietly into a chair under our big umbrella. Buzz Lightyear stayed home among the limes, bananas, and beach badges in a wooden bowl on the kitchen table. There was no way it could be heard over the rough surf.

Even though the ocean was freezing, I dove in with Ollie and got battered around until I had a shelf of sand above the underwire in my bathing suit. While I was drying off, sitting among the adults in a horseshoe of chairs, I spotted my friend Mona walking down the beach. She's a publicist I've known since my *You* days and had always been one of my favorite lunch dates. Mona can volley reading recommendations with the fluency of an auctioneer.

We hugged and I introduced her to my family. She made a perfunctory comment about how we all looked alike, then reached out to shake each of my parents' hands: "Ed, Joan, your daughter is just lovely. You did nice work."

My mom beamed. "We like to think so!"

My dad nodded, but he didn't smile. Was he in pain? Was the bulge on the side of his neck just the angle of the sun, or could it possibly be the tumor, already flouting the round of aggressive radiation it was being zapped with?

I was about to awkwardly explain why my dad wasn't able to say anything when Mona asked, "So, how's it going at Scroll?"

"It's great! I mean, it's a big change but . . . opening great bookstores? What more could I ask for, right?"

"You know what? I hate to say this, but I'm not drinking the Kool-Aid along with everyone else. These people own *shopping malls*. They're *retail*. What do they know about books?" Mona broke into rough, hysterical laughter—the kind that doubles as a cough. "And yes, I know they're selling first editions. But still. It's like this fake world—*ew*."

The rest of us were silent, but I knew everyone was listening, even the kids. The sandcastle building had come to a grinding halt.

My dad tilted his Hoyas cap back on his head in the manner of a street punk cruising for a brawl. He crossed his arms atop his no-longer-ample chest.

"Wow. I haven't thought of it like that"—although I had, fleetingly—"but it's not fake, actually. It's going to be a booklover's paradise." I launched into a manic description of the chaise longues, the gluten-free pastries, and the subscription program. I knew I was making a spectacle of myself, but I couldn't stop.

"Oh yeah, I've heard all that."

The conversation ended awkwardly, with a hasty fake plan to catch up with each other the next day. Then Mona strolled away, her perky straw hat disappearing into a sea of colorful umbrellas.

Nobody said anything for a minute, and then Will jumped in. "All I can say is? Fuck that. We are *not* hanging out with her." Mary and I made a show of telling him not to curse in front of the kids.

• • •

That night, I heard Margot's voice as I was climbing the ladder up to our sleeping loft above the living room. "Mom? Can you come here?"

She was hard to find among the cousins sprawled around in sleeping bags and on air mattresses, but when I finally tiptoed to the top bunk she shared, head to toe, with her cousin, I was taken aback by how tall Margot looked in the tiny bed. The year before, we'd squeezed Georgie in here, too.

"What is it, lovebird? You should be sleeping."

"Mom, why did that lady say that to you on the beach?"

"She was just being silly. She doesn't like Scroll."

"Did she hurt your feelings?"

"A little, yes. But people have a hard time with new things. It's what makes my job exciting but also hard sometimes."

"You really like your job, though, right?"

"I do, lovey. Now go to sleep. We have a lot of shells to collect tomorrow."

"Okay—but Mom?"

I leaned over to dust sand off the bottom of my feet. "Yes, Margot."

"Are Audrey and Susanna coming down this year?" Usually the two of them came to Long Beach Island for a day and we'd take the girls to the rides at Fantasy Island. Audrey is the only one of her siblings who has the stomach for amusement parks.

"No, sweetie. With Pop feeling—well, not so great, we thought it would be best if it was just our family this time. I thought I explained that—"

She lowered her head back onto the pillow and closed her eyes. "That's fine. Audrey says we're too old for the Tilt-A-Whirl anyway."

When I was growing up, I fell asleep every night to the sound of my dad in the room below mine, chuckling in front of *The Honeymooners* and

Johnny Carson. Now the wet rasp of his breathing kept me awake. The noise drowned out the swish of cars on the boulevard and the shush of the waves on the other side of the dunes. It was the gurgle of a throat that would never clear. It was the sound of suffering.

> **Susanna:** How are you guys holding up? Thinking of you constantly.
> **Me:** The cousins are skim-board phenoms, taking the island by storm.
>   Adults are more subdued; nice to all be together. You?
> **Susanna:** The usual. College kids quitting for a better offer, so basically
>   me on my feet all day, ringing up *Fifty Shades of Grey*. What *is* it with
>   that book?
> **Me:** Ya got me. I'm halfway through *The Light Between Oceans* and
>   LOVING. IT.
> **Susanna:** That one's selling like hotcakes, too, thankfully.
> **Me:** Speaking of lighthouses: we're off to Barnegat. Love to all. TTFN. Xx
> **Susanna:** You, too, especially your sweet dad.

My dad was anything but sweet, but illness had the effect of making people describe him that way.

The drive off the island was brutal. We got stuck in the interminable crawl of renters vacating houses as close to the ten a.m. deadline as possible, so there was nothing for me to do but stare out the window and replay our horrible leave-taking. "We'll be back next year," I said, when all the luggage and buckets and beach towels were crowding out the view through the back window of the minivan, and the kids were on the roof deck gathering the shells they'd collected during the week.

"Of course we will," said my mom.

My dad picked up Buzz and pressed it to four different sites on his neck before finding a spot that would cooperate. His eyes were hooded with exhaustion: "Not me."

As we passed the Ferris wheel at Fantasy Island—lights out, at a standstill until the next week's wave of kids climbed aboard—Margot piped up from the backseat. "Pop *really* isn't feeling well."

"I know, sweet pea. What makes you say that?"

"He just doesn't have any . . . juice. It's like his batteries are running out." This was from Oliver. I swallowed hard, determined to hold it together.

Nicholas adjusted the rearview mirror so he could see the kids in the backseat, then reached down to clasp my hand. "Remember how Mommy told you that Pop's cancer is back? That's what's making him so tired."

"Oh."

"Daddy?"

"Yes, George?"

"Does Cornelius have cancer?"

"No, why?"

"He's so tired, too. He sleeps *all the time*."

I laughed. "Don't worry. Cornelius might be an old man, but he's as healthy as a horse."

To: scrollglobal@scroll.com
From: gregrockwell@scroll.com

Today, I'm really happy to announce a new milestone for Scroll. The gaming company Joystick will be joining the MainStreet family. We absolutely could not think of a more perfect partner for Scroll as we both share a love of entertainment and an appreciation for the authors and video game creators who bring us our favorite escapes, be they in words or pixels. Whether you're turning pages or enabling your avatar to save the world from the forces of evil, both mediums are rooted in imagination. And as Albert Einstein famously said, imagination is more important than knowledge. Peace out, players.

Oliver was waiting most nights when I got off the train, either standing at the bottom of the little gravel hill next to the playground or sprinting

down the path that runs alongside the train station parking lot. He only
had to cross a single one-way street—North Edison—to get to the tracks.
If the train rolled in a minute early, I could see him, pausing carefully on
the corner and looking to the right. Spotting him from the train window
was the highlight of my day.

One night, I climbed off the train with an older woman. She stopped
on the platform, put on a pair of reading glasses, and flicked open her flip
phone. Her black tote bag had clear pockets containing pictures of little
people wearing colorful polar fleece and radiant smiles—grandchildren,
I figured.

Would *I* still be on this train when my own kids were parents?

Usually, Oliver showed up with a lacrosse stick or a basketball, but
that night he was empty-handed, arms hanging slack by his sides as he
submitted to a hug he tolerated without reciprocating.

"Mommy, can you stay home tomorrow?"

I opened my mouth to remind him that the next day was a work day—
but yay, we only have two more work days till the weekend—when the
woman with the tote bag said something I couldn't hear.

"Excuse me?"

"I said, 'Do it.' "

I pictured my Outlook calendar: Genevieve was OOTO, Rashida
was WFH, the Marketing Team was off site working on the budget for the
next quarter. (I should mention: in all my years working at *You*, I never
once heard about a budget.)

I shrugged.

"Okay, yes," I said to Oliver. "Yes. I'll stay home tomorrow."

As soon as we were out of earshot, he asked in his froggy whisper,
"What did that lady say?"

"She told me to take you to the lake tomorrow. And you know what?
I think that's a great idea."

"Is she a witch?"

"No, I don't think so."

"Just old?"

• • •

"This is Genevieve Andrews at Scroll. Please leave a message."

"Genevieve, this is Alice. I'm not feeling well today so I'm staying home. I'll be checking my messages, so let me know if you need anything. You have my number."

My first-ever mental health day. Of course, I felt terribly guilty, which made me feel vaguely ill, so I really *wasn't* feeling well.

We stopped at the deli and then headed to Deer Lake in Boonton, about forty minutes away. Nothing has changed there since the 1980s: same paddleboats, same pedal toilets in the outhouses, same tired woman serving limp french fries to a new generation of hungry swimmers. The minute I pulled into the parking lot, I felt like I was on another planet.

Susanna had jumped at the chance to join us for the outing. Between us, we had eight sand chairs, two Playmate Wheelie Cools, three mesh bags of sand toys, two umbrellas, nine varieties of sunblock (in lotion, spray, and stick form), and a kite. On the beach, we met up with another neighbor—a mother of four boys—and a friend from spinning whose twin girls are friends with Georgie.

"Ladies, what do we think about the new principal?"

Susanna was a class mom, so all eyes turned to her.

"Hard to say. I'm waiting to see what else he's going to do besides making North Edison two-way."

My neighbor laughed. "Well, it's nice to know his priorities are in order. Is he at all concerned about our kids' abysmal language arts scores?"

"Ha. What do you guys know about Tutor Shack? The Walsh kids go there and Stacy says they're suddenly journaling *on their own*. She can't keep enough composition notebooks in the house!"

Susanna chuckled. "Give me a break. Kids don't need a tutor to learn how to write; they need to *read*!"

And we were off, galloping into a full-blown momversation: day camps, educational and otherwise; skin care, running the gamut from acne treatment to wrinkle cream; use of alcohol and tobacco (how to respond when your kids ask if you ever smoked pot; whether you would ever serve alcohol to teenagers); volunteer opportunities for kids (Habitat for Humanity in Guatemala versus myriad less expensive options closer to home); and lice—always lice. Does Listerine really kill the bugs? Is it true that some people emit a pheromone that repels them altogether? Is the Filament lice lady as competent as the one in Brooklyn, who can guess your nit count *without even touching your head?*

I settled back in my Adirondack chair, enjoying the familiar cadence of the banter: respectful disagreement, gentle advice, the occasional over-the-top compliment: "Oh my God, you're The. Best. Mom."

There are two swimming areas at Deer Lake: one roped-off area for little kids, which is shallow and has a slide; and a deeper area with lap lanes, a bigger slide, and a faraway float. You have to pass a deep-water swimming test if you want to brave the big slide—no big deal for Margot, who stroked effortlessly out to the float in the middle of the lake on the first day of the season. But Oliver still hadn't made an attempt; he steadfastly refused to expand his horizons beyond Georgie's side of the lake.

In the late afternoon, after we'd eaten our salads and doled out granola bars to the kids, Susanna made a visor out of her hand and looked over to the lap lanes. "Is that Oliver?"

Skinny arms windmilled in a steady crawl in front of a modest whitewater wake. Instantly, I recognized Oliver's capable, cautious form: he was in the midst of the deep-water test, with three tanned, muscley little boys cheering him on from their perch at the bottom of the big blue slide.

By the time I'd made my way over to the deep end, he was back on dry land, shivering and grinning from ear to ear as a towheaded lifeguard pinned him with the special badge worn by advanced swimmers. I tried not to make too big a deal because this is how Oliver rolls: he gets it in his head that he's going to do something, he does it without hoopla, and then he's easily mortified by praise. I kissed the top of his spiky wet head, then the tip of his ear. "I'm proud of you."

The boys spent the rest of the afternoon leaping off the floating dock in the middle of the lake. Again and again, four boys in tandem, interchangeable as little seals hurling themselves into the water: cannonball, jackknife, pencil dive. Repeat.

As we packed up to go home, the other moms (with the exception of Susanna) made plans to meet up again the next day. While my friends were at the lake together, lighting their citronella candles and settling back for an afternoon in the Adirondack row, I'd be at work, wearing a wool cardigan to combat the icy blast of industrial-strength air conditioning.

Margot: "What do you think I should do when I graduate from college?"

Me: "I don't know, what do you want to do?"

Margot: "Have six kids?"

Me: "And what else?"

Margot: "I'm thinking the six kids will keep me pretty busy."

Me: "Well, yes. Six kids are a lot of work."

Margot: "Not for me, they won't be. I'll marry someone who does all the work, like Daddy."

Me: "Okay, then. Good luck with that."

FALL

14

I missed the kindergarten ice cream social, the first day of school, the first PTA meeting, Cornelius's bordetella vaccination, and Nicholas's dinner with a promising new client, New Jersey's leading manufacturer of pet beds.

But I was hunting down some great books for Scroll and was embracing my new mantra, "You can't be all things to all people (or animals)." The key to taking a stab at doing it all was getting comfortable with rarely hitting the bull's-eye—in fact, being hopelessly left of center most of the time.

Genevieve and Rashida were constantly behind closed doors, giving the rest of us a chance to breathe and a much-needed break from the constant pummel of inscrutable e-mails.

Matthew ripped open a packet of pumpkin seeds. "Have you noticed that Genevieve has canceled the all-hands meeting two weeks in a row?"

"I guess. Why?"

"Don't you find it strange that they don't want to know what we're up to? Something's afoot, I'm telling you."

"Aren't they just working on budgets for next year?"

"Sure, but will that budget have room for us? That's the question."

"You're a conspiracy theorist. Just do your work."

To: scrollnewyork@scroll.com

From: scrollpublicity@scroll.com

This week marks our first Wacky Wednesday! Wear polka dots and come pose for a group photo in the bullpen at 2 p.m. Let's show Cleveland our Scroll spirit!

Going forward, Wacky Wednesday will be a weekly tradition. Attached please find a spreadsheet containing themes through Wednesday, 12.19. The schedule includes stripes, florals, ruffles, argyle, plaid, boho, hobo, hippy, pajamas, nautical, among others. Ideas welcome. NOTE: For home team, Yankees/Knicks preferred, but does anyone have Indians/Cavs wear for team-building purposes?

Participation in Wacky Wednesdays is strongly encouraged. There will be scones.

15

To: alicepearse@scroll.com
From: pearseparents@gmail.com

Al, Mom & I have an appointment with Dr. Davis on September 18 at
2 p.m. This is the big reveal about whether or not the radiation has been
working. I realize it's right in the middle of your workday, but if there
is any possibility of you joining us, I know it would mean a lot to Mom.
No pressure whatsoever. I'm proud of you out there, being a woman of
letters.

Back at the old homestead, the pumpkins are coming up nicely, I'm
keeping Cozy Shack in business with my steady diet of rice pudding, and
we're looking forward to using our new Blu-Ray as soon as I can make
sense of these damned remote controls. We now have more remote
controls than we have living creatures in this house, including cats. Next
time Nicholas is in the neighborhood, I may ask him to give me a brief

tutorial. Will tried to set me straight via Skype but I'm afraid his strengths lie with sculling.

Do let me know about the date with Dr. Davis. He has expanded his collection of golf memorabilia since your paths last crossed, so that's something to look forward to.

Kind regards,
Dad

To: pearseparents@gmail.com
From: alicepearse@scroll.com

Kind regards? Dad, I'm your daughter, not your accountant. Of course I'll be at the appointment. If you can get rice pudding down, you might want to experiment with the Vitamix. You can even put chocolate in there! Along with your veggies. I don't want you to get scurvy. Xxoo

To: alicepearse@scroll.com
From: pearseparents@gmail.com

Scurvy is a disease resulting from deficiency of vitamin C, which is present in rice pudding in trace amounts. So I should be all set but thanks.

The minute I got home, I knew something was wrong. Not tragically so, but just *off*. You develop this sixth sense as a mother, especially with a recently minted middle schooler on the premises. Her charges against you may not be one hundred percent legitimate, but you know when you're about to hear them.

"Mom, I texted you like *fifty* times and you didn't answer." Margot stood at the top of the stairs with her arms crossed, leg jutted. In tween yoga, this pose is known as "how stupid can you be."

"Thanks, Margot, my day was fine. How was yours?"

Jessie grabbed her keys, quietly waggled her fingers, and headed out to her car. I knew she'd text me later if she thought of anything I needed to know—which reminded me: why hadn't Jessie responded to the last few group texts between the two of us and Nicholas? For the past week, she'd started a new string, replying only to me. That was odd. I made a mental note to find out what was up, and also to thank her for her meticulous organization of the craft cabinet, which usually looked like a larger, more colorful outpost of the junk drawer.

My mom was in the kitchen, packing up the supplies she brought every Tuesday night to make her famous spaghetti and meatball dinner: a cast-iron pot (even though we have the exact same one in our cabinet), Boston Bibb lettuce and homemade vinaigrette, and a lacy red and black polka dot apron that is very Shirley Temple meets Mayflower Madam. Once my mom left this garment hanging on one of the hooks where we keep our car keys and Nicholas said, "Is there some way we can incorporate this into our repertoire?"

Now my mom pointed at the kitchen ceiling, which is the floor of Margot's bedroom, and whispered, "I'm not touching this one with a ten-foot pole."

"What happened?"

She shook her head and made a beeline for the front door.

"'Bye, Mom. Thanks for coming."

"Pour yourself a big glass of wine. Oh, and Alice, I forgot to tell you: there's a Halloween party at the museum. Come as your favorite inventor. I thought the kids—"

"Halloween? Are you *kidding*? Mom, I'm not up to that yet. I still have beach chairs in the trunk of my minivan."

"Oh. Okay. Well, I'll remind you closer to the time. And hey, did Daddy e-mail you about—"

"Dr. Davis? Yes, I'll be there."

"Great, great. Night, sweet girl."

Nicholas and my mom crossed paths on the front stairs. I could tell by Nicholas's terse hello that I was in the doghouse with him, too, but I had no idea why.

As soon as it was just our family in the house, Margot exploded, "Lucky for me, *Daddy* checks his texts during the day. I'm not sure what I would have done if he hadn't answered."

"Wait, can someone please tell me what's going on here? And Margot, don't take that tone with me." One of those lines I thought would never come out of my mouth, and there it was.

"What Margot is trying to say is, she wanted to reach you to let you know she needed a piece of poster board for her social studies project, which is due tomorrow." Nicholas raised his arm to show me a white plastic bag with red poster board rolled up inside. "Don't worry, I picked it up."

He spoke calmly, but I could tell he was annoyed in solidarity with Margot, and this made me livid.

"I would assume this project wasn't assigned today, Margot?"

"No, she told us about it last week." ("She" meaning the teacher.)

"So you could have given me some advance notice about this drop-dead deadline?"

"Yes, but—"

"Like on Saturday? We could have gone to the stationery store together? Or I could have given you money so you could have walked over by yourself after school."

"But the other moms—"

"Margot. I don't care about the other moms. I'm *your* mom. And this is your dad, and he handled it. So stop pouting and finish your project. I don't want to walk into an ambush when I come home from work. I've had a long day."

Margot stomped up the stairs, but I chased behind her and yanked on the back pocket of her jeans. Suddenly I realized they were on the snug side and also way too short. The old Alice had been vigilant about providing clean, well-fitting clothes for her children. The new one? Not so much. Our entire household's worth of socks were permanently unmatched in a laundry basket at the foot of my bed.

"*Don't* walk away from me, Margot. Schoolwork is *your* job. Your school supplies are not my responsibility. You need to plan like a business manager."

I let her proceed to her room; the door didn't slam, exactly, but closed firmly.

"Jesus, Alice. Plan like a business manager? Margot is eleven."

"Wait, why is this *my* problem? I didn't have a chance to look at my phone all day. This happens to you all the time, and I don't get mad at you for not being in touch. She needed poster board; she has poster board. Thanks for getting it, by the way, but: problem solved."

"I think you know what the bigger problem is," Nicholas was in full lawyer mode. "You're so distracted, the rest of us barely register. You're constantly checking your work messages when you're home, but it doesn't seem like we're on your radar at all when you're at work."

I glanced down at my phone, which lit up the front pocket of my flowered tunic.

He had a point.

I had no trouble falling asleep that night, but suddenly I was wide-awake at 3:18 a.m., and then I visited Facebook.

Everybody else was baking pies, jumping in piles of leaves, wishing their parents a happy fortieth anniversary, and hopping a plane to LA (JFK → LAX) to deliver an important presentation to Pixar.

I considered updating my own status. This is what it would have said: "I'm lying here awake in the middle of the night, wondering how much weight I've gained and how long it's been since my kids have seen the dentist. She stopped sending reminder postcards. Our carpet has dog puke on it, our minivan has a gnat infestation, our board games are all missing pieces, and we eat nachos for dinner."

Or I could go with a crowd-sourcing approach, which tended to attract the most commentary: "My dad's tumor used to be the size of a golf ball; now it's the size of a tennis ball. Do you think he'll make it to his seventieth birthday?"

Somebody out there would have an answer, but I decided to keep my status (or lack thereof) to myself for the time being.

The sacred and the profane, not necessarily in that order.

Eventually, I whispered in Nicholas's ear. "Are you awake?"

"Now I am." I turned my back to him so he could wrap his arms around me.

"I'm really stressed out."

"Why?"

"I feel like I'm doing everything wrong. I can't keep track."

"Of what?"

"Everything."

"Alice, come on. You have so much going on. Too much. Everybody who has kids and a job feels like you do, not to mention having a sick parent."

"But not like *this*. I miss the kids. And I don't even want to *see* my dad—it's just too heartbreaking. And this job—it's not like I thought it would be."

"The kids are fine. They'll be self-sufficient and scrappy. Your dad . . . well, *he* seems to be in good spirits, so we need to follow his lead, don't you think? I think you're doing great with all of this—and as for your job? I know it's important, but honestly, you have bigger things going on."

"Really?"

"Really."

Now I lay on my back, my forearm against Nicholas's. I remembered lying in Margot's bed when she was a toddler and petrified to be alone in the dark in her bedroom. Every night we tucked her in and she'd sob inconsolably. "The chirps! The chirps! I'm ascared of the chirps!" We had no idea what she was talking about and we really wanted her to go to bed so we could watch *The Bachelor*. One night, I went back into Margot's room and crawled under the covers beside her. When she cuddled up against me and stopped whimpering, I heard the chirps: the high staccato sounds of an opera singer warming up with the voice teacher who lived upstairs.

"Margot, that's just *music*," I explained.

She let out a shaky sigh and closed her eyes. Problem solved.

Those were the days.

"Nicholas?"

"Yes?"

"There's one more thing."

"What is it?" He propped himself up on one elbow and peered down at me in the dark.

"I'm worried about *you*."

"Why are you worried about me?" He sounded genuinely amused. I didn't want to ruin the moment by starting a fight, but he deserved to know what was on my mind.

"I think the stress of your job is . . . taking a toll."

"What are you talking about? I'm so relieved to work for myself, and sure, I've had some bumps in the road, but—"

"I'm just worried about you."

"Yes, you said that already. And I'm telling you, I'm *fine*."

I don't know why it was so hard to talk about the elephant in the room; maybe because it was squatting directly on top of my lungs. I took a deep breath but still felt like I couldn't take in enough air. "Nicholas, you're drinking too much."

"*Excuse* me?" Every iota of tenderness had vanished from his voice.

The elephant was out of the bag. Or was that a cat? Louder now: "I said, *you're drinking too much*."

Nicholas turned away and pulled the sheets all the way up to his shoulders so he resembled a neatly wrapped burrito. "We are not having this conversation."

Oh, but we *are*, I thought. The only question is: When?

•   •   •

"Genevieve, can I interrupt for a minute?"

She cocked her head almost imperceptibly in my direction, keeping both eyes on the Design Within Reach Website. "Yeeeeah—hang on. I'm just drilling down on some of Rashida's concepts."

"Actually, that reminds me. I didn't notice any bookshelves in the new schematics, did you?"

"No, there weren't any."

"Is there a new plan for displaying the first editions? I think it would be a mistake to put them behind glass, but I guess I can see the rationale . . ."

"I'm afraid I can't answer your question at this time." Genevieve's face remained impassive. And I don't mean she looked bored or angry: the expression was total absence of interest to the point where I wondered if I'd imagined my own end of the conversation. It seemed possible that she was still waiting for my response. I was familiar with the many countenances of Genevieve, but that morning was the first time I saw The Mask. It gave me the same feeling I had when I first saw the clown in *Poltergeist*, a moment I remember vividly: sleepover, fourth grade, Beth France's basement aglow with the horror. That night, I went straight to the olive-colored rotary phone and asked my dad to come walk me home. Now I clutched my notebook as if my life depended on it.

"Well, anyway. I came by to let you know I'll need to miss the technology meeting this afternoon. I have somewhere I need to be."

"Oh?" Meeting attendance was of paramount importance to Genevieve, especially when the assemblage would be broadcast in Cleveland.

"It's a personal matter. I . . . well, my dad had cancer a while back—"

"Yes, you mentioned that at the sales conference."

"Yes. That's right. Anyway, so the cancer is back and the prognosis is not great and—"

"Where?"

"Oh, well this appointment is at Sloan Kettering, but my dad lives—"

"No, I mean, where is the cancer?" The Mask melted into an expression of pure compassion and Genevieve now leaned toward me in the pose made famous by Judd Hirsch in *Ordinary People*—elbows on knees, legs apart. But her responses were bloodless. As Gertrude Stein said, there was no *there* there; it was as if she was following the stage directions for a character described as a sensitive, in-touch boss.

"Throat cancer. We'll find out today if it's spread."

"Did he smoke?"

"He did. Yes." We were now in my least favorite part of any conversation about my dad's health. I watched for the invisible light to go on in Genevieve's head: *I don't smoke, so I'm safe*. But she threw me a curveball.

"Man, smoking is a *bitch*. My dad died of lung cancer when I was nine." She said it matter-of-factly, the same way she might have said, "I have brown eyes" or "*The One Minute Manager* is my bible."

"I'm so sorry to hear that, Genevieve. I had no idea."

"Yeah, well. It is what it is." She shrugged. The conversation was about to be over. "Do what you need to do. And good luck this afternoon."

The hospital was exactly as I remembered it: same scrum of people in scrubs, huddled outside the front door with their cigarettes; same interminable elevator ride from the dark entryway to the cheerful main lobby. You couldn't help but feel that you were ascending into an alternate universe when you arrived. Not heaven, by a long shot, but at least somewhere safe, where the people in charge would get to the bottom of your problem. That had been my experience in the past.

I found my parents in the tasteful waiting room, which was furnished in blond wood and soothing colors. They were sitting side by side, faces slack—not visibly agitated or worried, simply present but preferring not to be. My mom wore a long, lacy dress and a marcasite choker; my dad wore khakis, a blue button-down shirt, and a navy blazer. They believed in dressing nicely for doctors, Sunday mass, and airplane travel. Now they were like nervous fliers on standby, awaiting news of available seating and also the exact destination of their plane.

"Hi, guys." I gave them each a quick hug. They smiled briefly and my mom murmured thanks for coming; the room was as quiet as a library, so we kept our greetings short. Then we settled into our soft leather chairs, where we feigned enjoyment of Sloan Kettering's impressive collection of magazines. Unfortunately, we were transferred almost immediately to the inner sanctum of exam rooms, where there was no decent reading material and thus no way of keeping up a pretense of relaxation.

We waited a long time for Dr. Davis to come into the exam room, and you could cut the tension with a scalpel; there are only so many times a trio of nervous people can pick up a little plastic model of a head and pretend to find it interesting. My mom kept offering Chapstick, Kleenex, hand lotion, and Certs. I refreshed the home page of the *New York Times* so many times, there was nothing left to read except news from the AP and Reuters.

At first, I tried to engage my dad in conversation about the headlines, but he shook his head slowly and lay back on the paper-covered table and closed his eyes. I hated seeing him like that—his face slack, his still-tan skin taking on a gray cast in the fluorescent light. From where I was sitting on a small, round stool, I could see straight down the hole in his throat. Thinking about what was down there made me queasy.

Dr. Davis finally breezed in on a wave of white coats belonging to four fellows in otolaryngological oncology. "Joan, Ed." He gave them each a firm handshake, warm as a hug, and then turned to me. "What, no babies anymore?"

"Not this time."

He introduced us to the fellows, who were attentive but eager to get down to business. My dad was an interesting case: not only had he had his larynx removed, he also had a replacement esophagus made from a length of his own intestine. One of the fellows rifled through his chart with an expression of naked curiosity on her face. She shook her head and said under her breath, "Such a shame."

I thought, here we go again with the smoking.

"Karen?" Dr. Davis glanced sharply at the fellow, who wore an immaculate pink cardigan under her white coat—two articles of clothing whose high maintenance simply blows the mind of a slob like me.

"It's just, I'm looking at Ed's history here—"

"You mean Mr. Pearse."

"Yes, sorry, Dr. Davis. I'm looking at Mr. Pearse's history and realizing that if he presented with the same tumor today that he had ten years ago, he most likely wouldn't have to undergo such a radical surgery. Now we have alternatives to the total laryn—"

"*Karen.* That's enough." Dr. Davis rolled his stool to the edge of the exam table so he was roughly eye-to-knee with my dad, who was now sitting up. I couldn't bear to look at his face. Of course, I knew there had been advances in the treatment of throat cancer since my dad lost his voice, and of course, if any hospital were the front-runner in offering them, Sloan Kettering would be the place. But in that particular moment, when we were already bracing for the worst, the idea of a near miss was too painful to contemplate.

I kept my eyes trained on Karen, willing them to shoot daggers across the tiny room. She didn't seem to register my scrutiny or to be taken down a notch by Dr. Davis's admonition. Her own dad was probably slaloming in Aspen or developing arty black-and-white photos in his personal darkroom. Karen had all the facts at her fingertips but she wasn't fluent in the root words of her profession: worry, regret, anger, fear, and hope. Always hope.

The doctor took my dad's hand in his, not in a patronizing way but in the manner of two old comrades who root for rival Big East teams and respect each other immensely. It was as if they were alone in the room and the rest of us were watching through one-way glass.

"Ed."

My dad nodded, mouthing, "Howard."

"Your tumor is not responding to radiation."

My mom took notes so she could relay all the information to Will. I glanced at her, expecting to see tears drop on the page or at least a droop in her shoulders. But she was already in battle position: ramrod straight, pen poised, steadily nodding her head like an attentive student. *Fortune favors the prepared mind.* If she was the kind of woman who was inclined to cross-stitch sayings, Louis Pasteur's words would have hung over the mantel in her living room.

The fellows shifted from foot to foot, politely admiring the seams on my dad's neck and his ingeniously created and immaculately maintained stoma, a joint collaboration between Dr. Davis and my mom. I just sat there, blank as a piece of paper, letting the words land: *out of options at this point, questionable spots on the lungs, make you comfortable, palliative care, pain scale, hospice.* They never really tell you to get your affairs in order, but that was the gist of the conversation.

My dad listened quietly, eyes wide behind his thick glasses.

Dr. Davis explained that it would become more difficult for him to use Buzz Lightyear as the tumor grew. Swallowing would become difficult, too. Dr. Davis would have his GI guy install a PEG in my dad's stomach—a simple outpatient procedure—so my dad could feed himself through a tube. Eventually we would do it for him. He would require a special formula for diabetics, and a special pump to clear out mucus and bile from the stoma when his immune system went into overdrive.

In conclusion, "Of course, this will all take time. I'm just giving you the big picture."

My mom put down her slim aqua pen. "It doesn't sound very big."

"What doesn't sound very big?"

"The picture, I mean. How much time are we talking, Doctor?"

My eyes wandered to the ceiling. One, two, three, four panes of light. They reminded me of our family, gathered around the square table in my parents' kitchen. Ed, Joan, Will, Alice.

"We don't put a number on it, Joan. I mean, look at him." Dr. Davis grabbed the arch of my dad's foot and swung it gently back and forth.

"Ed Pearse is not someone to be underestimated." I was grateful he didn't call my dad a fighter, a cancer image I abhor. "This guy amazes me. Always has."

I pictured my dad walking up our hill in his summer suit—tall, smiling, funny in his dry Irish way, full of opinions and advice, easily persuaded to take a detour for an ice cream cone. When you're a kid, you think you're going to have this deep well of time with your parents when you grow up and you're all on equal footing. When I had kids of my own, I thought that time would come when my kids grew up and I had a little more freedom. I imagined myself as a fifty-year-old woman, strolling around the duck pond with my eighty-year-old dad. I might have looped my arm through his.

Now I knew, this was not to be.

16

Oliver: "A scientist came to our school to tell us about her job."

Me: "Really? What does he do?"

Oliver: "She."

Me: "What?"

Oliver: "The scientist was a lady."

Me: "Oh. So what kind of work does she do?"

Oliver: "I don't know."

Me: "I thought you said she told you about her job."

Oliver: "She did. She grows mold on plates. That's all I remember."

Me: "Interesting. Think you'd ever want to be a scientist?"

Oliver: "No. I'll be too busy in the NBA."

He pulled his Nike Elite socks all the way up to his knees. His calves had lengthened and slimmed since the last time I noticed. My chubbiest, chattiest toddler was now this lanky boy of few words, whose feet I could smell from across the room.

• • •

Jessie loved Nicholas's trademark five-alarm chili, so one night I invited her to stay for dinner when it was on the menu. The chef himself had a late meeting with a client, followed by drinks with another. Dom, the guy we met at the Lawyers for Justice dinner, turned out to be a connector in the New Jersey sense of the word—meaning he was a *macher* in the world of Filament lacrosse and had put the word out among his former high school teammates that Nicholas should be their go-to guy for bankruptcies, real estate closings, wills, and contract disputes. Suddenly, Nicholas was busy.

Jessie nodded brightly at Margot, who flipped her new sparkly retainer out of her mouth and placed it on a napkin so we could all admire it while we ate. "Did you tell your mom about your field trip?"

"Mom, we're going on a field trip." Margot lackadaisically stirred sour cream into her chili, telegraphing disapproval of the whole meal through her noncommittal grip on the spoon.

I tried to keep my tone light; Jessie and I rolled our eyes at each other. "Yes, I gathered that. Can you tell me *where* you're going on your field trip?"

"The Edison Museum."

"That's exciting. When?"

"I don't know. Next week, I think." Margot looked pained. Was the chili *that* spicy?

"Well, we'll have to ask Nan what days she'll be volunteering so we can figure out if she can lead your tour!" I sounded like a perky mom from a peanut butter commercial, but my kids were too grouchy to be cast as Skippy fans. They slouched around the table, exhausted and bedraggled, which was exactly how I felt.

Margot took a long gulp of her water and her blue eyes met mine over the rim of her glass. "Mom, I'm pretty sure the days won't match up."

I didn't push it. My mom had her hands full anyway, taking care of my dad. Was she still volunteering at the Edison Museum? I realized I had no idea, then felt terrible for not knowing. What kind of daughter was I? Or mother, for that matter? Here I was with the very people I'd been looking forward to seeing all day, and I couldn't wait for them to go to bed. I made a mental note to call my mom when the house was quiet. As if that would ever happen.

"So what else, guys? How was school?"

"Good."

"Good."

"Good."

I tried again, channeling advice I expected I might find on a parenting website, if I had time to read parenting websites. Ask open-ended questions! "Did anything exciting happen?"

"I got a scratch-and-sniff sticker on my math worksheet."

"My shoelace broke so I had to borrow sneakers for gym."

"We learned about an artist who cut off his ear. Now can I be excused?"

One by one, they dumped their bowls into the sink and filed out of the kitchen: to the backyard, to the playroom, to the bathtub. Jessie and I scraped greasy napkins into the garbage, then loaded cutlery and Fiestaware into the dishwasher. She paused and put a hand on my shoulder. "Alice, you know they're just tired, right?"

I shook my head and sighed, watching a swirl of kidney beans and bell pepper disappear into the black hole of the garbage disposal. "They just seem so . . . *blah*. You know what I mean?"

"I do. But I swear, they're chatty when I pick them up from school. By the time you get home, they've exhausted every ounce of energy on homework and art projects and sports." Jessie gestured out the window, where Oliver ran in circles with his lacrosse stick. She wore a ring on every finger and her nails were painted fluorescent yellow. For the second time that week, I wore a black wool turtleneck; it was hard not to be a little envious of Jessie's eclectic style.

"I know. I guess I just miss hearing all the news."

"But you know the important stuff."

But I wanted to know more than the important stuff about my kids: I wanted to know the little things, too. And I wanted to have a job where I earned a respectable paycheck and was an active participant in meetings and could occasionally hang out in the office kitchen talking about Sharon Olds and Anne Sexton. And I wanted to spend time with my dad in long, uninterrupted stretches, playing Scrabble at the dining room table without the deadline of an orthodontist appointment looming.

I'd internalized the message of all the brown-bag lunches and bean suppers I went to at the women's center in college: *Yes,* it really is possible to do anything, be everything. But maybe if I hadn't dozed through physics for poets, I would have been a little more up to speed on the limitations of time. You can't create more of it. You can sleep less, plan more, double-book, set the alarm for a 5:30 a.m. spin class, order winter coats for your kids while you're on a conference call, check work e-mail while your family is eating breakfast—but ultimately there are only so many hours in one day, and you have to spend some of them in bed. In an ideal world, you share that bed with someone who is sober, but this isn't always the case.

"Hey, Alice, did Nicky tell you what happened the other night?"

It took me a minute to figure out whom Jim was referring to, but then I realized: he meant Nicholas, my husband. Who never goes by Nicky. "Um, no, what?"

"After basketball, when the guys were drinking at the Shannon Rose? Ask him. It's epic. Let's just say, your husband was in rare form. I had no clue he could break-dance."

Jim continued loading six-packs of Red Stripe into the freezer at the liquor store. I'd taken a detour there on my way home from the train station; this was one of those days whose ending I couldn't face without a hefty goblet of merlot. Actually, lots of days fit this description—karmic justice for all the times I'd rolled my eyes at my dad when he headed straight from the train station to Shop Rite Liquors for booze.

Now I understood.

But what was Jim talking about?

Every fall, Nicholas plays basketball in a Sunday night adult league at a Catholic boys' school in West Orange. Once or twice a season, I'll bring the kids to see him on the court. I'm always dazzled by his grace; Oliver always wonders why the game seems so much slower than the ones he watches on TV. Nicholas's teammates are a motley crew—guys in their late twenties and early thirties who are clinging to their golden high school years. After games, they go out to a bar, usually one we'd never go to together. I know the basketball guys are a hard-drinking crew and that they're occasionally unfaithful to the sweet, big-haired girlfriends who faithfully show up for their games.

If Nicholas was drunk enough to break-dance, what else could have happened? And how had he gotten home?

I clutched the neck of my Monkey Bay and headed toward my house. It took me a few minutes to get there because I stopped on every corner and checked my e-mail, monitoring the influx of messages from Genevieve. She wanted the agenda for a meeting I'd set up and a debrief on a meeting I just had two hours ago. Then Will sent me three texts about an herbalist in Chinatown who had some luck with cancer patients—did I think we should try to get our dad in to see him?

Before I even opened the screen door to shout hello to my kids, I hunkered down on the front porch, addressing as many of these issues as possible. By the time I went upstairs and found Nicholas reading to Georgie—*Bedtime for Frances,* her favorite and a semi-excruciating read after a long day—I forgot to ask what Jim was talking about.

Instead, I realized this was the third day in a row I'd only seen Georgie in a nightgown. She'd been wearing a different one when I

left the house that morning; for all I knew, she might have worn it to
school.

Dad: Good day today. PEG safely installed. I can now pour food directly
into my stomach. Kids will be in awe.
Me: I'm in awe. Thanks for letting me know.
Dad: Hope you're well. LOL.

Every day, on the train into the city, I made my to-do list on the right-
hand side of a notebook page—a list of meetings and appointments I
had during the day. On Mondays, when Genevieve and I had our regular
nine-thirty 1:1, I would also list topics I wanted to cover with her. She
liked to hear about what I was reading, and she wanted to know how
industry folk reacted to my descriptions of what Scroll had in store for
the book-buying public. The excitement was contagious, especially since
I'd surreptitiously snapped a few photos of the Sim on my iPhone and
shared them with a few trusted editors. One followed up on our lunch
with an e-mail copying her entire office, saying, "WHEN CAN WE
COME?!?!?!?!"

One rainy Monday, before I had a chance to dive into my list, Genevieve said, "Lance and I went to the best Ethiopian restaurant this weekend. Bunna? In Bushwick? You *must* try it."

"Good to know—I love Ethiopian!"

"Actually, we should all go there sometime. Would you be up for that?

"You mean the team here . . . ?" I gestured around me, indicating
Keith, Mariana, Matthew.

"No, me and Lance, you and Anthony."

"You mean Nicholas?"

"Nicholas, sorry. You guys could bring your kids! This place has an
amazing brunch." She looked tentative, as if she'd never made plans with
a parent before and didn't know the etiquette.

I smiled politely, trying to envision Georgie with a mouthful of injera;

we had a hard enough time getting her to eat Nutri-Grain Eggos. "Sure. Maybe . . . after the holidays?"

"Great. We'll circle back then." Genevieve sat back in her chair and adjusted the broach on her lapel. It was in the shape of a cowboy boot, with tiny rhinestones forming a star on the toe. Then she said drily, "So. Joystick. You heard about the acquisition?"

I nodded while jotting exclamation marks next to the name of a famously curmudgeonly agent who had submitted a novella by his top-earning author for ScrollOriginals. "The video game company? Of course."

"And . . . ?"

"And what?"

"What did you think?"

"Honestly? I couldn't care less. As I told Greg, I'm really not a fan of video games. Why?"

Genevieve held up a surprisingly small hand, palm facing me. "Wait. You *said* that?"

"That I'm not a fan of video games? Yes."

"You said it to Greg's *face*?"

"I did. Is that a problem?" I reached up to turn my earring, wondering idly if my double pierce was still viable after a decade of neglect.

Now Genevieve brought a palm up to her forehead, which she cradled with her eyes closed. "Oh, Alice. Tell me exactly how this conversation unfolded."

I closed my notebook; it looked like we weren't going to be getting to my list anytime soon. "I just told him I don't allow video games in my house. I might have said they're like crack for kids . . ." My voice trailed off.

"That's enough." Genevieve spoke in the tone I use with Margot when she's asking if she can sleep over at Audrey's house after I've said no twelve times. She quickly shook her head and looked back at me with a shadow of a pitying smile on her face. "Alice, can I ask you a question? Does your honesty ever get you in trouble?"

This seemed like a rhetorical situation, so I didn't answer. "Genevieve, Greg asked me about video games *before* the Joystick acquisition. I thought it was just a casual conversation. I had no idea—"

"See, that was your mistake. There *are* no casual conversations at this company. *How* have you not learned that by now?" She took a sip of her tea, eyeing me over the rim of her Scroll mug. ("Unfurl Yourself.") "Yeah. Okay. I'm just going to lay it out for you. Greg mentioned the pivot?"

"Yes. I had no idea what he meant."

"This is the pivot: We're introducing a gaming component to our lounges. We're moving away from carbon-based books altogether and swapping out first editions for video games. The market research shows, our demo wants something for their kids to do while they shop."

I thought of the most popular nail salon in Battery Park City—the one where Margot used to watch *SpongeBob* while I got a pedicure. The only customers there were moms; I wore earplugs so I couldn't hear the din of the flat-screen at the back of the store. Serene and spa-like, it was not.

My mouth went dry. "Will we still have the SSR areas for VIP readers?"

"That's TBD, but probably not. We'll need that real estate for the rugrats. Apparently some of the games have an interactive component, so we have to allow for wiggle room. In fact, now that I think of it, that might be a good name for the kids' area. Wiggle Room." Genevieve created a Post-it on the screen of her laptop and then typed in the two words. She turned back to me with a sympathetic expression on her face. "Alice, I realize this isn't ideal. It's not what I signed on for; I'm sure you feel the same way."

I was too preoccupied with logistics to commiserate with Genevieve. "Wait, what about Mariana?"

"What about her?"

"I mean, what will she do if she's not hunting down first editions?"

"In light of the discontinuation of our ScrollFirst program, Mariana will be now transitioned over to Environmental. She'll be a direct report to Rashida, with a focus on creating a nut-free, egg-free menu for our youngest customers." Genevieve sounded like she was reading from a script.

"How does she feel about that?"

"Mariana is a team player. She's willing to shift gears, just the way Rashida did when she pivoted out of Analytics."

I nodded, noting that the hands of the giant clock on the steeple outside Genevieve's office were creeping toward ten o'clock. We'd gone over our allotted time. At Scroll, the person who set up the meeting was responsible for making sure it ended promptly; in this case, that would be me.

She continued, taking a deep breath. "Alice, I have to tell you, given your experience with this age group, Greg has asked that you play quarterback on the video game initiative."

"What do you mean by my experience with this age group?" I needed to hear her say it.

"I mean, you're a mom." We sat there in silence. "So we're going to tap into your expertise in regards to how kids behave on a screen: what do they want to see, do they want to play alone or with a partner, what lighting conditions are optimal, do kids stand or sit while they play, which games do they want to see, that kind of thing. MainStreet marketing has already started crowdsourcing this data and building out a spreadsheet; you should familiarize yourself. It's called MMO. You can find it on the Sharepoint."

"MMO?" I'd learned not to bluff my way through the acronyms; where one appeared, others were sure to follow.

"It stands for Mom's Morning Out. This is the experience we want to create for our customers."

"But Genevieve . . ." I paused to swallow, hard. I thought of Virginia Woolf, tucked into my overhead bin in her plastic wrap. "I don't even like video games."

"Yes, Alice, we've established that already. This mandate comes directly from Greg, who apparently is aware of your feelings."

I leaned back on her stiff white couch—a far cry from the sumptuous recliners down the hall. "Wow. This is—a big change. This isn't the Scroll I've been selling to the publishing community. People are so excited about—"

"You're going to have to deliver a different message to your contacts. But for the time being, this pivot is confidential and I would ask you to keep it that way." Genevieve leaned forward, conspiratorially; for a fleeting second I thought she was going to tell me it was all a joke. "Listen, Alice, I know this will take some time to wrap your mind around. But at Scroll, we're expected to think like MBAs. We assess where our business is heading and what our customers want, rather than what we want them to want, and we all pitch in to keep it on track."

I opened my notebook again, moved aside its fussy brown ribbon placeholder and wrote "MMO" on a blank page, underlining it twice. I thought of Nicholas, stretched out on our living room couch in front of a coffee table full of empty beer bottles. No matter where I was in the house, I heard the *plink* of a bottle cap landing on wood.

"Of course, Genevieve. I'm a team player, too."

"Alice, can I give you some advice?"

"Sure."

"Try not to get to attached to your idea of how you thought things would be at Scroll. Getting set in your ways is the first step toward mediocrity. You have to be nimble."

Oh, the humiliation of getting a lecture like this from someone seven years your junior.

Genevieve smile-smirked and brushed an invisible shred of lint off the front of her blazer. Suddenly, she gave the impression of being a corporate true believer, a company woman—or at least someone who would play this role, method-actor style, until she mastered the performance.

Befriend, then berate.

I pictured my kids lined up in the window, their little faces alight with pride as I headed off to the train.

The bells inside the steeple started ringing, and Genevieve paused to wait out the clanging. In the space of those ten tolls, her face fell. I glanced at a picture of her on the bulletin board—Genevieve and Lance and their two dogs, Jane and Austen, all four of them wearing shirts that said "Who Rescued Who?"—and realized, suddenly, how much older she looked now.

"Understood. I'll get on MMO as soon as I've had a chance to complete my deep dive on literature—does that sound good?"

"Okay, but please bear in mind that we need to indicate to Cleveland that we're on the bus."

"Oh, of course. Yes. I am on the bus."

"Good to know. And Alice? You're doing a great job."

This was such an unexpected revelation, I never thought to ask if the bus was going to an arcade.

On the train home that night, my phone started vibrating. I withdrew my hand from a greasy bag of Zaro's popcorn and licked the salt off the fingers of one hand while I navigated from e-mail to texts with the other. By now, I was adept at balancing the phone on one thigh—a multitasking move I thought of as semi-hands-free.

To: alicepearse@scroll.com
From: genevieveandrews@scroll.com

To recap our meeting that started at 9:30 and ended at 10:42, you will take ownership of the MMO push for the New York office. Going forward, half of your time will be dedicated to reimagining the Scroll experience to include video games, sturdy furniture, and child-friendly cuisine. [Note: Packaged snacks should be in biodegradable wrappers ONLY. No

lollipops due to choking risk.] Please adjust your goals in GatheringPlace
to reflect this change. Thanks.

To: alicepearse@scroll.com +11 others
From: quinlanfamily@yahoo.com

DON'T FORGET TO DROP OFF YOUR CHECK FOR GIRL SCOUTS! WE
HAVE LOTS OF FUN TRIPS PLANNED FOR OUR GIRLS, INCLUDING
AN OVERNIGHT CAMPING TRIP, RIVER RAFTING ADVENTURE, SOUP
KITCHEN VOLUNTEERING, SENDING LETTERS TO OUR TROOPS, LOCAL
PARK CLEAN-UP, GARDEN BEAUTIFICATION AT SCHOOL, ASSISTANCE AT
SPECIAL OLYMPICS AND KNITTING BLANKETS FOR CHILDREN AFFECTED
BY THE LANDSLIDE IN CHINA. PLEASE LEAVE CHECKS IN MY MAILBOX BY
FRIDAY 9AM SHARP!! XOXOXOX, KARA

The prospect of writing a check for $75, driving it across town, and
dropping it in Kara's mailbox filled me with ennui. I had a million excuses:
We were out of checks. I couldn't find my car keys. What was the amount,
again? I deleted the message, blocking out the memory of Margot happily
organizing boxes of Samoas, Thin Mints, and Trefoils in our living room.
Wasn't she too old for Girl Scouts anyway?

Jessie: Just a reminder, Margot needs a bagged lunch for her trip to the
Edison Museum tomorrow. No cutlery or containers—everything
has to be disposable. No lunchboxes allowed.
Me: You're a godsend. Thanks for the reminder!

Was it weird that Jessie had this information and I didn't? Or that she
knew where to find Oliver's shin guards and I didn't?

•   •   •

"Daddy, do you know how small a butterfly is?" Georgie whispered into Nicholas's ear in the middle of the night. Since I was awake anyway, I led her by one small, warm hand back to her room.

Then I nudged Nicholas. "Are you awake?"

"Now I am."

"What happened at the Shannon Rose?"

"You're seriously waking me up in the middle of the night to ask me about this?"

"Sorry, but I ran into Jim at the liquor store and he told me to ask you—"

"Alice, what is your *problem*? I'm *sleeping*. I have that meeting in Princeton tomorrow: I have to be *awake*. Can't this wait?"

He had a point.

I waited until he was snoring quietly, went downstairs, and opened Facebook on my laptop. I clicked through pictures posted by a girl I grew up with and hadn't seen in real life since fifth grade. Her family was at the Tennessee State Fair. There were her four snub-nosed kids, the exact ages now that their mom was when we'd both collected troll dolls. They were in the dunk tank, posed by a paddock of cows, painting gourds, and pouring layers of colored sand in jars.

Twenty-six pictures later, a flicker on the left side of the screen caught my eye. Who else would be joining the party so late at night except a friend in a distant time zone?

My dad, that's who. A little bubble popped up on my screen. "Can't sleep?"

"No," I wrote back.

"Why?"

"Oh, the usual. Work, money, kids. You."

"You know me, I'm always up."

"I mean, I'm up late worrying about you."

No response.

"Dad, are you still there? . . . Hello?"

I didn't need to look again at the left side of the screen to know that he was gone. I was relieved; the last thing I wanted to do was have a gooey heart-to-heart, especially over Facebook. What was there to say, really? I wondered if he was scared, but I didn't really want to know and I knew he didn't want to be asked. From the day of my dad's first diagnosis, he had insisted on forging ahead, living his life: ordering mysteries from the Book of the Month Club, mapping out the next season's perennials on graph paper, collecting spare nickels and pennies in Maxwell House coffee cans until he had enough to wow his grandchildren at the change machine at the bank. What was it like, having nowhere left to forge? I felt like my back was against a brick wall; I couldn't imagine how cornered my dad must have felt.

Back in bed, I heard the Chartwells truck back into the school parking lot, getting ready to drop off a week's supply of milk cartons and square slices of pizza. I heard the earliest train idling in our station, its shrill whistle silenced thanks to a petition circulated by a neighborhood woman who called herself a peace activist.

I fell asleep as the sun came up.

"Alice, here is the password for downloading Joystick games to your laptop: SimPlayParabola. Thanks, Chica!"

I found this written on an unsigned Post-it stuck to the center of my computer monitor one morning. I'd never seen Genevieve's handwriting before.

Late one afternoon, David came into my office and closed the door behind him. He sat down quietly in the chair behind mine and held up his hand in the universal "stop" gesture when I swiveled around to hear the reason for his visit.

"It's nothing. I just need to take a minute."

"What's wrong?"

"I had a one-to-one with Genevieve and . . ."

He closed his eyes and took a deep breath. I glanced at the clock on my computer and made a split-second decision to miss the 6:09 train; I could catch the 6:42 and still be home in time for baths.

"What happened?"

"Genevieve says I fiddle with my glasses in meetings. She told me to stop."

I stifled the urge to laugh. *This* was useful feedback? I thought of the executive editor at *You*, who taught me how to edit when I was around David's age. She'd call me into her office and gesture for me to take a seat while she made her way through an article, making careful marks with a mechanical pencil. At the time, the process seemed excruciating, but now I felt grateful to have had a crackerjack mentor.

"David. You need to take that advice and file it away. It's only as significant as you allow it to be. So fine, you occasionally fiddle with your glasses. Does that negate all the ways you're doing a great job? Half the time I have to remind myself that you haven't been at this as long as I have."

David kept his eyes closed. I imagined Oliver, fifteen years in the future, sitting in that chair, on his way home to split Thai takeout with three roommates in Bed-Stuy. Yes, it was annoying to me to be patronized by a youngster like Genevieve, but for someone at David's stage, the scrutiny and criticism could take a serious toll.

"And *none* of us really know what we're doing here, that's the thing you need to keep in mind. We're all making it up as we go. Not one person in the world has more experience setting up a bookstore-slash-gaming lounge than we do."

David laughed, reluctantly. "I know. I'm just trying so hard and she only ever points out . . . the bad stuff."

"Bad stuff? If the worst thing she can think of is this crap with your glasses? I'd say you're in good shape."

"I guess."

"Genevieve is like the man behind the curtain. Don't let her scare you."

When David left, I looked over at Matthew, who took off his noise-canceling headphones. He no longer stood at his tall desk; now he had a tall chair to match.

"Did you catch any of that?"

"Enough."

He rolled his eyes at me, pantomiming holding a gun to his head.

17

When he had his first surgery, my dad had no idea that he was going to wake up without a voice. He knew he had a tumor in his throat, and he went into the hospital to have it removed before starting chemo. But the tumor turned out to be much bigger than expected, and it was wrapped around his larynx in such a way that everything around it had to come out. Immediately.

As Dr. Davis put it, "We found ourselves a little surprise, so we had to get a smidge more aggressive than we anticipated."

This was the understatement of the century. My dad was never able to make noise again—no talking, laughing, whispering, humming, singing, or whistling. He had never been able to carry a tune, but he'd always been a big whistler. In what the hospital social worker cleverly referred to as the "new normal," he also had to breathe through a hole in his neck.

I don't remember who broke the news to him. I remember shiny yellow cinder-block walls in the recovery room. I remember aluminum chairs padded in turquoise and little packages of Keebler graham crackers stacked in a plastic basket on the windowsill.

When the weight of the news descended on my dad, he was ferociously angry in a red-faced way that would have been almost comical if it hadn't been so scary and wildly out of character. This was our mild parent—the one who, when he'd had a voice, never raised it.

After the surgery, my dad threw his meal tray of clear liquids across the room and the little sealed cup of Jell-O exploded loudly against the wall. He gave a nurse the finger, and when the surgeon came into the room, he refused to open his eyes. We handed him a legal pad to write on—because, of course, he'd come to the hospital prepared to get some work done while recovering—and he scribbled one word with such conviction, it left an imprint on every sheet all the way to the back of the pad: "LIVID."

I escaped to the hospital parking lot, where I leaned against a concrete construction barrier and cried so violently, I thought I might never stop. I was pregnant with Oliver, and this was the first time I felt him move.

The social worker said, "Your children will help your dad get through. When a door closes, a window opens."

But I knew better. My dad wanted to make noise. He was a talker, an analyzer, a debater, both a collector and dispenser of knowledge. Babies weren't his bag. Even as his daughter, I knew that I'd become more interesting to him as I'd gotten older and had more to talk about. At that moment, I would have traded the little butterfly of my own baby for one more conversation with my dad.

A few days after the laryngectomy, my dad handed the legal pad to my mom. (Dry erase was a relatively new invention and tricky for a left-hander to maneuver.) This time, the message said, "I need help and you can't give it to me." So my mom turned to the yellow pages—on par with the Bible in her faith system—and located the Voiceovers. They were a support group for people who'd had laryngectomies.

"They call themselves larys," she explained, after she'd talked to the leader of the pack, Tony Capossela, a butcher who spoke with the help of an electrolarynx. My dad would have to wait six weeks before he could use one, too. Given the margins of his tumor, we knew he wouldn't be able to learn to speak through his esophagus—the other alternative for laryngectomees, where you produce sound by sucking in air and expelling it again, almost like burping.

A week later, the Voiceovers welcomed us to their annual Harvest Banquet at Mambo's Grille and Chill on Route 46. It was not the kind of establishment my parents normally frequented, but they soldiered across the parking lot, arm in arm in their L. L. Bean jackets, while I struggled to tie the big grosgrain ribbon on my maternity coat. We were greeted at the door by a man with acne scars all over his face and a stoma cover crocheted in navy.

"Hello, sir," he buzzed at my dad. "We're sorry for you that you're here, but awfully glad to meet you."

He moved his electrolarynx away from his neck and held it like a microphone, pressing the button on the bottom to make it buzz. Then he brought it back to his neck. "That's me laughing. You'll get the hang of it."

Imagine attending a party where more than half the people can't talk normally. It was surreal, with men and women of all ages buzzing around the place or burping out their words while piling on croutons and pimento-stuffed olives at the salad bar. My dad worked the room with his legal pad, jotting down bits of advice gleaned from the larys: how to stand in the shower so your stoma isn't flooded with water; where to order backup batteries for an electrolarynx and summer-weight covers for your stoma; a reminder to register with the local police department—because if you ever need to call 911, they won't be able to hear you.

My parents took it all in, their faces serious. I didn't know whether to laugh or to cry.

•   •   •

We went back to the Harvest Banquet every October. This year, Tony did a double take when he saw my dad slowly shuffle into the dining room at Mambo's.

"Ed, what the hell, she got you on some kinda diet?" He planted a kiss on my mom's cheek and pulled her into a tight hug.

My dad pursed his lips and shook his head. No need to fuss with Buzz. Everyone in the room knew the signs of a recurrence, and weight loss was chief among them. Plus, my dad had fresh burns on his neck from radiation, and his color, as my mom had long feared, was now off—more of a mottled yellow than his usual ruddy pink. Otherwise, my dad's appearance was meticulous: shiny penny loafers, blue blazer, striped shirt, comb marks in his hair.

"Well, even looking like a scarecrow, we're glad to see you guys. Don't forget to put your money in for the Tricky Tray. We got tickets to *Beauty and the Beast*, a new car radio donated by Sully, a personal training session with Trish. You'll want to win."

My mom took my dad by the hand and started leading him to a booth. "We will. Thanks, Tony."

I felt awkward eating in front of him, but my dad made a *That's ridiculous* face and gestured for us to get in line at the buffet. By the time we were done, my plate was laden with marinated artichokes, mandarin oranges, and cubes of jack cheese—all the fixins' that push the envelope on the definition of salad. My mom's plate demonstrated characteristic restraint: a pile of brown-edged iceberg topped with goopy balsamic vinaigrette, with a handful of abused-looking pickled beets for garnish.

"Dad, is there anything we can order for you? I mean, a hot towel at least?"

He opened a blank screen on his phone and tapped out, "No worries. Here on a full stomach. ☺"

"When did you learn how to use emojis?"

He typed back, "Margot taught me."

Then he tapped to the notepad app, where he already had a list of questions ready to roll: "What are the kids going to be for Halloween?" and "What's the Book Lady reading these days?" and "How is it going for Nicholas?" My dad pointed to this one and waited.

"So far, so good. He's gathering some good clients. And he does *not* miss Sutherland, Courtfield. Not even for a minute." This was all true. The work wasn't as sexy as what Nicholas had been doing at the firm— and there were certainly no spur-of-the-moment trips to Luxembourg for top secret meetings. But the new clients paid their bills on time, and suddenly strangers were thumping his back wherever we went.

"Such great news—he deserves it. Who needs that pressure cooker? He seemed so happy and relaxed when he came by to help Daddy with his paperwork last week." My mom leaned over and smoothed my dad's lapel, irritating him.

"Wait, what paperwork?"

"Oh, just—"

My mom was about to answer when my dad started pecking away at his phone. We waited until he held it up for us to read: "Some business related to my estate. I needed a notary."

"You mean, your will?"

He nodded, grimacing slightly and holding his hands out in a gesture that telegraphed, "What are you gonna do?"

How to respond? "Well, gee, Dad. Way to be on top of it, I guess." I wasn't surprised that Nicholas had helped out, but I did wonder why he hadn't mentioned it to me.

18

Judy and Elliott came to town for Columbus Day weekend. Work at Scroll didn't stop for observance of the discovery of the New World, so Nicholas was on his own as houseguest cruise director. I was a little relieved to board the train on Monday morning; my office felt like a respite. Normally I loved my in-laws' energy, but now it was a painful reminder of my own fatigue.

The gang came to meet me for lunch, a tense affair where Nicholas ordered two Bloody Marys and the kids were whiny and peevish and all in a lather about ordering banana cream pie for dessert—which, for some reason, Nicholas vetoed.

I suggested that we all go to a Halloween pop-up store on Sixth Avenue to pick out costumes. Margot gravitated toward the slutty section and Oliver fell for the grim reaper carrying a bloody chainsaw, leaving me to wonder what had happened to the butterflies and basketball players of yore. Luckily Georgie remained smack-dab on the puppy and wholesome witch continuum.

We finally settled on modest and adorably matching zebra costumes for the girls and a blue, face-obscuring unitard for Oliver. While I paid an astronomical sum for this bounty, Margot started agitating for a set of bloody fingernails on display by the cash register. "Absolutely not. We're already spending a lot of money on costumes. You don't need these."

"Please? They're so creepy and cool. Just one pair?"

"I said no. We're not made of money."

"You're so *mean*." This was a new response to any perceived injustice. I hissed crazily, "You will *not* talk to me like that. Stop behaving this way or you will *not* have a Halloween costume. *At all*."

I delivered the Vulcan death grip to her upper arm, a particularly harsh version where my fingernails nearly dug into the skin.

With every customer in line and my in-laws looking on, Margot's eyes filled with tears. "Sorry, Mommy. Please can I still get a costume?"

"Fine, Margot. But you pushed me. And you've *been* pushing me. Imagine me like a rubber band—you can only stretch so far and eventually I'm going to snap back. I'm human."

"Alice, relax. Can you just sign the receipt?"

Nicholas seemed to have only witnessed the part where I lost my temper, not the part where Margot nagged and rolled her eyes and generally acted like exactly the kind of adolescent I swore I would never have. You'd think I would have learned my lesson by now, having also pledged at a certain point that I would never be the parent of a toddler who threw chicken nuggets on the floor at restaurants.

"Fine," I said. "We're done here. I have to get back to work, anyway."

"Alice, it's hard, we totally get it, we know you have so much going on—"

I stomped past Judy and her good intentions and stormed out of the Halloween superstore.

By the time I got back to my office, I'd boiled the whole incident down to a funny anecdote.

"Just be glad your kid is happy to be a panda," I told Matthew. "Before you know it, he'll be Freddy Krueger."

That night, Oliver waited for me by the platform in his blue man costume. Through the mesh face-covering, he said, "You were terrible today." It was like receiving negative feedback from a Martian.

"I'm sorry I left like that, but you guys need to learn that money doesn't grow on trees."

"Okay, but we just wanted the bloody fingers."

"So you can't always get what you want. That's life."

"Well. You were still mean. Do you like my costume?"

Some background: when Oliver first learned to talk, I offered him a cookie after dinner one night. He shook his head. "Two cookies."

"No, I'm offering you one cookie."

"Two cookies."

"Oliver, you can have one cookie or no cookies."

"No cookies."

I still don't know why I dug in my heels about that extra cookie, but to this day I think of that conversation as a metaphor for Oliver. He is dogged.

Which is how I found myself on the walk from the train station to our front door, arguing with a blue man about fake bloody fingers.

I was about to fall asleep when Nicholas's hand moved off my shoulder and started to explore.

"You have *got* to be kidding me."

"Um, no . . ."

"Seriously, Nicholas, now is not the time *or* the place."

"Actually, Alice? This *is* the place. But why don't you let me know when the time is right? I'm sick of getting it wrong."

"Good night."

19

Georgie's first tooth fell out while Nicholas was washing her hair in the bathtub. It disappeared into the suds like a little pebble, and we let out such a whoop, Oliver came running. "George, the tooth fairy is coming tonight!" He was over the moon with excitement, even though our tooth fairy is so lame, she forgot to come the last time he lost a tooth. (The next morning he came downstairs, grumbling, "The tooth fairy was a no-show.")

Later, I lit a lavender-scented candle (helpful for insomniacs, or so said SleepBetter.com) and I was settling in to read on the couch when I heard the all-too-familiar sounds from the kitchen: Refrigerator door opening, check. Clink of glass bottle on counter, check. Bottle opener removing bottle cap, *hiss*, check.

"Nicholas, you're having *another* beer?"

"Yes. Is that a problem?" Suddenly, he stood in front of me, hands on his hips, looking rakish in a white undershirt. I knew exactly what he would smell like if I pressed my nose into the dip between his neck and collarbone: Tide, Head & Shoulders, shaving cream. My favorite cocktail in the world—now tinged with a hint of alcohol, no matter the time of day.

"It *is* a problem, yes. Nicholas, when was the last time you went one day without drinking? You practically pass out after dinner—"

"Pass out? Seriously?"

"Yes. Seriously. I know how many cases you're going through. I can count."

"That's rich, Alice. Did it ever occur to you that I'm *exhausted*? You're gone all the time, I'm trying to hold it together for the kids, I'm knocking on doors all over town *hoping* to find someone who's about to declare bankruptcy—how do you think *that* feels? You'd have a couple of beers, too."

"Oh, really? Remember when we had three kids under the age of six? And Cornelius was a *puppy*? Did I toss back multiple martinis when you were in Geneva for two weeks and Georgie had whooping cough? *No.* I held it together, Nicholas. That's what I need you to do."

"Seriously, Alice? I'm sorry I'm not a pillar of strength like you are."

I stalked out of the room so briskly, my candle snuffed out. I hissed, "I am *sick of this*."

From the top of the stairs, a voice pleaded, "Can you guys stop? The tooth fairy might get scared."

To: alicepearse@scroll.com
From: genevieveandrews@scroll.com

Had a dream about my dad last night, which made me think of your family. How are you all holding up? How is your dad? He sounds like a great guy; I hate that you (and he) have to go through this. It really sucks. Update me when you have a chance.

Jessie had to leave early to practice for a wedding expo at the Paramus Park Mall, where all the local bands would audition their best songs for betrothed couples. I came home early and we had a quick debrief in the front hallway as she headed to her car, guitar case in hand, hair gelled into blue spikes. "Cornelius's ear smells funny; I'm worried he might have an infection. Margot is finishing her algebra homework; Oliver needs to be tested on his spelling words, and Georgie is at Violet's. I told Susanna we'd be there around five." Jessie said this all in one breath, no hesitations. Then added, "Hey, thanks for getting home early. I hope that wasn't too much trouble."

"No trouble at all. Break a leg tonight. I know from personal experience, you'd be good luck for any bride and groom."

When I arrived at Susanna's, she was in the sunroom off her living room, frantically punching numbers into a calculator with oversized buttons made of rainbow-colored plastic gems. She had a pen behind each ear and a pencil stuck in a bun at the back of her head. The floor was littered with printer paper, graph paper, file folders, and paper clips. Apparently the Blue Owl didn't share Scroll's strict rules about office supplies.

"What are you doing holed up in here?"

"I'm just figuring some things out about the store." She looked like she was about to cry—and when I sat down next to her and wrapped my arm around her thin shoulder, she did. "Oh, Alice, I really don't want to get into this with you."

"Stop, Susanna. What's going on?"

"Nothing immediately, but you know we've been struggling. I'm not sure I'm going to be able to make rent and Paul thinks I should just throw in the towel." She ran the cuff of her gray cardigan across the bottom of her nose. I thought of her on a low green stool, reading *The Twits* to a circle of rapt kids at story hour. *If you have good thoughts they will shine out of your face like sunbeams and you will always look lovely.* I remembered Georgie's little overalled rump resting in my lap as we listened; the other exhausted moms leaning against bookshelves and smiling at the familiar lines. Mom's morning out—that was mine.

"Things will work out, don't you think? The holidays are coming and—"

Susanna scrambled to her feet, grabbing an armful of papers.

"Thanks. I appreciate the sentiment, but honestly? You're the last person who should be reassuring me. Whether you want to admit it or not, Alice, *you* are part of the problem."

She pointed at me, then left the room.

One Friday, Nicholas encouraged me to come to work with him for a day. In the peace of his spare but attractive office, I checked my black keychain toggle for the sixteen-digit code that would grant me access to the virtual private network (VPN), then waited a full ninety seconds while my computer labored to connect to a remote server in Cleveland. (Remember dial-up Internet? Same speed.) Then I navigated through the Inventory folder to the spreadsheet named GameOn (GO). The numbers unfurled slowly on my screen, one column at a time.

The data pertained to Joystick's one hundred best-selling video games, including sales figures, median household income, median age of players, and average playtime per game, per level. The spreadsheet also included a one-line description of the object of each game—*Player storms enemy compound to capture evil drones* or *Assassins unite in the name of conquering gremlins on the planet Vibra*—and letter grades indicating levels of violence, profanity, gambling, and sexual content. Many games were designated CV, for "comic violence."

This information overload landed me back in high school chemistry class, studying the periodic table with a pit in my stomach. I clicked the arrow in the lower right-hand corner, scrolling left to gauge the width of the spreadsheet. It was endless.

Nicholas and I split a sloppy joe for lunch—the New Jersey kind, made with tongue, roast beef, Swiss cheese, Russian dressing, and coleslaw, on thin slices of rye bread. He gestured toward the beer refrigerator at the deli—"Want one?"—then grabbed two Dr. Brown's Cel-Ray sodas when I gave him a look.

"How's your work going?" Nicholas asked.

"I'm analyzing data about video games. How do you think it's going?"

"Hmm. Sounds tedious." I could tell Nicholas's mind was somewhere else—definitely more focused on his sandwich than he was on my professional woes.

"It *is* tedious. Also, I don't understand the value proposition—"

"Did I really just hear you use the term *value proposition*?"

"Yes, you did. Why are you acting like this? I feel like you're laughing at me."

"Al, I'm not laughing at you. I'm just wondering if we're ever going to have a conversation again that isn't about Scroll."

"That's not fair. How many times have I hashed out a work decision with you? I haven't asked you to return the favor in over a decade."

I tried to say this lightly, but I knew there was nothing funny about our conversation.

"Yeah, but you know the difference? I've gone through periods of a few weeks or—okay, I'll grant you, a month here or there—when I've been obsessed with work, or maybe working around the clock and checking my BlackBerry at all hours. You're *always* in that mode. Even when you're here, you're not here. And every time I roll over in the middle of the night, you're on your phone. I feel like you're just *gone*."

"Wow. You're one to talk."

"Excuse me?"

"I mean, I'm sorry you feel that way." I felt a momentary twinge of guilt, but it was quickly replaced by annoyance as Nicholas helped himself to more than his fair share of the mesquite potato chips we were supposed to be splitting.

"No, I don't just *feel* this way—it's a fact. You're obsessed with your job, Alice. I get it that you're excited about trying something new. And I'm excited *for* you, and I've said that a million times. But you can't ever seem to stop thinking about it. Here we are out to lunch, just the two of us, and all you want to talk about is MMO or GO or whatever it is. Isn't there something else we can talk about?"

Our table was next to the dairy case, so we got blasted with cold air every time someone reached in for a carton of milk. I pulled on the hood of my sweatshirt and hunched into it.

Nicholas continued, "Alice, I don't want to pile on, but when I was at your parents' a few weeks ago, it really wasn't a good scene."

"What do you mean, it wasn't a good scene?"

"I mean, your dad wanted to go over these papers in the dining room but it took him like ten minutes to get in there from the living room. He kept stopping and holding on to the wall. And your mom seemed nervous and talked nonstop, and that made him really mad."

"And? What else is new."

"Then when we were finished, he just kind of zoned out in front of the TV and your mom had to pour food into his tube. He was too tired to do it himself."

"Ugh. That makes me so sad." *Bereft* was a better word for it. Gutted. Devastated. Guilty that I wasn't at my parents' house 24/7; guilty that work was my constant alibi, not my kids; guilty that Nicholas had to step in to fill the void.

I could picture the scene so clearly: my mom, ministering to my dad, television droning in the background. Peel away one layer and the picture was different: same room, same chair, my mom handing my dad a warm metal bowl of popcorn to eat while they watched *Rear Window* together. This would never happen again. The realization was a sucker punch, one I couldn't explain to Nicholas, whose parents were vibrant, healthy, and jointly enrolled in a Senior Scholars class on Beat poets.

He went on. "The thing I can't stop thinking about? Your dad was watching the X Games."

"Okay. Enough. I get it."

My dad was a fan of *Masterpiece Theatre*. The thought of him zoned out in front of the X Games after finalizing his will—I shook my head, hoping to erase the image like an Etch A Sketch. "I wonder if they're going to need more help soon. Like a private nurse or something."

"I think they will." They were intensely private, my parents—creatures of habit and routine. It was impossible to imagine a stranger in their midst, rinsing syringes in the sink or using Will's old beer funnel to pour Ensure down the tube to my dad's stomach. Surely a nurse would have her own funnel, sterilized, without the "Don't Tread on Me" flag on its side. I imagined the soft pad of nurse shoes in my parents' hallway and felt physically ill.

Nicholas and I took a few minutes to polish off our chips and then he continued: "So, to change the subject for a minute."

I knew he was about to spring something on me. "Yes . . . ?"

"The basketball guys are going to a tournament in Atlantic City, and I want to go."

"So what's the problem?"

"There's no problem; I'm just telling you."

Of course I was fine with Nicholas going to a basketball tournament; I'd certainly been known to sneak away for a weekend with college friends. But his timing was suspect, and he was, as I would say to Margot, taking a tone, which I didn't appreciate.

"Well, great. When are you going?"

"It's not for a while. The last weekend in February. Of course we'll see how things are with your dad. And you'll be all right with the kids?"

"What do you mean? They're my kids! We'll be fine. We'll have fun."

"Great. I'll let Jim know I'm in."

Despite the semi-cordial end of the conversation, its antagonistic undertone was unsettling.

To: scrollglobal@scroll.com
From: gregrockwell@scroll.com

Hey guys, when you report to work today you'll notice some new security/trackability systems we're implementing. Employees will now run their palms beneath our new Biometric Time Clock. Don't worry, it doesn't bite! This technology allows us to take attendance and keep track of all kinds of stuff like what time you arrive at work, what time you leave, how long you take for lunch, and whether or not you flossed your teeth that day. Haha, maybe not so much with the floss. But we are, at heart, a retail company, so I'm sure you will be understanding when upon occasion we play by retail rules. Clock in, clock out. We just like to know what "yous guys" are up to. I'm looking at you, New Yawk!

Getting a Saturday appointment for a checkup with our pediatrician is like landing a reservation at the coolest restaurant in town. You have to call three months ahead to the minute and then wait on hold while the receptionist sifts through desperate pleas from all the other working parents.

We'd secured an appointment in the inner sanctum while the rest of the world was still home watching *Phineas & Ferb* and reading the *Star-Ledger*. Georgie stood in front of the eye chart, naked except for her blue underpants with a monkey on the butt. One hand cupped over her right eye, she recited what she saw: A cup. A star. A diamond. A hand. A circle. A square. A heart.

A nurse pointed to the bottom of the chart. "That's great, Georgie. Can you read the words at the very bottom, right here?"

"Sure. It says 'Only eagles can read this.'"

A rogue sob ripped out of my mouth. Georgie spun around on one heel, her pigtails flaring out from her head like Pippi Longstocking's.

"Mommy, are you crying?"

"No, sweetie, I just have something in my eye."

I had no idea she knew how to read.

20

I turned the ringer off on my phone and spent a Saturday morning raking leaves, then shoving each pile into a brown lawn bag and lugging it to the curb.

When I finished raking, I checked my phone. Six missed calls. Two were from Genevieve. On a Saturday. What could be so urgent? And then a text: "Alice: You need to demonstrate your commitment to MMO. Please prepare a white paper on your findings within the next three weeks."

A white paper was the Scroll equivalent of a term paper—six pages, in a prescribed font (Calibri), with footnotes. I wrote back, "Sounds good! I will!" I couldn't resist the exclamation point.

No mention of the mugs of bourbon Genevieve and I had swilled in her office the night before, toasting the Mistake by the Lake, Nicholas's least favorite nickname for Cleveland. I was getting used to Genevieve's Jekyll-and-Hyde approach to management. She might be your best friend in the elevator, but you never knew when she might mount her bully pulpit of virtual communication.

The fifth call was from my mom: "Alice? Are you there? We're on our way to urgent care at Sloan Kettering. Call me."

The sixth was from my brother: "Has Mom gotten ahold of you yet? Why are you so impossible to track down? Dad is having trouble breathing. They're on their way to the hospital. Can you please call me when you know anything? Mary is on call tonight, but I'll head down there tomorrow."

Will, our mom, and I were sitting in a semicircle around our dad's bed, slowly adjusting to hospital time, where you lose track of hours, days, even seasons. Nicholas was at home with our kids, or maybe Jessie was with them; I was hazy on the details. There was no hope of keeping our bearings, sailor-style, with an eye on the horizon; the roommate had the window. Everything on our side of the room was salmon-colored, even the drop tile ceiling.

Suddenly, an unfamiliar doctor yanked open the curtain that divided the room in two. He flipped open my dad's file, balancing its metal-hinged spine on one palm like a pizza, then looked at my mom. "Terminal pneumonia?"

"Actually, my name is Joan," she responded firmly. The eleventh commandment: Thou shalt command respect. I love that about her.

The doctor's face remained impassive as he whipped a pen out of his coat pocket and started jotting notes on the file. "The patient has terminal pneumonia, yes?"

My brother stood up, towering over the doctor. In his ratty Bowdoin sweatpants and loosely laced boots, he was more pissed-off hockey player than middle-aged oarsman. "If he does, this is the first we're hearing of it. What the fuck is terminal pneumonia?"

I waited for my mom to sound the siren of the language police, but she was silent.

The doctor clicked his pen closed, slipped it back into his pocket, and made sure it was clipped securely to the fabric above his name, which was embroidered in royal blue script. "This terminology denotes pneumonia occurring in the course of another disease near its fatal termination."

Then, with near-comic efficiency, he turned on his heel, slid the salmon curtain closed, and disappeared.

"Gee, thanks," I said loudly. I wanted to follow the doctor into the hallway and bang his small head against the granite countertop of the nurse's station, but I thought this might upset my mom.

Will turned to my dad. "Dad, can I get you a—"

Our patient was asleep.

Without making eye contact with my mom or my brother, I slipped my phone out of my pocket and started entering my four-digit password. Will leaned over, grabbed the phone, and threw it across the room, where it landed in the garbage with a thud.

When I was nine, Oliver's age, my dad surprised Will and me with a trip to Great Adventure, an amusement park an hour away. He shook us awake on a school morning and said, "Get in the car, guys, we're going to ride roller coasters."

Will ran into my room in a rumpled OP T-shirt and Jams. "Is this a joke?"

It was not a joke. We couldn't have been more overjoyed if our dad had surprised us with a puppy or the double-decker tree house we coveted. We piled into our blue Buick Regal and waved good-bye to our mom, who was as shocked by the spontaneity of the plan as we were—and, no doubt, equally thrilled to opt out.

"Dad, why are you *doing* this? Is something wrong?" I kept checking the exit numbers on the turnpike to make sure we were, indeed, heading south. Could this be an elaborate ruse to get us to go somewhere educational, like Richmond Town on Staten Island? Our parents loved places like that, with exhibitions on churning butter and one measly gift shop candy stick as the only reward for hours of boredom.

My dad smiled. From my vantage point diagonally behind him, I could see his eyes crinkle. "Just a change of pace, that's all."

"*Fraidy cat*," Will hissed, from the other side of the backseat. "You'll probably want to ride the teacups the whole time."

But for all his big brother bravado, Will was the one who didn't have the stomach for the scary rides. Chastened, he stuck to the flying swings and the log flume, which soaked the two of us again and again while our dad took Polaroid pictures from a nearby bench.

When it was my turn to pick a ride, I opted for multiple solo stints on the Gravitron, a stomach-turning paean to the power of centrifugal force. It was a cylindrical contraption lined with black padded panels. You picked one, leaned against it and held on for dear life as the ride started spinning at breakneck speed: around and around, sometimes upside down. Except you didn't actually need to hold on at all—you were glued to that wall. You couldn't lift a limb if you tried.

"Holy cow!" I squealed as the floor panel slipped from the bottom of the Gravitron. This was part of the excitement, but it was terrifying nonetheless. My dad, my brother, and their twin cotton candies dissolved into a watercolor blur on the other side of the fence. The clouds and the sky melted into each other; so did the carousel and the Ferris wheel and the white spine of a roller coaster. I felt weightless, as if I might burst through the back of my panel—a buck-toothed meteor in pink glasses and a terry-cloth jumpsuit.

I tried to open my mouth but the firm hand of gravity held it shut.

This was how I felt in my dad's hospital room: heavy and helpless, pressed against the wall. The bottom had dropped out. I wanted the ride to end, but it went on and on.

I took the 6:57 train to work so I'd be able to get more work done before going to the hospital in the middle of the day. After work, I FaceTimed with my kids ("Look guys, there's FAO Schwarz!") while walking to the subway that would take me back to Sloan Kettering, where I stayed until it was time to get back on the subway to Penn Station to catch the 9:35 train home. The schedule was head-spinning, literally.

I spent half my day underground and the other half reading brochures. They were everywhere in the hospital, splayed artfully on tables and hanging on the wall in Plexiglas racks: *Hospice Care: The Simple Facts* and *End of Life: Helping with Comfort and Care* and *Hope: It's the Thing with Feathers*. (Okay, I made up that last one. Apologies to Emily Dickinson.) I read every word of these missives and even brought in a pot of stinky paperwhites for my dad's windowsill, since all the self-actualized sick people in the brochures had them.

As for how I felt, aside from harried, devastated, and distracted? As for what it was like to present age-appropriate updates about my dad to my kids without losing it completely? The line that kept running through my head was *I'm too old for this*. It was an odd response, because I wasn't old; I was on the young side to be losing a parent, just as he was young to be lost. But I felt ancient and bone tired, as if I was trudging uphill through molasses in ill-fitting boots. What was waiting for me at the top wasn't anything I wanted to see, but I still had to get there.

"Alice, I heard about your dad. How is he doing?" Mariana was rinsing grapes in the office kitchen, the picture of bright-eyed beauty with her smooth hair and crisp white blouse.

"Aw, thanks for asking. He's not so great, actually." I tapped the lid of the Keurig impatiently and checked the water reservoir to make sure it was full. Isn't this supposed to be instant?

"I'm sorry to hear that. He's still in the hospital?"

"Yeah. We're hoping he'll be home by the end of the week."

"And then he'll . . . be on the mend?"

"Then hospice will come and . . . yeah. That's how he's doing."

"Wow, Alice. I hope you're making time to be good to yourself."

"I guess I am. I'm trying."

"Maybe a manicure? A massage?"

"Yeah, I should do that."

"Well, I'm so sorry to hear all this."

"It's okay, thanks for asking."

"At least he's lived a full life?"

I threw my shitty coffee at the wall and walked out of the kitchen.

No, in real life I smiled and said what you say when someone you like is trying her best but simply doesn't speak the language: "You are absolutely right."

On the seventh day, it was time for my dad to go home. "There's really nothing else we can do for him here," said a nurse, so apologetic that I felt compelled to reassure her he would be in a better place. Then I realized I'd jumped the gun on that line—my dad was still alive, after all.

I left work early and met my mom in the hospital cafeteria so we could read more brochures and have a cup of tea before bracing for impact. While we were choosing our Earl Grey tea bags from a collection of soothing blends, we noticed Dr. Davis, still wearing his little surgery beanie and looking exhausted as he waited in line at the carvery station.

"Howard! Come join us. We insist!"

My mom was visibly relieved to have a fresh face in our party, but I sensed Dr. Davis's reluctance. We were no longer the family of one of his most successful patients, the one whose e-mail he passed along to larys looking for purpose in the new normal. We were the caretakers of a marked man.

Dr. Davis pulled out a chair for my mom and then slid into the one beside her. "Ladies. Apologies for my appearance; it was a long night." He had tiny pinpricks of blood on the front of his scrubs.

"Please. Look at *us*!" My mom had pinched-looking wrinkles radiating from her top lip, and she was wearing a massive maroon sweater that belonged to my dad.

"So today is the big day, I heard. I need to stop by and give Ed my best."

"He'd like that." This was a lie. My dad hadn't opened his eyes when a priest came to visit or even his own sister. I had to resist the impulse to tell him that he was being rude, as I would have with my own kids.

"And you're set with . . . whatever you need? The social worker gave you all the information, literature, what have you?"

We nodded yes. We spared Dr. Davis the story of how the social worker chirped cheerfully at my dad, "You're one of the easy ones. Not one complaint!"

To which Will responded tartly, "Yeah, because *he can't talk*."

We chatted for a few minutes, and then my mom surprised me by asking the question whose answer we'd been tacitly searching for in the brochures. "Dr. Davis, I know you don't want to put a number on it, but how long do you think we're talking?"

He rubbed his tired face with an open hand, leaned back in his chair and crossed his arms over his chest. "Joan. That's impossible to predict."

"Just guess," I said, dreading the answer. "So we can pace ourselves. So Will can plan."

"I really can't say."

My mom reached over and cupped her hand around Dr. Davis's elbow. "Howard. We go way back."

"Joan." He cleared his throat. "A month? Two months, at most."

In such a low moment, his humanity was one of our greatest gifts. My mom and I stared at each other across the table. She shook her head slowly; I closed my eyes.

Then my phone buzzed, reminding me to dial into a conference call on workplace ethics. I sequestered myself in the empty hospital chapel and made the call.

•   •   •

The house was dark when we pulled into the driveway. My mom was in the passenger's seat of my minivan and my dad was in the second row, asleep among the soccer cleats and empty Smart Food bags. I shook him awake and guided him up the back steps with one arm around his waist. He shook his head at the new hospital bed and opted to sleep in his favorite recliner instead. My mom and I split a container of cottage cheese at the kitchen table, and then I went home to road test video games while Nicholas boiled spaghetti for Georgie's Strega Nona party the next day. We didn't talk much, but his presence was a comfort. I knew my mom felt the same way about my dad.

To: alicepearse@scroll.com
From: genevieveandrews@scroll.com

Will you be in tomorrow? Please be sure to track your absences in GatheringPlace. A missed half day results in lower productivity, so we need to be sure we account for that, especially as HR is now tracking data from the hand scanners. Thanks.

I rolled my eyes at this one, the evil twin of the message sent by Genevieve to my Gmail account: "Alice, please do what you need to do. I've got your back."

Susanna: Hope the homecoming went smoothly. Just wanted to let you know, Paul & I are bringing over dinner tomorrow. Let us know if you'd prefer lasagna or navy bean soup. Both will be accompanied by bread and salad. I have a key.
Me: Lasagna. Thank you so much.
Susanna: I love you, A. I know you're channeling your inner Winston Churchill.
Me: Keep calm and carry on?
Susanna: When you're going through hell, keep going.

@alicepearse . 1m

"Do any human beings realize life while they live it—every, every
minute?" Thornton Wilder, Our Town

(No retweets, no favorites, two followers lost.)

The next morning, I called my mom as soon as I woke up and she told me
that my dad had slept soundly. He was resting comfortably, watching the
news. They were looking forward to a visit from Linda, their new nurse,
who would give them an overview of what to expect. We joked that there
should be a brochure called *What to Expect When You're Not Expecting
Much*.

Then my mom said, "Let yourself off the hook today, Alice. I think
we're in fine shape."

This was a relief.

21

At Scroll, I received plenty of e-mail but very little real mail—or, I should say, carbon-based mail. A few weeks earlier, I'd been thrilled to receive an invitation to an evening of readings by first-time novelists at the Center for Fiction. This was a place I'd read about in *Publishers Weekly* and heard about from fellow publishing friends, but I'd never been invited to a gathering there before.

The invitation was hanging on the metal shaft of my office lamp with a WWHD (What Would Hamlet Do) magnet. I noticed it when I arrived at work and decided, spur of the moment, to go to the event. I *should* be good to myself, right? So I sent an e-mail to Nicholas, letting him know I'd be out late; then a text to Jessie just in case Nicholas had to work late; then, after some rejiggering of the evening's swim team car pool, I was all set. Not exactly spur of the moment, but a mom's best approximation.

The Center for Fiction turned out to be exactly the kind of high-ceilinged, parquet-floored, book-lined venue I'd imagined it would be. When Matthew, David, and I arrived, the cozy upstairs room was already abuzz with intelligent-looking people who looked like they've been born in a John Cheever story, educated in a Donna Tartt novel, and now lived the full Jonathan Safran Foer life—or so said their tote bags, touting food co-ops and imperiled far-flung outposts of the New York Public Library.

Most of the folding chairs were already taken, so we settled into the second row, directly behind the authors themselves. I felt a soft tap on my shoulder.

"Alice Pearse? Is that you?"

It took a second of rifling through memory files before I placed the woman behind me, but of course, underneath her tortoiseshell glasses and artistically highlighted hair, she was Bonnie, one of my fellow Vermont waitress roommates. She had been an early adopter of recycling. Somewhere on one of my triple-stacked Ikea shelves, I still had her slim, pink-spined copy of Eudora Welty's *One Writer's Beginnings*. I remembered Bonnie canoodling on our sticky velour couch with her college boyfriend, a twinkly-eyed boy—a twin—who had died in the World Trade Center.

In more than fifteen years in New York, we'd never crossed paths before, but I knew from careful scrutiny of the deal announcements in Publishers Lunch that she had migrated to a top spot at a respected literary house.

"You're at . . . ?" Bonnie mouthed hurriedly, as the first author approached the podium. She tilted her head to one side, quizzically, exactly as she had the night I botched the restaurant cash register so badly, I had to forfeit all my tips to the bartender in over-rings.

"Scroll," I whispered.

"*Scroll?* That awesome, super-fancy new bookstore place?"

I nodded and shrugged at the same time. I still wasn't at liberty to go public with the pivot, but it was hard for me to keep up the pretense that we were going to be the Starbucks of bookstores. I now suspected we were going to be the Dunkin' Donuts of video games, with e-books and organic sprinkles.

The readings started. The novels were some of my recent favorites— *The Snow Child*, *Girlchild*, *Seating Arrangements*. Hearing snippets of each one in the voice of its creator was a little bit like meeting the parents of a dear friend for the first time. I settled back between Matthew and David and lost myself in the words, my face relaxing into the same expression my mom wears in church: there but not there, seeing but unseen. Between authors, when the audience clapped politely, I glimpsed back at Bonnie and recognized her rapt look. We'd landed in the right place, a far cry from the shabby restaurant where we'd toasted our bright futures with Zima.

During cocktail hour, the long line for the bar snaked across the front of the room in such a way that my colleagues and I were forced to stand on the raised platform where the writers had waited their turn to read. We were the only guests standing up there, six inches above everybody else, so we only spoke to each other. We had easy access to oversized bottles of Yellow Tail chardonnay, but we were separate from the rest of the crowd in a way that made me uneasy. After a few plastic glasses of wine, Matthew said, "Is it just my imagination, or are people staring at us?"

"Maybe. We're like tributes."

David laughed, and then his face became serious. "Alice, your dad. What's going on with him? I've been meaning to ask."

"He has cancer. He just got out of the hospital—"

We were separated by a pair of women on their way to dismantle the podium; from across the divide, David mouthed, "But he'll be okay?"

I mouthed, "I hope so!" Convincing someone that your parent is *not* going to be okay is such an arduous task.

My gaze fell on Bonnie as she circulated through the crowd, passed like a beloved baby from one cluster of literati to another.

I thought of the back cover of *Highlights* magazine, where readers are invited to circle what's wrong in the picture. I'd circle the three of us.

"Hi, Mommy? This is Margot? Um, I forgot to tell you this morning, but I need a pack of unlined three-by-five notecards for tomorrow. For my oral report on Clara Barton? Don't forget: *unlined*. Also, do we have any red felt? The sticky kind? I need to make a red cross for my apron. And if we don't have the sticky kind, can you sew the cross onto the apron when you get home?"

"Alice, this is your mother. No news to report. Daddy is resting comfortably. I think he's really happy to be home. We'll talk tomorrow."

The 9:37 train was pulling out of the station when I arrived, so I had to wait for the 10:37. As anyone who has spent time there knows, an hour in Penn Station is the equivalent of three hours in charming Grand Central or even generic Port Authority, which at least holds the promise of bathrooms aplenty and the adequate Sedona chicken sandwich from Au Bon Pain. Penn Station offers no such creature comforts. Like a middle-aged, working-stiff Cinderella, I ate my Auntie Annie's pretzel hotdog slumped against the wall.

Then I called Nicholas. He sounded groggy, like I'd woken him up. "Hi, Al. How was your thing?"

"Fun. Guess who I saw?"

"No clue. Who?"

"Remember Bonnie who used to work in the dining hall? She was in our Shakespeare class?

"I think so. She was from Santa Fe?" When he said this, I remembered Bonnie's tote bag from college: a tooled leather number with a flap of Native American tapestry across the front. It was a cut above my Jansport backpack; Bonnie was going places even then.

"That's the one. She was sitting right behind me. She's a really big deal now."

"Well. Good for her. I think you're a really big deal, too, for what it's worth." I could hear him smiling through the phone. "My parents called to see how your dad is doing. They're wondering how they can help. Any ideas?"

"I can't think of anything. I mean, there's so *much* to do, and then on the other hand, there's *nothing* to do. It's surreal."

A young couple walked by, fingers hooked through each other's belt loops. The woman was laughing so hard, she had to stop and hold her stomach. The guy placed a hand on her lower back and rested his forehead on her shoulder so they formed a human pretzel of hysterical glee. When was the last time I laughed like that with Nicholas? I couldn't remember.

"Al, are you still there?"

"Yes."

"Are you okay?"

I sighed. "Nicholas, I miss him already and he's not even gone."

"I know. Listen, I'm waiting up for you. Come home."

When I finally arrived at 11:15—two hours after the Center for Fiction event ended—I stumbled tipsily up the front steps and then had to ice my shin.

As I left the house again to walk Cornelius, I noticed a mug on the porch next to one of our green Adirondack rocking chairs. I leaned over to grab it, and an ashy liquid spilled onto my wrist. The mug was full of cigarette butts—maybe fifteen of them floating in an inch of foul water. I stood there for a minute, looking out at the recycling bin by the curb, knowing it was stacked to the brim with Sam Adams bottles. Nicholas hadn't stopped drinking since our conversation; he'd just gotten more careful hiding it from me. Every night when I kissed him hello, his breath smelled like Aquafresh.

I sat down in the rocking chair, remembering all the afternoons Margot attempted to break the Guinness World Record of hula-hooping (74 hours, 54 minutes) while Georgie napped in my arms in this very spot. Inside, Nicholas turned off lights: kitchen, dining room, sunroom, hallway. Eventually, he poked his head out the front door and said, "You ready for bed?"

I held the mug over my head like an angry Statue of Liberty wearing a dress from Lord & Taylor. "Nicholas, is this Jessie's?" I actually hoped that it was.

He sat down in the rocking chair next to mine, sighing as he landed. "No, it's not Jessie's."

"You're telling me that these are your cigarettes?"

"Some of them, yes."

"So now you're *smoking*?"

"No, not really, I—"

"Wait, *some of them*? Can you tell me who the others belong to?"

"They're Susanna's. She came over after the kids went to bed—"

"Okay. Let me get this straight." I leaned down to place the mug on the floor of the porch. I could hear the blood rushing through my ears. "You're telling me that you and my best friend were sitting here on our front porch, *smoking*, while my dad is in a *chair* six miles away, *dying* from cancer he wouldn't *have* if he *HADN'T SMOKED*?" I spoke between massive, heaving sobs, the kind that sound like hiccups but aren't funny. I leaned down again, picked up the mug, and hurled it over the porch railing and into the yard, where it landed among the skip laurels, stubbornly intact.

Nicholas opened his mouth to speak, but I kept going. "Also? Why is *Susanna* coming over after the kids are asleep? Is there anything you need to tell me?"

He laughed, but not in a nice way. "I'm not even going to dignify that with an answer."

I thought of the couple at Penn Station, how they'd kissed each other for the length of the escalator ride up to Madison Square Garden. If we had a few seconds of downtime, Nicholas and I were more likely to be checking our phones. Still, in my heart of hearts (wherever that is), I knew he wasn't a cheater. He was just a drunk.

"Nicholas, this has *got* to stop. You're drinking and smoking and who knows what else—just *falling apart* at the very moment I need you to— I don't know—be a *man*! You can't be sitting here on the front porch like some good-for-nothing, playing quarters and smoking like a chimney all the time—" I was on a roll and I could have kept going, getting myself more and more riled up, but Nicholas put a gentle hand on my arm.

"Alice. Take a deep breath."

I stopped.

Our neighbors' living room light went off, and I wondered if they were sitting there in the dark, watching us have it out. I'll admit, I've observed their occasional marital spat with interest.

Nicholas started rocking in his chair, eyes fixed straight ahead on the windows of Georgie's classroom across the street. "You're right. I've been drinking too much. I'm not in such a great spot myself, as you know, but I definitely need to cut back. And I will. I promise."

"I thought you were going to cut back after we talked last time and instead you started hiding your beer under the back porch."

He glanced at me, smiling briefly. "I'm not an alcoholic, Alice. I was just too lazy to bring it in from the car and I didn't want to listen to your grief. But you're right. And these cigarettes—"

"Which are *disgusting*, by the way, aside from being completely unacceptable in the home of the daughter of a cancer victim; not to mention Margot being at such an impressionable—"

"*Alice.* Will you just listen for a minute? Susanna brought them over. She stopped by to talk about—well, she thinks the Blue Owl might have to declare bankruptcy, and she wanted my advice. She was pretty upset."

"Fine. Still—"

"She's really in trouble. Even if she can get more customers into the store, she owes quite a bit of money and, honestly, it's not looking good—"

"Yeah, but that's still no reason to be smoking." I was losing steam. I knew Susanna smoked occasionally in her garage; it certainly wasn't her best habit, but who was I to judge? At least Susanna found time to shop for her kids' Christmas presents; I'd delegated this responsibility to Jessie, who tactfully texted from Sports Authority, "Are you sure O wants the LeBron jersey? Pretty sure he had his eye on Chris Bosh."

"Alice, these are tough times. We need to work harder at getting through them together."

I rocked back and forth in my chair. Down the street, the last train of the night idled in the station. *Clang, clang, clang.* It pulled away, heading to the next town.

"Alice? Did you hear me?"

"Yes."

"And?"

"I'm still mad, but I love you."

"I love you, too. I'm sorry."

We went upstairs and this time I didn't push him away when we turned off the light. Fade to black.

22

For the first thirteen years of our marriage, Nicholas and I avoided hosting all major holidays. Actually, we hosted Christmas the year we got engaged, and the whole affair was so egregiously mistimed, we ended up serving the turkey (rare) at eleven p.m.

Now, given my dad's health, we finally decided to take the plunge for Thanksgiving. The conversation went like this:

Nicholas: "Don't you think it would be fun to host Thanksgiving?"

Me: "Who would cook?"

Nicholas: "Me."

Me: "Everything?"

Nicholas: "Can you be in charge of desserts?"

Me: "Homemade chipwiches?"

Nicholas: "Done."

Me: "What about my dad?"

Nicholas: "What about him?"

Me: "What if he can't get up the stairs?"
Nicholas: "Will and I can carry him."

On Thanksgiving morning, Margot bossily supervised Georgie's painstaking lettering of the placecards; Oliver and Nicholas basted the turkey; I made the chipwiches and chocolate mousse, checking my recipes no fewer than fifty times and leaving our first-generation iPad splattered with heavy cream.

As I straightened up the kitchen and unloaded the dishwasher for the final time before the onslaught, I realized I hadn't been alone in this room for months, let alone actually cooked in it. When had Nicholas rearranged the drinking glasses? Or was it Jessie? And when did we get this mysterious yellow plastic contraption that Georgie said was a pineapple corer—and why?

I thought back to a simpler time, to all the afternoons I'd sat at the kitchen table with Cornelius curled at my feet while the kids ate their Earth Valley chocolate chip granola bars after school. The light comes in just so at that time of day, making the kitchen glow in a way that reminds me of the day we first saw the house and knew it would be home. Now I felt like I barely lived here anymore. But at least, since it was Thanksgiving, my phone was quiet. Apparently, even Greg took a break to eat turkey. Or maybe tofurkey.

At the appointed time—actually ten minutes early, as is our way—my brother's Subaru pulled up in front of my house and his family emerged, bearing tin-foiled platters, pie plates, and Pyrex dishes: cranberries, stuffing, bacon-wrapped figs, creamed spinach. A few minutes later, my parents arrived in their Toyota. My mom was behind the wheel—an unfamiliar sight—but even through the windshield I could tell that my dad was better than he had been in weeks. To begin with, he was awake, and he didn't have the usual furrow between his eyebrows, *and* he wore a button-down shirt instead of his usual Georgetown sweatshirt.

Slowly, carefully, my dad made it up our front steps on Nicholas's arm, then smiled warmly at our kids, who clustered nervously in the front hallway. They took a moment to assess his decline since the last time they'd seen him a week earlier, and then—expectations recalibrated—ran out to the yard to play basketball with their cousins.

Mary and my mom were already arguing about how the gravy should be made. All was not exactly right in the world, but at least everyone was under one roof and alive.

The meal was delicious. We abandoned the dining room and instead brought our plates to the living room so we could be near my dad, who was settled in front of the fire. He couldn't eat anything but jotted "Mangia!" on a legal pad when Margot said she felt bad gorging in front of him. It was the first holiday in twelve years when Nicholas and I didn't have to pop up multiple times midmeal to refill a sippy cup or hunt down a missing Dora spoon or produce a peanut butter and jelly sandwich.

I looked around at my family and felt really, truly happy.

Oliver announced glumly, "My homework is to go around the room and say what we're grateful for."

My mom groaned. "Oh, you all know that's not really my speed."

"Mom, he's hardly asking you to bare your soul. Just think of one thing that makes you happy." Even in near-middle age, I recognized the look on Will's face from childhood: trying not to cry. All the adults were determined to keep the mood light, but it was impossible not to trip on the fact that this would be our last Thanksgiving with my dad. The turkey tasted different, carved a little too thick by Nicholas.

Will swallowed hard, his Adam's apple plunging toward the collar of his Patagonia sweater. "Okay, I'll get started. I'm grateful that we're all here, especially this guy."

Margot jumped in next. "Me, too. I'm grateful for Pop."

Then it was Georgie's turn: "For mashed potatoes. For Pop. For Cornelius, even though his breath stinks." She reached down to pat the dog, who hung around waiting for her to drop a scrap of turkey on the floor.

We all looked expectantly at my dad, who pointed his finger straight at my mom. I almost said, "No, it's *your* turn," but then I realized what he meant: *she* was what he was most grateful for. The rest of us nodded, lips pursed stoically, knowing this simple gesture was one of the most romantic of their impressive forty-five-year run.

When the wave of gratitude reached me, I felt the need to lighten the mood. "I'm grateful that I took a big leap this year, and that Nicholas helped me do it. I couldn't be doing this job without him and my fabulous kids."

I smiled at Nicholas, who was nursing a seltzer while rolling a scented pinecone awkwardly on the tablecloth next to his plate. He flashed me a quick grin back.

"Why does everything have to be about your *job* all the time?" Margot's face dissolved into a full-blown snit, and there was an uncomfortable silence. Will might have rolled his eyes, or I might have been overly sensitive. We continued to go around the room, but the moment was gone.

That night, Will and Nicholas helped the cousins extract the wishbone from the turkey carcass. It was a disgusting operation, and I knew my one wish would never come true, so I went down to the basement to make a phone call. It went straight to voice mail: "Hey, it's Jessie. Leave a message after the beep and I'll get back to you."

I leaned against the dryer. "Jessie. It's me. You're probably in the middle of dinner but I just wanted to say thank you. I couldn't do . . . *this* without you." I gestured at the detergent bottles and retired lunchboxes and pairs of crisply drying jeans as if she could see what I was talking about. I really hoped she knew what I meant.

23

Susanna sent a video to my Scroll e-mail with this note: "I know you hate things like this, but promise you'll watch. Just promise. You'll be glad you did."

I clicked play. To the tune of the *William Tell* overture, a woman on a stage launched into all the things she says to her kids every day: *Get up, get out of bed/Wash your face, brush your teeth, comb your sleepy head/ Here's your clothes and shoes . . .*

Oh, sure, I thought; this one went viral years ago. Why had it taken so long to reach Susanna?

We'd had an ugly morning at our house, where I harangued everybody about leaving shoes all over the house and swore I was going to charge one dollar for the return of every item I picked up off the floor. I may have used bad language. I tripped over Cornelius and then yelled at him, too. Two out of three kids had been in tears when I left for the train, and by the time I arrived at the station, I already had a text from Nicholas: "Seriously, was that necessary?"

I pressed play again.

And again.

As I was about to watch the video a fourth time, I sensed eyes on my back. People were staring: Matthew, from his tall chair; and Genevieve from the doorway, where The Mask was hardening—this time with a raised-eyebrow twist.

Because, of course, my headphones weren't plugged in.

Sheepishly, I said to Genevieve, "It's funny though, right?"

"I guess, a little. Maybe if you're forty-five and live in Des Moines."

I was having trouble linking to the ANT drive, where we shared all our files with Cleveland, but after the video snafu I was too embarrassed to ask anyone for help. Usually I tried to spread my technical problems among my colleagues, so as not to impose on anyone too heavily. I'd bothered everyone enough for the day.

"Hello, you've reached MainStreet Computer Services. May I have your name?"

"Alice Pearse."

"Hi, Alice Pearse. Can you read me your twelve-digit IP address? Look under—"

"I have mine memorized. It's—"

"Memorized?"

"I call you guys a lot." I recited the number.

"Great, thanks. What seems to be your problem?"

Take your pick, I thought. "I got a prompt to change my password and now the new one isn't letting me log in."

"Okay, that should be an easy fix. Do I have permission to take over your screen for a second?"

"I wish you would."

"Great. A window will open; just click 'Accept.'"

A few seconds went by. I opened a bag of gummy bears and grabbed a handful, keeping one eye on the screen.

"Hello? I'm sorry to report, I'm not seeing a window."

"Really?"

"Really. The window is not opening."

"Huh."

I fished out all the orange gummy bears—my favorites—even though I'm certain all the colors taste the same.

"Alice? Still no window?"

"I don't see one."

"Can you hang on a quick sec? I think I need to refer your case to my manager."

24

In the new, new normal, my dad slept most of the time and was attended to by hospice volunteers, nurses, and my mom, who tracked his every painkiller and calorie in a Mead composition notebook. The one time I peeked inside, my eye fell on "Changed socks, brushed teeth, 10 a.m." I closed the cover before I fell into the Grand Canyon of heartbreak contained inside.

The first floor of my parents' house was transformed from its familiar mash-up of mission style and Victoriana into a style I thought of as modern healthcare chic. The living room was cluttered with medical equipment on wheels: hospital bed, walker, commode. There were cans of formula stacked in cardboard flats and boxes of gauze pads in all shapes and sizes. The kitchen counters were covered with a buffet of syringes, beakers, binders and of course, brochures. *Your Guide to a Peaceful Death at Home,* and the like. (Was it possible to get extra credit for reading all the literature?)

One day I walked into the house without ringing the doorbell and found my dad getting a sponge bath from Linda, the nurse who drove a

Camaro. He didn't see me, but I saw him. He towered over Linda, still well over six feet tall but frail, with skin draping off his back like ill-fitting curtains. What bothered me more than seeing my dad naked was the way Linda gently wiped the back of his neck with a pink washcloth from my parents' bathroom. The gesture seemed so hopeless, swabbing at that area when the tumor was inches away, impenetrable and tenacious. I imagined it looked like one of the plastic pencil-topping monsters my kids begged for at Filament Stationers: mean and green, with hairy, rubbery tentacles and one beady eye.

Silently, I held up my hand like a stop sign so my kids would stay behind me in the kitchen. I don't know how they knew to be quiet, but they were.

I whispered, "Pop needs a minute," and they followed me, single file, back to the minivan. We sat there for a minute and then went back into the house as if we'd just arrived.

"Hellooo? Anyone home?" I abhorred the forced cheer of my own voice, but I figured levity was the least I could offer my parents, who were getting battered from every angle. As if cancer wasn't depressing enough, their roof was leaking; there was a bucket in the front hallway, collecting drips.

"Alice, is that you? I'm on the phone with the insurance company. I'll be down in two shakes of a lamb's tail!" (Yes, my mom really talks like this.)

Oliver and Georgie made a beeline for the hospital bed, which my dad refused to use. "Let's play doctor and you have a freckle in your armpit!"

"No, let's play pirate! This is our ship."

"No, it's a trampoline!"

"How about it's a pirate ship with a trampoline for pirate babies?" Oliver, ever the peacemaker.

Margot and I rounded the corner and found my dad in his armchair, fully clothed, hair combed but parted on the wrong side. Linda bustled around the room, filling a pillowcase with laundry.

"Hi, Dad." I stood there, awkwardly, arms at my sides. I didn't want to hug him in case he was in pain.

He smiled and closed his eyes.

Margot glanced nervously at Linda; then, as casually as if she was offering a knock-knock joke, she said, "Pop, can I swab your lips?"

He nodded his head, yes. I couldn't watch but made a mental note to tell Nicholas about the easy grace of Margot's gesture. At her age, I would have hidden in a closet with a book, willing myself into another world.

I offered to help Linda, who said, "Just be with your dad. It's good for both of you."

Throwing a load of stoma covers in the washer was so much easier than sitting quietly, which required bravery and patience. My dad was too weak to use Buzz or to maneuver pen and legal pad or even dry erase, so his responses were limited to thumbs up, thumbs down, and the occasional exhausted eye roll. But he did seem to enjoy company, so I kept up a constant steam of commentary about Nicholas, the news, and the weather. I read from the *New York Times* until I was hoarse, skipping the obituaries and avoiding articles with death, illness, or tragedy in the headline.

Eventually the kids got bored and went upstairs to watch *Charlie and the Chocolate Factory* on the iPad. My mom was napping in her room—which is what it was, all of a sudden: just hers.

When I couldn't think of anything else to say to my dad, I placed my hand on top of his on the arm of the chair. In the movie version of this scenario, my dad's hand would have been suddenly dwarfed by mine; in reality, he still looked healthy and freckly from a summer spent watering the garden. In any case, the pose didn't come naturally; we weren't usually affectionate with each other. But this was necessary and comforting—the least I could do. I knew we would never have a final heart-to-heart conversation. He would have no last words. But we did have this: our fingers laced neatly together, everything that needed to be said already said.

I waited for my dad to doze off, and then I studied his face. Bushy eyebrows, dimpled chin, nose a pointier predecessor of my own. Smile lines, worry lines, smooth apple cheeks. For me, memorization was the first stage of grief.

Nicholas stopped by every morning to bring in the paper. Once, my mom called and said, "Your husband is out there in his suit, shoveling snow off the roof." I admired his dedication while secretly worrying he wasn't spending enough time at his new office. No matter how weak my dad was, no matter how far he slipped into a world where we couldn't reach him, one thing remained the same: every night, our red mailbox was filled to the brim with bills. Verizon, taxes, gas, water. Time and money marched on.

There was also the issue of Nicholas's drinking, which still happened every night. Beer was now off the menu—presumably because the bottles were too obvious—so now Nicholas drank vodka tonics that could be mistaken for seltzer from a distance. At dinner, Margot took a sip and said, "Ick, Dad, something is seriously wrong with this Sprite."

He never mixed these drinks when I was in the kitchen, but I could hear the sound of the ice clink in the glass from wherever I was in the house, and my entire body registered the noise. Once I touched a socket that was missing its cover and afterward my whole hand felt tingly for an hour; that's how Nicholas's surreptitious bartending made me feel, only the tingles weren't numbness, they were the simple syrup of rage.

One night when we were brushing our teeth before bed, I said, "You know, I'm not an idiot."

"Excuse me?"

I spit out my toothpaste and stepped aside to let him do the same. "I said, I'm not an idiot."

"What makes you say that? I mean, I know you're not, but why—" He handed me a length of floss.

"You've had three vodka tonics since I got home, and who knows how many before that. You can save yourself the trouble of hand washing the shot glass—I know what you're up to."

"Wow, nice detective work, Alice." He stalked out of the bathroom and into our bedroom, with me trailing like the angry haranguing wife I'd never wanted to be.

"That's all you have to say?"

"Right now? Yes."

I shot him a poisonous look, then sighed as I opened drawer after drawer and realized most of my clothes were downstairs in the laundry room. "Nicholas, I appreciate everything you do for my parents and I'm asking you to do this for me: can you *please* cut back?"

He didn't answer my question. Instead, he tossed one of his T-shirts across the bed. "Here, wear this."

It was the one he wears on our anniversary every year: "I ♥ My Awesome Wife."

Distress Quiz for Family Members of Cancer Patients
During the past week I have . . .

- had trouble keeping my mind on what I was doing.
- had difficulty obtaining a good night's sleep (seven or more hours).
- felt completely overwhelmed.
- felt fearful about the future.
- felt loss of privacy and/or personal time.
- been edgy or irritable or lost my temper with others.
- felt strained between my work and family responsibilities.
- relied on alcohol, cigarettes, or prescription sedatives to manage my stress levels.
- been upset that my relative has changed so much from his/her former self.
- All of the above.

25

We had a new hire named Tracy. Even though I'd been an interviewer on her Chain, I wasn't sure what she did. One day, I poked my head into Tracy's office. "Just wanted to say hi and see how it's going so far."

"Great, I'm drilling down on these new hires in Cleveland. Some are my direct reports and I haven't even met them yet!"

"Well. I'm sure they'll love you." A flash of disappointment: Tracy's use of Scroll lingo didn't bode well for our friendship.

"It's all good. I'm a bottom-up manager, so I'll let them show me what they need. Hey, want a brownie?" Tracy gestured toward a shoebox on her desk. It was lined with wax paper but there were still grease stains along the bottom corners of the box.

"No, thanks. Who sent you a care package?"

Tracy explained that her college roommate in Kansas had baked these brownies so she'd have an icebreaker to help ease her into her first week of work. "Come on, you have to try one."

"Thanks, anyway. But they look delish."

"Seriously, take one. My friend would be offended!"

The truth is, I'd just joined Weight Watchers. I'd gained a few pounds since starting at Scroll—too much sitting in a chair. Even though Tracy and I had already established that we both graduated from high school in 1991, it seemed weird to impose my weight-loss strategies on her at this early date, although I did take it as an indicator of our possible future friendship that she had inspired such loyalty in her brownie-baking friend.

"Alice, you must take a brownie. I insist."

This was getting awkward, so I grabbed a brownie and took a bite and exclaimed that it was the most delectable thing I'd ever tasted. Then I held the rest of the brownie in my hand while I wrapped up the conversation as quickly as possible. Not only did I not want to exceed my daily points value, I was also a little grossed out by not knowing anything about the provenance of the brownie. What if Tracy's friend's cat slept in that shoebox?

The minute I extracted myself from Tracy's office, I headed straight for the bathroom. I had to use it anyway, and while I was there—I don't know what possessed me—I dropped the remainder of the brownie into the toilet. And then, to make matters worse, the toilet wouldn't flush, so I made a split-second decision to abandon ship and just leave it in there. Not the smartest choice.

Imagine my surprise, when I opened the door, to find Tracy standing there in the bathroom with a big smile on her face, waiting to go into the same stall I'd just come out of. "Hello again! Hey, did you see there's a Diane von Furstenberg sample sale . . ."

There were two stalls in the bathroom, and it seemed like a breach of office etiquette for her to proceed into the one I'd just left, but that's what happened.

Tracy's cheerful chatter faded away as I busted out to the hallway as quickly as possible. I couldn't imagine what she thought when she saw the brownie in the toilet. Both alternatives were too embarrassing to contemplate.

•　•　•

"Hey, Margot, guess who I heard from today?"

"Who?"

"Your principal! She wants me to come to the middle school to talk to your classmates on Career Day."

"What did you say?"

"I said I'd love to! I'll take the morning off—"

"Mom, please tell me you're joking."

"I'm not joking. I thought you'd be happy."

"Mom, *are you kidding me?* This is the most embarrassing thing, like, ever. You can't come. You just can't."

"Margot, do *not* speak to me in that tone. I'm coming to Career Day whether you like it or not."

"OMG, I'm going to be *mortified*. Mom, you can't do this to me, I'm begging you. Please."

"I am speaking to your classmates on Career Day. End of story."

"*Mom, you're ruining my life!*"

Cue the door slamming. Wow. Did that really happen? Why, yes. Yes, it did.

I visited the Blue Owl with my kids on a Saturday morning after spinning, looking for excuses to mingle among real books instead of digital files of books. We stocked up on Clementine, Lemony Snicket, Origami Yoga, Camp Confidential—pretty much every book presented to me, I piled by the cash register. Discomfort with my place of employment made me suspend my stringent spending rules.

While Susanna wrapped *Jenny and the Cat Club* (a birthday gift for Georgie's friend), I ran into a woman I knew from Oliver's hip-hop class. She said, "Alice, how funny, I was *just* wondering when you're going to host another meeting of the No Guilt Book Club!"

I cringed, glancing at Susanna, who appeared to be all ears, even from the back.

"That's right, we haven't done one in a while. Susanna and I will have to put our heads together and figure it out."

"Please do. I'd love to come!"

The birthday present was meticulously wrapped in owl paper and topped with a curly green ribbon. Susanna and I avoided each other's eyes as she handed it over. "So what do you think?" I asked. "Should we put a date on the calendar?"

She waited until a pair of arriving customers moved past the cash register and spinning card racks, toward the nonfiction section at the back of the store. Then she answered, "I'm sorry, I can't do another No Guilt night with you, Alice. I have an obligation to the store and—well, you know."

"*Susanna.*"

"*Alice.* This is business. I don't want to collaborate with you here anymore; I'm sorry, it's just too weird. It feels like a deal with the devil."

"So I'm the devil?"

"Scroll is . . . okay, maybe not the devil, but I don't want you in here, scouting for ideas for your stores."

"Is that what you think I'm doing?" My gaze took in the gleaming wood of her shelves, built by Paul, and the peaceful crowd of customers browsing round tables in the center aisle of the store. At a recent meeting at Scroll, we'd discussed the logistics of distributing noise-canceling headphones to all our customers. They'd need them to drown out the din of the video games and the heirloom popcorn machine we'd have in the kids' area. No, I wasn't stealing ideas from the Blue Owl; I was mourning a dream that would never come true.

But I couldn't say this to Susanna. Instead, I grabbed a copy of *14,000 Things to Be Happy About* from a cardboard stand next to the cash register and added it to my pile of things to buy. She rang up the items without meeting my eye.

•   •   •

Georgie's kindergarten teacher, Miss Pasquariello, sent home a monthly calendar so parents could sign up to volunteer in the classroom. When Margot was in the same class, I used to go in and help with "center time" every Monday and Wednesday morning. Hard as it was to squeeze the bump-that-would-yield-Georgie onto the Lilliputian kindergarten chairs, I looked forward to an hour of cutting out snowflakes or helping Margot's classmates form simple sentences using the letter of the week.

By the time Oliver was in kindergarten, I'd reduced my volunteer commitment to once a week—but never was a child so happy to see his mom show up in the classroom doorway! The beatific look of joy on his face almost made up for all the time Oliver spent as a toddler collapsed in a heap on the floor, wrapping his body around my ankles. For years, every time I looked down, I saw a flash of train engineer–striped overalls.

When I received the December calendar from Miss Pasquariello, I decided it was time I took an interest in Georgie's education. I added my name for a Thursday morning, estimating that the forty-minute commitment would land me at work sometime around lunchtime. I made myself OOTO on Outlook and declined an invitation or two for meetings scheduled at that time.

On the morning of my much-anticipated volunteer commitment, I received a text from Genevieve at 7:11 a.m.

> **Genevieve:** You going to the analytics debrief at 11? Please fill me in after.
> **Me:** I have a family obligation at that time.
> **Genevieve:** OK.

To her credit, Genevieve had a healthy respect for the challenges of being a working mom. Once when she ran into me by the elevator at the end of the day, she said, "Now you're off to your second shift."

I smiled appreciatively, feeling like a specimen under glass.

•   •   •

Georgie jumped for joy when I told her I was coming in. She requested a special hairdo (two paths of hair clips leading into braids) and a special outfit (powder-blue tutu paired with pink chihuahua shirt).

Walking the kids across the street to school had become a novelty, and I was surprised by how much more congested our street was now that traffic ran in both directions on North Edison. The street teemed with minivans and Priuses, each bearing oval magnets indicating the memberships, political leanings, and vacation destinations of its occupants: MV (Martha's Vineyard), ACK (Nantucket), OBX (Outer Banks), FUSC (Filament United Soccer Club), SDFC (its rival), a green paw print indicating Panthers swimming (Margot's team), GOBAMA!, COEXIST, and of course the plain A in a sage green circle, indicating allegiance to Louisa May Alcott School.

I stepped gingerly across the street and buzzed at the front door. Just inside the front hallway, I ran into Kara and another mom, who were transforming a bulletin board into a starry backdrop for a collection of projects by second-grade Van Goghs.

"Alice!" Kara leapt off her step stool and gave me a tight hug, demonstrating subtle Bar Method muscle. "What are *you* doing here?"

I ignored the slight—because, truly, I knew it wasn't meant as one—and took an instant to appreciate how pretty these women are, with their well-tended figures and neat, studiously casual clothes. In my too-short color-block minidress, I felt as though I'd arrived at a casual party in costume.

When I walked into her classroom, Georgie was sitting on the floor with her class, listening to Miss Pasquariello read *My Mama Is a Llama.* She ducked her chin shyly when she spotted me. I recognized the kids' sitting position as criss-cross applesauce—not Indian-style; I've spent enough time in kindergarten classrooms in recent years to be aware of this important linguistic shift.

While the kids listened to the last few pages, I stepped over to the window, where there was a string weighted down with pictures clothes-pinned under a sign saying "How My Family Stays Healthy During Cold and Flu Season." I scanned the crayon drawings of people with gigantic heads washing their flipper hands and found Georgie's masterpiece toward the end of the exhibit, half obscured by a spider plant in a twine hanging holder.

Immediately, my cheeks got hot with shame. Georgie's caption, as dictated to Miss Pasquariello: "We stay healthy by sharing toothbrushes." It was true that our dental hygiene had slipped in the past few months; in fact, by recent calculations, we had only three toothbrushes in the rotation. But I had never claimed this was anything but a failure on my part to get to CVS.

I ended up in the school library with Georgie and three other little girls in side ponytails and huge sparkly sneakers. The girls took turns reading *Frog and Toad*, one page each at a snail's pace. When it was Georgie's turn, she caught my eye and smiled. Suddenly, it didn't matter that I wasn't a PTA regular and that I only sent in napkins and cutlery for every school party.

26

If Linda could arrange to stay late on Tuesday nights, my mom still came over to make spaghetti and meatballs for the kids. I tried to let her off the hook, but she insisted. I suspected she was also on the receiving end of constant reminders to do something nice for herself, and ordinary time with her grandchildren seemed to fit the bill.

Our tradition was to have a glass of wine together when I came home from work, but sometimes I was so tired I pretended we didn't have any wine on the premises. One night, my mom helpfully pulled a bottle of red out of her Mary Poppins bag. "Time for a quick slug?"

"No, thanks," I said.

"Seriously? Are you sick?"

"I'm fine, Mom. Just tired."

"This job—Alice, you really need to get some rest."

"It's not just the job. It's—"

"Too much, if you ask me." She wound a scarf around her neck: around and around and around, until it looked like she was wearing a ruffled purple neck brace. "Well. Your meatballs are in the fridge. Make sure you read a good book and get to bed early." This prescription was a constant refrain from my childhood. There was the Holy Trinity we learned about in the CCD program at Our Lady of Agony, and then there was the one Will and I absorbed by osmosis at home: work hard, read a book, go to bed early.

Suddenly, it occurred to me: my mom was a round-the-clock caretaker, yet here she was making dinner for my family. "Wait, Mom, how are *you*?"

She looked exhausted, with new pink pouches under each eye and an unnerving new slump in her shoulders. My dad had taken off his wedding ring for one of his many procedures and now my mom wore it on a chain around her neck. She sighed. "I'm soldiering on."

This response was classic Joan Pearse. Like my dad, she avoided talking about her feelings the way most people avoid root canal or the DMV. "Well, Dad is lucky to have you. You're doing an amazing—"

"Why does everybody say that? He's not 'lucky.' I'm his wife. This is what you *do*, dammit. You take care of each other. He would do the same for me." Her face reddened. Was she thinking what I was thinking? *He'll never have the chance.*

"Mom. I'm so sorry, I didn't mean—"

She shook her head and left without answering, bucket of cooking supplies in one hand and her meatball pot in the other, dangling by one handle. Before her car was out of the driveway, I'd uncorked her wine and poured a large glass for myself.

Employee review season was approaching, so Genevieve briefed me on how it worked. I would solicit six to eight colleagues to deliver feedback on my performance, and I would accept invitations from six to eight colleagues who wanted my feedback on their performance. Feedback would be collected on the basis of innovation, initiative, and inner spirit. Team members would then be ranked according to their performance. The highest performer would receive a bonus in the form of MainStreet stock, and the lowest would be put on a PIP (Performance Improvement Plan).

"Remember, Alice, these evaluations are not a reflection of how much you *like* a colleague. We want the good, the bad, and the ugly, with an emphasis on the final two. Because, of course, that's where true learning occurs." Genevieve's smile flickered on/off, as if it were connected to a light switch.

"Wow, okay. I'd rather share my thoughts in person, but if this is the protocol—"

"This is the protocol. The automated system is more efficient." She clicked out of GatheringPlace and ticked an item off a list on her iPhone. "Hey, how's your dad doing?"

"Thanks for asking, Genevieve. He's home now."

"And?"

"Well, the goal is just to make him comfortable at this point."

(My phone lit up with a text from Jessie: "Margot doesn't want to go to swimming.")

"That's really hard. How are you holding up?"

"I'm just kind of . . . numb, if that makes any sense." (My phone lit up with a text from Margot: "Do I have to go swimming? Pls Mommy? I rly don't feel good.") "As horrible as this sounds, I just wish I knew when . . . how long it's going to be. The uncertainty is exhausting. Do you put your life on hold or do you keep going because this—he could be in this holding pattern for another month?"

Genevieve nodded knowingly. "I mean, I barely remember the very end when my dad died. But it seemed to go on forever, and for a long time that was the only way I remembered him—so, so sick." She stared at a spot on the ceiling and then snapped back to attention, as if she had forgotten I was there. "Does he have the death rattle yet? Your dad?"

"Um . . . I'm not sure what that is."

"It's this terrible sound a dying person makes as they near the end. Like maracas."

"Gee, nobody has mentioned the death rattle. I don't think he has it."

"You'll know it when you hear it. Don't say I didn't warn you."

(Text from Nicholas: "I told Margot she can skip swimming.")

The *death rattle*? Perhaps this was to the end of life as the mucus plug is to the end of pregnancy: a final humiliation nobody warns you about until there's no going back.

I went back to my desk and started soliciting feedback on my performance. "Dear Matthew, I would appreciate your thoughts on my work. Would you mind visiting GatheringPlace to provide an evaluation of my strengths and weaknesses? Thanks for your time. I would be happy to return the favor."

Then, a second message to Matthew's Gmail account: "Matthew, if you leave out the time I cried in our office, I'll leave out the time you gave Genevieve the finger behind her back. Deal?"

To: alicepearse@scroll.com
From: gpasquariello@filament.k12.nj.us

Dear Mrs. Bauer,

Georgie got a little teary in class today and she told me that her grandfather is very sick. I gathered from some of the details she shared that he may be near the end of his life. I told her how my mother passed away yet is still with me always. Forgive me if I've overstepped; I'm not sure of your belief system—Georgie says she is "half Jewish, half Christmas."

My days are always brightened by Georgie's big laugh. I'm certain yours are, too, especially during this difficult time.

Sincerely,
Gina Pasquariello

My first order of business when I arrived for a visit with my dad: before I even ducked my head into the sunroom to say hi, I went directly to the living room, where I examined all the framed photographs on top of the piano. My parents at the ribbon-cutting ceremony for Will's kayak school; my parents on their wedding day; me and Nicholas on the London Eye, with Big Ben in the background; my dad standing next to a home-grown sunflower that came up to his shoulder. Looking at these pictures was like picking a scab: I couldn't stop, but I knew I should try to "stay in the moment," as people kept urging me to do. The past was a gaping black hole with no end in sight.

WINTER

27

Our office holiday party happened in two shifts. The first part took place during the day, when we met in the conference room to exchange gifts. They were to be wrapped and then added to a grab bag. If you didn't like what you got, you could swap with the person on your right. You couldn't swap with the person on your left or across the table. You could not spend more than $10.

These instructions were conveyed to us in a series of e-mails from our office manager, Jane. On the day of the party, she donned a headband of reindeer antlers and spent the morning alone in our blank conference room, hanging red and green lanterns from the ceiling. When the decorating was done, she sent a sternly worded e-mail, instructing us not to peek, even though nobody seemed the least bit interested in peeking.

During phase one of the party, I landed a mug bedecked with the Scrabble tile *S*—for Scroll, of course. Other colleagues opened packs of dry-erase markers, a copy of *Fifty Shades of Grey*, a $10 gift card from Target. I talked to the faux British guy from marketing, who worked the word *zed* into every conversation and dropped the second syllable from the word *literally*. His response to everything I said: "Alice, you are such a pip."

When the rest of us returned to our desks, Jane meticulously Saran-wrapped the mountains of leftover sandwiches, stored them in the office kitchen, and followed up with a series of e-mails reminding us to eat them. The mom in me wondered why we'd ordered so much food, and the employee in me wondered why, if we were all team players, nobody had offered to help with the cleanup.

The evening portion of the holiday party was at a bar on the Lower East Side. The location wasn't easy to find because I came of age in an era when the Lower East Side was off-limits, with the exception of Russ & Daughters on East Houston Street. My time at the party was limited because I had to catch the 6:09 train back to Filament for Georgie's holiday sing-along. (This is not my favorite school event, but one can't really tell one's five-year-old that one would rather be drinking creative cocktails than attending the show a kid has been practicing for since Halloween.)

I positioned myself by the deviled eggs and downed one glass of wine very quickly. Genevieve encouraged me to order another, so I did. She was in a celebratory mood, wearing a feather boa and sipping a Red Stripe.

The room was packed with people who were normally too busy to chat. Suddenly, I was having a great time.

At 5:40, I said my good-byes and slid tipsily into the back of a taxi, which became ensnared in a tangle of traffic.

At 5:58, I looked up and we were still eleven blocks from Penn Station, at a standstill. The taxi driver looked like he wanted to bang his head on the steering wheel.

"Do you think we'll make it to Penn Station by 6:09?"

"No."

"Really? I have to catch a train to New Jersey so I can go to my daughter's holiday show. I have to get there."

"Then you must run." The taxi driver stopped the meter and I handed him a wad of cash. "Run, woman! Run."

I started to sweat. I ran past FIT, past Panera, past American Apparel. I muscled my way through intersections crowded with tourists, weaving around pedicabs and food carts and halal men who in turn dodged dramatically out of my way.

When I finally arrived at Penn Station, I leaned down and unzipped my boots and made the rest of the mad dash only in my navy blue tights. This was no time for a low heel. By the time I plummeted down three flights of stairs to Track 2, the conductor was clanging the bell signaling all aboard and I made it onto the train without a second to spare.

I could feel the sweat trickling down my back, cold inside my winter coat. Every tendon in my neck hurt from tensing forward through the rush. My ribs hurt from the unaccustomed strain of running #thisis38.

I tried to catch my breath but couldn't escape the haunting realization that I'd almost missed Georgie's concert so I could have a second glass of wine. My friends and I are always telling each other not to feel guilty—*ever*, about anything. "Don't go down that road," we say. Because of course if you do, you'll never come back.

If I'd missed that train, there would have been no choice.

I located Nicholas and settled into the hard wooden flip-bottom chair beside his. From behind, I felt a few unidentified hands patting me on the shoulders; someone whispered, "You made it." The lights went down, catching sparkles on the glittery snowflakes circling from the ceiling.

Georgie was in the first row, front and center, wearing a blue and purple shiny dress that had been handed down from Margot, purchased years ago for my mom's sixtieth birthday party. Jessie had styled her hair in the half-up, half-down style, with the up part consisting of tiny, perfect braids.

When Margot and Oliver participated in this kindergarten holiday show, they'd located themselves as far from the limelight as possible, and to the extent that I caught a glimpse of an eyebrow or forehead, I saw just enough to know that they were mortified and miserable up there in front of the whole school. I'd expected the same level of dread from Georgie.

But she was radiant during the show, with a huge smile showing off her Chiclet teeth. She might have been the most delighted kid in the grade. She was resplendent.

I settled back and grabbed Nicholas's hand. There are certain times when you think you might burst from happiness and this was one of them.

We were hosting our fifth annual holiday party, and the dining room table was laden with petit fours, brownies, crab dip, pulled-pork sliders. Normally this is my favorite night of the year, but now I felt like my house was crowded with friends who had committed the unforgivable offense of having healthy parents. I could just imagine the pairs of boomers, strolling the boardwalk together or shaking up a Boggle set with veiny but vital hands.

I scanned the crowd, looking for Nicholas. There was Jessie, every inch the cool rocker chick in a leather minidress, tattoos glowing in the candlelight as if in Technicolor. She was deep in conversation with Susanna, who took a long sip of Kim Crawford sauvignon blanc, her favorite. From the concerned looks on their faces, I suspected they might be talking about me.

I found Nicholas on the back porch, using a long pair of tongs to break up bags of ice. I grabbed Oliver's soccer hoodie from a hook by the back door, stepped outside, and closed the door behind me. The porch should have been romantic—strung with fairy lights, a dusting of snow on the floor—but I had a funny feeling in my stomach. Not worry, exactly; more like homesickness, even though I was in my own home, surrounded by beloved people.

"Hi."

"Hi. You look pretty." I wore a red dress—too tight, too short, the best I could do. I'd found it at the back of my closet while browsing for clothes to wear to my dad's funeral.

"Thanks. I just overheard Tim and Bill talking about your tournament—by the way, they ate all the Swedish meatballs. Anyway, it sounds like you guys have a lot of fun stuff planned."

Behind us, the bathroom light went on. Through the window, we saw Margot in front of the mirror applying . . . was that *lipstick?* Top lip, bottom lip, fake pout. She seemed to know exactly what she was doing.

"What tournament? The Atlantic City one?"

Nicholas's response confirmed that something was off. Why was he stalling for time?

"Um . . . is there another tournament I don't know about?"

"Alice, we play every Sunday night. Sometimes games; sometimes tournaments. I don't always tell you which is which."

Nicholas was certainly putting a lot of muscle into the ice. When he looked up, he stared blankly through the porch screen to the swing set, now covered in snow. An empty swing set is one of the most tragic sights in the world; even before we surprised our kids with this one, we agreed to rip it out the minute they lost interest.

I sighed. "Nicholas. We're getting off the subject. Tim and Bill were talking about the Atlantic City tournament and it sounded like they were saying something about meeting up with a bunch of girls."

"I have no idea if that's part of the plan. I'm just going for the basketball."

"Nicholas—"

"Why do you keep saying my name? I know you're talking to me."

"Fine. My point is, do you really want to be involved in this thing if those guys are going to pick up . . . women?"

"Who cares if they're picking up women? It's none of my business."

"It doesn't make you uncomfortable that these guys aren't . . . *loyal?* I mean, the conversation they were having was pretty gross. And when they realized I was listening, they stopped talking, which led me to believe they expect you to be part of their plan."

In my peripheral vision, I noticed Margot heading for the back door. It figured; our kids have strong radar for arguments and scandals. The less I want them to have certain information, the more determined they are to seek it out. And they'll innocently follow up later, in front of my mother or one of their teachers: "Mommy, what did Daddy mean when he called that guy a juicebag?"

"Alice. I am not having this conversation with you. I've never given you a reason not to trust me. Ever. I'm going to this tournament. I deserve this after all I've done around here in the past few months."

There were many problems with this response. Nicholas was right: he's never given me reason to doubt him, but what did he mean about *everything he'd done* in the past few months? Had I not been doing all those same things for him?

"Nicholas. It's not like I've been sitting around eating bonbons."

(Why do people always go with the bonbon example? Has *anyone* actually sat on the couch eating bonbons, *ever?*)

I wished I could find a way to articulate my freezing-cold trudge to the train station and then the twenty-five-block windy walk from Penn Station to my office. (Of course I'd crunched the numbers—the long trek through midtown was faster than the subway followed by a shorter trek along the windy base of Central Park.) While Nicholas was snug in his Accord listening to the *BBC Newshour*, I was wrapped in two scarves, wearing supposedly attractive snow boots, puzzling together the day's news from the block-long ticker in Times Square. Ninety minutes, door-to-door. You could lose your mind on this commute.

"Yes, I get that and I've been supportive every step of the way. But when I tell you I need a break—"

"And I'm *giving* you a break!"

"What do you mean, you're *giving* me a break? Like you're my boss? I'm—"

The back door opened, bringing with it light, a rush of warm air and faraway laughter. "You *guys*. All you do is fight."

"Margot—"

We both said her name at the same time, but I won. "Lovey, please stay out of this. Daddy and I are having a conversation—"

"Yes, I heard you giving him a hard time." She gestured at the house behind her. "Mommy, tonight is supposed to be *fun*."

I glanced to Nicholas for reinforcement, but instead of coming to my defense in parental solidarity, he looked tickled to have someone on his team.

"I was *not* giving him a hard time. You know what, Nicholas? Let's talk about this later."

"Great. Let's do that."

28

The floor of the quiet car was slippery with dirty, melted snow, so you couldn't put your bag on the floor. I sat with my Orla Kiely tote on my lap, and on top of that a massive, crinkly paper shopping bag from Old Navy, filled with the winter's second round of hats and gloves for each kid.

Someone's phone was ringing and I was about to join the disgruntled crowd—"This is the *quiet* car!"—when I realized the ringing was coming from my bag. The caller was my mom. I sent her directly to voice mail and then listened to the message: "Alice? I think you need to come home."

I dropped my backpack in the hallway and kissed each of my kids. Georgie was sitting on the bottom step, freshly bathed and smelling like Suave. "Tell Pop I'll save him a seat," she whispered.

"He knows," I whispered back, perplexed but touched by her promise.

I reversed out of the driveway so quickly, I ran over a hockey stick and a snow shovel.

I called Nicholas from the car and reminded him that we needed

to bake cupcakes in ice cream cones for Oliver's class party to celebrate the conclusion of the second-grade read-a-thon. "The cones I
bought don't have the recipe on the back, but I'm sure you can find it at
BettyCrocker.com," I barked into my phone, pausing at a stoplight to
rifle through the glove compartment to make sure I had a spare contact
lens case.

"I'll take care of the cupcakes; please don't worry." Nicholas's voice
was husky. "Alice, do you think this is it? I just saw him this morning. He
flashed me a peace sign when I left."

I checked the rearview mirror before switching lanes but still managed to cut off a driver who then leaned on his horn and honked at me for
the next half mile.

"I have no idea. On one hand, he's suffered enough. On the other—
well, the other hand is unimaginable." My eyes filled, but I didn't trust
myself to lift a hand to wipe them. The angry tailgater was still in close
proximity, now with a hairy middle finger thrust out his window in the
direction of my minivan.

"Alice, remember: I adore you."

"I adore you, too."

A scalding hot tear slipped down my cheek.

I stood in the ocean, chin-deep, worn out from treading water. I faced
a massive wave, gathering speed as it rolled toward shore. I took a deep
breath and dove into the middle as the water crested over my head.

Be brave.

Every light in the house was on when I arrived. Electric Christmas candles still shed their garish orange light in each window. My dad was in his
chair, feet propped on a leather ottoman, with his head tilted back and his
mouth open. He was wearing a yellow short-sleeved shirt and powder-
blue Carolina shorts in mesh. He didn't look like he was in pain, but he

also didn't appear to be entirely present, either. He had lost a lot of weight since he'd come home from the hospital. Now all of a sudden, he looked puffy.

"His kidneys are shutting down," Linda explained. "Honey, it won't be long."

My mom and I just stood there, staring at each other and then back at my dad.

Linda was on her way out, but she had a lot of instructions for us, as if we were preparing for a home birth. "This binder will walk you through what will happen. Remember, it's the most natural thing in the world. Should you have any questions or concerns, here's the number you can call, day or night, and hospice will advise you. There will always be someone at the end of this line. If he passes, you should call this number. If he appears to be in any pain, you should give him that shot from the fridge. I don't think he'll need to use the toilet, but I've put a wee-wee pad under him just in case."

A *wee-wee* pad? I tried to catch my dad's eye, expecting to trade mortified smirks, and then remembered . . . Oh. He wasn't in any condition to share private jokes.

I wanted Linda to leave, and I couldn't believe she was leaving.

When it was just my mom and me—which was how it felt, suddenly—I called my brother, who answered on the first ring. "Alice. How's Dad?"

"He . . . he really doesn't look good."

"Do you think I should get in the car and drive down there now?" By this point, it was eight o'clock.

I took the phone in the coat closet since I suddenly felt rude having this conversation within earshot of our dad. "Yes."

"You think I should drive down now?"

"Yes." It wasn't like Will to seek my counsel; I had the queasy feeling of being in over my head.

"I'm just thinking out loud. Mary is on call. If I drop the kids at her mom's, they can all drive down together in the morning, and I can be there in seven hours with no stops. Do you think—?" A rough sob ripped through the phone. I pictured my brother and our dad, listening to a Mets game on a small transistor radio in the backyard, their fists pumping in the air every time Keith Hernandez hit a homer. Will was the only person who knew the secret ingredient in our dad's recipe for Irish soda bread.

"I think that's a good plan. I'm staying over . . . in case."

"How's Mom?"

"She's making lists. She's listening to opera and sitting with him right now."

"Okay. Listen, I should—"

"Be safe, Will."

"You, too."

I put my hand on top of my dad's wide, warm head and I told him I would see him in the morning. He nodded weakly. Then I went upstairs to check my e-mail.

To: alicepearse@scroll.com

From: genevieveandrews@scroll.com

Alice, I know your plate is full right now but Greg wants answers on MMO and GO. Please finalize your white paper and drop a date on his calendar to present it to him via teleconference. It is imperative that we demonstrate commitment in the gaming space.

29

That night, asleep in my childhood bedroom, I dreamed Nicholas and I were renting our own beach house on Long Beach Island. When we went to collect the key from the real estate agent, we learned that we'd actually rented a houseboat by mistake. It was a huge sloop, with billowing sails and a slippery, varnished deck. Our kids skittered all over the place while we tried to figure out how to steer the unwieldy vessel into Barnegat Bay.

Suddenly I noticed my dad sitting in a lawn chair next to the old-fashioned wooden steering wheel—the same yellow and white chair that left checkerboard patterns on the back of his legs every summer. He was reading the *New York Times*, with the newspaper covering his face, but I heard him say in his deep, familiar voice: "You guys will figure out the way. It just takes time."

When I opened my eyes, my mom was sitting on the edge of my bed. Maybe she was there to wake me up so I could squeeze in a little studying before a Spanish quiz. *Hablo, hablas, habla, hablamos, hablan.*

Or was there an early student council meeting?

Then, I knew.

We stood together by my dad's chair: me, my mom, my brother. Will's coat was still on, his hands still holding a chill from outside. I held them in my hands and choked out, "He hung on for you."

Will nodded, his lips tightly pursed, eyes glassy with tears.

Our mom's white hair commingled with our dad's salt-and-pepper curls as she leaned over, kissed him on the forehead, and said, "Good night, sweet prince."

Will said, "Bye, Dad."

I said, "I'll miss you every, every day."

It was the most gut-wrenching moment of my life so far, and also the most peaceful.

The future stretched in front of us like a long road.

To infinity and beyond.

I glanced at the clock in my mom's kitchen—it was all hers now. Four fourteen. Was it too late—or too early—to call the number at the back of Linda's binder? I dialed, haltingly, and a nasal voice answered: "Hospice. North Jersey. Reason for your call?"

"Hi. I'm calling because my patient . . . died."

"Patient name?"

"Edward Pearse."

"Middle initial?"

"V."

"Patient number?"

"Sorry?"

"Last four digits of patient's social?"

I handed the phone to Will.

• • •

My conversation with Nicholas happened in split screen: on one side, my husband leaned against our kitchen counter, left elbow in right palm, left hand on his forehead, massaging new worry lines and wiping his eyes; on the other, he was twenty-four and my dad pumped his hand up and down, up and down, right after their first Scrabble game. Nicholas was the winner, but my dad was the one who looked victorious. He had hit the jackpot of future sons-in-law and he knew it.

The gears shifted. We were on a conveyor belt, moving down a prescribed path toward the gaping maw of whatever came next.

The undertakers arrived. One of them was a puffed-out, grown-up version of a boy from the maintenance crew at the pool. I remembered him in a Co-Ed Naked Lacrosse T-shirt and Umbros; now he jingled change in the pocket of pleated khakis. "Are you . . . ?"

I reached out a hand, literally over my dad's dead body. "Alice. Mike, right?"

"Alice, I am so sorry for your loss."

Standing there barefoot in my mom's flannel nightgown, I had the sinking sensation that I might have hooked up with this guy behind the snack bar, wedged between two chlorine tanks. Didn't he have a goatee back then? Was there more to it than kissing? *Come on, nobody can see us.*

Mike and his sidekick warned me not to watch them work, but I watched.

As their minivan hearse drove down the hill, I glanced out an upstairs window and saw a cluster of neighbors at the end of a driveway across the street. They were in bathrobes, shaking their heads, with newspapers in blue plastic bags dangling from the same hands that once doled out my Halloween candy and babysitting money.

Ed Pearse. A good man. One of the best.

• • •

Nicholas arrived with our kids and Judy and Elliott. Later, as they efficiently disassembled the hospital bed and tucked my mom in under an afghan for a nap, I did the math and realized that my in-laws had driven through the night from Cleveland to be with us. I never asked how they knew it was time to come.

The kids eyed me nervously, as if I had a strange new haircut they couldn't quite get used to. I knew Nicholas had already told them about my dad.

Oliver looked me square in the eye and said, "Mommy, we're all really sad."

"I know, lovebird. I am, too."

Margot said, "Wherever Pop is, I bet he's talking a *lot*."

"I'm pretty sure he is."

Georgie pointed at the empty penny loafers by the back door. "Mommy, Pop forgot his shoes!"

I sat down at the kitchen table and cried through an entire box of Kleenex.

To: scrollglobal@scroll.com
From: genevieveandrews@scroll.com

I regret to inform you that Alice Pearse's father, Edward V. Pearse, passed away this morning after a courageous battle with throat cancer. He was 69. On behalf of our team, I will send an Edible Arrangement to the family.

I was on the Scroll Global list, of course, so the reply-alls rolled in. Responses included but were not limited to:

Thanks for letting us know, Genevieve.
Our Cleveland team is thinking of your New York team today.

Do you have a sense when Alice will return to work?

Do we know where Alice was on her evaluation of this week's GO list?

Poor Alice. Any idea if he smoked?

The food was breathtaking. Trays of fried chicken, cold cuts, and deli sandwiches; Pyrex casserole dishes accompanied by heating instructions for ziti, lasagna, quiche, shepherd's pie, moussaka; towers of brownies, lemon squares, rugelach, linzer torte. One well-wisher left a gigantic, shivery bowl of tapioca pudding on the back steps, and the dry cleaner dropped off a blender. ("Gee, eyeballs and smoothies. That's *my* idea of comfort food," said Will.) Judy covered these offerings with pink Saran wrap and arranged them in the refrigerator with military precision. We ate and ate and ate, and we were still starving.

The line for the wake snaked out the door of the funeral home and into the parking lot of the CVS next door. I stood in the center of an arc of intimidating, sash-bedecked flower arrangements with Will and my mom while Mary and Nicholas took turns keeping an eye on the kids, who toppled a watercooler during a game of leapfrog.

Waves of people rolled in, with no rhyme or reason to the order of their arrival. Will's former drum teacher walked in on the heels of my dad's first cousins; a dry-eyed great-uncle knelt on the prayer bench alongside my dad's barber, whose sobs were audible from the ladies' room. My college friends chatted with three of my dad's sisters, while my mom's brothers mingled with a town councilman my dad had never liked.

There were a few surprises: a stranger who said he'd shared a paper route with my dad in 1954 (he slipped my mom his business card in case she needed a life coach); a Town Car full of *You* editors ("Your friends are *hot*," said my cousin, eyeing their long legs and stilettos); a high school friend who had visited us one summer on Long Beach Island ("Your husband encouraged me to go to law school," she told my mom. "Now I'm a federal judge.") Great, I thought. And I'm peddling video games for a living.

Everyone offered a variation on the same lines: *I'm sorry to see you under these circumstances, I'm sorry for your loss, He put up a good fight, He's in a better place, If there's anything I can do . . .* My favorites were the ones who went off script: *He made a helluva martini* or *Ed Pearse was no-bullshit* or *He was a cheap son of a bitch.* For the most part, I was on autopilot, but I almost lost it when my dad's brother held on to my elbow and leaned down to whisper, "He was one proud father."

Mike materialized from behind a vase of calla lilies as I was leaving the funeral home.

"Alice?"

"Yes?"

"I just wanted to let you know—"

"Yes?" I didn't mean to be impatient, but Nicholas was waiting in the car and I felt gutted by the day. My feet were sore and my face was exhausted from the effort of wearing an appropriate expression for four hours.

"Um, I don't usually say this to families of people I've worked on but—" *Worked on?* The image was too gruesome to contemplate. "I mean, what I'm trying to say is, I knew your dad. I remember him from the pool."

"Really?"

"Wasn't he the dude who used to sit by the diving boards? Smoked a pipe, got super tan?" Mike shifted from foot to foot. Under the bright overhead light, I could see the smooth pink of his scalp.

"That was my dad." Past tense.

"He was a cool guy. A good listener."

"Really?" I learned this later; when I was a teenager, I couldn't be bothered to give my dad anything to listen to. In fact, most times when he came to the pool, I pretended I didn't know him.

"Yeah, I bummed a light off him one day and he told me I should quit smoking. We got into this whole conversation about money. About how people should spend what they have, not rely on credit. Dude was frickin' *smart*."

I smiled. That sounded like my dad. "So, did you quit?"

"I did. Cold turkey. Switched to dip, but that's it." Mike bowed awkwardly, one hand on his tie, which was printed with a dizzying pattern of dice. "Well. I just wanted to let you know. My best to you and your family."

He disappeared behind a door marked Employees Only.

I thought, if only my dad had followed his own advice.

I hadn't been on the altar at Our Lady of Agony since my days as a very reluctant acolyte—a stint that ground to a halt one Sunday when I accidentally poured red wine instead of water over a monsignor's hands. Now I was in the oak pulpit, eight feet above the rest of the congregation, eulogizing my dad with Will.

We took turns leaning into the microphone. As he described our dad's other religion—justice—I scanned the packed pews. There was our mom, regal in ivory lace; and Judy, Elliott, and Dr. Davis, Linda, Jessie, and dozens of Filament friends, including Susanna and Paul and their kids. Despite my poor attendance at their meetings, the entire executive board of the Louisa May Alcott PTA was there. Our relatives were easy to pick out since they all had snow-white hair and wore matching expressions of concern on their gentle faces. Even in grief, the elderly Irish look like they're smiling; my aunts and uncles were no exception.

In the middle of the church, three rows were packed solid with men and a handful of women in gray and navy suits. They were partners from my dad's law firm—litigators and tax lawyers and bankruptcy specialists whose names (last names only) had been legendary at the dinner table when I was growing up. I recognized some faces, mainly my dad's contemporaries, who had also been hired fresh out of law school in the late sixties: Curley, Progresso, Rankin, Marcus.

I remembered these men from visits to my dad's office. But despite their chumminess with him for nearly forty years, they'd been largely absent from his retired life and invisible during the past few months. Maybe it turned out that they had nothing in common beyond the law, or maybe they lacked the wherewithal to participate in conversation with someone who sounded like an automated recording, but their disappearance had been notable, and disappointing. These lawyers were the people who had spent the most time with my dad during his best years.

I knew, beyond a shadow of a doubt, that I would never see them again after his funeral.

Will motioned for me to step up to the microphone. My turn. I started: "Our dad was the first person in his family to graduate from college. From an early age, he instilled in us a sense of . . ."

As I talked, my eye fell on a familiar but incongruous woman at the back of the church. I blinked, hard, and my mouth went dry. She was backlit from the light pouring through the front door into the dim sanctuary. It was hard to make out her face, but yes, that *was* Genevieve leaning against the wall even though there was plenty of room to sit. She was dressed in full-body black—wide-legged trousers, double-breasted blazer—with the exception of a black-and-white striped boat-necked shirt that lent a sort of Marcel Marceau air to her getup.

Why was she here? And what was that thing on top of her head? For one brief, cringing moment, I thought Genevieve had a bird in her hair— not entirely beyond the realm of possibility since I remembered how birds occasionally got trapped inside this church—but then I realized: she was wearing a fascinator. Yes. A small, black, feathered number, perched atop her head at a rakish angle. Odd choice, I thought, before turning my attention back to my notes.

When I glanced over my shoulder after Communion, she was gone.

One by one, the guests left my mom's house. They promised to check in soon and made us promise to let them know if there was anything they could do.

News flash: nobody is going to give you an assignment. Just *do something*.

Amy, the daughter of one of my mom's tennis friends, worked quietly in the kitchen, sleeves rolled up, brewing pot after pot of strong coffee and stowing Mass cards and sympathy cards in a straw basket so my mom could read them later. Even though our mothers had been friends for decades, we weren't friends; she'd been a few years ahead of me in school. Up until this point, most of our contact had been through families she'd babysat for, whom she passed along to me when she lost interest in watching *227* alone on Saturday nights. I knew Amy was a teacher now, and the mother of toddlers, which meant that she'd lined up both a sub and a babysitter of her own so she could take coats and arrange crudité platters for our family. Her kindness was mind-boggling.

"I hope my kids grow up to be like Amy," I said to Will.

"Looks like they might take after me." He gestured with his chin at Georgie, who was running around the living room with a coffee stirrer dangling from each nostril. We both laughed, then exchanged a guilty look, then dissolved into hysterical giggles the likes of which we hadn't shared in thirty years.

We polished off the last of the cheesecake and pressed our index fingers onto the dessert trays to pick up stray crumbs from lemon squares.

Later, my brother and I drank Bailey's, paged through albums filled with Polaroids, and traded favorite family stories. I told Will about the drive our dad had taken me on the night before I left for college. "Where are we *going*?" I'd asked, annoyed to be missing a barbecue at the home of a friend whose parents could be depended upon to serve wine coolers. My dad pointed to the parkway sign nearest our house: "Exit 142A. Remember that. People will want to know."

"Typical." Will laughed softly and shook his head. "Remember the time we went to the top of the Empire State?"

I nodded; of course I did. It was a blisteringly hot Sunday, a day the two of us would have preferred to play Marco Polo in the deep end of the pool, but our parents insisted on a pilgrimage to the city. When we arrived at the observation deck, Will and I begged for quarters for the coin-operated binoculars, then took turns trying to spy on people in other tall buildings. The unspoken—and unrealized—goal was to spot someone naked.

Just as the binoculars were about to go dark, we reluctantly ceded them to our dad, who swiveled the eyeholes in the direction of the Weehawken waterfront. Will and I burst out laughing. What a waste of money! There was nothing to see on the other side of the river except a rusty Colgate Palmolive clock and the site of a duel between Aaron Burr and Alexander Hamilton. (We never learned about the Vietnam War in grade school, but we studied this duel every year, often with a reenactment in period garb.)

When we had collected ourselves, Will zipped up his Members Only jacket and said, "Dad, why would you want to look at *New Jersey*?"

Our dad shrugged, straightening his glasses. His answer was matter-of-fact, as always. "New Jersey is home."

Then I stepped up to the viewfinder, but there was nothing left to see. Our time was up.

The next morning, Margot helped me carry extra folding chairs out to the garage. As we were stacking them against a wall printed with raccoon paws, I noticed boxes of tulip and daffodil bulbs my dad had been too weak to plant in the fall.

He must have known then, I realized. Had he been scared?

Judy and Elliott wrapped my mom in a three-way hug, then started the long drive home to Cleveland. We said good-bye to Mary, then to Will, who squeezed his eyes shut and shook his head rapidly when my mom thanked him for all he'd done. Then the two of us stood in the driveway, waving until the Subaru was out of sight.

The yard was quiet. We dropped our arms to our sides. It was all over, but of course it wasn't. Not even close. The hardest part was just beginning.

30

To: alicepearse@scroll.com

From: genevieveandrews@scroll.com

I'm sorry I didn't get a chance to talk to you after the service. I'm glad I
could be there for you. Your family seems very sweet.

The same people who were so insistent that I should do something
nice for myself when my dad was sick were now adamant that I should
take all the time I needed before returning to reality. Unfortunately, none
of them worked at Scroll, where there were no bonus days for bereave-
ment, and the digital clock on GatheringPlace indicated that I'd exceeded
my time-off allowance.

Among my 822 unread e-mails, I found one from Human Resources
instructing me to file a trouble ticket for my unexplained absences or
risk being docked pay. The trouble ticket drop-down menu didn't include an option for "death in the family," so I filed my explanation

under "other/medical" and sent an e-mail to my team, saying I'd be back in on Monday.

"Really?" said Nicholas. "Alice, so what if they dock your pay? You need to take care of yourself."

"No, it's fine. It'll be good to get my head back in the game."

My eyes had been excruciatingly sensitive to light, and my vision was blurry even with contact lenses, so I made an appointment with my eye doctor on the morning of my first day back. Dr. Mandelbaum lowered his equipment to my face and asked me to put my chin on a perch lined with tissue paper.

"Your ophthalmologist sister-in-law is correct: you do indeed have two scratched corneas, my friend. No contact lenses for a week, be sure to wear sunglasses when you're in bright light, and I'll give you a prescription for drops to apply three times daily." He snapped off his rubber gloves and started scribbling on a little blue pad.

"Okay," I said, already dreading appearing in public in my cat-eye glasses, which had been cool on Lisa Loeb circa *Reality Bites*. "Can you tell me how this might have happened?"

"Any recent trauma to the eyes?"

"Not that I can remember."

"Any significant stress you can think of?"

I sighed. "Well, my dad just died."

Dr. Mandelbaum looked up sharply from his ablutions at the sink. "That'd do it." He glanced quizzically at my chart. "He must have been quite young."

"He had cancer years ago and it came back."

"My word, that is terrible news. You take good care, okay?"

I promised I would, and then sat there alone in the dark, tears leaking from behind my burning eyes, as Dr. Mandelbaum's voice boomed in the next exam room: "What seems to be the problem?"

• • •

When I arrived at my office, the team was gathered in the conference room for a meeting that wasn't on my calendar. Matthew gestured to the seat next to him and touched my shoulder briefly when I sat down. "Glad to have you back. Lunch?"

"I'd love that."

The TV monitor flickered to life and there were the Clevelanders, lined up at a table like judges at a spelling bee. Greg gave a mock salute and said, "Alice. Glad you're up and running."

"I'm glad, too."

Except I wasn't really up and running: my eyes were watering and stinging so badly, I could hardly keep them open. Reluctantly, miserably, I leaned down to my backpack, withdrew a pair of giant black sunglasses, and put them on over my regular glasses. Dr. Mandlebaum's assistant had pressed them on me along with the receipt for my co-pay. ("Hon, I insist.") I'd resolved on the spot to tough it out until the drops did the trick, but my eyes didn't stand a chance in the fluorescence of the conference room.

When I looked up again, everyone was staring at me—including Genevieve, whose eyes suddenly looked bright, alert, and youthful. "Sorry. Minor eye injury."

Greg's voice filled the room even though he was halfway across the country. "So, Stevie Wonder, you want to get started?"

"Get started?" I glanced desperately at Matthew. What was this meeting about, anyway?

Genevieve snapped to attention, glancing nervously at the big screen. "Yes, Alice, we're eager to hear your three most innovative ideas for how our lounges can exceed customer expectations."

"My three most . . ."

"Innovative ideas, yes. Did you not get the ask? I sent it last week."

Talk about baptism by fire. It was bad enough to be wearing two pairs of glasses. Now I was completely unprepared?

I considered winging it, but I was in no condition to improvise. Matthew's hand found my knee under the table, a vote of confidence.

This was all too much. My eyes smarted.

"Alice? Would you prefer for us to begin with another team member?"

"I . . . I don't have any ideas."

"*None?*" Greg's booming laugh vibrated the glass in our windows.

"I'm so sorry, Greg, Genevieve." I pushed the glasses and sunglasses up on my nose. "I'm not prepared for this meeting. You should come back to me another day."

Matthew leaned in to the diamond-shaped speaker at the center of the table and started talking. While everyone else's attention shifted to him, Genevieve's eyes remained on my face. Her face reddened as she stared at me with a look of confusion, then annoyance, then rage. The Mask. From behind my dark lenses, I stared right back.

Genevieve never mentioned the funeral in person; neither did I. After the disastrous meeting, she gave me a wide berth, but she did send me a terse e-mail that alluded to having a conversation about "deliverables" at our next 1:1.

When I walked by David's desk, he said, "Welcome back, Alice. Feeling better?"

"Yes, thanks." I paused. "Wait. You know my dad died, right?"

"Yes! Sorry, I just didn't want to remind you. Did you get the Edible Arrangement?"

"We did—thanks." Translation: it sat in the middle of the dining room table for three days and nobody touched it.

"Nom, nom, nom, right?"

"Yeah, definitely." Translation: "Actually, not so much. Pineapple impaled on a toothpick doesn't make anybody feel better, ever."

Matthew requested a thorough debrief on the events of the previous week, down to the specifics of my dad's final hours: "I mean, did you *know* it was the end?"

"Yeah. Pretty much."

"Were you scared?"

"No."

"Did he have any final wishes?"

"It never came up, Matthew."

"Any regrets?"

"My dad? Actually, he said he wished he'd eaten more."

Matthew took a big bite out of a jelly doughnut, sprinkling the front of his shirt with confectioner's sugar. "A man after my own heart. So, what's your mom going to do now?"

"I don't know. She's pretty exhausted from the past few months. She'll probably take it easy, she has a lot of friends . . ."

"Will she sell the house?"

"Oh, I don't think so. Nicholas is sorting out the estate. I think she'll be fine."

Matthew swiveled his chair back to face his computer monitor. "Well. If she's looking for something to do, Starbucks is always hiring. Lots of retirees go that route."

"I'll keep that in mind, thanks."

On the train home that night, I fell into such a deep sleep, I missed my stop. When I stumbled off in Upper Filament, bleary-eyed and disoriented, Susanna pulled up alongside me. "Hop in, I'll take you home," she said, lifting bags of takeout Chinese off the passenger seat. She cupped her hand around the back of my neck and we drove back to my house, listening to Norah Jones sing "Come Away with Me" on Lite FM. I made no attempt at conversation and that was okay.

Dear Alice,

You've been on my mind constantly since last week. On the way back into the city, the *You* girls and I were saying your dad must have been an

amazing man, considering how well you turned out. Will doesn't seem
so bad either; he's definitely got that sage outdoorsman thing going on.
And your mom! She had a million people to talk to, yet somehow found
a chance to tell me the story of your parents' engagement. I love that *she*
was the one who popped the question.

I have no idea what you're going through right now, but I'm certain the
Pearses and the Bauers will carry you safely to the other side. I'm here,
too; don't forget.

Love to Nicholas and the menagerie,
Annika

I slowly closed the embossed card from my former boss at *You*, taking
a moment to appreciate her artistic handwriting. It amazed me how some
people knew exactly what to say.

I felt like I'd been in a holding pattern for so long, I needed to snap
back into action with a vengeance. Unfortunately, the effort of doing so
left me dizzy and disoriented. Also, the world looked monochromatic, as
if a primary color were missing from the spectrum.

Now that the formal machinations of mourning were behind us, we
had to navigate on our own.

31

The middle school principal was depending on me for Career Day, so I went. Even I was bored by my presentation, which focused heavily on Scroll's pastries and cold-pressed juices. I still didn't have the green light to let anyone know we would be selling video games; at least among tweens, I'm sure this news would have been warmly received. I talked about how I'd always loved to read, how I used to try to sell books to my own family, so the job at Scroll really was a dream come true. Yawns all around. One kid whipped a pick out of his back pocket and added some volume to his hair.

Finally, Margot's section of the sixth grade filed in and filled the scuffed-looking desks and squeaky chairs. She gave me a halfhearted wave, which I returned just as halfheartedly, in an effort not to be too embarrassing. I was pleased to see Audrey in the mix—I had no idea that they were in the same social studies group. But Audrey didn't say hi; she sank low into a seat at the back of the room between two girls who were clearly her acolytes. Oh, I thought. Audrey is the alpha girl! You're never too old to spot one. Her shirt slipped off her shoulders, *Flashdance* style, revealing a turquoise bra strap. That was new.

About halfway through my presentation, just as I was about to pass around a few incarnations of an updated Scroll logo so the kids could vote on the one they liked best, Audrey leaned toward her friend and lifted a hand to cup around her mouth. She whispered behind the hand, but her eyes told the full story: they were on Margot's reddening neck, cruelly squinting. The girls in the back row snickered. Margot's miserable eyes met mine.

That was all I needed to know about why I wasn't welcome at the middle school. Of course I was mortifying and old and my job wasn't all that exciting—those things are just a given when you're the mom of an eleven-year-old girl. But who wants her mom to see her getting picked on by the girl who knows her best?

My heart broke for Margot.

32

Nicholas decided we should invest in new kitchen cabinets since our current ones were in danger of falling off the walls. He said, "We deserve a little pick-me-up after the past few months, don't you think?"

I agreed reluctantly. I still wasn't entirely comfortable with our financial situation, but we had received a modest inheritance from my dad. "He'd definitely want us to put the money into our house," I offered, even though I knew this wasn't true. My dad had strenuously objected to the purchase of a microwave; he certainly would have wanted us to keep our money in the bank.

Suddenly, we were looking at six-burner stoves, walnut floors, imported mosaic tile, and high-end light fixtures consisting of incandescent bulbs hanging from the ceiling on a piece of cloth-covered string.

"Huh," said my mom, distractedly, when I showed her the printouts from Schoolhouse Electric. "Not much has changed since 1880."

Our whole family crowded around the kitchen table to admire blueprints drawn up by a kitchen designer named Marjorie. We would have skylights and high hats, wainscoting and crown molding. We would have one water spigot inside our refrigerator and another over our stove so we wouldn't have to tax ourselves carrying heavy pots back from the sink. The pièce de résistance would be an island in the middle of the room, topped with a nine-foot, live-edged slab of reclaimed wood. (Reclaimed from where? And what was the alternative to a live edge?)

I added the price tag for all this opulence to my list of things to worry about in the middle of the night.

I was at Market Table in Greenwich Village with an agent named Lisa. We were getting to know each other over thimbles of watermelon gazpacho—a "gift" from the chef, delivered by an unctuous waiter who prefaced his recitation of specials by asking, "Any allergies, intolerances, or aversions?"

"Oh, God," said Lisa. "Too many to list."

I knew we'd get along.

"So how do you like working for Genevieve?"

"She has a really hard job, dealing with Cleveland. We used to be closer but . . . I'll leave it at that."

"When does Scroll open, anyway? We're counting the days back at my office."

"Actually, we haven't nailed down a particular date yet, but soon. I hope."

"Good, because I'm on the prowl for an old copy of *Middlemarch* for my husband. I'm hoping it will be the first of many purchases at Scroll."

I smiled weakly, picturing the team of antiquarian book experts who had been hired to cart away all the first editions from the Sim. The bookshelves had been disassembled, too; we needed the space for flat-screen monitors and egg-shaped rubber chairs. The fate of our own dream books was unclear; I still had Virginia Woolf squirreled away above my desk.

Lisa went on, "So what's it been like for *you*? I can't imagine a more fun job."

"It's been exciting, I guess. I mean, there are some . . . changes afoot that I can't talk about yet."

"Well, I can't wait to curl up on one of those recliners!"

Georgie: "Are we going to see Pop soon? "

Me: "No, sweetie. Remember, he died?"

Georgie: "Yeah, but I drew him a picture of his garden."

Me: "You can give it to me. I'll hang it on the fridge."

Georgie: "So, wait, now you have *no* dad?"

Me: "Nope."

Georgie: "At *all*?"

Me: "Right."

Georgie: "Sophie has two dads."

Me: "She's lucky."

Georgie: "But it really stinks to have no dad."

Me: "You know what? It really does."

33

The condolence cards rolled in, fast and furious. "A memory is a keep-sake of time that lives forever in the heart." "Sharing in your sorrow." (How, exactly?) My favorite one came from a soft-spoken woman I knew from the parent holding pen at gymnastics: "We don't know each other well, but my dad died six months ago. Shall we go out one night and get drunk?"

Back in September, I'd signed up to help organize a fund-raising comedy night at Margot's school. The time had come to make good on my promise, so I agreed to coordinate invitations for the event. I assumed my job would consist of notifying parents by Evite, until I received an e-mail inviting me to Kara's house for an evening of invitation assembly.

Invitation *assembly*?

I rolled my eyes and tilted my computer monitor so Matthew could see the clip art bottle of chardonnay at the bottom of the message.

I headed to Kara's straight from the train station, having eaten a piece of pizza en route. When I arrived, the foyer smelled like lemon, and a fire crackled merrily between andirons shaped like black labs. Kara enveloped me in a hug made all the warmer by her sumptuous moss-colored cash-mere sweater. "Welcome, sweetie. So glad you could make it."

"Please—it's the least I can do."

"Alice, the service was beautiful. What a tribute. And those flowers!" She held an index finger under one eye and then dragged it down her cheek, feigning the path of a tear.

"Thanks, Kara." I followed her into the dining room, where a row of women were seated around the table, folding and assembling invitations of the sort I'd only ever seen associated with weddings: tri-fold, RSVP card, envelope for the RSVP card, vellum overlay, little vellum pocket to hold the whole shebang, and then a mailing envelope you opened and closed by wrapping a red string around a metal grommet. It was quite an operation.

On a sideboard, a sales rep from Ava & Mabel Accessories arranged her wares on black velvet trays: a turquoise necklace draped alongside a pair of coral hoops; a row of rings fashioned from little gold snakes with emerald eyes. The sales rep's son is on Oliver's soccer team, and she's a regular fixture at evening events for moms—the modern incarnation of a Tupperware lady. She has a soft touch, draping a complicated lariat around your neck when you least expect it, then relying on a chorus of women to assure you that you deserve to buy this special treat. In fact, you owe it to yourself.

My seat was in front of a masking-taped mark on the table. My job was to line up the invitation over the masking tape and then fold it right at that spot over a wooden ruler so the crease was straight and sharp. I introduced myself to the woman on my left, whose job it was to insert the RSVP cards into the RSVP envelopes, faceup. A few had been inserted facedown and Kara kindly requested that the woman take another stab at it. I already knew from our interactions through the Girl Scouts that Kara is big on kindly requesting things.

"I'm Margot Bauer's mom," I said, by way of introduction.

"I'm Katie Rourke's mom," said my neighbor who, like many moms

I know, turned out to be named Melissa. "I think Margot is in Katie's photography class."

(Margot is taking photography?) "She *loves* photography. And of course, I've heard all about Katie."

"Forgive me if this is an odd question, but did Margot recently lose a grandparent?"

"She did. My dad died last month."

"I've been there," Melissa said, simply. "It gets easier."

"Thanks. I appreciate that."

Suddenly a silver cuff bracelet encircled my wrist. The Ava & Mabel rep stepped back as quickly as she had approached, allowing me to behold the splendor in peace. The cuff was smooth to the touch and surprisingly light given its chunky appearance. I liked the way it made my wrist look delicate and powerful all at once.

"That's a *must*," said Kara. "Seriously, ladies, how fabulous does this bracelet look on Alice? Not many people have the bone structure to pull that one off."

The jewelry rep stood by and beamed.

Another mom leaned across the table, grabbed a two-bite brownie, and nibbled daintily around its edges. "Alice, that was made for you. Hand over your credit card."

It was a painless transaction. I hate shopping, and I rarely wear bracelets, but the combo of the wine and these warm women made me want to commemorate the moment.

The mom who was responsible for sliding each completed invitation into a clear cellophane bag and tying it with a pre-curled magenta ribbon said, "Didn't Kara do such a great job with these?" She gestured at the tidy package in her hand.

"Oh, she really did," said Melissa. "All you need is one glance at the organization of her mudroom to know you're in the presence of a genius." I'd never seen Kara's mudroom but I knew the type: a profusion of adorable hooks, a red metal locker for each child, rows of gingham-lined rattan baskets with their contents labeled on mini chalkboards. The real pros have custom shelving for cleats, ice skates, and Wellies, but I didn't think Kara would take things to that level; she had a thrifty side to her that I liked.

Our conversation settled into the usual mom subjects: best Poconos ski slopes; how old your daughter should be when she starts shaving her legs; the new Peruvian place on Bloomfield Avenue versus the new fusion place on Valley Road; who may or may not be getting divorced; who may or may not be pregnant; whose kids have lice and whether or not the family is taking appropriate precautions to contain the problem; who has lost a significant amount of weight and how they have done it; whether or not you should buy your minivan at the end of the lease or trade it in for a new one; which teachers give too much homework; which teachers are phoning it in.

Every so often, the conversation turned to jewelry. The sales rep flitted in and out of the crowd, pairing her "pieces" with just the right woman. By the end of the night, her trays were bare. She loaded them back into a big black suitcase, passed around her cards, and invited everyone to host a trunk show of their own. I knew Kara had landed herself a boatload of free jewelry: that was part of the deal.

By the time I left at midnight, my fingers were numb from the folding, but I felt strangely content. When I said goodbye to Melissa—a quick kiss on the cheek, the standard exit between moms—she grabbed my upper arms and said, "Remember: there is no statute of limitations."

Kara looked back and forth between us, confused, but I knew exactly what she meant.

SPRING

34

Georgie came downstairs at 6:42 a.m. wearing a pink satin butterfly nightgown and the blue flowered bike helmet she got for Christmas. She asked the same question every day: "Could we ride bikes? *Pleeease?*"

The answer was always no. There were still two inches of snow on the ground; on top of that there was slush; on top of that, frozen slush.

Now I peeked out the kitchen window and noticed a long, clear strip of blacktop in the school parking lot across the street. There were still snowbanks along the periphery of the building and in the shady areas of the playground, but there was enough of a thaw to allow for a quick spin before school.

"Fine," I said to Georgie. "Put on your boots and I'll grab your wheels."

"Can Cornelius come?" As usual, he was right by her side, his mouth hanging open in a canine proxy for a smile, wearing the half-tragic, half-adorable expression that is his trademark.

"Fine. Grab the leash. It's on the hook by the—actually, can you ask Daddy where the leash is? I haven't walked Cornelius in a while."

When I unearthed Georgie's hand-me-down dirt bike from underneath a stack of saucer sleds in the garage, I remembered that Nicholas had removed the training wheels at the end of the previous fall. Georgie's maiden voyage without them had been wildly unsuccessful, ending with a Ziploc bag of ice resting atop an angry scrape on her leg.

We reached the parking lot at 7:01.

Georgie threw a leg over the seat of the bike, hiked up her nightgown, and gestured for me to stand back.

"Are you *sure* you want to do this right now? You haven't even had breakfast."

"I'm sure. I'll eat after."

And she was off, pedaling first herky-jerky and then smoothly, sailing away from me with a barbaric yawp—"Mommy, I'm doing it!"

Cornelius barked raucously, the dog version of cheering.

I stood there with a big grin pasted on my face, marveling at the topsy-turvy carnival ride of my life. *Can you see me now?*

All of a sudden, I heard Margot, Oliver, and Nicholas cheering from my bedroom. The social worker was right: a window had opened.

35

I had an idea, and I settled down on our green, greasily fingerprinted couch to get to work on it after dinner. Nicholas sat down next to me with his laptop to watch YouTube basketball clips. He was drinking a glass of water, no bubbles.

"Nicholas, I'm trying to get some work done."

"Sorry, I was just looking for quality time with my wife. Hey, so when I was at your mom's today—"

"You were at my mom's today?"

"Yeah, straightening out some tax stuff. Didn't I tell you?"

"No, you didn't. Nicholas, shouldn't my mom figure out some of this stuff on her own? Or call someone from my dad's firm?"

"Um, why should she pay someone when she has an expert attorney in the family?"

He was in a jokey mood; I wasn't. "Nicholas, I love how much you're helping my mom, but you also have your own business to worry about."

"You're kidding, right?"

"No, I'm not. I don't want you to risk—"

"Alice. Your mom needs help. I'm going to help her. It's the right thing to do. Period."

I made lists, jotted notes, and scrutinized the Ava & Mabel website for information on their fee structure and training program. I watched video testimonials from several of their sales reps, each along the theme of "Hosting at-home jewelry parties allows me the flexibility I want as a mom." I felt a little bit like a character from a movie, hunkered down in my Garnet Hill pajamas, working feverishly into the night. Add empty containers of Chinese takeout and chopsticks shoved sexily into my hair, and I could have been the star of a romantic comedy. Unfortunately, my co-star went to bed without saying good night.

I was shouldering my way through a crowd in front of Radio City when my phone lit up with my brother's high school graduation photo. I'd snapped a picture of it at my mom's house: Will's mullet alone was worth a laugh, not to mention his white coral necklace and Jimmy Buffet T-shirt.

"Hey, it's me."

"Hi. I know."

"What are you up to?"

"Walking to work. You?"

"At work. Slow morning."

"Oh." I pictured Will in his wood-paneled office, inside a weather-beaten red fisherman's cottage on the edge of Casco Bay. From his window, he had a view of the pine trees and church steeples of Orr's Island and the Cribstone Bridge to Bailey Island, spanning a cove known as Will's Gut (no relation). He was only seven hours north, a straight shot up the coast, but he might as well have been in Siberia.

"Alice, you know what amazes me the most? The way you're supposed to go back to normal, but *everything* has changed. You feel so fucking *empty-handed*."

And suddenly he was right there, falling in step beside me on the sparkly gray sidewalk. His presence was, indeed, present enough.

"Totally." I sighed. "Do you think he can see us now?"

"I have no idea. I wish I knew." Will paused to crack his knuckles—a sound that was as irksome over the phone as it was in person. "You know what else? I get like half as many e-mails and texts now. He used to send me about fifty—"

"I know. Me, too."

"Did you read them all?"

I shook my head, no. The word made me so ashamed, I couldn't even say it out loud.

I ran into Genevieve as we were getting off the elevator. She had a pinched look on her face, like she didn't know me and wasn't quite sure why I was smiling at her.

"We need to talk," she said.

"Okay, are you free right now? I actually had something I wanted to discuss with you." I tried to keep an upbeat look on my face, but my insides felt like they were filling with lead. How was it possible to be thirty-eight years old and still as afraid of someone as I was of my fourth-grade teacher?

"Yes. I need a high-level overview on where we stand with gaming. The Environmental Team wants to revamp the Sim, stat, and they feel they don't have the buy-in from you that they need."

We walked down the hall and into Genevieve's office. Since we didn't have a meeting on the calendar, I knew better than to sit down on her couch, so I stood awkwardly in the doorway and slipped off my gloves and hat. This was not a conversation to be had with a pompom on my head.

I will not cry at work. I will not cry at work. I will not cry at work.

"Genevieve, before I tell you what I have in mind, I have to ask: have you actually *looked* at any of Joystick's video games?" I knew Genevieve had some technical difficulties of her own, and I wasn't certain she knew how to navigate through the ANT drive to the SharePoint to MMO to KidVid to GO.

"I don't need to play them. If Greg wants to sell them, we'll sell them."

"But the vibe is so antithetical to what we originally set out to do—I mean, it's a complete about-face. Are video games really the best—"

"*Best* is a subjective term."

I held my head very still so the tears wouldn't slip down my cheeks.

"Genevieve, I'm not sure you've had a chance to delve in beyond the spreadsheets, but trust me—*Conflagration* is not about playing with matches. The player is an arsonist, tasked with setting fires in unsuspecting homes while families are sleeping. The object is to burn down as many—"

Genevieve held up a surprisingly small hand.

"That's the thing, I don't need to delve in beyond the spreadsheets. Greg needs to know that we're on board and he's starting to wonder. We need to give him what he wants."

"I know, I get that, but these are games for *kids*—"

"At the end of the day, we're here to make money. Whether or not you approve is beside the point."

"But what if I have another way to make money? One that's better suited to my background and the original mission of Scroll?"

"Alice. We're not going back to the original mission of Scroll. We're selling books *and* video games. You need to wrap your mind around that."

I took a deep breath. "Fine, but can I still tell you about this other idea I have?"

Genevieve closed her eyes and said "Fine" without opening them. "Shoot."

"Okay. Here goes." I flashed back to the jewelry rep's big, empty black suitcase. "Imagine a Tupperware party—but instead of buying containers, or jewelry or candles or whatever else people sell at parties—you buy books. A Scroll rep comes to your house to present the season's best books to your best friends. She gets a discount and the host earns points for free books depending on how many titles her guests buy. We know women love to drink wine and talk about books, but lots of us have no idea what to read. With ScrollBests, we bring the books to you."

Genevieve opened her eyes. "Huh. Interesting. Have you run the financials?"

I unfurled my very first self-generated spreadsheet and went through it, column by column, number by number. Genevieve wasn't enthusiastic, exactly, but she listened politely. When I was finished she said again, "Interesting. Do you think you can take a stab at convincing Greg?"

"I know I can."

This was as close as I had ever come to being forceful with Genevieve and I sensed a degree of admiration.

"Then I suggest you book a trip to Cleveland. In the meantime, Alice, you need to demonstrate your commitment to MMO. Otherwise . . ."

"Otherwise what?"

"Otherwise we need to begin a conversation about your role at this company."

This was a classic Scroll dodge. When you didn't want to talk about what was actually being talked about, you talked about beginning the conversation about it at a later date.

To: alicepearse@scroll.com
From: annlee@scroll.com

GREG WILL BE ON CHEESE & WINE TASTING TOUR IN THE LOIRE VALLEY DURING THE DAYS YOU MENTIONED. HE CAN SEE YOU ON FRIDAY, FEBRUARY 26, AT 10AM. PLEASE ADVISE AS TO WHETHER OR NOT YOU WOULD LIKE ME TO HOLD THIS DATE. ☺

Greg's assistant, Ann, communicated exclusively in capital letters. You would have thought she was yelling at you, except for the happy-face icon that showed up at the end of each message. When I met her, I'd been shocked to discover that Ann was meek and soft-spoken.

Susanna: I think there was some kind of incident with the girls. Not sure what happened but Audrey says Margot is ignoring her. Do we want to discuss?

Me: Let's each take care of our own, k? I don't think we need to hash it out.

Susanna: Gotcha.

It was taco night on Flower Street and everyone was bickering over a pad of Post-its. Ollie had turned twelve of the little slips of paper into flashcards so he could learn his seven times tables.

Margot claimed these Post-its were hers, to be used exclusively for a language arts project where she was supposed to jot down unfamiliar words while reading *Dandelion Wine*.

Even Georgie leapt into the fray. "Yeah, *Ollie*," she said derisively. "And that's *my* paper clip you used to hold together your tine tables."

"Ollie, we're sick of you stealing our stuff. Mom, Ollie always steals our stuff." Margot folded her arms across her chest and glared in my direction over the little bowls of condiments Jessie had set out on the table: chopped tomato, guacamole, shredded cheddar, sour cream.

"Why are you bringing me into this, girls? Give Ollie a break. It's not easy being in a sister sandwich. And you're talking about Post-its. We have hundreds of them, and we can get more if we need them."

"Ugh, it makes me sick how you're always on his side just because he's a *boy*. It's totally misogynistic." Margot rolled her eyes and blew out a quick burst of air that would have lifted her bangs off her face if she'd had bangs. I thought of Margot holding each of Ollie's chubby hands and perambulating him around the living room of our old apartment before he learned to walk.

"Enough." Nicholas ended the conversation, thankfully. We crunched away at our Ortega shells in silence until finally the kids chased each other upstairs, in the thick of a new fight over who would get the first bath.

"So, Genevieve wants me to go to Cleveland to present my Book Lady idea to Greg."

"Really? Does that mean she liked it?" Nicholas took a swig of his drink. He was sticking with one per night, but I still kept a careful inventory of the liquor cabinet.

"Who knows."

"When are you going to Cleveland? And will you please visit my parents? They're worried about you."

We heard a loud crash from the bathroom upstairs, then Margot's voice: "Everything is okay, guys! Georgie knocked the conditioner out of the tub. I'm cleaning it up!"

"Thanks!" we said in unison.

"So, Cleveland . . ." I started.

"Yes! Do it. I'll hold down the fort. We'll barely notice you're gone."

"Thanks, but now that's the thing. Ann says—"

"Who's Ann?"

"Greg's support. She says—"

"Wait, *support?* What are you talking about?"

Usually I had an endless appetite for laughs at the expense of Scroll terminology, but now I was impatient. "Ann is Greg's assistant, Nicholas. They call them 'supports' in Cleveland. It's more . . ."

"Supportive?"

"Yes. Inclusive. Anyway—"

"I'm imagining Ann carrying Greg around in an adult-sized Baby Bjorn, patting him on the back between meetings and feeding him dog biscuits."

"Nicholas! Here's the thing: I need to meet with Greg on the Friday of the weekend you'll be in Atlantic City. So we'll both be away. I was thinking of asking Jessie if she could spend the night, and I'll fly home early Saturday so I can be here in time for Oliver's game."

"Sounds great. I mean, we'll have to talk it over with Jessie, but I think the kids would love that." He threw an arm around me at the sink. "Aren't we so high-powered? Both out of town at the same time?"

A door slammed upstairs. "OLIVER! I TOLD YOU TO STAY OUT OF THE BATHROOM!"

Margot was like Ann, minus the happy-face emoji.

The Scroll travel gods were smiling upon me: they agreed to a slightly higher-priced hotel than they were usually game to spring for. I quietly decided not to tell Judy and Elliott that I'd be in their city—it was such a short trip after all. My mom agreed to be on standby on the home front and even refrained from pointing out that the date of my meeting with Greg would have been my dad's seventieth birthday. We'd talked about going out for fried clams in his honor.

Jessie was game to sleep over on the one night my trip overlapped with Nicholas's. But later she texted, "Can we talk tomorrow? I know the timing isn't great, but I have two things I need to check in with you about."

I was on the train—wasn't I always?—when I received this message.

I wrote back, "Everything OK?"

Jessie's response: "Yah, but a friend's film company is looking for a receptionist and I'm going to interview for the job on Monday at eleven. Will be back in time to pick up kids."

My heart stopped. Me: "Got it. Keep me posted."

Jessie: "Just feel like I should have the interview. Really looking forward to my sleepover with the kiddos."

Me: "Totally get it."

I stared out the train window at the gray tree branches that look like arms reaching up to the sky. In the distance was the Newark Cathedral, bathed in the rosy glow of sunset. From inside this vacuum-sealed train car, I could almost fool myself into believing it was warm outside.

I thought of the countless nights I'd walked home from the train station to find Jessie playing soccer in the front yard with Georgie or hanging out on the porch with Margot, listening to the latest in middle school crises. I hadn't signed a permission slip or looked at Georgie's homework since I started my job at Scroll. Suddenly—and, I'm embarrassed to admit, for the first time—I wondered what all my outsourcing had been like for Jessie.

Also, what was the second thing she wanted to check in about? I'd forgotten to ask.

There was Oliver, waiting at the train station. The embankment up to the tracks was slick with ice, so he stood on the sidewalk next to the parking lot, wearing royal-blue snow pants, with Cornelius on a sled.

"Hi, gentlemen."

He smiled.

"You had a good day?"

"Yeah. We had an assembly about mummies."

"And did you guys have ravioli for dinner?"

"Yeah."

"How are Margot and Georgie?"

"Annoying."

"And Jessie?"

"She's fine. She let us play Angry Birds on her phone."

"Fun. So what else happened today?"

"Nothing. We have to do a report for women's history month."

"I'd write about Susan B. Anthony."

"It can't be someone you know. By the way, what's infinity?"

We reached the corner of North Edison and Flower, and we clambered over the mountain of snow that had been pushed to the side of the road by the snowplow.

"It's complicated. It means something that goes on forever, like numbers."

36

"Hi, Mrs. Bauer?"

"This is Alice."

"This is Elaine Murphy? I'm the school nurse at Alcott. No need to panic, but I wanted to let you know, I have your daughter, Georgie, here in my office. I'm afraid she was sick to her stomach in art class."

"Oh, no! What happened?"

"Well, at first Miss Pasquariello thought it might have been a reaction to the smell of the papier-mâché—that's potent stuff, you know—but then Georgie got sick again in the hallway."

"In the hallway?"

"Yes. And then one final time in my office, on my cot. On the pillow."

"Oh, no, poor girl. I'm *so* sorry to hear that. I'm going to call my husband and ask him to come by and pick her up right away."

"That's the thing, Mrs. Bauer, we already tried Mr. Bauer. He isn't answering. Neither is your babysitter or Georgie's grandmother, who is listed as a contact on Georgie's emergency card."

"My mother? You called her already?"

"Yes, ma'am. Georgie said you wouldn't be able to come. She told me to try her grandmother."

"Oh. What did my mom say?"

"No answer. So, can you?"

"What?"

"Come pick up your daughter." Mrs. Murphy said this slowly, as if she was talking to another kindergartener.

"Yes! Of course. I have a meeting in fifteen minutes, and then I'll get on the next train which is . . . oh, I think . . . 2:37? Arriving at 3:13?"

"Ma'am, school is over at 3:00."

"Shit, you're right. I mean—sorry! I'm leaving my office now."

From the backseat of a yellow cab, I dialed Nicholas. No answer.

My phone lit up with a call from Jessie. "Hey, Jess."

"Alice? I just got a voice mail from the school nurse. Did she reach you?"

"She did. I'm on my way home right now. I'm in a taxi—we're just about to—"

"Oh, I'm so sorry! I would have been happy to pick up Georgie—poor little muffin—but I'm on my way to Brooklyn to grab an amp from a friend. We have a wedding on Saturday and—"

"No, it's fine." Actually, as long as I kept my eyes off the meter, it was kind of peaceful to be hurtling down Route 3 in the middle of the afternoon, my life in someone else's hands. "Hey, Jessie, do you have any idea where Nicholas might be?"

There was a silence. We passed Raymour and Flanigan and I experienced a momentary yearning to be the kind of person who has a matching brass-handled bed set. I never imagined I'd be on the brink of forty and still storing my clothes in a dresser I found in the trash on Lexington Avenue when I was twenty-two. "Jess? Are you still there?"

"Alice, that's the other thing I wanted to talk to you about."

For a second, I thought she was referring to the state of my bedroom furniture. "Wait, *what*?"

"It's Nicholas. I think he—"

"Wait. Hold that thought." I put my hand over the phone, leaned forward, and stuck my face through the bulletproof partition separating the back seat from the front. "Excuse me? You'll want to take the Bloomfield Avenue exit, coming up on your right in about two miles after the Tick Tock Diner. Jessie? I'm back. So, you were saying Nicholas . . . ?"

"Alice, I don't know how to tell you this, but he's been drinking during the day in the basement. He comes home and goes down there through the bulkhead doors in the yard—I guess so the kids can't see him. When I went down to switch the laundry yesterday, he was on the couch. Passed out."

I swallowed hard and closed my eyes. "Are you sure he wasn't just taking a nap?" Denial is not just a river in Egypt. But I really believed Nicholas was sticking with one drink a day.

"He's wasn't taking a nap, Alice." Jessie's voice switched from apologetic to annoyed; I imagined this was the tone she used with tipsy wedding guests experiencing stage lust for the lead singer. "There's a jug of vodka hidden behind the elliptical machine. I've been wanting to tell you, but I haven't been able to get you alone."

I don't know which bothered me more: the fact that Nicholas was coming home from work to get drunk in the basement or the fact that he knew I would never find his stash if he hid it behind the elliptical trainer, which I never used.

Ten minutes and $102 later (not including tip and tolls), I found Georgie in the principal's office, clutching a little tied-shut plastic bag containing her puked-on overalls. She wore an unfamiliar Hello Kitty sweat suit, borrowed from the shoebox of another kindergartener; naturally, the clothes in her own shoebox were way too small.

Her face lit up when she saw me.

Nicholas's car was in the driveway.

After I tucked Georgie in on the couch to watch *Alvin and the Chipmunks*, and after I gave Cornelius a quick belly rub and gently stirred the stew in the slow cooker, I clomped downstairs to the basement. I half hoped the sound of my boots would wake Nicholas, but he was out cold on the couch when I found him, exactly as Jessie said he would be. Smashed into a cushion covered in used dryer sheets, his face looked slack, as if it had dropped from the sky and landed that way—*splat*. He wore his work clothes and dress shoes, the mocha wingtips we chose together from Johnston & Murphy when he worked at Sutherland, Courtfield. The only way to describe the Smirnoff bottle on the floor by his side was half-empty—and normally I pride myself on having a half-full perspective on the world.

I nudged Nicholas's shoulder and stood over him, arms crossed. "Wake up." No reaction. I leaned down and enunciated, loudly, right in his ear. "*Nicholas. Wake. Up.*"

His eyes opened and took an instant to focus. Then he lifted himself to a seated position, looking confused, then scared, then embarrassed. He opened his mouth to speak, but I held up my hand.

"Please don't. I don't want to hear what you have to say. I just want you to know, Georgie is sick. You were too drunk to answer a call from the school. I want you to ask yourself one question: are you the person you want to be? *Right now?*" Nicholas hung his head and rested his elbows on his knees.

I turned on my heel and headed for the stairs, stalking past a dusty ExerSaucer and a Tupperware bin of Matchbox cars. I missed my dad, but I missed my husband more.

Behind me, he muttered, "Are you?"

At our weekly meeting, Genevieve suddenly had a lot of questions about Filament. "I'm curious, you guys have an Anthropologie and a Williams-Sonoma out there, right?"

"We certainly do! Both within walking distance of my house, in fact." Just that morning, Nicholas had assured me that our prime location justified every penny we were now pouring into the kitchen—and there were many. Pennies, that is. The kitchen was a safe subject, a distraction from the real issue, which we hadn't discussed since our showdown in the basement.

"What about foot traffic? You have that?"

"Of course. People move to Filament because it's a walkable suburb. Our neighbors don't even have a car." Now I was confused. Was Genevieve considering a move to New Jersey? Perhaps she had been inspired by her trip out for my dad's funeral?

"Interesting. Very interesting." She clicked on the larger of her two monitors and waved her hand at a picture that popped up. "Welcome to the future home of Scroll Filament!"

"Excuse me?" It took me a minute to place the squat building in the photograph, but a tiny sliver of blue awning next door brought it all home. "Is that . . . ?"

"Yes, it's an empty property we're considering. Of course, we'll have to see how we do in our beta markets, but the location team has concluded that Filament contains a critical mass of target customers—what they call the Desperate Housewives." She unleashed a short bark of a laugh. "Shit, you probably *know* them."

"That store—" I leaned forward on Genevieve's couch, squinting at the picture on her screen. "Isn't it a—"

Genevieve nodded. "A deli? Yes, currently. But MainStreet can erase the smell of salami in no time, don't you worry."

Of course. I was looking at the deli owned by Phil Mercadante. Nicholas's client, who had dropped off homemade mozzarella with the first payment on his legal bill.

"Are we at all concerned that this storefront is adjacent to a bookstore? The Blue Owl?" My voice went up an octave on those last three words, dangerously close to cracking. I pictured Susanna on my front porch, handing over a piping-hot quiche and the hot mitts to hold it.

Genevieve rolled her eyes. "Are you kidding? We'll show Filament readers how it's done: fast, cheap, good coffee. Their kids will be begging for video game tokens. Game over for *that* bookstore, right? So, listen—" She leaned forward, offering me a Peppermint Pattie from a little ceramic bowl. "Everything we've just discussed is in the cone of silence, right?"

"Yes, of course." The night before, I'd seen Susanna restocking shelves as I crept by outside in the dark, on my way home from the train. In the old days, I might have popped in for a glass of wine left over from the No Guilt Book Club. Now there were too many subjects to be avoided—the future of the Blue Owl, the rift between Margot and Audrey—so I kept going, shivering under a Harry Potter umbrella.

"Okay, I need to move on to less fun stuff. I know you've been jammed up, and I want to take your temperature about when you'll be up to speed."

"Well, I'm doing my best—"

"Can I stop you right there?"

You just did. "Of course."

"Sometimes our best isn't good enough, Alice. We have to push ourselves to excel. We're innovators, right?"

"Right." Actually, the status quo suited me just fine.

"And what do innovators do?"

"Innovate?"

"We turn adversity on its ear. You've had a setback, Alice, and now I need to know your head is in the game. Because people are wondering. Your hand scan records indicate majorly reduced hours." She made a V of her index finger and middle finger, pointing at her eyes, then mine. "*Is your head in the game?*"

"Well, to the extent it—" A *setback?* A drubbing was more like it.

The Mask was on. "Is. Your. Head. In. The. Game?"

"Yes. My head is in the game."

"Fabulous. And seriously, when things settle down we still need to make a plan for Bunna."

"Excuse me?" I thought Genevieve was referring to another acronym I'd forgotten.

"Remember? The Ethiopian brunch we were talking about?"

Now I had whiplash. That conversation felt as if it had happened in another century, on a different planet. "Of course. Yes, let's do it."

"Let's."

Berate, then befriend. Different pattern, same mixed message.

Dear Alice Pearse:

Please call 1-800-WESTELM to schedule delivery of 6 GORDON BACKREST BAR STOOLS (@$260 x 6 = $1560). Thanks from your friends at,

WEST ELM

Nicholas: I need to leave early tomorrow morning. Can you take the kids to school?

Me: Sure. What's up?

Nicholas: Meeting your mom at probate court. Also she says she has something wrong with her "World Wide Web," so I'll swing by the house after.

Me: Okay, thanks.

Nicholas: You sound annoyed.

Me: Not annoyed. You're a great son-in-law.

Nicholas: But?

Me: Nothing. Just remember, you're *my* husband, too!

Nicholas: I'm going to pretend you didn't say that.

The house was blissfully peaceful when I walked in the door. It would devolve into chaos the minute Jessie left, but for now the big kids were finishing their homework in their rooms and Georgie was coloring in the dining room. Jessie stirred sausage into the farfalle; all we had to do was pull out our chairs and sit down. The napkins were neatly folded into triangles next to each plate.

She looked at me apologetically, and even before she spoke, I knew what she was about to say. "So. I got the job."

"You got the job! Congratulations!"

Forcing this enthusiasm was like disgorging a chicken bone stuck in my throat, but I owed it to Jessie for her years of loyalty and especially for the time she turned around on the parkway years ago when she was on her way to a gig and I texted her from the emergency room to say that Georgie had a broken leg.

Jessie had been there for me and now I had to be there for her. The timing couldn't have been worse; I couldn't think about how Nicholas and I would break the news to our kids, who were already in the midst of puzzling through another massive loss.

"I'm still not sure if this is the right thing." Jessie started folding the dishtowels into a little pile, which I knew she would then top with an upside-down juice glass. I knew all her little habits, as she knew mine. "And I know you guys are going through a lot right now, with your dad and—well, with Nicholas."

I waved away those concerns as if they were mere roadblocks—when in fact, they loomed in front of me like twin Mount Everests. I remembered another gem of wisdom from Susanna (this time via Robert Frost): "The best way out is always through."

"Jessie, if this *is* the right thing, you need to do it. It will be hard for us, too. Too hard to think about. Are you excited about the job?"

"I guess so. Maybe. I don't know. But I think it's time for a change of scenery—"

"Wait, before you finish, let me just say: things around here will change. We've been . . . overwhelmed. But we're turning over a new leaf, getting our act together . . ." My voice trailed off as Jessie waved her hands for me to stop. I was humiliated by my own desperation, but she was worth fighting for. I knew that much.

"Stop, Alice—it's not you guys. Please don't think that. You're like family. It's just that the kids are getting older, and it feels like I should be thinking about the next step. I need to figure out what it is."

I wanted to tell her that the next step was for us to blunder forth into the teenage years together, consulting each other about curfews and driving lessons the same way we'd been confabbing for years about healthy snacks and the right time to pull the plug on the pacifier.

"Jess, you're still very much needed here, if that's what you're wondering. Please, *please* don't leave because you think we don't need you. Only if you feel like this new job will open doors for you. We understand that we can't offer much of a career future beyond a ticket to three high school graduations. But what a hot ticket that is!" I forced a small smile. I knew I needed to think about Jessie's future, not just mine or my kids'. If you love someone, set her free.

Jessie's eyes darted miserably to our refrigerator, wallpapered with pictures of the kids from a long-ago Halloween (ice skater, basketball player, ladybug); at the top of the Empire State Building; huddled together in a chubby-faced trio one afternoon at Deer Lake. According to my quick inventory, Jessie had been our babysitter when each one these photos had been taken.

She swallowed audibly—a small gulp. Suddenly, even with her edgy nose pierce and heavily lined eyes, she looked like a teenager. "Alice, I really think I need to do this."

I closed my eyes in an extended blink, willing them to hold their tears for later, if I had any tears left. I remembered Jessie from our first meeting at Starbucks: the way she bounced up to the counter to collect her Frappuccino, the huge smile on her face when I described Margot and Oliver. For an instant, I pictured Jessie the first time she met Georgie as a newborn—a light going on, pure adoration. I had to pull a blackout shade over that memory.

"Jessie, I think you need to do this, too. Can you stay until—"

"The Atlantic City tournament? Yes, definitely. Alice, I—"

"We're happy for you. Truly."

I wanted to tell her how I'd noticed and was so grateful for all the little details she'd attended to over the years: the half-eaten lollipops preserved lovingly on a saucer in the fridge; the finger paintings drying over the edge of the tub; the bowling and roller-skating and sand art birthday parties she'd cheerfully attended on Saturday and Sunday afternoons, always with the most sought-after and beautifully wrapped gift. I'd looked forward to seeing her at the end of every day almost as much as I looked forward to seeing my own kids. Fine, I'd never pinched Jessie's cheeks or inhaled the smell of the top of her head—that would have been weird—but I loved seeing her in the front yard, running bases with Georgie as I made my way home from the train.

I couldn't say any of this without crying, so I said nothing.

I couldn't imagine what it would be like for my kids to see someone other than Jessie waiting for them on the front lawn of the school. The thought of them scanning the crowd for her face killed me.

We hugged.

She yelled "Catch you on the flip side" to the kids, as she always did. Cornelius tried to follow her out the door, as he always did.

As Jessie walked to her car, I remembered that she was the one who had shoveled this path the last time it snowed.

Nicholas wanted to wait to break the news. He poured himself a tall glass of water (this was something good, at least) and said, "Let Jessie sleep on it; does she even have an official offer?"

"I think so. Nicholas, now that we know, we can't keep this from the kids. What if they hear us talking and find out Jessie is leaving?"

"We'll make sure that doesn't happen. I just think we should give it a night, talk to them in the morning maybe."

I said I'd wait—but for some reason I didn't. I plowed ahead in the middle of dinner and dumped the news on the shoulders of our worn-out gang. "You guys? I have something hard to tell you."

They immediately perked up. They love bad news, especially when it has nothing to do with them. Unfortunately, in this case, it had everything to do with them. I ignored Nicholas's look of caution. "Well, you know how Jessie graduated from college a few years ago and has been trying to figure out what she wants to do after she's finished being our babysitter?"

"Of course," said Oliver. "But she's not finished being our babysitter."

I soldiered on. "Well, that's the thing—"

"Jessie *is leaving*?" Georgie burst into tears. "*But we love her!* Doesn't she *know* that?"

"Wait, hang on a minute. Jessie got a new job, and she's really excited about it. She's so sad to be leaving us. It's going to be a big change for everyone, but Daddy and I are proud of her."

"WTF," Margot muttered under her breath. Before I had a chance to address her semi-profanity (did acronyms count?), Nicholas nodded in Oliver's direction.

At first I thought he had fallen asleep at the table, but then I realized Oliver's chin had dropped to his chest because he was crying. Silent, shoulder-heaving sobs, big fat tears rolling down his cheeks. Nicholas and I exchanged a miserable glance and blundered through the rest of the conversation. Even though it was still freezing cold outside, we took them out for frozen yogurt for dessert. While they piled on their toppings, Nicholas said quietly, "I asked you not to tell them tonight, but I guess my opinion doesn't count."

I didn't respond; we sat in silence, both stewing.

37

Mom: "I put aside a few of Daddy's ties, if you want them."

Me: "I'd love them. But I thought we were going to do his closet together?"

Mom: "And when exactly would that happen? Don't worry. I rolled up my sleeves and did it. Also just dropped off shirts to have them made into a quilt."

Those shirts: blue, white, striped, their collars battened down with little buttons. I forced my memory to zoom out, like the long lens of a camera. You had to keep the picture at a wide angle—that was the trick. The devastation was in the details.

38

Two nights before I left for Cleveland, I was scrolling through uninspiring babysitter listings on Care.com when Nicholas reminded me about our appointment to refinance our mortgage. I quickly recalibrated my Tuesday morning: I would head into work around eleven, when the morning press of trains would already have tapered off, so it would be quicker to drive into the city. I had a metrics meeting at eleven. No matter how I traveled, I'd be cutting it close.

The morning did not go according to plan. The representative of the mortgage company was an hour late, after calling periodically to report a huge backup on the parkway north. She named exit numbers—"I'm driving by Exit 135 at a snail's pace"—which I knew were bunk because I'd turned into the kind of obsessive person who fact-checked late arrivers with the traffic report on 1010 WINS. According to the radio, traffic on the parkway was moving along smoothly.

As the mortgage lady shuffled through her papers on our dining room table, arranging pages marked with little plastic tabs for our signatures, she said, "I'm so sorry I kept you waiting. They said there was a rubbernecking delay."

I said, "That's interesting, because I heard on the radio that the parkway was clear this morning."

Nicholas gave me a look that said, *Seriously?*

The mortgage lady looked up from her paperwork, surprised, then wounded. She aggressively twisted her little shell earring, then shifted in her seat to avoid Cornelius's wandering nose. "All I know is, down by where I live, there was traffic. It was bad."

"Yeah, well, not according to the radio. I'm just saying."

"Alice, do you want to initial the pages first and then I'll do mine?"

Nicholas was openly hostile, sliding the papers across the table with force. My behavior was unacceptable and I knew it. But these two with their normal jobs had no idea what it would be like to be late to the metrics meeting—the burning shame of walking into that room and facing the big screen of grim Clevelanders, their every pore and flared nostril magnified in the camera's glare, then the wrist-slapping e-mail Genevieve would dispatch to the entire team, reminding us that punctuality was paramount. Or the alternative: missing the meeting altogether and having to schedule a confab with the miffed marketing team so they could give me a private tutorial on the data they'd shared with the group. I knew from experience, it was harder to feign understanding in an intimate setting.

"Alice? This is Mom. Just sitting here at the kitchen table feeling a little blue. Call me if you have a chance. Love you."

I arrived in the city at 11:15, having screeched through the Lincoln Tunnel at such a fast clip, the transit cop on the Manhattan side flashed his headlights as I tore by. The minute I settled into my white leather chair,

Genevieve called on me to interpret the data listed in column GG on the Smart Board. I stuttered over the explanation—something to do with pricing—but tried to avoid specifics, mainly because I had no idea what the numbers meant.

When I was finished, Rashida piped up cheerily but not cheerily, "Okay, so everyone? It would be fabulous if you could take a read of this material and digest it *before* you come to the meeting? It's available on the SharePoint. If you have trouble accessing the files, you can file a trouble ticket and we can remedy that for you. But it's top priority for us all to be on the same page when we get together. Otherwise we lose ground, right? Right. Awesomesauce."

Matthew was at an appointment with his acupuncturist, so I closed our door and called my mom. "I'm having a really bad day."

"Hang on a minute." Three steps across the kitchen, and she was turning down the volume on *Rigoletto*, which blared from a Bose radio courtesy of WQXR. The kettle was on. I'd been in the center of this scene so many times, I knew it by heart. "Al? I'm back. What seems to be the problem?"

"I'm really stressed out."

"I know that. You've *been* really stressed out." Her tone was breezy, stating the obvious. For some reason, the observation didn't bother me, but when Nicholas had the same response, my nostrils flared and I breathed fire. *Really? You're no picnic either.*

"No, I mean, I'm so stressed, I feel like my head is going to explode."

"Alice, your head isn't going to explode." I pictured my mom in her kitchen, spooning a peppermint tea bag out of an old mug printed with fading green letters: Very Charming Very Lucky Very Irish.

"Mom?"

"Yes?"

"I don't think I like this job."

Silence. I heard her blow on the tea, take a quick sip. "Yes, I gathered that."

"Would you think I was a loser if I left?"

"A *loser*?" I had to hold the phone away from my head, her voice was so loud. "Have you taken leave of your senses? Alice. You're a *winner*, always. You're my girl." She said this as if daughterhood was a career path unto itself, with a paycheck and vacation days, maybe even a modest pension. Come to think of it, this didn't sound like a bad gig.

"Thanks. Well. You're my . . . mom. Obviously." Why couldn't I say something nice in return? You're a winner, too? Hail Joan, full of grace? But the words wouldn't budge.

"Alice, are you still there?"

I waited for a bleating police car to make its way down 55th Street. "I'm here. Do you think Daddy would think I'm giving up on Scroll too soon?"

"Absolutely not." There was a pause, then a little catch in her voice. "No. He wouldn't."

"Thanks." Suddenly, I remembered her voice mail from earlier in the day: "Feeling a little blue." The woman had just lost her husband and here I was, prattling on about my occupational ennui. It didn't seem right, but I was mother enough to know she wanted to be supportive, and daughter enough to appreciate her strength. It occurred to me that the Irish stiff upper lip deserved the same global acclaim as the gift of the blarney.

"Alice, Daddy thought you were doing too much."

"Really?" My mom already had a habit of attributing her own opinions to my dad when it was convenient. *As your father always said, when you find an antique Limoges candy bowl, you should snap it right up.*

"You better believe it. Also, remember what Edison said."

"What was that?"

"He said, 'My mother was the making of me.'"

My eyes burned. "Okay . . ."

"Remember, *you* are the making of your kids. That's important stuff."

I felt better when I hung up the phone. At least if my head did explode, I'd be in good hands while it healed. My mom would brew bottomless cups of tea and lend me the pick of her hat collection: wide brim with cherries, black sequined beret, the gray felt cloche that was her cur-rent fave. I remembered her gently placing a Mets cap on my dad's head when we were leaving Sloan Kettering for the last time, how she tugged the bill into place with one hand while the other cupped the back of his neck.

I was down one parent, but I still had a lot to learn from the one I had left.

At five o'clock, I crept out of my office and made a beeline to the parking garage under the Gershwin Theatre on 50th Street. My head was spin-ning with all the data decoding and dishwasher unloading and laundry folding I would have to do after I put my kids to bed.

I hastily shoved my ticket through the bulletproof plastic at the sleepy attendant and hopped on a halting elevator down to the subterranean level where my minivan awaited. It was one of those elevator rides where you keep jamming the number with your finger even though it's already lit.

I arrived on my level and marched distractedly to my blue Honda Odyssey. As I rounded the driver's side, I almost bumped into a tall chest-nut horse tied to the wall in the adjacent parking space, between my mini-van and a cherry-red Fiat.

For the first time all day—all year, maybe—I stopped. I stood completely still.

The horse was well fed and carefully groomed. He was staring straight ahead at the pocked cement wall, his ears barely clearing a caged bulb hanging from the ceiling. They twitched in time with the slow drip of water in some far-off corner of the garage.

Did he belong to the NYPD or was he just taking a break from his responsibilities to a carriage driver in Central Park? He wasn't wearing a saddle, reins, blinders or any other equine accessories. Why was he tied to a wall six floors below ground? I opened the car door gingerly, afraid of spooking the horse. But his limpid, mournful brown eyes barely regis-tered my sound or movement. He looked resigned.

As I put my key in the ignition and glided up the steep, dark ramp, I started to cry. I mean, *really* cry. Hiccups and snot—the whole deal.

Why had I tethered myself to this job where I was so unhappy?

Why had I checked my e-mail when my dad was downstairs, dying?

How many times had I pretended to listen to Nicholas or our kids when I was really agonizing about work? I was no more a Scroller than that horse was a car. The more I tried to assimilate, the more impatient, scattered, and unreliable I became. I couldn't believe I'd treated the poor mortgage broker with the condescension and disdain that permeated Scroll like a flu.

The whole way home, I puzzled through the logistics of how that horse would get out of the parking garage. He wouldn't just step onto the elevator; he would have to plod up five slippery exit ramps to the mouth of the garage. It would take time, but he would put one foot in front of the other and he'd end up in the right place.

This was how I'd get out of Scroll. I promised myself.

The kids were full of complaints about the grilled chicken legs Jessie made for dinner. After she left, they amped up their whining: "I don't like drumsticks. Why can't I have macaroni? When is Daddy coming home? This dinner is slimy." Even though I generally tried to hold it together in their presence, I started to cry again.

"Mommy, what's wrong?" Margot snapped out of her adolescent funk, immediately back to the sweet girl who used to wake me up every morning with a kiss on the forehead. "Do you miss Pop?"

Georgie piped up, "You must be sad because your dad is dead."

Oliver put his hand over her mouth. "Georgie! That's desensitive!"

All six eyeballs were on me: four blue, two green. I swallowed hard. "You guys, I'm not happy at my job."

They looked at me blankly. This was an adult problem, and not the one they had been expecting. I told them about the horse in the parking lot. Now I was speaking their language; they love animals.

"The hard thing with the horse is, he's *trying* to be a car," said Oliver. "But he's a horse. That's probably very hard for him." From the mouths of babes.

"When did you know you didn't like your job?" Margot asked.

"I can't put my finger on it. It's just been gradual, but now I know I need to start thinking about what I'll do next." Boiling my life down to their level was a useful exercise; I felt grateful to have such an attentive and sweet board of directors.

"Will you be home to pick us up after school like Morgan's mom?" Okay, so maybe the honeymoon didn't last long. I resisted the urge to tell Georgie that Morgan's mom was having an affair with her paddle tennis coach.

"I don't think I'll be home all the time, but I'd love to find a job where I'm around more and where I'm less stressed out."

"And maybe where you don't have a phone?" Georgie pointed to mine, which was next to the cookie tray of chicken legs. The sound was turned off, but it lit up every few seconds as new messages rolled in.

I pictured the ramps stretching in front of me and above me, stacked on top of each other. One step at a time, ramp by ramp.

39

Leaving for Cleveland was surprisingly easy—a big change from the last time I'd headed out there, for orientation, when the kids had asked a million questions about who would pick them up and who would read *Freckleface Strawberry* before bed. This time, Filament Taxi arrived at 8:06, which happened to be the exact time I normally headed out for the 8:16 train, so I yelled up the stairs to the kids as I did every morning. "Love you guys! Be good for Jessie!"

"We will!" The chorus was cheerful. They were excited to have Jessie sleep over; she'd promised them a dance party to end all dance parties, complete with a disco ball and limbo contest. This seemed like a fitting way to end our happy seven-year run with Jessie at the helm.

Nicholas walked me to the front door and gave me a brief, impersonal hug. We'd been cordial but distant—spouse colleagues—since our encounter in the basement, and my rudeness to the mortgage broker hadn't helped matters. We hadn't talked—I mean, *really* talked, aside from the logistics of child minding and pet care and who would pick up the dry cleaning. When Nicholas conspicuously unloaded a six-pack of O'Doul's nonalcoholic beer into the door of the fridge, I made an "I'll believe it when I see it" face. Every time I felt a moment's relief about his new temperance movement, I flashed back to Georgie, gamely waiting for me in the principal's office while he dozed drunkenly across the street, only five hundred feet away. This wouldn't be an easy image to forget.

"Good luck out there." Nicholas held me at an arm's length and then kissed my cheek.

"Thanks. Have fun at your tournament."

"Thanks."

He opened the door and gestured for me to walk through. Halfway down the walkway, which was now covered with a chalk hopscotch board, I turned around and said, "Nicholas, when I get home, we really need to have a state of the union conversation."

He leaned against the doorframe and crossed his arms over his chest. For a guy who'd come off a year-long bender, he looked pretty great: thin and strong, with a hint of a beard. Just as I was appreciating the badass scruff, he nodded curtly. "Trust me, Alice, I know that."

On the way to the airport, I noticed that the school drop-off line was fifteen cars deep at the end of Flower Street. Despite my proximity to the school, I rarely saw it; by the time the cars started lining up, my train was sliding down the gritty corridor between Bloomfield and Watsessing Avenue.

But Nicholas constantly complained about the gridlock, and I read friends' irritated status updates on Facebook. "Sat in car line for 30 min this morning. Anyone else wonder what would happen if an emergency vehicle needed to get through? Between the Denalis and the snowdrifts, good luck with that," wrote Kara, sparking a polite passive-aggressive war among the moms. I could picture them at granite kitchen islands all over town, sliding aside their Chobani yogurts and crafting careful but pointed—oh, so pointed—responses. "Perhaps you should consider dropping your kids one block away? Let Owen get his feet wet for a change?"

I knew one thing about being a working mom: you forfeited the right to weigh in on a subject like this one.

The flight to Cleveland was transcendent in every way. I'd long been suspicious of the claims of regular business travelers that it's a hardship to be away from home for a couple of days, to slog through an anonymous hotel lobby with no hope of seeing a friendly face at the end of the day. Fine, I get that, even though I, personally, have never felt anything but joy at the prospect of someone else making my bed or leaving a stack of fresh folded towels by the tub while I'm out.

But flying alone? I can't imagine it would ever get old. Once you've been a parent, trudging through airports lugging kid paraphernalia—car seat, Pack 'n Play, baby gym, booster seat—you never again take for granted the freedom of strolling toward your gate unencumbered.

I sidestepped the comically fast-paced people mover, collecting Toblerone chocolates, edamame, a mini-tray of takeout sushi, and two cans of Diet Coke on my way. I even took pleasure in the smooth glide of the purple rolling luggage I'd borrowed from Margot. It had been a Christmas gift from Judy and Elliott; in a rare burst of sweetness, she'd insisted I take it, even though my trip would be so short, I could have crammed all my clothes in a backpack.

Judy and Elliott didn't know about my trip to Cleveland. I was going to be in town for less than forty-eight hours, most of them gobbled up by Scroll. I knew Nicholas was annoyed about this, especially since he'd just spent an afternoon rewiring my mom's sound system to accommodate a turntable; thankfully, he was tactful enough not to comment.

I was landing at eleven, meeting with Greg at four, and catching an early morning flight back to New Jersey on Saturday, slated to arrive at Newark Airport at seven o'clock. My plan was to take a taxi from the airport to the train station, hop on a train to Filament, and be home in time to take Oliver to his basketball game. I didn't dare take a taxi all the way home from the airport since I'd been reprimanded for flouting the frugality tenet in my expense reports.

When my flight landed at Cleveland Hopkins, I stopped at an airport outpost of a famous local candy store, Malley's, to buy an assortment of chocolates as a going-away present for Jessie. First I grabbed a modest tray; then I splurged on an outrageous triple-layered affair of dark chocolate, milk chocolate, and truffles, all encased in a satin box tied with a garish purple ribbon.

As I was paying, my wallet slipped out of my hands and change spilled all over the counter, bouncing off the back of the cash register and plummeting to the floor in a loud, chaotic mess. It took me five minutes to collect my coins while the put-together twenty-something clerk rearranged the cardigan around her neck and surreptitiously checked her teeth in the mirrored chrome of the cash register. The last thing I picked up was a hair clip of Georgie's: turquoise plastic, with a bear playing the banjo at its center. This I tucked into my pocket for good luck.

I kept my head low as my taxi wound its way down the gray strip of highway leading to Scroll Headquarters. Even though Cleveland is a big-enough city, I was paranoid about getting spotted by Judy or Elliott or one of their sharp-eyed friends. It was a little sad and also a little exhilarating to pass the Cleveland landmarks that I'd visited as a new girlfriend, a fiancée, a wife, and later as a mother—but never before seen through the eyes of a midlevel, stressed-out, anonymous businesswoman wearing a blue Marimekko shift and navy wedge heels. Unfortunately, the dress was cut in such a way that it rode up too far when I bent over, which I absolutely could not do since my tights had a hole in them in exactly the wrong place. But when did I have time to go shopping for a new pair?

Ann had given security a heads-up about my arrival, so they didn't eye me with the suspicion and derision I remembered from orientation. This time they only requested two forms of ID alongside my blue employee card, which they advised me to wear around my neck on a lanyard they handed over surreptitiously. The lanyard was bright yellow, with 100% Wacky stitched around it in navy thread. The security guy and I both knew that I wasn't supposed to have one of these since I hadn't participated in the requisite battery of wacky tests at MainStreet's annual Down-Home BlockParty. This small act of generosity could very well have cost the man his job.

Ann told me to go straight to SodaFountain for my meeting with Greg. She said this with a straight face—she said everything with a straight face—and I was too nervous to smirk, as I normally did when the nostalgic names of Scroll conference rooms came up in casual conversation. SodaFountain, HardwareStore, CobblerShoppe.

When I arrived at SodaFountain, a guy in a hoodie was scribbling on the whiteboard with a squeaky red marker and everyone else at the table was tapping away at their laptops. Greg glanced up laconically from his spot by the dog treat buffet. He was wearing a T-shirt that said "Main-Street: Old is the New New."

"Hey, we're just wrapping up here. Everyone, you know Aileen Pearse from Scroll New York. Aileen, this is everyone."

"Actually, it's Alice. Hi, everyone." Seriously? Given Greg's prominence in my middle-of-the-night stress sessions, it was unfathomable to me that he still didn't know my name.

One by one the Scrollers filed out of SodaFountain, until I was alone with Greg. I smoothed my dress underneath me as I sat down, painfully aware of how short it was and noticing his quick flick of a glance at my legs. The room went completely silent, vacuum-sealed like a can of tuna when the last person out closed the door behind him. With my eyes closed, I might have mistaken this room for a church, instead of a drop-tile-ceilinged conference room on a bustling corporate campus in the middle of a midsized city on the banks of a Great Lake.

"So." Greg lifted his heather-blue hood onto his head, leaned back in his chair, and folded his hands under his chin in the manner of a student awaiting instruction.

"Well, thanks for meeting with me. It's good to be here. I'm always amazed by how short a trip—"

He glanced quickly at his wrist, where there was no watch. "Genevieve said you wanted to talk to me about an idea?"

"Yes. I've been thinking about the possibility of offering at-home book parties in conjunction with Scroll's rollout across the country. We can train a team of tastemakers to select the best titles each season, and then dispatch them to sell these books at pop-up literary salons hosted by individuals in their network. Like the Pampered Chef with a cultured twist."

"Huh." Greg looked skeptical at best. "Keep going."

"My thinking is, women, wine, and books are a proven formula. Under this model, we bring the books to the women. We narrow the choices. They can sit back on the couch and relax while our Book Lady plays matchmaker—"

"Why should these moms trust this Book Lady?"

"She's one of them, for starters. She's from their community, a friend of a friend maybe, so she knows which books will go over well in her world. Picking a book can be overwhelming for busy women. The Book Lady narrows the field, and she can sell you an e-book or a carbon-based—"

"No carbon-based. Has Genevieve not debriefed you on our Paper Is Poison initiative? Beyond biodegradable napkins, we're not going to have a shred of paper in our stores. Ever. We won't even take cash."

"That wouldn't be a problem in my model. Less for the Book Lady to lug around."

Greg shifted in his white chair, indicating the end of this part of the conversation by switching the leg he crossed over another, ankle to knee. "The human touch can be costly, Alice. I'll take this under advisement, but before we spitball anymore, I'd like an update on where you are with the Joystick initiative. I'd like to re-message the publishing community as soon as possible, and I'm going to need your enthusiasm to do that."

I cleared my throat and sat up straight in my chair, so my back wasn't even touching its white webbing. "Greg, I'm going to be honest with you. I'm not enthusiastic. Actually, I think the whole thing is a really bad idea."

Greg rolled his eyes. "Genevieve tells me you've had some issues with the content you've been asked to vet?"

"Yes."

"And . . . can you tell me a little bit more about that?"

I glanced quickly at the whiteboard, where the word "EXELL" [sic] was written in green dry-erase marker. "Well, I find the games offensive and in bad taste."

Greg placed his whole palm over his face and massaged it like he was thinking long and hard. But with all my practice testing kids on spelling words, I recognized this move as a stall tactic. He gestured with his hand, *Get on with it.*

"You could say my problem is three-pronged." (I thought the prongs might win me some points.) "First, I don't think my skills as a reader and as an editor are well utilized when I'm choosing video games to sell in our stores. Second, I don't think we should scrap our original mission, to create a peaceful lounge where people can read and buy books. Parents need a break from Romper Room."

"And?"

"And what?"

"You said there were three prongs. What's the third?"

I took a deep breath. "The third prong is the content of the video games. I don't feel good about that either."

Greg shrugged laconically. He furrowed his brow, exaggeratedly quizzical. "Come on, Alice, these are just games. All in good fun."

"I get that, but—I don't feel good about selling games where kids blow up buildings or kill each other."

I opened my notebook and pulled a piece of paper from its front pocket. Knowing how important it was to have data points and hard evidence to back up my claim, I'd copied and pasted sales figures and descriptions of Joystick's thirty top-selling games onto this paper. Now I unfolded it and started to read to Greg. "Here's their number one best seller: *Urban Bomber.* 'The object of the game is to steer a 747 loaded with explosives into as many tall buildings as possible before getting shot down

by military helicopters. The more buildings you topple, the more casualties you rack up. The more casualties you rack up—' "

"I get the idea, thanks. But Alice, if these are the games kids want to
play, we need to address that desire as a retailer." He smirked. "We're a
business, remember. How are we going to make big bucks? That's what
I want to know."

I knew what Genevieve would say. I could hear her voice all the way
in Cleveland, urging me to remain neutral. But in this instance, with so
much at stake, that approach seemed like yet another attempt at trying to
be something I wasn't.

There was another voice in my head, louder than Genevieve's, and
it belonged to my dad, who had lost his voice and struggled mightily to
find it again. I pictured him in the early days after his laryngectomy, remembered how he moved his lips to speak and no words came out. Not a
sound. Watching him get yanked back to the new normal had been devas-
tating. Again and again and again.

You have a voice. Use it.

"Greg, I don't have an answer to your question. I feel like I was hired
to be an architect and now you're asking me to be a plumber. From a business standpoint, I guess I understand why you want to sell video games,
but from a human perspective, I don't think I'm the right person to curate
the selection or to sell this pivot to the public. From a maternal perspective, what would I tell my kids if their jobs took such an unexpected—
and, I'll be honest, offensive—turn? I'd tell them to speak up."

I sat back in my chair and took a sip of antioxidant water from a biodegradable cup made of reclaimed plastic. I felt for Georgie's hair clip in
my pocket. The room was quiet again.

Happy birthday, Dad.

Outside, two Scroll employees threw a Frisbee in the courtyard while
a golden retriever puppy ran back and forth between them, frantically
trying to catch the plastic disc in his mouth.

Greg still reclined in his chair, frozen again in a relaxed pose but alight
with tension and disapproval and annoyance. Like a paper clip snapped

out of shape, his small mouth reorganized itself into a cool smile. "Well, then. You're a valuable member of our team, Alice. I hope you find a way to make this work."

I walked back to Ann's cubicle, feeling a little bit proud and a little bit mortified and mostly just really, really hungry. At *You*, I had been a team player. I got along well with others. I did as I was told. Now the stakes were higher. I'd given up too much on the home front to spend my waking hours putting guns (even virtual ones) into the hands of kids. I hadn't carried my five-month-old through the rubble on 9/11 to do this for a living.

I remembered the rows of lawyers at my dad's funeral. Former friends, stars of his favorite stories, filing out of the church in silence. Work was important, but it wasn't everything.

Before I rounded the corner to Ann's desk, I stopped in the empty hallway to yank up my tattered, disobedient tights, which felt like they might forfeit altogether and land in a disgraced pool around my ankles.

"Whose groovy purple suitcase is that?" Through a little cut-out in the wall, I saw a guy leaning into Ann's desk in the universal stance of a man talking to a woman at work: bent in half at the waist, face propped on hands propped on elbows.

"That's Alice's. She's just out for the day from New York." Ann's voice was curt, as always.

"Really? Looks like she's planning to move in. This thing is a steamer trunk!"

Laughter all around.

"What can I say? She's a mom."

More laughing.

"Obviously."

What can I say? She's a mom.

Margot had personally introduced me to each zippered compartment, showing me where to store my shampoo and how to pack an extra pair of shoes, soles out, so they wouldn't get the rest of my clothes dirty.

My eyes prickled.

Why yes, I thought. I *am* a mom.

The hotel was garden-variety airport chic, decorated in subtle oatmeal hues and featuring one of those ingenious shower rods that bow out to give you more space while you bathe. I ordered an early dinner from room service—caprese salad and penne à la vodka, which arrived on a little doily soaked in oil. After I finished eating, I called Nicholas, hoping to catch him before he headed out on the town for the night. After five rings, my call went to voice mail.

Then I checked my work e-mails. Among the sixty-seven metrics reports and OOTO notices and announcements from GatheringPlace and expense reimbursement queries was the message I had been expecting from Genevieve. She kept it simple; I had to hand it to her for that.

To: alicepearse@scroll.com
From: genevieveandrews@scroll.com

Please drop a 1:1 on my calendar so we can discuss your meeting with Greg. If it's important to you to have a job that is 100% aligned with your sense of self, we should talk about the fit.

That night, I slept well for the first time in months.

My alarm went off at 5:15 a.m. I pressed snooze twice and ended up in a mad dash to get to the airport on time. When I boarded the plane, I snapped at the Continental gate attendant, who seemed puzzled by the disparity between my driver's license photo and the woman standing before him ("It was taken a long time ago, okay?"), and then I spilled coffee all over my jeans as soon as we were in the air. The sense of peace I'd felt the night before had been supplanted by a terrible unease. How would I get out of this mess?

CLE → EWR.

40

The train from Newark arrived in Filament at 8:32 a.m. I'd been in constant contact with Jessie by text, so she knew what time to expect me. What I did not expect, when I climbed off the train, was to see Oliver running down Flower Street toward the station, coat unzipped and flying like a cape behind him, hell-bent on meeting me before I made it down the path to North Edison.

I watched him from half a block away, as if I were watching a movie about somebody else's lanky, sweet, freckled boy: pausing for the slightest second on the corner of North Edison, looking to the right, only to the right but not the left—the street was two-way, now, remember?—and then stepping into the street without seeing the green Ford Flex muscling its way toward him at top speed from the other side of the school.

The car was going too fast; Oliver was going too fast.

Once again, I opened my mouth and made noise.

In a split second, his life flashed before me: a newborn baby, red and wailing in a Plexiglas bassinet at NYU hospital while the sun rose over the East River and nurses listened to his freshly minted heart; the black-felt cat costume he wore on his first birthday; his bossy commands at bed-time: Sing my song, Kiss my lips ("Tiss my whips"); Oliver in preschool, racing into the gym at the end of the day, into the crowd of waiting adults, his face bright with joy; cheek to the floor, giving a chubby plastic dump truck the universal boy *vroom* sound; a gentle, dimpled hand resting in the middle of Georgie's back, teaching her how to dive; Ollie on the beach in Maine, emerging from the water at Cedar Beach to place gray rock after gray rock in a red bucket, each one a beloved addition to a collection curated according to standards only he understood; Oliver scoring a goal at a lacrosse game; Oliver opening his eyes in the morning and looking at me for a second like he had never seen me before; Oliver waiting by the bench in front of the school, alone.

Sweet prince. Baby bird. Little fish. Blue-eyed boy.

All the names; all the days, hours, minutes, and seconds.

I thought, *This* is infinity.

Oliver stood frozen in the middle of the road like a mannequin boy wear-ing a Filament Brights cap and a black and red winter coat from a bargain basement sale at an expensive ski store. Look closely and you could see the dirt on the cuffs and along the zipper from slide tackling on frozen ground. He's a boy who plays outside every day, wearing away the grass on every inch of the front yard, no matter how cold it is. He never stops moving. And yet, there he was, at a standstill, watching with a kind of shocked curiosity to see if the Flex would stop in time.

I watched, too. It was the longest wait of my life. One word popped into my head: *empty-handed*.

With a screaming symphony of brakes, the car came to a halt three inches from Oliver. The sound brought him back to life, and he ran back to the curb he'd come from, the one closer to home, instead of running straight into my arms. It was an odd choice, a reflex, but I noticed.

The driver of the car was a man in his sixties: thin face, gray crew cut, thick old-fashioned glasses, a modern version of the scientists who narrated reel-to-reel films about the solar system when I was in grade school (*Can we watch it backward?*). The window projected a map of naked tree branches onto the driver's face. But I could still see him, shaking his head at me, tight-lipped. Then he drove away.

Without looking both ways, I crossed over and gathered my boy in my arms.

41

The rest was easy.

No, actually, it wasn't easy.

But it was clear: the motherhood equivalent of love at first sight. Sometimes you just *know*. And so you rearrange your life around what you glimpsed through a little window that opened for one second to show you a glimpse of something you might never get to see again. Even so, you know you will never forget the view.

Oliver and I held hands and walked home. Margot came bounding down the stairs and I realized another thing: she needed a bra. My mind started to dance the familiar outsourcing jig—would Nicholas have time, could I ask Jessie to take her? And then I thought, *No, this is my job*. I remembered my mom's cool hands on my back, adjusting thin straps in the dressing room at a Lord & Taylor that is now a Gold's Gym. Not a happy memory, exactly, but a necessary one; more of a transaction than an occasion. My daughter deserved the same.

"Mommy, how was your trip?

"Did you bring presents?"

"Did you see Grandma and Grandpa?"

"Did you know we have a turtle in our classroom?"

We said good-bye to Jessie. The plan was for my mom to watch the kids while we looked for a new sitter. Jessie had to take her flying leap into the next phase of life, but first, I rested my chin on the shoulder where all three of my kids had rested theirs.

"How can I possibly thank you for all you've—"

"Alice, don't. It's too much." She pressed a finger against her lips and shook her head, gesturing toward Margot, Oliver, and Georgie. They were silent, lined up at the bottom of the stairs with glum looks on their faces. I knew they resented me for encouraging Jessie to take the new job, but I hoped they would understand someday that it wouldn't have been right to hold her back.

Someday they'll understand. How many times does this phrase run through a mother's head?

"But, seriously, I want you to know, I'm incredibly grateful for—"

"I know you are. I am, too." She brushed a strand of half blue, half sandy-brown hair out of her face. I knew she was trying to cultivate a more professional look, letting her hair go back to its natural color. This seemed like a prudent idea, but I couldn't shake the image of a colorful parrot with its wings clipped.

Jessie spread her arms out wide and gestured for all three kids to pile in. Then she wrapped her arms around them and squeezed them together until they squealed in protest. "Jessie, you're suffercating us!" From the back, all I could see were six hands clutching Jessie's back. I had to look away.

When it was my turn, I followed her lead and tried to keep it simple. "I love you, Jessie."

"I love you, Alice."

The feeling was remarkably similar to the one I had when I broke up with my first boyfriend in a diner parking lot: brokenhearted, but with the perspective to be grateful for all the events that had led to this moment. In both cases, I had been certain we'd stay close. In this case, that turned out to be true.

Nicholas came home late Saturday night. The kids were already asleep when I heard the familiar clomp of his feet on the front steps. I met him at the door wearing his brown North Face sweatshirt, holding Cornelius's collar so he wouldn't lick Nicholas's face raw. I was so happy to see his wide smile and the beloved, friendly crinkles around his eyes. Beyond happy.

"Well, hello! I thought you weren't coming home until tomorrow!"

He wrapped me in his arms in the exact spot I'd said my good-byes to Jessie twelve hours earlier. "We lost our game, and I didn't feel like going out. One night was enough. Also, it sounded like you . . . ?"

We still hadn't had a thorough debrief on my conversation with Greg, but I'd delivered the gist via text.

"It sounded like what?"

"It sounded like the Cleveland trip didn't go so well."

"I wouldn't say it went *badly*. It was just . . . eye-opening."

"In what way?"

Now we were sitting on the couch next to each other, feet up on the coffee table, with Cornelius lying contentedly underneath. I took a deep breath. "Let's see, I don't even know where to start. To begin with, I hate my job." I figured I'd begin the conversation on neutral territory.

He chuckled and nodded. "You know, on my drive to AC, I was thinking I can't remember the last time I saw you read a book. That's not normal."

"I can't concentrate. I keep thinking I'm just sad about my dad or worried about you, but it's more than that."

"I wish you wouldn't worry about me. I'm—"

"But that's the thing, how can I *not* worry?" Okay, so we were going to dive right in. Cornelius lifted his nose off his paws and gave me a heavy-lidded stare. The look on his face said, *My God, woman! This again?* "Nicholas, I get it that you've had some huge changes in your life. So have I. But you went from being a guy who had one or two beers at a party or maybe a little bourbon with your dad, to a guy drinking hard liquor in the middle of the afternoon. In our unfinished, disgusting basement!" I tried to keep my tone light—I really, really didn't want this to turn into a fight—but the weight on my shoulders reminded me of the stocks Will and I once posed in at Old Sturbridge Village.

"Alice, that will. Never. Happen. Again. It's been—what? Three weeks? I've turned over a new leaf, I swear—"

"I know. I believe you. I guess what I don't understand is, if you could quit cold turkey like that, why didn't you do it months ago? Why did you ever get started in the first place? When I first met you, you barely even drank. *That* was the guy I fell in love with!" I hesitated, hoping he wouldn't point out that the girl he fell in love with weighed 125 pounds and pretended to like reggae.

Nicholas stared straight ahead at the row of blue and yellow tiles above the fireplace. We'd laid them ourselves while our kids napped, then built a fire and fell asleep in each other's arms on the couch.

Now he turned his eyes to meet mine. "Here's the thing. My job situation was disappointing, then stressful, but then just as I started to realize it was a good thing—maybe the best thing, to be out on my own—your dad—" He stopped. His eyes were red and a little watery; for a fraction of a second, I wondered if he was high. But then I recognized the look on Nicholas's face: pain. Those were tears in his eyes.

"Wait, what about my dad?"

"Well, he got sick again and that was awful, to see what you were going through. But also—Alice, I loved him, too."

"I know that." I stopped. *Of course* he had loved my dad, the same way I loved his. We'd known each other's parents since we were barely adults ourselves. I pictured Elliott's face as he told a funny story, the puckish O of his mouth while he waited for his audience's laughter to subside. He wasn't my dad, but he was pretty close. How would I feel if he were sick? (Knock wood a million times.)

"Can you let me finish? My point is, I wanted to be there for you; I tried to be there for you, and I think I was. But the drinking—it was a way to lighten my own load, and then it just got . . . out of hand, I guess. I feel terrible about it, and embarrassed, especially about the time with Georgie. That was the end."

I'd known Nicholas for twenty years; we'd been married for thirteen. I could count on two hands all the times he'd been unreliable or unpredictable during that time—and at least one hand's worth had occurred in the six months leading up to this conversation. I'd been prepared to give Nicholas the benefit of the doubt, but now I realized, he deserved total absolution. Given the miracles he'd performed as a son-in-law, he might have qualified for canonization.

"Nicholas, I believe you. And I feel terrible that I was so wrapped up." I smoothed a still-black wave of hair behind his ear. "I never really stopped to think how much you'd miss my dad, too."

He grabbed my left hand and held it between his in an impromptu, late-night, middle-aged approximation of a vow renewal. "We can do better. Let's promise."

"I promise."

"Me, too." He leaned to pet Cornelius, who looked relieved that the discussion hadn't escalated into a fight. "Alice, on a more mundane note, can we please get back to your job?"

I groaned. "Yes. What about it?"

"I think you should start looking for a new one."

"The problem is, I have no idea what I want to do next."

"Then I think you should quit and take some time to figure it out."

This option hovered in front of me like a mirage. "I feel like I can't. We need the money. Then, on the other hand, the equation doesn't add up. This is not a job worth missing out on life for."

"I know."

"How do you know?"

He laughed. I loved the way his face looked from where I was sitting: still every inch the boy I'd fallen in love with, but also the face of a man who would crawl through a window to shovel his in-laws' roof on the way to work.

"I just know. For what it's worth, not to kick you while you're down, but it hasn't exactly been easy living with you lately."

I fought the urge to dispute his claim. "What about our finances?"

"We'll figure it out. Our straits are not as dire as you seem to think they are. I'm building my business. It takes time. But it's going well so far. And if we've learned anything this year, it's that life is short. You need to be happy."

"I know. It's just . . . I was so proud when I got this job. It makes me sad to think how wrong it turned out to be."

"There are other places."

"I know." I paused. "Nicholas? I hope you know how much I adore you."

He smiled. "I adore you, too."

The next thing was hard to say without crying. "Also, I hope it goes without saying, but my dad loved you. He loved you like a son, and a dear friend."

"I know, Al. I never doubted that."

I laid my head in his lap and he gently slid the elastic out of my ponytail.

42

Monday morning was sunny and warm, and the crocuses were out. The train conductor called out the name of each station in a deep baritone that sounded almost operatic. When I bought a single ticket, he waived the usual surcharge for making a purchase on the train and reminded me to get my new monthly ticket on the way home.

Genevieve was late for our 1:1, but she swooped past my office on her way in from the elevator and gestured for me to follow. When I closed her door behind us—click—she paused, trench coat in one hand, hanger in the other.

"No."

"Yes."

"You're leaving?"

"I am."

"You're *not*."

"Genevieve, I think we both know this isn't working. I'm not the person you need for this job."

She sighed. She had become so hard-nosed—the antithesis of the chatty bookworm I'd fallen for at the Union Square Café—but she was still just the messenger delivering tidings from Cleveland. "I know how hard it's been for you to make this all work, with your family and everything."

The shred of sympathy I had for Genevieve began to evaporate. Suddenly I knew that we would never break Ethiopian bread together, and this realization came as a relief.

"I don't want to give the impression that I'm leaving to spend more time with my family, like some sort of disgraced politician. Genevieve, I'm leaving because the position you hired me for doesn't exist."

Her glare didn't scare me anymore.

"And I'm not naïve enough to think that my job needs to align one hundred percent with my sense of self. I've never had that in a job, or expected it. But I know what my talents are and they're not needed here. I'd like to find a place where they are needed. This isn't that place."

Genevieve nodded. "You know, you'd be a natural in sales, Alice. All the work you've done here has underscored that."

She wasn't my friend. Never had been; never would be.

"Thanks." (No exclamation point.) I noticed that her nails were dull, bitten to the quick. There was a greenish cast to her skin, as if she hadn't been outside in weeks.

We talked logistics.

There was a departure protocol, of course. I would be contacted by my human resources representative—alas, not Chris Pawlowski, who had offered me the job; he had been fired in the interim and was now suing Scroll for wrongful termination. I would have an exit interview. My computer would be collected and scrubbed clean. My outstanding expenses would be paid. My blue badge would be surrendered. I would be referred to the Employee Resource Center if my final paycheck didn't materialize within a specified amount of time.

Finally, I held up my hand to stop Genevieve's litany, which was starting to have the ring of Miranda rights. "I appreciate all this. I'm sure we'll figure it all out."

"If you have any questions, you can look for answers in Gathering-Place or the wiki. And Alice, I'm sad about this. I wanted to make it work."

"I know."

At lunchtime, I bought pears from the fruit guy and ate them on a marble slab bench by the LOVE sculpture on the corner of 55th Street and Sixth Avenue. While tourists posed for pictures—shyly, outrageously, one guy sticking his tongue out of his mouth into the V of his index and middle finger—I called Nicholas. "It's done."

I heard him smile. "How do you feel?"

"Numb? Relieved? Worried I'm never going to find another job."

"You will. You did the right thing. You couldn't stay there. Remember the first tenant: Winners Get It Right."

To: scrolleveryone@scroll.com
Cc: humanresources@scroll.com, payroll@scroll.com,
   techserve@scroll.com, publicity@scroll.com
From: genevieveandrews@scroll.com

Alice Pearse's last day with us will be on April 17. We thank her for her service and wish her the best of luck in future endeavors. Please refer any questions to the Employee Resource Center or file a trouble ticket.

One by one, my New York colleagues filed into my office, closed the door, and recited their own litanies of frustration. They were universally supportive of my decision, especially Matthew, who followed up with this e-mail: "You'll be missed, Pearse." I looked over at him, two feet away, glued to his laptop, sitting in a defeated slump at his standing desk. At least I'd leave Scroll with one friend. Matthew and I were soldiers together in the same war, and I wouldn't forget him when I landed on my native soil.

I didn't hear from anyone in Cleveland.

• • •

I went straight from the train to the bookstore. Susanna was reading on a high stool by the cash register. When she heard the jingle of the bells on the door, she looked up, then looked momentarily surprised to see me. Maybe I'd been avoiding her; maybe she'd been avoiding me. The rift between our older girls remained unexamined, and I tried not to notice or care that Audrey's birthday had come and gone without an invitation to the annual hibachi party at Benihana. Friendships wax and wane; I knew that. I didn't want to be a stage manager mom, although it was harder than I expected to be relegated to a bit part in Margot's life.

I walked to the middle of the store, stopping at the counter between a rack of Blue Owl bookmarks and a little bowl of Werther's caramels. "Susanna, I quit."

"You—*what?*" She leaned forward and grabbed my shoulders, knocking over the wooden stool behind her. "*What?*"

"It wasn't the right place for me. I don't want to be the horse in the parking lot."

Knowing nothing about the pivot or the spreadsheets, Susanna threw her arms around me and said, "You were too good for them."

This time, she was the one who cried. Over her shoulder, I watched two burly men lug a deli counter out of Mercadante's.

My kids were nonplussed.

"Does this mean we won't redo the kitchen?" asked Margot.

"No, we won't redo the kitchen. But I'll be around more while I'm looking for a new job and I'll be able to come into your classrooms for book clubs—"

"Mommy, did you know Cornelius can go down the slide by hisself?"

"Actually, Georgie, I did *not* know that. Thanks for telling me. Are you glad I'll pick you up at school more?"

"I guess. Will Jessie come, too?"

"No, lovebird. But when I find a new job, we'll find a new babysitter and she'll be really nice, too."

Oliver looked up from his baked ziti. "Mommy? I need to bring an abacus to school on Friday. Do you have one?"

"No, I do not."

"Mommy, do I have to eat this kale? It's so . . . ruffly."

It's lucky I wasn't expecting a ticker tape parade.

The next morning, I woke up and felt the most exquisite sense of relief. Then I turned to Nicholas, who was also awake and staring up at the ceiling.

"Good morning."

"Good morning to you, too. Do you feel like this is the first day of the rest of your life?" He rolled over and lifted my chin with his index finger. Suddenly we were eye to eye—so close I could see faint flecks of yellow in his irises.

"I do. Nicholas?"

"Alice?"

"Are you worrying about the money?"

He sighed and rubbed his face. "No. I mean, yes. Long term, do I hope you find a job you love where you have a fat paycheck? Yes. But short term, I think you need to give yourself some breathing room."

"Breathing room?"

"A month, maybe, or the summer. Just to figure out where you *are*. You deserve that."

Georgie skidded into our room like Kramer from *Seinfeld*. The day was upon us.

43

To: alicepearse@scroll.com
From: genevieveandrews@scroll.com

Please provide me with a list of names and contact information for the
contacts you've been working with. We'll take it from here, thanks.

I picked up a batch of dresses and skirts from the dry cleaner and
wondered when I'd have a chance to wear them again. I threaded Georgie's ponytail through the little hole at the back of a baseball cap and
realized I'd be home to see her turning cartwheels in the outfield during
her softball games. As I started boxing up my office, flowers arrived from
Susanna. The note said, "Congratulations! No more horsing around."

The Sunday before my last day, we all drove into the city to collect my
belongings. It was the first time my family had seen my office and I felt
oddly proud to give them the grand tour: this is the kitchen I flooded with

coffee; this is the airshaft I dropped the bathroom key into, this is the toilet where I flushed the brownie.

It was bittersweet. I felt relieved and I felt like a failure. I felt as though I was moving back home after dropping out of college.

While Nicholas and I carted boxes to the elevator, the kids appropriated some Expo markers and used them to draw Martians on the glass window next to my office door.

"Can we leave them, Mommy, please?"

"Fine," I said, remembering the dismissive conversation I'd overheard in Cleveland. *What can I say? She's a mom.* There were worse ways to be remembered.

> To: scrolleveryone@scroll.com
> From: alicepearse@scroll.com
>
> I left *You* with a mock-up of a magazine cover featuring my face on Maria Menounos's body. I leave Scroll knowing how the retail business works, from the ground up. Thank you for answering my questions, solving my technical problems, and being my friend while I was here. No matter how much you think you might miss me, please do not hit "reply all" if you're moved to respond to this e-mail. That can be your farewell gift!

> To: alicepearse@scroll.com
> From: genevieveandrews@scroll.com
> Subject: last day
>
> Do you want to grab lunch?

> To: genevieveandrews@scroll.com
> From: alicepearse@scroll.com
> Subject: Re: last day
>
> Sure, I'd love to. What time?

To: alicepearse@scroll.com
From: genevieveandrews@scroll.com
Subject: Re: Re: last day

Are you okay with eating in my office?

To: genevieveandrews@scroll.com
From: alicepearse@scroll.com
Subject: Re: Re: Re: last day

Sure. When should I come by?

To: alicepearse@scroll.com
From: genevieveandrews@scroll.com
Subject: Re: Re: Re: Re: last day

1 p.m. I'll have a turkey with pesto, an apple, and a seltzer.

I collected the meal from Pret and brought it back upstairs.

When I arrived at Genevieve's door, she was wrapping up a phone call. She indicated that this was the case by reaching her arm out and making a swirling gesture with her index finger, a move that made me feel like I was the waiter and she was a customer requesting the check.

In the same vein, I arranged her order on the desk: sandwich, apple, bottle of seltzer, straw, napkin folded in half. I almost bowed, in the way of trendy waitstaff, but then thought the better of it. With the meal all teed up, I settled into my usual spot on the couch, feeling a jolt of joy when I realized that I would never again sit in this spot—ever *ever*, as Georgie would say. I released my egg salad sandwich from its clear plastic container and nibbled daintily around the edges while holding my hand underneath to prevent stray yolk from falling to the floor.

Lunch at the Union Square Café this was not.

Alice Pearse is holding steady, approaching her final one hundred meters. She looks strong, head held high. She has one more hurdle to clear before—

"Sorry, sorry, sorry." Genevieve returned the receiver to its cradle with a loud *thunk*. "I was just schmoozing with Greg. I finally had a chance to play *Urban Bomber* last night, and oh man, what a hoot—" She paused midsentence, realizing who she was talking to. "Sorry, I forgot you're anti—"

I had just taken a big bite of egg salad but I waved away her discomfort with one hand. In a full-mouth cheap trick I forbade my kids to employ at the dinner table, I let the other hand hover in front of my lips and spoke before I swallowed: "Please. No judgments. Suicide bombers just aren't my . . . cup of tea."

Genevieve shrugged. "And I get that. But the sound effects in this game are truly phenomenal. You feel like you're *right there.*"

I imagined her in a dark room, her face lit by the glow of the game. Then I remembered the cozy blanket of Georgie as she sprawled on my lap while I read *Officer Buckle and Gloria* and *A Bad Case of Stripes.* That had been the highlight of *my* night. Or maybe when Margot beat me in Hangman, or maybe when I planted a kiss on Oliver's eyelid right before I went to bed. It was a toss-up, really.

"So." Genevieve cleared her throat. Her sandwich remained on the desk, untouched. Considering that it was too late for me to get reimbursed for the meal, eating with gusto seemed like the least she could do. Suddenly I remembered Genevieve's youthful voice chirping, "Bon app!"

"So. I guess this is it." I folded my napkin and returned the uneaten half of my sandwich to its container, making a mental note to pack it in Margot's lunch the next day; egg salad was her favorite. But sulfurous leftovers in the middle school cafeteria? Maybe not the best idea.

"I guess it is. Alice—" Genevieve cracked open her seltzer, then winced as the bubbly water exploded all over her laptop and down the front of her shirt. Naturally, I'd given the bottle a vigorous shake in the elevator. (Mature, no. Satisfying? Absolutely. Listen, I wasn't born a mom.)

She regained her composure and smile-smirked at me. "Alice, I really can't wait to hear about your next adventures."

"I really can't wait to find out what they are." I smiled right back, for real. *Genevieve Andrews is no match for Alice Pearse! The Jersey native is nearing the finish line in a full-on, all-out sprint! The end is in sight!*

Genevieve looked away, her tired eyes finding their way to the drop tile ceiling, which wasn't as pristine as it had been when I first started: the white was now mottled with a rusty-looking stain. Blood, perhaps?

I started to feel giddy. Visions of exclamation points danced in my head!!!

Suddenly, Genevieve was all business. "Alice, I'll need to collect your first edition, please."

I reached into my bag and pulled out *A Room of One's Own*, still trapped in its transparent pocket. I'd removed it only one time, that very morning, to insert a three-by-five notecard in the middle of the book. The card was printed with three words, written in pencil so as not to harm the beloved old pages: *ALICE WAS HERE*. I didn't care who found this proof of life. As my girl Virginia said, "Literature is strewn with the wreckage of those who have minded beyond reason the opinion of others."

I knew there was a room of my own in the future, but it was somewhere else—far, far away from Scroll.

Quietly, as gracefully as I've ever done anything, I gave Genevieve a farewell hug. I'm not sure we actually touched each other, but our arms went through the motions and our faces wore appropriate neutral expressions. Then I deposited my laptop and ID tag on her desk and exited her office.

I said good-bye to some people, not to others. I wished them all the best. And then I exited the building.

When I emerged from the revolving doors into the early spring day, I turned around and looked up at the tall box of glass. I wondered how long it would be before I worked in a skyscraper again, how long before I would drink a fresh cup of coffee in a quiet midtown conference room. Would I have an office again? A view? A business card? Direct deposit?

I walked by a shoeshine guy, Korean delis, luggage stores, camera stores, three Duane Reades, the back of the Winter Garden Theatre, Ray's Famiglia, Red Lobster, Ruby Tuesday's, all the places I'd walked by so many times in either an angry huff or a sad slump on my way home from Scroll. Now I threw my shoulders back and lengthened my stride, grinning from ear to ear like the star of a romantic comedy after her first date with the love of her life.

The sun was setting on the way home, draping a blanket of pink clouds over the Meadowlands and the Newark Bears stadium and the back lots of downtown Bloomfield.

As the 6:09 train approached Filament, I deleted my Outlook account from my iPhone. The touch of one red lozenge of a button and it was gone. No more reply-all messages referring to a joke that had happened in an office halfway across the country; no more OOTO notifications from a stranger letting me know that they were missing a half day of work to renew their driver's license; no more dizzying columns of numbers.

I scrolled to the top of a year's worth of text conversations with my dad and deleted that too. I worried I'd regret it, but I couldn't imagine a scenario where I wouldn't feel terrible for all the messages I never responded to, all the links I never clicked. Besides, those texts were no more his real voice than Buzz Lightyear had been. That voice was still in my head, getting louder every day as the memory of his suffering receded. This was the silver lining of loss.

I turned off my white noise app, plucked out my earbuds, and listened to the sound of the real-life train whistle. I knew every curlicue of graffiti on every cement wall we passed. I looked for the EMTs smoking cigarettes behind the rescue squad and into the windows of offices whose layouts I imagined I knew as well as my own. When the conductor came around to collect tickets, I handed mine over before he asked.

We hadn't planned it, but I wasn't surprised to find my kids waiting for me when I climbed down the steps to the platform. Three rosy faces aglow with expectation and excitement; three wide smiles revealing baby teeth, big new permanent teeth, and one upper row fenced in by a retainer. Margot quietly slipped her hand into the pocket of my coat, and Oliver and Georgie each grabbed a hand.

"Congratulations, Mommy! You made it."

"Thanks, lovebirds. I did."

In a four-person tangle, with the promise of spaghetti on the table and Choco Tacos in the freezer, we walked home.

EPILOGUE

Of course, we had to cancel the renovation. Marjorie came by to pick up a monogrammed tape measure she'd left behind and, on her way out the door, paused for one final assessment of our dilapidated kitchen. I braced myself, resisting the urge to apologize for the Tupperware piled willy-nilly on top of the fridge.

"You know, Alice, this is one of the ten happiest houses I've worked in."

"Really?"

"Really."

We splurged on the dishwasher of Nicholas's dreams: Bosch, whisper-quiet, three racks. It works wonders on wineglasses (all mine).

I made a list of people to talk to about jobs: agents, editors, even a friend who writes copy for a wig catalog. The list was longer this time, and I found that people e-mailed me back more promptly than they had the year before. A few wanted the scoop on what had happened at Scroll— how could I have walked away from such an exciting opportunity? Those people were probably sorely disappointed to hear my epiphany about the horse in the parking garage. But most just seemed eager to welcome one of their own back to the fold. Book people stick together.

My high-powered publishing friend, Bonnie, and I became friends on Facebook. She invited me for lunch at the Grand Central Oyster Bar. She wrote, "If bucket lists had been a thing in 1995, ours would have included oysters Rockefeller. Let's do it."

I listened for the 8:16 train every morning. Most of the time, I was happy not to be on it.

My mom needed a hip replacement; all those years of climbing marble museum steps had finally taken their toll. When the doctor delivered the news, she was sitting on his table, wearing paper shorts. Reading glasses on, notebook out, she dutifully transcribed every word of the treatment plan: surgery, two nights in the hospital, four days at a rehab facility, six weeks of physical therapy.

The doctor turned to me. "How's your schedule looking? Will you be able to help Mom out?"

I thought of my dad in a hospital bed, in a hospital gown, tears streaming down his cheeks. No sound.

That would not happen again.

"Of course. My brother will be here, too. We're a team."

On the last day of school, I pored over report cards, admired final art projects, served real Oreos, not Newman-O's, and then hustled everybody into the minivan so we could get to the pool.

Georgie and Oliver were in a vicious spat for the duration of the six-minute drive, and Margot's eyes remained glued to her phone no matter how many times I tried to engage her in conversation. Maybe I had too much riding on the afternoon, but something in me snapped. "You guys, can we just treat each other *like human beings?*"

I yelled so loudly, the tendons in my neck ached for days. (Name a parent who hasn't suffered from this affliction and I will show you someone who is not my friend.) It was a depressing turn of events but also cathartic, and a powerful reminder that there is no scripted fun where kids are concerned. You have to be nimble.

After dinner, when the four of us were eating ice cream cones at the snack bar, Georgie said, "It's funny, because Jessie never yelled at us."

After the deli closed, a Christian Science reading room moved in next door to the Blue Owl. I never found out why Scroll didn't take the spot, and I never told Susanna they'd planned on opening there. In the front window of the reading room was an easel with this quote from Mary Baker Eddy: "Home is the dearest spot on earth, and should be the centre, not the boundary, of the affections."

Amen. Even people who are half-Jewish, half-Christmas can get on board with that.

I collected book review assignments and worked on them during Margot's early-morning swim team practices. In one ear, I heard Genevieve's voice: "No exclamation points. Think like a business manager. Are you on the bus?" In the other, the booming, Polish-accented voice of Margot's coach: "You can do it! Go for it! Kick, kick, kick!" Her encouragement was directed at a pool full of winded kids, but the message had a cleansing effect on me, drowning out a litany of self-doubt. I would get back in the game. I just needed to figure out which story

I belonged in, and I gave myself until the end of the summer to think about how it would unfold. As Thomas Edison said, "There is a time for everything."

Dear Jessie,

Happy birthday! I remember when you couldn't even buy a bottle of wine. Or *vote*! But you were always wise beyond your years.

25! Wow. Let's see . . . do I have any useful advice?

First of all, enjoy your straight, dark hair because soon it will be threaded with kinky, coarse gray. And go easy on your eyebrows—you'll miss them when they thin into pale shadows of their former selves.

If you're planning to spend the rest of your life with someone, make sure he's funny. You might find that your definition of *sexy* changes over time; but what makes you laugh will stay the same. Money, looks, ambition, success—those change, too. Funny has legs.

Also, please don't waste time wondering whether it's possible to "have it all." Banish the expression from your vocabulary; make sure your friends do, too. A better question is What do you really *want?* Diving headlong into the second quarter of your life without asking this question is like going grocery shopping without a list. You'll end up with a full cart but nothing to cook for dinner. Figure out what you feel like eating, and then come up with your own recipe for the whole messy, delicious enchilada.

Also? Everyone reminds you to call your mom. Call your dad, too. Not one day goes by when I don't wish I could call mine.

You are a beautiful human being. We are all so lucky to have your
particular sparkle in our lives.

Love,

Alice

Even though the card I wrote it on cost $6.95, I never gave this
note to Jessie. I crumpled it up and hid it at the bottom of the recycling
bin. In the end, I collaborated with Margot, Oliver, and Georgie on an
acrostic for Jessie's birthday. I'm pretty sure she recognized my contribution:

Jaunty

Excellent

Savvy

Sweet

Intelligent

Essential

In two months, Jessie went from receptionist to office manager to fi-
nance lead at her new company. She was the first person to see a picture
of Georgie missing both front teeth.

Greg followed me on Twitter.

Matthew was miserable at Scroll, but at least he had his own office. We toasted sticktoitiveness over dinner. It was one of the tenants,
after all.

MainStreet became embroiled in a high-profile lawsuit with the city of
Cleveland for illegal disposal of waste and noncompliance with the man-

datory recycling program. As a cost-cutting measure, the Rockwells had sanctioned late-night dumping of bottles, cans, and cardboard into a Dumpster behind Walmart. They were caught on camera by a local activist group, Occupy Main Street. As an editor, I applauded their commitment to the space between Main and Street.

As of this writing, the Scroll stores have not yet opened in New York or Chicago.

Nicholas and I left Margot in charge at home for the first time and the kids were thrilled to see us go. We ended up having so much fun at dinner that we missed our movie.

At the beginning of August, two struggling Pennsylvania paper companies consulted the same bank about borrowing money to save them from bankruptcy. The bank had been so impressed with the work Nicholas did for the Mercadantes, they recommended him as an outside counsel, who could handle negotiations with other lenders.

"Not to go all retail on you," I said, "but this bank sounds like a promising anchor tenant, don't you think?" Nicholas and I were lounging on the front porch after the kids went to bed. Above our heads hung Georgie's latest art project: CDs decorated in Sharpie, spinning dizzyingly on fishing wire. The neighborhood reflected in miniature as they turned: school, skip laurels, silver sky. I shuddered to think of books becoming as superfluous as CDs.

Nicholas took a sip from his O'Doul's. "Definitely promising. I think I can safely say, I'm in good shape."

"What a huge relief."

"You know, Alice, I never thought we were as close to the poorhouse as you did, but I'm glad you're glad." Nicholas wrapped his arms around me from behind and leaned his head down to kiss my neck. I turned around and reciprocated. Soon we migrated upstairs to spare the neighbors a show.

Afterward, lying in bed, I rested my cheek on his chest and took a deep breath. "Nicholas?"

"Yes?"

"You know the money from my dad?"

"Yes?"

"I know what I want to do with it."

"You mean, instead of putting it in the bank for college?"

"Well, that, too. But I want to give some of the money to the Blue Owl."

Nicholas propped himself up on one elbow. I gently removed my hair from under it. "Really?"

"Really. I know Susanna is behind on rent, and I want to help her catch up. If I've learned anything this year, it's how much I want the kids to grow up knowing stores like hers."

"She'll never take money from you, Alice. You know that."

"But you're her lawyer now. Can't you arrange for her to have an anonymous benefactor?"

"Like Magwitch? How very *Great Expectations* of you. Yes, I think I might be able to arrange that. The question is, how will you ever pay my fee?"

I smiled. "I'm sure we can figure it out."

It was the summer of Rainbow Loom. Kids sprawled on every available surface—bellies poking out of tankinis, little necks tan beneath baseball caps—weaving rubber bands into bracelets and anklets. Demonstrating a new crafty side, I learned all the stitches and waited in line with other moms at the toy store to meet shipments of new elastics. I even invested in a clear plastic tackle box so we could keep our tie-dye rubber bands separate from our glow-in-the-darks and glitters.

Susanna and I were at the pool, sharing a paper cup of french fries while our kids sat out adult swim, bent over their looms. Margot and Audrey worked on a fishhook design, alternating who got to pick the color. Theirs was an easy détente; I worked harder to forget that mean glint in Audrey's eye, knowing I had to move on.

"Hey, Alice?"

"Hang on. *Oliver!* You need to wait until the kid in front of you is *off* the diving board before you climb on the ladder!" I turned to Susanna, who rubbed her ear where I'd yelled directly into it. "Sorry, what were you saying?"

"While you're looking for a new job, would you want to pick up a few hours at the store? The weirdest thing happened—some Filament bigwig made an anonymous *donation* to the Blue Owl! I'm caught up on rent and, believe it or not, I think I can afford to hire a part-time salesperson. It wouldn't be much—"

"When can I start?"

We talked logistics. The pay was hourly and astoundingly low. But I had an idea for how I might be able to earn more money, even if I would never approach the salary I'd earned at Scroll, not to mention the stock options. I leaned forward in my chair. "Susanna, have I ever told you about the Book Lady?"

We hired a new babysitter. I bought new shoes and a new notebook.

When I arrived for my first day of work, visible rays of light crisscrossed through the store, turning the shelves into a rainbow of spines: thick, thin, shiny, matte, striped, printed with small pictures and designs, lettered in gold. The effect was dazzling. I already knew the bustle of the Blue Owl on a weekend afternoon, or after closing with customers in work clothes lingering over platters of Triscuits and cubed cheese. But, I realized, this was my first time in the store before it opened and, instantly, I knew it was the best time to be there—the bookseller's equivalent of watching your kids sleep. I could feel the peace in my bones.

•   •   •

My dad is not everywhere, as people promised he would be. He isn't with me, no matter how many times I search for his face in the melee of Penn Station or listen for his voice at my mom's house, where Buzz Lightyear slowly loses its charge in her sock drawer. Still, I've joined the well-meaning chorus perpetuating this myth for others who are on the brink of losing someone they love. My dad is everywhere and he is nowhere. My world tilts on a different axis, orbiting the sun of my own family—but still, I feel his warmth.

In August, my mom rented a beach house on Long Beach Island. Much to the surprise and delight of our kids, we rented a surrey with a fringe on top, which Nicholas and I pedaled past the site of the cottage from the year before. It had been destroyed by a hurricane, reduced to a stretch of sand marked on four corners with cedar stilts. Even though the scene was desolate and depressing, I felt reassured by the sight of those four sturdy columns.

That night, we watched the sunset from my mom's new rental. There was a small, square deck on top of the house—nothing fancy, but just the right size for all of us to gather under a wonky blue umbrella: my family, Will's family, my mom. We were sandy-footed and still damp from the outdoor shower. There weren't enough chairs or Tostitos; the corn for dinner needed to be shucked. The kids wanted to go to the water slides, the adults wanted to go to the lighthouse, and my mom wanted to know who had eaten the last piece of fudge. It was a typical night on a typical family vacation, the same one we'd been on at least twenty times before.

When the fiery sun finally slid beneath the telephone wires and into the blue envelope of Barnegat Bay, I wasn't watching. My eyes were on Nicholas, who suddenly looked relaxed and young enough to be my trophy husband, and then on our kids, all three piled in one chair, their tangled limbs dotted with crops of fresh freckles.

I'll admit, when I fantasized about a room of my own, this wasn't what I had in mind: a mossy deck on top of a small house at the side of a four-lane boulevard at the Jersey Shore, with charcoal smoke drifting up from the grill in the yard. Still, in that moment, I was in the exact right place and I knew it.

Nicholas caught my eye and gestured at the bay, the pink sky, and our family. Over the high-pitched chatter of cousins, he mouthed, "Nice view, right?"

I smiled and nodded. The view was breathtaking.

ACKNOWLEDGMENTS

Thank you to my husband, Ethan Amadeus Skerry, who did not read every draft of this book like all the other spouses you read about on pages like this one. Instead, he believed that I would someday have a chance to write one of these pages and that was enough—in fact, it was everything. Thank you to Louisa, Simon, and Frankie, three grouches and beautiful humans, who introduced me to noise-canceling headphones and understood the plight of the horse before I did. Thank you to my mom, Maura Egan, and my sister, Kate Egan, who moonlight as dear friends. Thank you to Jonathan Wayne, Amy and Phil Skerry, and Jessica Horvat—beloved winnings in the in-law jackpot.

Before I wrote a page of this book, I sheepishly, hopefully changed my computer password to "youcandoit." Thank you to all the people who helped me believe this was true, especially Rebecca Banerji, Tory and William Brangham, Dina Cagliostro and David Ganz, Abby and Ken Colen, Stephanie Gore, Kate and Caleb Epstein, Anya Epstein, Claudine Coto Knautz, Molly Lyons, Harriet Marcus, Claire Martin, Wendy Naugle, Terri Trespicio, and Jane and Eric Winston.

For encouragement, suggestions, laughs, and more encouragement, thank you to my agent, Brettne Bloom, and my editor, Marysue Rucci. You are two of the most talented people I know, and I'm humbled by your belief in this book. Elizabeth Breeden, your efficiency and enthusiasm made everything more fun.

Thank you to the commuters and conductors on the Montclair-Boonton Line, where most of this book was written. Some writers have Yaddo or MacDowell; I have New Jersey Transit, whose horns are the soundtrack of home.

Finally, Jack Egan, your legacy lives on. I hope you read me.

ABOUT THE AUTHOR

ELISABETH EGAN is the books editor at *Glamour*. Her essays and book reviews have appeared in *Self, Glamour, O, People, Publishers Weekly, Kirkus Reviews, Huffington Post, The New York Times Book Review, LA Times Book Review, The Washington Post, Chicago Sun-Times*, and *Newark Star-Ledger*. She lives in New Jersey with her family.